COLD MOON OVER BABYLON

MICHAEL McDOWELL was born in 1950 in Enterprise, Alabama and attended public schools in southern Alabama until 1968. He graduated with a bachelor's degree and a master's degree in English from Harvard, and in 1978 he was awarded his Ph.D. in English and American Literature from Brandeis.

His seventh novel written and first to be sold, *The Amulet*, was published in 1979 and would be followed by over thirty additional volumes of fiction written under his own name or the pseudonyms Nathan Aldyne, Axel Young, Mike McCray, and Preston MacAdam. His notable works include the Southern Gothic horror novel *The Elementals* (1981), the serial novel *Blackwater* (1983), which was first published in a series of six paperback volumes, and the trilogy of "Jack & Susan" books.

By 1985 McDowell was writing screenplays for television, including episodes for a number of anthology series such as *Tales from the Darkside*, *Amazing Stories*, *Tales from the Crypt*, and *Alfred Hitchcock Presents*. He went on to write the screenplays for Tim Burton's *Beetlejuice* (1988) and *The Nightmare Before Christmas* (1993), as well as the script for *Thinner* (1996). McDowell died in 1999 from AIDS-related illness. Tabitha King, wife of author Stephen King, completed an unfinished McDowell novel, *Candles Burning*, which was published in 2006.

D0723135

By Michael McDowell

NOVELS

The Amulet (1979)★
Cold Moon Over Babylon (1980)★
Gilded Needles (1980)★
The Elementals (1981)★
Katie (1982)★
Blackwater (1983; 6 vols.)
Jack & Susan in 1953 (1985)
Toplin (1985)
Jack & Susan in 1913 (1986)
Clue (1986)
Jack & Susan in 1933 (1987)
Candles Burning (2006) (completed by Tabitha King)

PSEUDONYMOUS NOVELS

Vermilion (1980) (as Nathan Aldyne)
Blood Rubies (1982) (as Axel Young)
Cobalt (1982) (as Nathan Aldyne)
Wicked Stepmother (1983) (as Axel Young)
Slate (1984) (as Nathan Aldyne)
Canary (1986) (as Nathan Aldyne)

SCREENPLAYS

Beetlejuice (1988)
Tales from the Darkside: The Movie (1990)
The Nightmare Before Christmas (1993)
Thinner (1996)

★ Available from Valancourt Books

COLD MOON OVER BABYLON

MICHAEL McDOWELL

VALANCOURT BOOKS

Dedication: In memory of Marian Mulkey McDowell

Cold Moon Over Babylon by Michael McDowell
First published as a paperback original by Avon Books in 1980
First Valancourt Books edition 2015

Published by Valancourt Books, Richmond, Virginia
http://www.valancourtbooks.com

ISBN 978-1-941147-63-4
Also available as an electronic book.

Cover art by Mike Mignola
Cover type design by M.S. Corley

Set in Dante MT

Look down fair moon and bathe this scene,
Pour softly down night's nimbus floods on faces ghastly,
    swollen, purple,
On the dead on their backs with arms toss'd wide,
Pour down your unstinted nimbus sacred moon.

—Walt Whitman
Sequel to Drum-Taps

Prologue

One hot afternoon in July of 1965, Jim Larkin and his wife JoAnn were slowly paddling their small green boat upstream on the Styx River that drains the northwestern corner of the Florida panhandle. Having spent the several hours around noon lazily fishing in a favorite spot, half a mile downriver from their blueberry farm, they were bringing back enough bream for themselves and half the town of Babylon besides. Jim's widowed mother, Evelyn Larkin, was back at the farm, taking care of their son Jerry, eight years old, and their infant daughter Margaret, born only the year before.

JoAnn Larkin, who had pale skin and dark red hair, and always wore dark red lipstick and matching nail polish even when she was working in the patch, had already started to clean the fish, and was idly scraping scales back into the water. Her husband, Evelyn Larkin's only child, paddled slowly, and kept his face turned away from the sun. He had to be careful about burn, and considered that it was a sore trial for a farmer and his wife to have fair skin.

"What's that?" JoAnn said curiously, and pointed at something in the water, twenty feet away.

"It's a croker sack," Jim Larkin replied, and turned the boat a little so that they would come nearer it.

"It's not one of ours, is it?" she said. "I don't think it's one of ours. Who'd be throwing our croker sacks in the river?"

"I don't know. We ought to take it back. Good croker sacks are getting harder to come by every day. Looks dry. Must have just fell in from somewhere."

JoAnn leaned over the prow, and snared the sack. She swung it over the side of the boat, and set it between herself and her husband. The string that held the top together had already come loose in the water, and the sack fell open in her hands. With dampened rattles, five snakes slithered out over the lip of the burlap.

The man and woman drew back in fear, pushing frantically against the rattlesnakes with their feet. Each was bitten several times, and probably would have suffered more had not their thrashing panic overturned the small boat.

Jim Larkin dived deep, and in a few seconds attempted to come up for air. Among the dead bream that floated on the surface of the water, he could see the snakes coiled and waiting. Their tails swaying slowly in the water beckoned him upward. He lost consciousness and drowned.

JoAnn Larkin swam to a sandbar, crawled across it, and fell into a sand-sink, which are as common as leeches along the margin of the Styx. She was sucked in slowly, and all the while never left off calling her husband's name. But she gave over all resistance to the sinking sand when she saw his corpse rise suddenly to the surface of the water, and bob among the dead fish. His head was thrown back, his eyes wide, and one of the snakes pushed its way into his slack mouth.

Their bodies were never recovered. JoAnn Larkin's skeleton, white and contorted, still lies frozen in the sand a dozen feet below the surface of the Styx. Jim Larkin was spun a couple of miles downstream, and then wedged into a rocky crevice in the bed of the river; there the normally sluggish black waters of the Styx, rushing through this submerged ravine, industriously pried the rotting flesh from his bones.

Evelyn Larkin had nothing of her son and daughter-in-law to mourn over and bury. The overturned boat, protecting the nested croker sacks and two drowned rattlesnakes, told no plausible story of their deaths. One July morning they had rowed down the Styx and simply failed to return.

Though she had no remembrance of her parents, Margaret Larkin never went swimming in the river, for fear that she would be dragged down to the bottom by her drowned mother and father. And her brother Jerry never after crossed the bridge over the Styx without glancing uneasily among the pilings, dreading to see there his parents' decayed corpses. Yet they said nothing of these irrational terrors to one another, nor to their grandmother, who never lost the feeling that her son and daughter-in-law were still to be found somewhere in the river's meandering length.

Eventually, a small cenotaph was raised in the Larkin family plot in the Babylon cemetery. It was marked with the names of the couple and bore the simple legend: LOST UPON THE STYX. 14 JULY 1965.

PART I

CROSSING THE STYX

Chapter 1

Three roads lead out of Babylon. The first takes you to Pensacola, forty miles to the southeast. In Pensacola are the Escambia County Courthouse, the discount liquor stores, the dog tracks, and the dazzling white beaches of the Florida Gulf coast. The route is well traveled.

The second road out of Babylon heads southwest, to Mobile, only sixty miles away. Babylon is in the very upper corner of the panhandle of Florida, with the Alabama border only ten miles to the north and the west alike. People from the town go to Mobile to buy their Christmas presents and to have braces put on their children's teeth.

But a third road leads out of Babylon as well, a small winding third-grade road, grudgingly maintained with county funds. By it, you get to other towns just over the line in southwestern Alabama, towns that are quieter, and poorer, and even smaller than Babylon itself.

The forest encroaches so thickly on this third road that tree roots split the asphalt, and large single oaks in places completely overshadow both narrow lanes. Three-quarters of a mile out of town, this road crosses the murky Styx River, a wide slow stream with occasional short stretches of black-foamed rapids that empties into the even slower and murkier Perdido River a few miles to the west. The Perdido forms the extreme western boundary of Florida with Alabama.

The bridge over the Styx, built just after World War I, consists of thick planks set across iron rails; these rest on three sets of wooden pilings. When a plank splits or rots through, it is replaced by Jerry Larkin, the only man living within a mile of the bridge. The county cut a large number of these boards for that purpose, and left them with Jerry, so that its road crews would not be bothered with this remotest area of Escambia County. The Styx River road is not so well traveled that it needs much repair from one year to the next, but planks disappear from the bridge with annoying frequency.

The land around Babylon is thickly wooded, boggy near the rivers and numerous streams, and soft spongy with many centuries of rotted pine needles everywhere else. A few wild dogwoods bloom in the spring; acorns fall from the oak trees in the autumn, but otherwise the seasons appear pretty much the same, for the land is green all year round with the ubiquitous pines. These trees are so thickly spread that the sun is kept from all but the top branches. The lower limbs brown, wither, rot, and drop off. Around the Larkin house, for instance, is a stand of long-leaf pine, three or four hundred in number, eighty feet tall, but with living branches for only the uppermost twenty feet or so. The house is in perpetual shade, and never knows the sun. But the Larkins don't mind, for the trees don't shadow their blueberry bushes, and they keep the house protected and cool through the oppressive six-month summers of this part of the country.

The Styx River, because of its slow movement, and its frequent sandbars, stagnant marginal pools, and dead courses, is infested with mosquitoes, leeches, and snakes. This whole part of Escambia County is sparsely populated, and almost no one lives along the rivers. Higher land is for building: away from the insects and the danger of spring flooding. Although the Styx meanders a course that is nearly forty miles long, only four persons live actually within sight of it. One is an old black woman whose shack is perilously near the junction with the Perdido. She is deaf and mad.

The other three live just on the other side of the single bridge that spans the Styx. Old Evelyn Larkin and her grandchildren, Jerry and Margaret, are there because of the blueberries.

Blueberries grew wild in the bogs and swamps of this part of the country long before the Spaniards arrived, but they were not cultivated until about the turn of the century. They grow best in well-drained land that is yet very damp, and an ideal situation for blueberries was that portion of the Larkin property along the Styx River: several clear acres that sloped from the old farmhouse down to the river's edge.

The plants are enormous and very old, with eight or nine bushes, seven to eight feet high, to the single root system. No one remembers now who first planted them or whether they had grown wild there before. Evelyn Larkin's husband had owned them and the house when she married him, and she could not now recall how he had come by them.

These overgrown luxuriant plants were not arranged in orderly rows, but were an intricate unplanned maze over five acres, so confused that sometimes even Jerry and Margaret lost their way. For fifty years the Larkin blueberry farm had practically run itself. The soil was rich, and the climate of the Florida panhandle perfectly suited for the cultivation of the fruit. The plants had to be kept trimmed, and the berries had to be picked. No fertilizer was used because none was needed, and it seemed unlikely that there was any way to improve the yield of the plants, which by the middle of June were heavy laden with the succulent dark blue berries. Jerry and his sister Margaret shooed the birds away and killed snakes that crawled along the paths and pulled up seedlings of pine and oak that had settled into the ripe spongy ground—but there was little else to do. At harvest, it was the custom for the local Boy Scout and Girl Scout groups to come out to the farm and pick the berries all day long. They were paid ten cents a pint for their labor. Jerry drove the berries to Pensacola, and they were shipped north. It had never been a really profitable concern, but it was all that they knew.

For a dozen years after the disappearance of Jim and JoAnn Larkin the seasonal berries had seen the remainder of the family through the year. This was certainly well, for it had been demonstrated by Evelyn's husband many years before that the land was really good for nothing else. But for some years now inflation had reduced their margin of solvency. In the late spring, just before the beginning of the picking season, Evelyn had found it necessary to take funds from the sacred account of her husband's insurance money to get them through. She hadn't known what they would do when this resource was expended, and had hoped continually for a pronounced rise in the price they were paid for the berries, but that remained stable when everything else went up. Then, just three years before, floods in April had done serious damage to the first floor and foundations of the house, and had killed off nearly a quarter of the plants. The last of the insurance money was employed on repairs to the house, and beyond that, a bank loan had to be secured to support them the following year, for the crop that summer was much smaller than usual. Evelyn trembled nightly. They had no financial cushion now, but were forced to make monthly payments on that large loan. Several times in the past year she had been late on the installments, and now had received notice that May's was past due. April's had not been paid at all. The berries wouldn't bring in cash for another two weeks.

The future of the farm wasn't bright either. Jerry Larkin, though he was afraid to speak of it to his grandmother, had noticed a gradual deterioration of the blueberry plants. The foliage was as lush as ever, was if anything thicker and more profuse season by the season, but the yield was lower each year, and the berries of decreasing size and quality. The bushes had simply grown too old.

One morning, in a part of the patch that he knew was not visible from Evelyn Larkin's bedroom window, Jerry attempted to dig up one of the plants, a large specimen that he had tagged as having a particularly small number of berries. He was able to dig a trench around it to a depth of about six inches, but could not go deeper; the roots were a solid cordon below that, fibrous and fine individually, but tough and unyielding in aggregate. Dynamite might get the bush out, but nothing else. And this root system, he realized, must underlie all five acres, like the marrow of a bone. No new improved strains of bushes could be planted and expected to grow.

As an experiment, he had tried cutting off one of the bushes at the ground. His father had explained to him that the roots would quickly replace the missing plants with new shoots. After a couple of years, Jerry was glad that he had not tried this experiment extensively, for though the bush grew back quickly enough, the berries were still lower in quality than those on the surrounding plants, and often shriveled in the sun before they could be picked.

Jerry came to the conclusion that the ground below was tiring out at an accelerative rate. He tried increasing amounts of expensive fertilizer, following the advice of the county agricultural agent (who Jerry came to suspect didn't know much about blueberries), but the ground soaked it in without apparent effect. It seemed likely that more fertilizer than Jerry could afford would be required to feed the thousands of cubic feet of roots beneath this gently sloping ground.

After the deaths of her son and daughter-in-law, Evelyn Larkin had managed the farm herself, with the help of one hired man. When Jerry graduated from high school, he took over the farm, and the salaried worker was let go. Although Evelyn depended upon the blueberry patch for her sustenance, she had an aversion to the place. Too often when she was working down among the oldest, largest bushes on the edge of the Styx, she grew nervous about snakes, and found herself staring for long minutes at the muddy waters of the river. When her grandson tactfully suggested that she not bother herself any longer with the blueberry patch, Evelyn retreated gratefully to the farmhouse.

Jerry knew that eventually the blueberry crop would fail entirely, or at any rate, with inflation and increased competition from new farms, it would cease to support them. He hoped fervently that he would be able to survive financially as long as Evelyn Larkin lived—but he could not hope beyond that. After his grandmother died, and he was miserable just thinking of such a time, he would sell the place for whatever little it would bring, and move well away from Babylon. He wondered what sort of job was available to a man who knew everything there was to know about blueberries—and very little about anything else. Sometimes in the winter he worked at a filling station or at the grocery store as a bag boy, when such positions could be had— but they would not support him, he knew. And understandably, these jobs were now going to those younger than himself.

Margaret, of course, was another problem. Though she seemed now not much more than a child, in four years she would graduate from high school. Jerry had always hoped that at that time she would be able to go away to college. Now he was certain there would not be money to cover such an expense. Margaret would simply have to make it on her own. She could go to the university in Tallahassee, or in Pensacola, if she could obtain a scholarship; if not, she would have to find work. Jerry had wanted to make things easy for his sister, but he understood now that Margaret was probably in for as rough a time as he had of it.

Jerry was not overly intelligent, had not done well in school, but he was hard-working and responsible. He was in a perpetual state of indignation that no one except Evelyn Larkin and his sister Margaret thought that the orderly running of the blueberry farm was any accomplishment. Over the last several years he had grown sullen as well, depressed by his blocked diminishing future. He would not desert his grandmother, and had resolved he would care for her as she had always cared for him. Two changes only he saw in his life to come, both inevitable: the death of Evelyn and the deterioration of the farm into bankruptcy. Evelyn Larkin marked the growing intractability in her grandson, but because she was assured of his continued affection for her, and because he never mentioned the possibility of leaving her, she set it down to "growing pains."

It was Thursday, the first of June. Margaret had graduated from junior high school the week before. At the ceremony in the gymnasium, Evelyn had wept and smiled with pride; Jerry had appeared overheated and uncomfortable. The next Monday, the first Boy Scouts would come out to the house after school and carefully pick the first ripening berries. Jerry and Margaret would pick too, and supervise the boys. The following week, many more berries would ripen, and the Girl Scouts would be enlisted as well. The front yard would be littered with bicycles. At her table on the back porch Evelyn would keep a record of the number of pints picked by each Scout, and would cover the baskets with cellophane wrappers that bore the name Babylon Farms and a crude drawing of the Styx River bridge. Early in the morning, Jerry would drive to Pensacola with the berries that had been gathered the day before.

The picking would continue at this rigorous pace for at least four weeks, and the Boy Scouts be dismissed. Then only Girl

Scouts would be allowed to come out, as gleaners, and Jerry would make the trip into Pensacola only every third day. After that, they would all lie back exhausted.

In the sweet empty weeks following the season, Jerry would go fishing every day—not in the Styx, but in the Perdido—and Margaret and her grandmother would sew. Throughout the year, Evelyn Larkin took in piecework to supplement the farm income, and as a kind of apology to Jerry for not working in the patch. She had taught Margaret as well, and they traded off time on the sewing machine. Margaret made all her own clothes. She bought her materials at a seconds store in Pensacola, and few suspected that her wardrobe wasn't store-purchased.

Margaret was small boned and dark complexioned (in contrast to her parents and Jerry), with regular features that could be considered pretty by the sympathetic. She was soft-spoken, and reserved to the point of secretiveness. Her quietness and small stature made her seem even younger than she was. She had never been an exuberant child, but in the past few weeks she had seemed downright morose. Jerry imagined that his sister was suffering some sort of adolescent female trauma that he knew nothing about. Evelyn, knowing that her granddaughter had undergone menarche the year before, supposed it was only the summer doldrums that would disappear as soon as the picking began.

Boredom was understandable. This was a week that was for the most part empty, the calm before the blue storm of the season. All the work had been done to prepare themselves and the bushes for the ripening. The cartons were stacked by the thousands on the latticed back porch, and Jerry had had work done on the station wagon, so that it would bear up beneath the daily loaded trips to Pensacola and back. He had talked to the Boy and Girl Scout troop leaders, and worked out schedules with them for the employment of the boys and girls. He had visited the shippers in Pensacola, and he had telephoned the distributors in Massachusetts and Illinois. Now there was nothing really to do but sit on the front porch, and pray that there would be no heavy rains in the six weeks to come.

Chapter 2

Evelyn Larkin was almost seventy. At the time of her marriage, she had been a cheerful woman, and had maintained that disposition even after her husband was struck dead by lightning in the pine forest. But during the three sorrowful anxious months in which she waited for Jim and JoAnn to return from their boating expedition, her eyes took on a cloudiness that never completely cleared. She was thin, nervous, prone to high blood pressure, and fell into small bouts of weeping once or twice a day of late.

Women who have worked their lives away on farms age quickly, and rarely live to be seventy-five. Or, reaching that age, they appear a full generation older. It is a hard life that often precludes even the meager satisfactions of old age. For it is impossible to retire on a farm—one works until death stays the hand. And, because of the structure of the Social Security system, Evelyn Larkin, who had never worked for wages, was entitled to only a very small monthly check from the government.

She fared better than most country women, however, because she had left off working outside the house. She cooked and cleaned, and she took in sewing; and those relatively congenial activities in the past ten years had slowed her physical decay. But Evelyn Larkin knew that she had not many years left. This was a frightful thought to her, but she sometimes spoke jestingly to her grandchildren of the time when she would no longer be there, in an attempt to prepare them for her death.

About five o'clock on the afternoon of the first day of June, Evelyn Larkin sat on the front porch of the farmhouse with Jerry. From here they could see the road to Babylon, fifty yards away. The large plot of ground before the house was crowded with the tall pine trees, but the underbrush had been cleared, and camellias and azaleas planted in clumps all about. The blueberry patch was just off to the right, and could be seen from the end of the porch. The Styx lay here and there visible through tangled shrubs and ground vines, and if you stood on the railing, you could just glimpse the bridge that crossed the river.

Evelyn sat in a rocking chair near the front door, monogramming a napkin with a cursive *A*. Seven others, completed, lay piled in a small basket by the side of the chair. Jerry swung noisily in a swing at the end of the porch away from the river. He had listlessly picked up a two-year-old copy of *Reader's Digest* from a wooden magazine rack near Evelyn's chair. The pages had warped from atmospheric dampness, and the cover was speckled with rot.

"I sure do wish Margaret would hurry up and get home," said Jerry languidly.

"I do too," sighed Evelyn. "I feel like starting supper, but I don't want to till I know she's here."

"Who'd she go to see?"

"She said she was going over to the high school to help Mr. Perry take care of something or other. She likes to help him and he's been real sweet to her. I hope she's not just getting in his way though. I would have thought that she'd be home by now. She left here on her wheel right after dinner."

"I wish you wouldn't call it a 'wheel,' Grandma. A bicycle's got two wheels, and you make it sound like it's just got one. Margaret couldn't have made it all the way into Babylon if she just had one wheel to do it with."

Evelyn made no reply. She was used to Jerry's frequent peevishness, and knew that he was only bored. She had tried to explain to him before, that when she was a girl, they called it a "wheel," and she still thought of it that way, but Jerry had complained so often of this usage, that she didn't bother explaining it any longer. However, she didn't say "bicycle" either.

"Jerry," she said instead, "let me run inside the house, and bring you out a lamp. I don't want you to ruin your eyes reading without a lamp. Light's beginning to fail out here."

Jerry tossed the *Reader's Digest* over his shoulder. "I'm not reading," he said. "Besides, you're sitting there doing embroidery without a lamp. You're the one's gone ruin your eyes, not me."

"Well," said Evelyn, "doesn't matter so much for me, my eyes have only got to last a couple of more years, but your eyes got to last you till you get as old as I am."

"Don't talk like that," said Jerry impatiently.

"I just hope Margaret gets home before dark."

"Not dark yet," said Jerry contrarily. "It's just because of the pines. If you and me walked out there to the highway, we'd probably be blinded by the sun."

"You think we'll be able to hear her when she comes over the bridge?" asked Evelyn.

Jerry shook his head. "Cain't hear anything from the bridge."

"Well, I just hope she gets back before it starts to rain."

"Don't say that, Grandma. I got two pints of berries today, and those were the first. The others are coming. I don't want it to rain. If it was to be heavy, we could lose a lot. I don't want you to say that." He stood out of the swing, and moved to the railing of the porch, leaned forward between two large pots of fern, and tried to make out the sky above the trees. "Sun's shining," he said, "though you cain't much tell it from where we're sitting, doesn't look like rain to me."

"Well," said Evelyn, realizing that Jerry was in fact very worried about the plants, "it probably won't rain, but Margaret ought to get back before dark. Fourteen-year-old girls ought not ride their wheels at night. People in cars don't always see people on wheels, especially when they're small like Margaret."

"She'll be back," said Jerry reassuringly.

They were silent some minutes. Evelyn rocked softly in the chair. The last napkin, not quite finished, lay pressed beneath her folded hands. Jerry moved from one end of the porch to the other, squinting up at the sky, and glancing anxiously around the corner of the house at the blueberry patch. At last he threw himself onto the sagging front steps, and folded his long arms above his knees. He was anxious for the afternoon to end and the evening to begin, and that wouldn't happen until Evelyn started supper, and Evelyn wouldn't start supper until Margaret returned from Babylon. It didn't so much matter though, because Jerry knew that he would be just as restless by the end of the evening, and would impatiently look forward to the hour when he could get into bed with some hope of falling asleep. The season was exhausting, but it filled the days and evenings, and there was no time for reflection. Until the accounts were reckoned in August, it was possible for Jerry to imagine that this year the farm would be making money. Jerry began to lose himself in hopeful predictions of the season's returns, placing them far above what he could reasonably expect.

"It's gone pour before I can get supper on the table."

Jerry said nothing now to contradict his grandmother, for he too had begun to smell the moisture in the air. He rolled his eyes upward trying to catch sight of the sky, but he didn't crane his neck, because he didn't want his grandmother to know that he was looking.

He lowered his eyes suddenly to follow the hasty approach of a powder-blue Volkswagen that had just turned into the long driveway.

Chapter 3

"You think it's Margaret?" Evelyn asked hesitantly and hopefully.

Jerry didn't bother answering. He knew that it was not. Margaret had left on her bicycle, and would surely return on her bicycle. Even considering, on the outside, that something had happened—a flat tire, or some such—Margaret would simply have walked back. Babylon was less than a mile away, though nothing but forest lay between the Larkin farm and the city limits.

A young girl was driving the Volkswagen; she waved cheerily out the window before she came to a stop beside the house.

"It's Belinda Hale," said Jerry, "it's not Margaret."

Belinda Hale hopped out of the car with a bundle of clothing clasped against her breast. She was of medium height, very blond, and what Evelyn called "well-developed." She was lively, garrulous, and very pretty. No one had ever seen Belinda depressed, though sometimes she was angry, frustrated, or petulant.

Belinda was the daughter of the sheriff in Babylon, Ted Hale. Belinda's mother had run off with an FBI agent a couple of years after Jim and JoAnn Larkin had been swallowed by the Styx. Belinda Hale loved her father, but not as much as he loved her.

"Ohhh!" she squealed, as she hurried up to the front steps. "Hey, Jerry. Hey, Miz Larkin! How ya'll doing? How'd the berries gone be this year?"

"Hey, Belinda," said Evelyn, "how're you?"

"Berries gone be fine this year," said Jerry modestly. "We're gone send you and your daddy a couple of pints just as soon as we start the picking next week."

"Well, I'm looking forward, I just cain't tell you how much I'm looking forward to that," cried Belinda. She smiled lusciously at Jerry, and then moved her gaze upward to Evelyn. "Miz Larkin, I brought you some things to do up for me. I found 'em in the back of my closet, about to put out shoots, Lord knows how long they were lying there, probably since two years and fifteen pounds ago, because they have ever' one of 'em got to be let out. I tell you, I am getting *huge*." She smiled at Jerry again, and patted her flat taut belly.

"That's fine, Belinda," said Evelyn kindly, "you got 'em marked where you want 'em?"

"I sure do. There's three skirts, and four blouses, and I was just wondering if you could change the emblem on my blazer." She mounted the steps so close to Jerry that her skirts brushed his cheek, and handed the clothing to Evelyn. She held up the black blazer for their inspection. "I don't suppose you would have heard it, because it only happened this very afternoon at three o'clock, and I am not gone really celebrate until tomorrow night, but I just got elected co-captain of the cheerleaders for this coming school year, which is a real honor since I am still only a junior."

"Well, well. Congratulations, Belinda, that's real fine. I know your daddy will be real proud of you."

"My daddy," laughed Belinda, "has put out an all-points bulletin . . ."

A little belatedly, Jerry echoed his grandmother's congratulations: "That's real good, Belinda . . ."

Belinda turned, and flashed a brief sweet smile at the top of Jerry's head.

"But the thing is," Belinda continued, "I get a special emblem because I'm the co-captain, it's twice as big as the one I have on now, and I want you to replace it for me, I put the new one here in the inside pocket, okay, Miz Larkin . . . ?"

"I'd be proud to do it, Belinda," Evelyn replied. "Won't you sit for a piece, Belinda? Jerry and I were just waiting for Margaret to get back from Babylon. She's on her wheel. You didn't pass her on the way, did you?"

"I didn't see anybody, Miz Larkin, not a soul 'cept Mr. Geiger, down under the bridge, fishing, as usual. I don't know how he keeps his business going. He ought to open a branch down under the bridge, 'cause he's there more than he's at his place in town." Ed Geiger ran a small sporting goods store between the police station and the barbershop.

Belinda had seated herself in a chair on the other side of the front door from Evelyn. She rocked in it with a quick steady rhythm, as if to show how energetically pleased she was to be there. "But he was just packing up when I came over the bridge. Does he catch much down there? Sometimes he brings fish to Daddy, and Daddy brings 'em home to me, I just throw 'em out, 'cause I hate to clean fish, and Daddy don't eat 'em anyway. I don't mind the scales, but I hate cutting off the heads. They stare at you. D'you ever notice how fish stare at you when you're cutting their heads off? And then your fingers stink to high heaven for the next eight days, like the fish were paying you back for doing it to 'em."

Evelyn didn't like to talk about fishing in the Styx, and so said nothing.

"Ed Geiger's down there a lot," said Jerry politely, "seems like every time I drive over the bridge, he's down there under it."

"Well," said Belinda, "I got to go." She stood. The chair continued to rock noisily.

"Don't run off," said Evelyn. "Wait till Margaret gets back. Margaret'll be sick at the heart if she comes back and we tell her that she missed you."

Margaret Larkin and Belinda Hale were not close. Belinda was two years older than Margaret, and Belinda's ebullience made her seem older still, while Margaret's reticence made her appear even younger than she was. There were two recognized social circles among Babylon's adolescents; Belinda Hale sat triumphantly at the top of the better, and Margaret Larkin languished somewhere about the middle of the other.

"Miz Larkin, I'd give anything in the world to be able to sit here and gossip with you and Jerry until the sun went down and we couldn't see each other in the face any more, but I got to get back to Babylon, and go fix Mr. Redfield's dinner."

"Belinda," said Evelyn. "I didn't know you were taking care of him like that." James Redfield was the richest man in Babylon, owner of the Citizens, Planters and Merchants Bank (usually referred to as the CP&M). He had been bedridden, however, since a serious automobile accident eighteen months back. "How is Mr. Redfield's neck these days?"

"Not so good," said Belinda gravely. "Miz Larkin, if you was to stick a loaded shotgun to his back, he couldn't turn his head enough to know it was you that was doing it."

"That's too bad," said Jerry.

"It is, it really is," said Belinda solemnly. Then she brightened: "But these days, it seems like I spend more time over there than I do at home. And Daddy doesn't like it one little bit. Of course, if Daddy had his way he'd cut off my arms and legs and strap me to his holster, and I couldn't *never* leave him then. But there's laws against cutting off people's arms and legs, or at least I tell him there are, so he won't be tempted to do it . . ."

"Your daddy loves you," said Evelyn indulgently. "He loves you like I love Margaret and Jerry."

"You be good to your grandmama," said Belinda to Jerry sternly, then laughed gaily. "Anyway, Mr. Redfield likes to have me around, and it all works out perfect, 'cause as you know I am planning to be a practical nurse, and I have already got the catalogs of every nursing school between New Orleans and Atlanta, even though I won't be going off for another two years like. But I am getting in a lot of practice on Mr. Redfield. He pays me too, so I am saving my money to go to school on. I don't want to be a drain on my daddy. And since I'm cooking for Mr. Redfield, I'm learning all about that too. Daddy won't eat nothing but steak and French fries."

"Is Mr. Redfield picky?" asked Evelyn, solicitously.

"*He* isn't," said Belinda confidingly, "but them two boys of his, I don't know about them. Seems like they won't eat anything. They eat like they was three years old, both of 'em, not like they were grown men. I don't put up with 'em either. I fix supper for Mr. Redfield most nights, and I fix enough for Ben and Mr. Nathan too, and I don't hang around to see if they eat it or not. I leave it on the table, and if they want it, they eat it. And then they got Nina coming in every morning to clean, and she takes care of Mr. Redfield during the day, and cleans up the dishes and like that, so I don't really know if they eat it or not. You'd think a thirty-three-year-old man like Nathan Redfield would eat a little dish of white peas that was picked that very afternoon, wouldn't you? But he won't, and neither will Ben—"

During this last, Belinda had advanced slowly down the steps. She now stood in the yard, smiling up at Evelyn and Jerry: "If I see Margaret on the way back, I'll tell her you're waiting for her."

"I just want her to get back 'fore the rain starts," said Evelyn.

"It's not gone rain," said Jerry.

"Radio said it was," said Belinda, and climbed into her car. She backed quickly out of the driveway and spun off toward Babylon. She honked the horn in farewell, and they saw her hand fluttering a moment over the roof.

"That girl talks like a five-dollar lawyer," sighed Jerry: "I got tired out just sitting here listening to her go on."

"She sure is pretty though," said Evelyn, and smiled at her grandson. "Maybe she'd like to go with you to the Starlite Drive-in one night, Jerry. Why don't you ask her?"

"Oh no, Grandma, I—" He turned away blushing. "You know," he said, to cover his embarrassment, "I haven't seen her much in that car before—she must have just gotten her license. And I've seen her in it everywhere these past few days."

"Well, she probably just turned sixteen. Margaret won't even be fifteen until October—the twelfth of October." Evelyn sighed and rose from her chair. "I'm going in to start supper. Margaret's sure to come back before I get it on the table. She's not late, not ever." She leaned forward, and rubbed the top of Jerry's head affectionately. "You stay out here and wait for your sister. But you come inside if you start to see lightning."

Evelyn gathered her sewing and the clothes that Belinda Hale had brought, and went into the house. The screen door slammed lightly behind her.

Jerry walked into the yard and dropped his head back, staring dizzily into the boughs of the pines far above him. Two drops of water splashed thickly against his cheek. He knew it had already begun to rain; it took a while before falling water worked its way through the thick pine canopy. He walked slowly to the highway, and saw that the asphalt had already turned black with moisture. His unobstructed view here of the shedding cloud cover told him that it was a storm that had blown up from the Gulf. Then, in confirmation, he heard the low-pitched thunder breaking to the south, over Babylon.

Chapter 4

The piney woods begin well inside the municipal boundaries of Babylon. The southern portion of the town is more densely populated, while the blacks, the two dozen or so Creek tribes-men, and very poorest of the whites have settled into the upper half of the township. Their run-down, unpainted houses with sagging porches are set well back from the road, deep among the pine trees. Chickens scratch about the foundations, and emaciated dogs sleep inside the abandoned automobiles that lie rusting in every side-yard.

On Thursday the first of June, the sullen silent children of these impoverished families stared at Margaret Larkin as she hur-riedly pedaled along the Styx River road, in the last few moisture-laden minutes before the storm broke.

The houses became less frequent as Margaret approached the town limits. She stopped only once, to speak to a middle-aged black woman who stood beside her mailbox at the side of the road.

Margaret balanced on one foot, but did not dismount; she greeted Nina by gasping her name, then paused to catch her breath.

"How you, Margaret? How's your grandmama?"

Evelyn Larkin, about three years before, had suffered a slight stroke, and Nina had nursed her for a month afterward. Since that time, Nina had never failed to inquire after the old woman's health.

Margaret replied that her grandmother was well, and invited Nina out to the house to pick all the blueberries she wanted, before the season became very busy.

Nina thanked Margaret for the invitation, and then both turned briefly to watch a vehicle approach and pass them on its way out of Babylon. It was a lumbering black hearse, about twenty years old, that had been converted into a fishing wagon. Half a dozen cane poles stuck out the back.

"Well," said Nina, "I don't know who that is, but they crazy to be going out right now. Fish bite in the rain, but they don't bite when there's lightning started. And you better get on home, honey, 'cause it looks bad for tonight. I sure hope it don't do nothing to your berries—"

Margaret laughed, a little nervously.

"You go on now, child," said Nina. "And you tell your grand-mama I'm thinking about her, and next time she comes into town she ought to stop and speak, and not just drive by."

Margaret replied that she would relay the message, and then hurried off toward home. She was outside the town now, and there were no more houses between her and the Styx River. The trees were dark beneath the gathering lowering clouds. A single car passed her; it had an Alabama license plate.

Margaret increased her speed when she felt the first few drops of rain. The wind in her ears deafened her. She glanced behind her several times to make sure that no car was coming up. The Styx River road had no shoulder, and she was forced to ride on the asphalt. Because the edge of the paving was ragged and broken away in places, she traveled in the middle of the lane.

She knew every slight turn in the road, could identify many single trees by the distinctive pattern of their branches, and was familiar with every clearing and small rise that she passed. This exact knowledge of the road made the trip shorter, for she always knew where she was and how much farther she had to go. She sighed with relief when she began to turn the bend that would bring into view the Styx River, the bridge that crossed it, and the second story of their farmhouse on the other side. She had a good chance now to make it home before the rain began in earnest.

Margaret sailed around the bend without pedaling; the bridge was only fifty yards away. She was always a little nervous to cross it, and was careful to pass over with her eyes focused on the road beyond. She particularly avoided staring into the black water that flowed beneath the uneven planking.

But her attention was distracted by a movement in the brush by the side of the road just ahead. She imagined that some 'possum or 'coon, disturbed by her approach, was about to take flight. She began to brake in case the animal ran in front of her.

A man leapt out of the dense shrubbery. He dashed into the middle of the road. His movement was at first so rapid that she could make out nothing of his appearance but that he was very dark. Then he was still, with his strong legs placed wide apart over the center line, his long arms rigidly outstretched to halt her. Above his black pants, the hair on his chest was so thick, the skin beneath it so deeply tanned, that she did not immediately realize he wore no shirt. Covering his head was a black leather hood, tight-fitting and fastened on the side, with slits cut above the eyes and nose. The mouth was zippered shut.

Margaret swerved to avoid him, but forgot to release the brake, and she spilled sharply onto the pavement, with the bicycle falling on top of her. She burned where she had scraped her legs, arms, and side. She kicked the bicycle off her, and called faintly for Jerry to come and help her.

She struggled to raise herself, but stumbled again with the pain of her fall. The man lunged forward, lifted the bicycle and heaved it into the bushes.

Margaret was on her feet, dazed, staring wildly across the bridge. She could see the window of her grandmother's bedroom, and again called, this time more loudly, for Jerry.

She hobbled toward the bridge, but stumbled when she looked behind her. The man in the black leather mask was almost on top of her. From behind, he took her by the shoulders, and lifted her from the ground. She tried to twist free, but his grip pinned her arms to her body. She kicked at his legs with her heels, but he held her at such a distance that her thrashings were ineffectual.

The raindrops were sparse but heavy, the familiar prelude to a substantial prolonged downpour.

Margaret trembled violently as they approached the bridge. She screamed but knew that Jerry would not hear her. She had learned as a little girl that voices did not carry from one shore of the Styx to the other. The sound was swept downstream.

Two cars had passed in the last ten minutes: the fishing hearse and the car from Alabama. Why didn't someone else come along? How could this happen within sight of her own house?

The man's gloved fingers had cut off the circulation in her arms. Margaret was ready to faint. She began to lose the sense of her situation. She stared in front of her, at the familiar bridge, the Styx River, and the window of her grandmother's bedroom. Her head wobbled and the scene jerked dizzily before her. It was strange, she thought involuntarily, to be carried about like this. She turned her head around, and choked with fright when she found the black leather mask almost touching her face. She could have counted the teeth in the zipper that was closed over the mouth. The eyes were black and flat, and seemed lashless. Individual drops of rain spattered violently against the taut black leather.

Her head jerked back, and she began to scream—in hope, for ahead of her, on the other side of the bridge, she had heard a car horn. There *was* someone else on the road, and maybe the horn meant that rescue was coming. Her grandmother had seen what was happening from her bedroom window, and sent Jerry down. Jerry had jumped in the car, and rushed out. He was blowing the horn to tell her he was on his way—

But it wasn't the horn of their car, she knew, and it wasn't Jerry. Margaret hoped her grandmother *hadn't* seen anything from the window. To see her granddaughter attacked might well have brought on a stroke. *But if it wasn't Jerry, who was it?*

Despite her continued struggles, her captor had advanced onto the bridge, but he halted at the sound of the horn. Margaret was confident that he would let her go now, and conceal himself in the shrubbery. She would limp home across the bridge, and tell her grandmother that she had had a little fall on her bicycle.

Margaret drew in her breath as she was lifted higher and turned sharply in the man's arms. *How could a man be so strong?* she thought. *How could he—*

Directly beneath her now were the slow, muddy waters of the Styx, and the sandbar where she and Jerry had once dug for pirate treasure—and left off for fear of coming upon their parents' corpses. The river was pockmarked with rain. Drops caught in her eyes, and she blinked them away. But while she was blinking, she was let go. She twisted her head around, and saw the sandbar come swiftly nearer. She thought of the pirate chest of gold and jewels that she and Jerry had never found, and she thought—

After the man in the black leather mask had hurled Margaret over the side of the bridge onto the sandbar beneath, he dived into the high grass that grew at the end of the bridge, and remained motionless while the powder-blue Volkswagen passed over, and around the bend toward Babylon. The black lashless eyes behind the mask narrowed and followed the receding car.

Margaret Larkin lay unconscious on the sandbar. The man in the leather hood climbed out of the grass and hurried into the trees. He emerged presently onto the road with a length of coarse rope. He picked the bicycle out of the bushes and carried it over to the side of the bridge, and then flung it over the railing so that it landed squarely atop the girl's frail body. The downturned pedal gouged deeply into her belly; she jerked and shuddered. The back wheel spun against her upturned cheek, shredding the flesh.

The man slid down a clay bank to the river, and then jumped across to the sandbar. He dragged Margaret and the bicycle entirely beneath the bridge. With a pocket-knife he ripped her clothing open, front and back, but removed none of it. Thick blood welled up in the long gashes cut on the young girl's body. He laid the bicycle flat, and placed Margaret on top of it. With the rope he had brought along, he secured her neck to the handlebars, her waist to the frame, and her feet to the back wheel.

He tested the ropes by pulling on the knotted portion over Margaret's belly. The girl's eyes flashed open, expressionlessly, and then closed slowly. The man waded a few feet off the sandbar into the water, and laid Margaret and her bicycle carefully onto the surface of the black swirling stream. He watched them sink slowly into the narrow channel in the middle of the river. Margaret's torn clothing fluttered briefly in the water, but did not sustain any air that would have impeded the submergence.

The man stood patiently on the sandbar beneath the bridge until no more air bubbles rose, and then stealthily climbed back up the clayey bank, and disappeared into the forest.

A few minutes later, the converted hearse pulled out of a long disused logging track, and moved back down the road toward Babylon. Its windshield wipers moved furiously against the driving rain.

PART II

MISSING MARGARET

Chapter 5

One or two others were perhaps larger, but no house in Babylon was so impressive as James Redfield's. The banker had built it at the insistence of his second wife, who died five months after she had walked through the front door with a complaint on her lips about the height of the concrete steps. Located at the end of a forest-surrounded cul-de-sac, the house was long and low, with cream-colored stuccoed walls and large dark-wood double doors with ornate brass handles in the Spanish style. All along the rear, the bedrooms and the den were walled with sliding glass that opened onto small patios, the pool, or the pine forest.

Land in back sloped down to a small nameless creek with gurgling rapids. Between the house and the four-car garage was an enormous swimming pool, enclosed by high stuccoed walls covered with white wisteria. James Redfield's pool, the first in Babylon and still the largest, had been thought a breathtaking extravagance—almost a wickedness—in 1955.

The house was located on the fashionable western side of the town, and the ten acres belonging to James Redfield abutted on the municipal boundary of Babylon. Just beyond the creek in back, the old man's substantial holdings began, nearly eight thousand acres of timber land between Babylon and the Perdido River. Few poaching hunters trespassed on this boggy land, despite the plenitude of wildlife; it was thought dangerous because of snakes and quicksand. For a few years in the late fifties, a moonshiner had operated his stills in a clearing about a mile from the Redfield house, but the apparatus inexplicably exploded and killed him. The woods were supposed to be haunted by his ghost, but no one would swear to having seen the specter. James

Redfield had never allowed logging here, because he didn't like chain saws and he didn't need the money; but within the past year he had been quietly approached by Texaco and offered a staggering sum to allow test rigs on the acreage nearest the river. Jay, only twenty miles to the east of Babylon, was a little oil boom town now, whose nighttime skyline was bright with flares from producing wells. The Texaco representative had assured James Redfield that no other landowner around Babylon had yet been approached, and he was asked to keep the negotiations secret for the time being. James Redfield was being particularly slow about these transactions in order to annoy his son Nathan, who was greedy for Texaco royalties; the old man himself had no use for the money.

Although the underbrush had been cleared and diseased trees felled, James Redfield's house still appeared to be isolated in the midst of the pine forest. The tall slender trees had swayed insistently and with a low-voiced moaning all the afternoon.

In the hour before a thunderstorm, the color of the forest deepens: the pine needles take on a dense vibrant greenness they possess at no other time, the slender trunks go black, and the leaden sky above sinks lower by the minute.

Belinda Hale pulled her powder-blue Volkswagen into the knob of the cul-de-sac, jumped out, and ran toward the side of the house. She pushed open a narrow wrought-iron gate, and stepped into a small patio. This space was about fifteen feet square, bordered with azaleas bearing the brown withered blossoms of the March flowering. Two chairs and a glider of wrought iron had been painted glossy black recently. The flagstone paving was covered by brown pine needles.

A portion of the patio was protected by the overhang of the house. Beneath this, and in front of the sliding glass doors that led into his bedroom, sat James Redfield, impatiently tearing apart tufts of pine straw that had fallen beside him onto the seat of the glider.

James Redfield was seventy, but looked older. His last accident, complicating the injuries he had received in another seven years before, had left him a very old man. He moved about only with difficulty, and most often in a wheelchair, had endless difficulties with his digestion, and suffered vastly in comparison with his few pleasures. Belinda Hale was the principal one left to him.

"You late, Miss Pie," said James Redfield, with narrowed eyes and reproachful sternness. His voice was high, a drawling wheedle, a deliberate parody of the tremor of an ancient man. He had affected it when he retired—again, to annoy his sons—and it had become his natural voice.

"I told you not to call me that, Mr. Red," cried Belinda, and turned to slam the iron gate behind her. She looked back at the old man: "I'm fat, and I know it, but I don't appreciate your calling attention to it . . ."

"Pretty soon, Miss Pie, I'm gone look out my window, and see your daddy carting you up here in a wheelbarrow."

"I did not come here this afternoon to talk about how much I weigh," said Belinda, with feigned huffiness, "but what I do want to know is what you are doing out here when the bottom is going to fall out of the sky in two minutes and forty-five seconds?"

"Nina brought me out here just before she left. She didn't want to do it, Miss Pie, so I don't want you to say anything about it to her, because I said you were sure to show up before the rain started. And here you are, just like I said you'd be."

"Well, Mr. Red, what if something had happened to me? What if I had decided to stay and talk to Miz Larkin and Jerry Larkin like I wanted to? What if I had just followed my own inclination, and stayed out there? Or what if I had had a ferocious accident on the Styx River bridge, and right this very minute I'd be singing hymns with the guppies? You'd be out here all by your lonesome, about to drown in a glider!"

All the while she was scolding him, Belinda raised James Redfield out of the glider, and guided his palsied way through the glass doors. She helped him onto his bed, where he lay back wearily. She removed his shoes and placed them in their accustomed spot, then went to close the doors that opened onto the patio.

"Don't do that, Miss Pie, I want to hear the rain." Belinda paused and stared out into the patio. A few heavy drops exploded against the iron chairs. The dark sky pushed against the tops of the pines.

"Mr. Red," she said softly, "I want some thanks, because I

just saved you from a watery grave out there on your very own private patio. Next thing I know I'm gone have to quit school and take care of you full time, because you sure aren't gone do it."

Belinda Hale had been tending to James Redfield for the past nine months, and the man had grown dependent on her daily ministrations. She plumped his pillows, and warmed Nina's leftovers for his dinner and prodded him to take his medicine and scolded him when he did not. When he fell asleep in the afternoon, it was to the sound of her voice; and when he woke a couple of hours later, it was with her speech growing louder and more coherent in his ears. He was an old man, and the attention of this lovely young girl flattered him, though he was careful at the same time to pay her well for the time that she spent at his house.

Ted Hale, the sheriff, didn't like his daughter's spending so much time at James Redfield's bedside; but he hadn't the courage to command Belinda to leave off her visits. The pay was generous, and Belinda put most of it into the bank—there was little chance of the cheerleader being caught up short in anything—and he could not have replaced it. Beyond that, Ted Hale had a great respect for James Redfield, who was acknowledged the most powerful and the richest man in Babylon—and he had thereby all the more respect for his daughter, who controlled the difficult invalid so easily. The sheriff was good friends with Nathan Redfield, James's elder son, who now ran the bank, and Nathan's greeting to him was always appended with praise for Belinda's indispensable care of his father.

Ted Hale knew that James Redfield was not on the best terms with his offspring, Nathan and Benjamin, and suspected that Belinda, whether by design or out of accidental charity, was acting as a buffer between father and sons. He sometimes subtly questioned his daughter on this point, but Belinda was careful to misunderstand and deflect her father's veiled inquiries.

The sheriff's surmise was in fact the case. Whole days went by when James Redfield saw neither of his sons, though both were unmarried and lived at home. Nathan was away at the bank during the day, and took lunch where he could be served a couple of strong drinks—Nina didn't approve of liquor, and would never allow it to be drunk with a meal that she prepared. For two years, Benjamin had been apprenticing as a teller at the bank, but his work was slow and inaccurate. Now his sole duty at CP&M was to drive to Pensacola three times a week to pick up bags of coins needed for Babylon's merchants, leaving at different times of the morning, but returning always half an hour before closing. He saved the bank a portion of its Wells Fargo fees.

Otherwise, Ben did little. From April through October he lay on the hot white sand in front of Nathan's condominium on the beach at Navarre, at the eastern tip of Santa Rosa Island in the Gulf of Mexico. When it was too cold for the beach, Ben watched television, and accompanied his brother to the dog track in Cantonment. Since his father didn't question him on the progress of his apprenticeship, Benjamin was never put to the extremity of lying.

In the evenings, Belinda fixed a small dinner for James Redfield, consisting principally of the leftovers from the noontime meal prepared by Nina. Nina was middle-aged, large-boned and coarse-featured, and was never seen without an expensive glossy black wig that she had purchased in New Orleans an hour before John Kennedy's assassination. Her bulging figure was confined in a blue uniform a size too small, and she was proud of being the only maid in Babylon to wear one. She was devoted to James Redfield, and had worked for him since the death of his first wife in 1954.

Occasionally Benjamin or Nathan would peek into their father's bedroom and greet him briefly. This was to demonstrate that there was no outright warfare between themselves and Mr. Red. When something particular was wanted, or some message had to be delivered, or a signature secured, they would sit briefly on the corner of the bed or at the other end of the glider. James Redfield didn't object to this lack of attention, for he found the interviews no more welcome than did Benjamin and Nathan. He was not lonely when he could count on seeing both Nina and Belinda in the course of the day, and few afternoons went by when he did not have one or the other to gossip with him on his patio. He appeared to use the two women as protection against his sons.

James Redfield had recently concluded that life had never been so satisfactory as it was now, even though he rarely left his small suite of rooms. He was secure and untroubled, no longer worried about the bank, and he saw no one he wished to avoid. Nina knew exactly whom to allow in, and whom to turn away at the door.

His two sons were the thorns in his flesh. He suspected that neither was up to any good, and thought that they were probably bad in different ways. But these fears remained necessarily vague, since they were respectful in his presence, and told him nothing at all of their lives. James Redfield's friends, no longer close to him, were unwilling to repeat what they had heard of Nathan and Ben, even supposing that they knew anything, and the old man was too proud to ask, afraid of what he might hear.

Nina professed ignorance of the ways of Benjamin and Nathan, and always exclaimed only, "I don't know for the life of me where they gone to, Mr. Red. You could switch me with a entire blackberry patch till I was standing in a puddle of my own blood, and I still wouldn't know nothing about them two."

Belinda was cagier than Nina, and told James Redfield only things, perhaps true, perhaps fabricated for the occasion, that would reassure him. She would say: "Why, Mr. Red, Benjamin was so nice to me last time I went in the CP&M, and I did a deposit and a withdrawal at the same time, and he didn't make one single solitary mistake, and he's probably right out there right now on the diving board about to do a belly flop—you want me to go see if I can find him?" Or, speaking of the elder son, she would say: "Mr. Nathan and my daddy said they were going out to supper in Pensacola tonight, Daddy knows this real nice place, and it's out on the pier, and you know there's nothing like salt water to give you a appetite for steak and potatoes, so Daddy *loves* to go there. I told Mr. Nathan not to let my daddy go out drinking any three-point-two beer, and Mr. Nathan pulled out this stack of Bibles, and promised me he wouldn't . . ."

James Redfield knew exactly what Belinda Hale was doing, but he lazily allowed himself to be reassured.

The rain fell heavily, and against James Redfield's wishes, Belinda closed the door onto the patio, leaving a space of only about three inches. As it was, she had to pull her chair close beside the bed so that they could hear one another over the noise of the falling water.

"Miss Pie, I do believe you make up stories that you think are gone make me feel good, I believe you do!" he cried in his highest pitch.

"I told you not to call me that, Mr. Red, or I am gone walk out that door into the blinding rain, and never set foot in this room again."

"I couldn't do without you, you know that . . ." said the old man, and Belinda smiled at him beatifically. He hoped he would be dead before Belinda went away to nursing school.

Mr. Red and Belinda talked half an hour more. (Only Belinda and Nina were privileged to use this nickname for James Redfield.) Belinda excitedly told the invalid of her success in being elected co-captain of the cheerleader squad, and Mr. Red wanted to write out a large congratulatory check, but Belinda wouldn't hear of it.

"Where you think I'm gone cash something like that? I take it down to the CP&M, and everybody there's gone know about it in two minutes flat, and they gone think I'm doing *night duty* here!"

In the midst of her laugh, there was a brief knock at the door. It was opened immediately, and Benjamin Redfield's tousled head of dark brown hair craned around. "Hey, Daddy . . ." he said softly.

"What you want, Ben?" his father demanded shortly.

"Daddy, Nathan just wanted to know if Belinda was in here." Ben stepped inside the door. He was of medium height, and below average looks, which however had improved after he had grown the moustache that Belinda had once playfully suggested to him.

"I'm here," said Belinda brightly: "You mean you couldn't hear me at the other end of the house?"

"I heard you," the young man grinned.

"What does Nathan want with Belinda?" asked James Redfield. Ben looked confused. Belinda winked at him, and he became even more flustered. "Daddy, I don't know, something about supper, I guess. Sure is coming down, hunh?"

"Somebody pulled out the stopper," cried Belinda, and stared dramatically through the plate glass. Rain beat against the cast iron furniture, and tore up the dirt in the flower beds around the patio.

Ben stood clumsily about, and his father sighed heavily. "Well Belinda's here, as you can see if you got eyes, Ben, but she is taking care of me, as I hope you can also see. Nathan's got two good legs, and a good back, and it looks to me like he could take care of himself. And why you run his errands for him I want to know?"

"Daddy," pleaded Ben. "I just came in here to speak to you, and to see if Belinda was in here with you. I didn't come in here to get blessed out."

"Mr. Red, why don't I go see what Mr. Nathan wants? I swear, Ben, you and Mr. Nathan are more helpless than Mr. Red." She smiled graciously at her employer, saying in a lower voice: "And *he's* just pretending 'cause he likes me to wait on him. The three of you would run Nina and me down to bloody stumps if we let you. I saw a water-baby in a prefab incubator that could take care of itself better than the three of you put together."

With a melting smile, Belinda rose from her chair, and marched to the door. "Ben, you stay here and talk to your daddy till I get back from seeing what it is that Mister Nathan Redfield cain't do for himself."

Ben, with a gesture of impatience and dismay, looked imploringly at Belinda. He had no wish to remain behind with his father. She cocked her head at him severely, and he moved irresolutely toward the chair that she had just vacated.

"Take him with you, Miss Pie, I don't have anything to say to him, and he don't have *nothing* to say to me."

"Daddy!" protested Ben.

"Mr. Red, you ought not talk about Ben in front of him like that. If you'd just sit and listen, Ben could tell you lots of things that you'd like to hear. He talks to me and I listen to him for hours on end, and it don't seem like twenty minutes have gone by, from start to finishing it off." Mr. Red said nothing, and Belinda shrugged. "Well, Ben," she sighed, "I guess you better come on with me. I declare, there are times I can get lost in this house, like I had never been in here before in my life. If the King of Sweden moved in with his wife and his twenty kids, you probably wouldn't even know they were here till you saw 'em taking up the swimming pool . . ."

Belinda pushed Ben out of the room, turned and smiled at Mr. Red, and then was gone herself.

Alone in the large, sparsely furnished, low-ceilinged room, James Redfield turned painfully in his bed, and stared out the plate glass doors into the patio. There the rain had formed wide pools, and the pine needles floated, a brown churning mat atop the flagstones. Pines just beyond the stuccoed walls swayed unrhythmically in strong contrary winds. The light was failing, and for lack of anything else to think of, James Redfield tried to determine, by the sound and quality of the thunder, which houses in Babylon the lightning had struck.

After a flash of lightning not apparently worse than any other, the second hand on the electric clock on the bedside table halted. James Redfield did not notice the loss of power, but braced his body against the inevitable thunderclap.

Chapter 6

The thunder that held James Redfield rigid and fearful on his bed had rolled up in thick overpowering clouds from the Gulf of Mexico, through Babylon quickly, and farther north to the Styx River. The waters of the stream were too disturbed to reflect the lightning, but all that part of the river not shadowed by overhanging vegetation or the planked bridge turned a shimmering leaden blue, and glistened like oiled snakeskin.

Evelyn Larkin stood at her bedroom window, and looked out over the blueberry patch to the Styx River bridge, watching for her granddaughter. The lightning flashed cold and blue, and bowed the trees crazily on either bank of the turbulent river. At the same time that she was impatient to see Margaret crossing the bridge, Evelyn hoped she had taken shelter in Babylon, and not ventured out. The Styx River road was awash. Lightning struck in the forest on both sides of the stream.

Below, Jerry Larkin stood motionless on the front porch. He could see little through the water that poured in an uninterrupted sheet from the roof, tearing up the flower beds, gouging splinters from the sagging steps. Without his grandmother having to ask, he had removed the great pots of fern from the ledges, where they were in danger of being overturned.

Jerry could not bring himself to look out the southern end of the porch, toward the blueberry bushes. It had rained this way three years before, when the crop was destroyed, when the Styx rose, when he had feared that the entire house would wash down to the Perdido.

With sudden resolution, Jerry loped to the other end of the porch. He stared toward the patch, and wondered then what he had expected to see. The bushes shook eerily; all were turned a light shade of green because the wind twisted the leaves wrong-side up. He knew that already the berries on the lower branches had been beaten into the earth, and that perhaps five percent of the crop would be ruined with each hour of rain that kept up with this force. His temptation was to run out into the patch, and see the berries destroyed; but among the destruction, his anxiety and frustration would only increase to a hoarse fever.

The screen door swung damply open. Jerry turned at the muffled sound.

"Jerry," said his grandmother quietly, "You come on inside. I see lightning. I don't want you out on the porch when there's lightning."

Jerry nodded with unaccustomed obedience, and followed his grandmother inside.

Evelyn turned to her grandson in the darkened hallway. His form was blackly outlined against the dark green and gray landscape visible through the front screen door. Stray raindrops blown across the porch filled the rusting squares of the screen.

"I'm worried about Margaret," said Evelyn with a calmness that Jerry could see was feigned. "I looked out my window, watching for her. I didn't see her. Jerry, I didn't want to see her. I don't want to think of her out in weather like this. I don't like to think of her crossing the Styx. Those planks could fall through."

"If Margaret had started out before it started to rain, she would have been here by now. Since she's not here, it means she decided to stay in Babylon. She's just waiting for it to be over. I'm surprised she hasn't called." He spoke softly to his grandmother, pausing between each sentence in hopes that his logical explanation of Margaret's failure to return would comfort her.

"Maybe we ought to call the school. I'm scared to use the phone when it's lightning like it is, but I've *got* to find out where Margaret is. I've *got* to make sure that she's safe." She walked into the small front parlor, and headed for the window that looked out onto the blueberry patch. On a small table before this window was the only telephone in the house.

"Call the school," said Jerry, "but I don't think anybody'll be there. I 'spect that Margaret saw it was about to come down, and went over to sit it out with some friend of hers, maybe Annie-Leigh Hooker or somebody like that." He followed his grandmother into the parlor.

From the directory, Jerry read out the number of the North Escambia County High School, but Evelyn's hands trembled so, that Jerry dialed the number himself. He handed the receiver to his grandmother.

Lightning striking close by illuminated the room with a cold blue light, and thunder following immediately on shook the house to its foundations. The windows rattled in their frames.

Evelyn stared at her grandson in terror. "It went dead," she whispered. "It started ringing and then it went dead."

Jerry took the phone, listened, then jiggled the buttons, twirled the dial, all without effect. "The lines are down," he said at last.

Evelyn moved slowly over to a chair, and sat weeping.

Jerry threw up his hands. "Grandma, don't cry, please don't cry. There's no reason for it. The lines have been down before. They're always coming down. I'll bet they were down in Babylon since the beginning of the storm, and that's the reason Margaret hasn't called yet."

"You think that's it?" asked Evelyn, and raised her head hopefully.

Jerry nodded. He threw himself into the corner of the couch, sinking miserably into the broken springs. He hated all this: The telephone lines down, Margaret unaccountably absent, his grandmother about to twist into hysteria—and behind it all was the growing conviction that a substantial portion of their blueberry crop was being destroyed by the rain. They had little money left, and soon they would have no hope of getting more. He reached behind him to turn on the reading lamp beside the couch: He wanted light in the room.

The light failed to go on. "Is that the bulb?" he asked automatically.

Evelyn stood nervously, and tried to turn on the television set. Again, nothing happened.

"Power lines are down too," said Jerry grimly. Evelyn broke into fresh tears.

"Oh, Grandma, don't go on like that! You crying won't do us a bit of good! It won't get Margaret back here any faster! It won't turn the lights back on!"

Evelyn turned away from him, and stifled her sobbing against the back of her hand.

"I'm sorry," said Jerry quietly, "just tell me where the candles are."

Evelyn didn't answer for a moment, but when she turned back toward him from the window, she had stopped weeping entirely. Her voice was low and even: "I'll get the candles, Jerry. I want you to take the car into Babylon and look for Margaret."

Jerry remained still, then said carefully: "No, I'm not going to do it. Margaret's inside somewhere, safe and sound, and she'll call us when she can. If I go out in that, I could have a wreck easy, and we *got* to have that car to get the berries to Pensacola. How are we going to afford another car if I have a wreck?"

"Do you want me to go?" said Evelyn slowly. "Because if you don't go, I will . . ."

"I'll go," said Jerry sullenly, and rose from the couch.

Knowing that nothing would keep out the water, Jerry didn't bother to put on boots or a coat. He took the keys from the hall table, and dashed out the front door.

Evelyn Larkin stood in the darkened hallway, convulsively

gripping the wooden frame of the screen door, and watched Jerry break through the sheet of water that crashed off the roof onto the front steps.

Most of the yard in front of the house was sheeted in standing water. This shallow pond was deepest over the depressed driveway. The station wagon got halfway to the highway—throwing up chest-high waves of chalky red water—before it stalled, then died. Evelyn turned away despairingly.

Jerry pushed open the car door, and strode awkwardly through the ankle-deep mud. He jumped up the front steps, avoiding those he knew to be rotten. The curtain of water falling from the roof closed mockingly behind him.

Jerry removed his sodden shoes and socks, rolled up the cuffs of his jeans, and stepped silently into the house. He climbed the stairs three at the time. On the way to his bedroom he paused at his grandmother's door. She stood, her back to him, staring out the window at the road into Babylon, and at the bridge that crossed the Styx.

They were trapped on the blueberry farm that night. The rain kept up, with a small abatement every hour or so that they hoped was a sign that the storm had passed over, but in a few moments the rain picked up again with increased vehemence. The power and telephone lines were not repaired, and the station wagon remained mired in the driveway.

Evelyn and Jerry sat together in the little parlor at the front of the house. But for the continuing lightning, two candles on the mantelpiece were the only illumination. They talked for perhaps ten minutes out of every hour, repeating for their comfort all the possible innocuous reasons for Margaret's having failed to return. Again and again, Evelyn declared her inability to rest until Margaret was back with her. But by eleven, she was dozing, though starting at the thunder, and protesting feebly at the disturbing dreams that came inexorably upon her.

She woke once, and found the room wholly dark. The clock on the mantel ticked loudly, and its faint green luminous dial read half-past one. The candles on either side had gone out, but she could smell the burnt wicks still.

She rose groggily, holding on to the arm of the chair, and

propelled herself to the window. This had been raised slightly, and the damp air blew softly through the azaleas that bordered the house. The rain had stopped, and the clouds broken to the south. The waning crescent moon shone lividly pale over the water that lay above the level of the grass in most parts of the yard. The house seemed to have floated into a shallow colorless sea.

A man leapt out of the bushes that clustered near the Styx River bridge. His black silhouette splashed silently through that calm sea toward the house.

Evelyn screamed for Jerry. She turned away, breathing heavily, and stumbled toward the hallway. She slammed the front door shut, and fumbled with the key in the lock. It fell to the floor before she could turn it. Evelyn dropped to her knees. With her face pressed against the door, she ran her hands frantically over the rough floor until she had retrieved the key. She pressed it back into the lock, and turned it forcefully. The bolt shot.

The old woman raised herself weakly and dizzily. She feared that the man would appear at the parlor window, or that she would hear his steps on the porch. She climbed the stairs to wake Jerry in his room. She felt that the intruder was standing at the front door, peering through the glass, watching her ascend the stairs.

Her heart beating dangerously fast, Evelyn pushed open the door of Jerry's room, and gasped his name. His bed was away from the window, and she could not see into that dark corner. Rushing toward the bed, she collided with a chair, and fell sprawling over the undisturbed covers. Jerry wasn't there.

Then feverishly the thought occurred to her that it was perhaps Jerry that she had seen leap through the bushes. With this timorous hope to strengthen her, she limped to her own bedroom and cautiously approached the window. She drew the curtains closed, then peered out of one corner onto the property.

There was now no movement near the bridge; even the wind had died down. But a feeble light moved erratically through the blueberry patch, the gleam of a weak flashlight. Evelyn threw her hand over her mouth, realizing in relief that it must be Jerry, checking on the berries after the rain. Earlier, he had been looking at the condition of the bridge. She pulled a small chair to the window, and gazed out of a little corner of a pane, still fearful until certain it was Jerry. At last she saw him directly below, coming to the front of the house. She hurried downstairs to unlock the door for him.

"Oh, Jerry," she cried, weeping though she had meant not to. "I was so frightened! I saw you in the yard, and I didn't know who it was!"

"I'm sorry," said Jerry. "I didn't think you were going to wake up. I went to check the berries. And I had a look at the bridge." He sighed, and moved into the parlor. "We're not going to have a good year. The storm came at the worst possible time." He shook his head morosely.

"What about the bridge?" his grandmother asked. "Margaret has to get across that bridge."

"About five planks gone, I guess. Three of 'em right together near our side, and the water's high, so it was a risk just going out on it. I'll work on it as soon as it's light out. I put up the Bridge Out sign on the other side, but I guess people in Babylon'll know enough not to try to get over the bridge tonight."

"What about Margaret?! What if Margaret tries to get home tonight, and she sees that sign and she turns back?"

"Margaret's not gone come out tonight. She'll stay wherever she is, and come back in the morning. By that time, I'll have the bridge fixed."

Jerry helped his grandmother up the stairs tenderly, bringing a candle to put on her bedside table. "I don't need it, Jerry darling, the moon is bright tonight. It doesn't matter anyway, since I won't be able to get a wink without Margaret in the house, even though I know she's all right, we just don't know where she is, that's all. I'm old, and I worry, and I just can't help it—I love you and Margaret too much for my own good."

Jerry hugged his grandmother goodnight, and went to his own room, softly closing the door behind him. He returned to Evelyn's room several minutes later, and said softly: "Go to sleep, Grandma. Go to sleep and we'll see Margaret in the morning. She may even be back by the time you wake up. Margaret gets up early, and she hates strange beds, she says. I'm going to close the curtains, Grandma . . ." He stood for a moment at the window, and glanced over the scene below him; the scrap of moon was reflected on the Styx at a point just a few feet downstream of the bridge, and was reflected calmly, though Jerry knew with what swirling intensity the water flowed tonight. He pulled the thin lengths of patterned fabric together and whispered, "I don't know about you, but the brightness of the smallest moon can keep me awake all night long . . ."

In times of heavy rain, the black waters of the Styx swell rapidly and flow with alarming swiftness. The stream is short but strong, and the land about it drains quickly through many thousands of unnamed, uncharted tributaries: Creeks, branches, brooks, runs of water that flow quietly into the river every twenty feet or so, along both sides of its course. Three small brooks, that dry up entirely in drought, trickle through the blueberry patch itself. Because of these innumerable fingers of water, the river rises quickly in storm, and remains high for some time.

On this night, beneath the Styx River bridge, the water rose inch by inch along the rotting pilings. Tree branches, new fallen or suddenly dislodged, were caught briefly against the posts, knocked one to the other, and then were swept crazily downstream, where no other bridge would interrupt their progress.

Margaret Larkin's bicycle was caught in a cold deep gully of the Styx, the wheels and handlebars lodged among slime-covered black stones. Silt was already beginning to fill in beneath this new obstruction in the river's course. Margaret's body, her head downstream, stirred gently, as if turning in delicious sleep.

Already, the young girl's clothing was being loosened by the flow of water down the length of her body. Fragments of cloth ripped by her killer's knife tumbled solemnly toward the Perdido. Margaret's eyelids and mouth had been pushed wide open. As if expressing wonder at sudden death, she gaped sightless through the black cold waters of the Styx to the moon overhead.

Evelyn woke at seven, past her accustomed hour, and felt ashamed that she had slept when she ought to have been worrying about her granddaughter. Jerry's conjecture that Margaret might be back by the time that she got out of bed made Evelyn tremble with the hope that if she went downstairs, she would find the girl sitting in the front parlor, making coffee in the kitchen or rocking slowly in the swing on the front porch. The old woman lay motionless hoping for noise in another part of the house, proof of Margaret's presence.

The house was still.

The window was open behind the thin curtains, and Evelyn heard an echoed hammering, that she knew to be Jerry nailing new planks onto the Styx River bridge. She rose and from the window stared at Jerry's kneeling figure on the distant bridge. The morning sun cast dappled green shadows all around her grandson. For a startled happy moment, Evelyn saw Margaret standing behind Jerry, waving her hands and remonstrating, but when the figure was suddenly no longer there, Evelyn realized it was only a trick of her imagination and the morning sunlight.

After she had dressed, Evelyn descended the stairs slowly. She pushed the button that turned on the overhead light in the dining room, to check if the power had returned; it had. She was just about to try the telephone when Jerry came through the front door. "I've already made the calls, Grandma."

"Where's Margaret," demanded Evelyn, "when is she coming back?"

"I called Mr. Perry. He said that Margaret helped him at the school until five, and then she left. He said she was on her way back here, on her bicycle. He said she probably stopped at some-body's house on the way because it looked like a storm, and she didn't want to get caught in it." Jerry did not tell his grand-mother that Warren Perry had sounded very worried, and that this explanation was one that Jerry had supplied the teacher; Mr. Perry had merely agreed to it hopefully.

"Where's Margaret . . . ?" cried Evelyn again.

"I called Annie-Leigh Hooker. She hadn't seen Margaret since day before yesterday. But yesterday afternoon Annie-Leigh was working at the store until six. She didn't get home until well after the rain had started, and so if Margaret went by her house, she wouldn't have known about it."

"Who else did you call? D'you call all her friends? Margaret has so many friends, so many people like her. Maybe . . ." Evelyn moved into the parlor, distracted.

"No," said Jerry softly, "I didn't call anybody else. I guess it makes sense now to go in and talk to the sheriff."

A little after eight o'clock, Evelyn and Jerry Larkin crossed the Styx River bridge on their way into Babylon. The waters of the river still were swollen and black. Large leafed branches and small dead animals floated downstream, knocked about under the bridge, and then tumbled unchecked down to the junction of the Styx with the Perdido.

As they went over, Jerry could hear the difference in sound made by the old and new boards. Maintaining the bridge was a bothersome responsibility, but it had never been so onerous as this morning. The old boards had been swollen with dampness, and gave rottenly beneath his slender weight. It was a wonder that any car made it over at all, Jerry thought. Small spots of sunlight flickered on the boards around him, and he grew dizzy staring into the black agitated water that flowed beneath the bridge. It swirled in strange eddies, with black foam. Holding onto the edge of a plank for support, Jerry had leaned down and stared into the water, which seemed thicker and muddier than he had ever known it in his life. A scarlet and green woodpecker, its head twisted backwards, pitched suddenly into sight, spun twice around one of the pilings, and then was cast up on the sandbar where once Jerry and Margaret had dug for pirate treasure.

Chapter 7

In the country around Babylon, where the ground is soft and rarely disturbed, rattlesnakes breed profusely, and are an ever present danger to hunters, the owners of livestock, and indeed to all who live near the piney woods. To rid the area of a substantial number of snakes, the Chamber of Commerce of Babylon holds a rattlesnake rodeo each year during the reptile's mating season. A prize is offered for the largest caught, and at the closing there is a barbecue at which everyone in town grimaces and tastes cooked rattlesnake meat and then decides that it cannot be distinguished from Kentucky-fried chicken.

The difficulty is that the snakes must be brought in alive. This would seem a nonsensical demand, since the point of the event is to clear the county of the vipers; but the hunters all declare there is no sport in simply killing them. A large wire cage, twenty feet long, ten feet wide, and six feet high is constructed behind the town hall, and there the live snakes are kept until the end of the Rodeo.

The snakes are easy to catch. Practice will teach you to find their holes; you become familiar with their favorite type of ground, and just the "look" of it all. The apparatus is not complicated: a sturdy broom handle with a wire loop at the end, which can be pulled taut. The loop is placed over the snake's hole, and then the ground just about is prodded sharply. The only trick is that when the rattler slithers out of the hole and through the loop, the wire must be pulled tight immediately. To fail to secure the snake just behind the jaws is potentially lethal. It doesn't matter how much the rattles flail in the air if the head of the enraged snake is kept far away. The rattler is then thrust into a large double croker sack—burlap bags used to store farm produce and fodder—and the loop let slacken. The operation is dangerous insofar as rattlesnakes are always dangerous to be near; but better to approach them with a broomstick and a loop of wire, than to come upon them unawares.

Sheriff Ted Hale had made it a rule that no boy under six-

teen was allowed to participate in the rodeo. This injunction was
to keep young boys from foolishly coaxing rattlesnakes out of
their holes—but Hale generously allowed those under the req-
uisite age to accompany their fathers and elder brothers on these
summer expeditions.

Ted Hale's office was a high narrow room at the back of the
town hall; it overlooked the rattlesnake pen. The walls of the
office were painted green to a height of ten feet, and had been
badly peeling for the past three years. Above a picture molding
was a three-foot section of white plaster that had yellowed with
cigarette smoke. A ceiling fan that was rarely oiled whirred noisily from March through November, but the sheriff was thank-
ful that it covered the incessant rattle and hiss of the snakes
throughout the month of July.

Three newspaper photos of a younger and slimmer Ted Hale
apprehending criminals—clutching them by their collars as he
might have held up a string of fish—were hung on the wall next
to the frosted-glass door. About twenty framed pictures of Belinda Hale were grouped on the other side: Belinda in the first
grade through the twelfth, Belinda at the junior-senior prom,
Belinda at the cheerleader clinic at the University of Mississippi,
Belinda in the rotunda of the capitol in Tallahassee shaking hands
with the governor.

On the morning after the worst thunderstorm that Babylon
had seen in a number of years, Ted Hale sat hunched over his
desk, trying to keep the crumbs of his second doughnut off the
file folders that were set before him. He already had spilled his
coffee on a letter from the head of the Florida Highway Patrol.
Hale was a large-boned man, who would never really be fat; but
he would never really be slender again either. His voice was low
pitched, and so slow that it gave him the constant air of consideration and cunning.

He was brushing the doughnut crumbs off his desk into his
lap, when the door to his office, about fifteen feet away at the
far end of the room, was opened. Jay Neal, his youngest officer, twenty-three, gangling, shy, and terrified of firearms, stood
with his hand on the knob, and was about to speak, when Evelyn
Larkin and her grandson rushed past him into the room.

"I told 'em you hadn't even finished your coffee," protested Neal in a shrill voice, but Hale ignored him.

"Hey, Miz Larkin," he said slowly. "How you doing, Jerry? I heard Belinda talking last night on the phone about how good your berries was gone be this—"

"Berries are gone," said Jerry shortly.

"Well—" began the sheriff.

"Sheriff," interrupted Evelyn impatiently, "we cain't find Margaret. We don't know where Margaret is—"

Hale motioned them to take the two chairs in front of his desk. They had been removed from the ruins of the Piney Woods Baptist Church Sunday school building after it burned, and still bore scorch marks on the ladder backs.

"What?" demanded the sheriff peaceably: "You mean you cain't find her? Margaret is what—one year, two years, behind Belinda in the school?"

"Margaret didn't come home last night," said Jerry. "She was at the high school yesterday, helping Mr. Perry grade some papers. She left there on her bicycle and she never came home."

"D'you call Warren?" asked the sheriff. Warren Perry rented out the tiny apartment above the garage in the backyard of the sheriff's house.

"I called this morning," replied Jerry. "He saw her ride off on her bicycle, a little while before the rain started. I called some of her friends, but they hadn't seen her either." Jerry thought it best to let the sheriff imagine that they had already made extensive inquiry.

"Well," said the sheriff thoughtfully, "weren't the lines down out at your place last night?"

Evelyn nodded: "Of course. Margaret would've called if she could have. The lines were back up this morning, and she didn't call. Something happened to her. We wouldn't be here if we didn't think something had happened to her."

"What you think could have happened?" asked the sheriff. "It's about two miles from the school out to your place. On a bike that's not more than fifteen minutes, and that's with stopping for a drink of water and a ice cream cone to boot. And there's no-where to get a ice cream cone or a drink of water from the high school out to your place. In fact, there's not much of anything there."

"That's why we came to you!" cried Evelyn: " 'cause we don't know! She left the school, and she didn't come home! She's not with any of her friends, so where is she?" Evelyn cast her hand over her mouth, trying to keep from tears.

"Well," said the sheriff, "maybe somebody saw her. Ed Geiger goes fishing out at your bridge. He was there yesterday, came back just before the lightning started. I spoke to him and he didn't say a thing then about seeing Margaret, though even if he had, I don't know why he would tell me about it. Belinda didn't say nothing about seeing Margaret either, when she was coming back from your place yesterday evening."

Evelyn nodded: "We thought it might be Margaret coming up, but it was Belinda. I wish Margaret had been with her . . ."

Hale turned in his chair a little, and brushed the crumbs out of his lap onto the floor. Quietly he suggested: "Maybe Margaret didn't plan on coming home."

"Where *else* would she go?" Evelyn demanded. "She knew I was fixing supper for her."

Jerry saw what the sheriff was after, and tried to think of a way to head him off before he upset his grandmother further. But before he could, Hale went on: "Maybe she just . . . went off."

"On a wheel!" cried Evelyn.

"Girls sometimes just . . . go off. Not thinking, that's all. And they just . . . go off. Sometimes they go off by themselves, sometimes they go off . . . with somebody."

Excitedly, Evelyn protested: "What are you talking about?! Margaret doesn't *run off*! She's only fourteen! Where would she go off *to*? Who would she go off *with*?"

Hale backed down when he saw that Evelyn didn't—or didn't want to—understand. "It was just a idea, just a idea." He stood. "We'll find Margaret. She was on a bicycle, she's around. Probably still in Babylon."

Sharply Evelyn cried: "You know where she is! Where is she?!"

Hale threw up his hands: " 'Course I don't know where she

is, Miz Larkin. I mean, she just couldn't have gotten far on a bicycle, in the middle of a storm like we had last night."

"Maybe," suggested Jerry softly, "maybe she had an accident."

"If she had, somebody would have reported it. We're not out in the middle of the wilderness. If Margaret had stayed on the road, and had a accident, then somebody would have found her and taken care of her. I'm gone look of course, but you got to do two things for me, Jerry . . ."

"Anything!" cried Evelyn: "He'll do anything you want him to. I couldn't sleep, sheriff, last night I didn't close my eyes . . ."

"What you want us to do?" asked Jerry, riding over his grand-mother's complaint.

"Jerry, first thing I want you to do, is take Miz Larkin home, and Miz Larkin, you stay there—"

"I cain't, sheriff, I got to help look for my little girl."

"You got to stay there, in case she comes back, in case she calls," said the sheriff calmly. "And that's that, Miz Larkin."

"What else?" said Jerry.

"Bring me back in a picture of Margaret. The one that went in the yearbook'll be fine."

"You know what Margaret looked like, sheriff!" protested Evelyn.

"I know Margaret, sure, Miz Larkin, but maybe all the men out there don't know her, and I want them to know who they're looking for." In a lower voice, he added: "And if for some reason we don't find her, we'll send the picture to Tallahassee to the highway patrol. We just need it for our records . . ."

"Records!" exclaimed Evelyn, with less control: "How many people are missing in Babylon that you got to keep records on 'em?"

Hale shook his head, and was thinking of how to get Evelyn Larkin out of the office, when the door opened once more, after a sharp familiar rap on the frosted glass.

Belinda Hale, in her cheerleader outfit and swinging her gold and black pompoms in a wide arc, leapt into the room. "Daddy," she cried: "I just came by to tell you that we are having an emer-gency cheerleader practice this morning, and—"

She broke off, and greeted Evelyn and Jerry with some small

surprise. She could see that Evelyn Larkin was upset, and looked to her father questioningly.

"Listen, honey," said Hale, "when you were coming back from Miz Larkin's yesterday, did you pass Margaret on her bike?"

Belinda shook her head, with great solemnity and pursed lips. "I surely did not," she said in a hoarse whisper. "Why? Did something happen to Margaret?"

Evelyn looked away. Jerry cast down his eyes. Hale shook his head slowly, an indication that Belinda should not renew the question. She licked her lips and rolled her eyes. Already backing slowly out of the room, she said with a brittle smile: "Daddy, I got to run, or I'm gone be late. Good to see you again, Miz Larkin, Jerry . . ."

After she left, Hale turned to Jerry and Evelyn: "Belinda won't say anything to anybody. She knows better. She's got a mouth, but she's also got a zipper to fit it."

Evelyn shook her head distractedly: What did anything else matter but Margaret's safety and return?

"Look," said Hale, glad that Evelyn had calmed down from her near-hysteria: "We don't even really know if Margaret is missing yet. Maybe she overslept at somebody's house. Maybe she's home now. You go back out there and see. If she's not there, give me a call back here. Tell Neal, and he'll tell me. I'm gone ride out your way, and see who's out there, and just see if anybody saw Margaret riding by . . ."

Evelyn nodded tearfully, and Jerry led her toward the door. There, Evelyn turned, and wiping the moisture from her eyes, said in a voice that Hale had to stand still to hear: "Sheriff, I love my little girl like you love yours. You find her for me. You *promise* me you'll find her."

"We'll find her," said Hale, and turned away. Glancing out the window, he saw Belinda waving to him from the corner of the rattlesnake pen. Behind him the frosted glass rattled as the office door was pulled shut.

Chapter 8

After leaving the sheriff's office in the Babylon town hall, Evelyn wanted Jerry to take her directly home, but Jerry argued against this. "No, Grandma," he said carefully and firmly, "we ought to go by the bank first. I've got a hundred dollars, maybe just a little more, in my savings account, and I'm gone take it out today. If there's any berries left after last night, I'm gone have to pay the Scouts when they start coming out on Monday. And we got to buy groceries this weekend too. We're almost out of gas, and since Texaco took their card back we got to pay for it in cash."

Evelyn shook her head in amazement: "Jerry, we don't have one idea in the world where Margaret is, and you are thinking about *Scouts* and *gasoline credit cards?!*"

"I'm thinking about those things 'cause I know Margaret'll be back. She's not lost—we just don't know where she is right now. I'd have to come back into town later anyway to go to the bank, and I'd just as soon do it now." His real motive, entirely unselfish, was not to leave Evelyn alone on the farm, when she was in doubt about Margaret.

"Well," cried Evelyn hastily, "let's go right now. The sooner we're done, the sooner we can get back out to the house. What if the phone is ringing right now? Jerry, I couldn't forgive myself if I thought that I was missing Margaret's call."

"If Margaret's calling now, she'll call back."

"What if she was kidnapped?" whispered Evelyn, and clutched Jerry's arm. They crossed the street blindly to the Citizens, Planters and Merchants Bank.

Jerry laughed hoarsely: "And what do they want for ransom: eight thousand pints of blueberries?"

While Jerry stood in line at the teller's window, Evelyn sat nervously on a leather couch in an alcove at the front of the bank. Several comfortable chairs were arranged about a low round table covered with magazines. A newly installed plate glass window looked out onto John Glenn Avenue. This had been called Main Street since the town was founded, but an emergency session of the town council had changed the name after the astronaut first circled the earth.

The bank had been built just before World War I, and the principal fixtures were handsomely carved of dark wood. But over the years the effect had been spoiled by the addition of common steel desks and other cheap furnishings. James Redfield, before the retirement forced on him by his automobile accident, had made plans to erect a new building. His son Nathan looked to follow through on his father's wishes, but not so quickly as James Redfield would have pursued them. Nathan didn't care much one way or the other what happened to the bank, as long as his salary continued to increase each year. The stock of the bank was owned almost entirely by his father, and Nathan as yet received none of the dividends.

The desks of the four officers of the bank were set behind a low mahogany railing. Nathan Redfield usually arrived at the bank about the time it opened, though he rarely remained until closing; he was forgiven this lack of conscientiousness because he was the acting president, because he stood to inherit the whole thing, and because there was nothing Nathan could do short of embezzling directly out of the teller's drawer that wouldn't still show him off to advantage against Ben.

The combination of Nathan's uncommon languid handsomeness and his father's money made it universally wondered at that he had never taken a wife. When it was brought up to him, Nathan said only that he would "wait till next June, and *then* they'd see a wedding . . ." Or, if June were inconveniently close, he'd say, "I'm seeing someone in Mobile just now, and we'll just wait and see what comes of that." Some people he gave to believe that he was keeping company with a woman in the midst of divorce proceedings, and for her sake had to keep the liaison secret. Others he told he had just that week put his order in at the Sears catalog store, and was awaiting delivery of the perfect spouse. In short, Nathan had such a line of tales and evasions that people didn't know what to think, and all the gossip was contradictory. Other men in town Nathan's age were married fathers, and they prodded Nathan to tell them of his sexual exploits in Mobile and Pensacola, but Nathan disappointed them

altogether, or his stories were too vague to satisfy their pruri-
ence.

It was certain, however, that no woman from Babylon was
suited to Nathan. Six years before, it had been thought that he
would choose one of the two prettiest women in town. Both of
these had had their hopes, and maintained a friendly rivalry. Both
were disappointed. The younger married the manager of the
shirt factory up in Brewton, and the other went long in the tooth.
Nathan flirted with the peroxided widow who tended bar at the
Lost Ways Inn on the Mobile highway, but they had never been
seen together outside the bar; in any case it was not thinkable
that Nathan would introduce such a woman to James Redfield as
his future daughter-in-law.

There was strangely no scandal about Nathan Redfield,
though it was odd that he was a bachelor. Only the dim-witted
and homosexuals—of the latter there were two in Babylon, who
lived next door to one another, and taught grammar school—remained unmarried at so advanced an age as thirty-three.

Mirabelle Hightower, a young Creek girl from the north side
of town, became pregnant in junior high school; it was supposed
in the Indian community that Nathan Redfield was the father.
But the girl was run down on the highway in the fifth month of
her pregnancy, and the question of paternity became irrelevant.
In any case the story had never circulated widely.

Nathan could call almost all of Babylon by its first name, but
had few friends. Those closest to him were the other officers of
the bank and the sheriff, men with whom he sometimes hunted,
or played dominoes, or got drunk. But most of Nathan's pleasures were solitary: He swam a great deal, which allowed him to
keep his figure, and he spent many afternoons at the dog track in
Cantonment, twenty miles distant. And, it was considered that
Nathan was performing an invaluable service to the community
by keeping a rein on his little brother, who wasn't fit to barb wire.
Ben might be unmanageable if Nathan married. But after twelve
years of speculation about what Nathan Redfield was really like,
without coming to much of a conclusion, Babylon gave it all over
with the easy formula: *Nathan Redfield pretty much keeps himself to
himself . . .*

This Friday morning, Nathan sat in his creaking swivel chair, with his feet propped gracefully on the corner of his desk. He leafed idly through a dog-eared copy of *Field & Stream*. He was dressed in a light blue shirt, with a wide blue striped tie that had been loosened at the collar before he even arrived at the bank. Hair at his throat was dark and thick. His blue cotton pants had been immaculately cleaned and pressed by Nina. Her care for Nathan's wardrobe was a kind of sarcasm, for she never tried to hide her distaste for the man himself.

Over the top of the magazine, Nathan cast a perfunctory eye at the uncrowded room, and caught sight of Jerry Larkin. He looked around more attentively then, stared a few moments at the alcove in the front of the bank, and presently rose with the magazine rolled tightly in his fist.

He moved casually through the small wooden gate and toward the alcove, as if to return the periodical to the table before the plate glass window. He tossed it onto a pile of others, and glanced at the old woman sitting on the couch.

"Oh hey, Miz Larkin, how you?" said Nathan, with an affable smile of surprise.

"Nathan, I'm fine, how you?" answered Evelyn automatically. Even if she had thought, she would not have replied any other way, for she had no wish for the town to know that Margaret was missing. But her distracted manner and thick voice betrayed her disquiet.

"Miz Larkin, I was hoping you were coming in today, because I have been meaning to talk to you. Jerry's gone be a minute at the window, he came in right behind the Western Auto deposit, and that woman they got over there never gets it right."

He sat beside her on the couch, and leaned forward a little to speak to her over the loud whirr of the air-conditioning unit just above them.

"Nathan?" said Evelyn cautiously, "what you want to talk to me about—you want to talk about that loan . . . ?"

He nodded slowly.

Evelyn looked around panicked for Jerry. He stood impatiently in the line, and was not looking in her direction. She tried to gather her wits: "Nathan, please let's don't talk right now.

This is a bad time for me to try to talk about something like this. Something happened this morning, and I just—"

"Well, Miz Larkin," protested Nathan, with a small smile and a becoming incline of his head, "I hate to say it, but we just got to talk. Now you know you have been behind on these payments since last October, sometimes a week, sometimes two weeks, sometimes longer than that. We've been over this before, you and me. Sometimes you pay what you owe, but most times you don't. You're already ten days behind on May, and we're not even gone talk about April, and Belinda Hale told my daddy that you weren't even going to start to pick your berries until Monday. So I don't s'pose Jerry is standing in line to put money *in*, is he? Because if he's standing there waiting in line to make a payment on his loan, I'll go over and shake his hand . . ."

Evelyn shook her head miserably: "Nathan, please let us come back next week, and we'll talk it over then. I don't know what Jerry is doing. We don't have the money yet, and I cain't think. I just cain't think when—" She looked away, not daring to complete her excuse.

"When what?" prompted Nathan.

Evelyn began to tremble uncontrollably, and couldn't speak at once: "Nathan, nothing . . ." she faltered.

"We cain't wait till the season's over, Miz Larkin, and I cain't imagine that the kind of rain we had last night did your berries much good."

"No, it—"

"And," continued Nathan, paying no attention to the wild manner in which she twisted her head about: "As acting president of the CP&M, I got to make sure that you've made provision to keep up with your payments on that loan. It was a large loan, and there was some question of giving it to you. You default on that loan, Miz Larkin, and you don't just lose your credit rating, you lose the whole kit and caboodle . . ."

"Jerry! Jerry!" cried out Evelyn. She had lost the meaning of Nathan's words as he continued mercilessly about the loan payments, and since Jerry had still not appeared to aid her, she called out for him, unmindful of what other customers in the bank would think of her outburst.

When Jerry had finished his transaction at the teller's window, he thrust the bills and the passbook into his back pocket, and hurried to his grandmother. He glanced suspiciously at Nathan.

"What's wrong, Grandma?"

She shook her head dismally, unable to speak. She looked up at Nathan, and Jerry stared sullenly at the young, handsome president of the bank.

"I take it you were just making a payment on your loan—the one that's already overdue," said Nathan.

"No," said Jerry defensively, though he rankled beneath Nathan's sarcasm: "Not yet. We got to wait until next week after the first berries sell. Berries were late this year. I made a little installment on it, though, and—"

"Your 'installments' don't amount to much, Jerry, twenty-five dollars a week on the three hundred fifty that's due every month. That doesn't work out just right, you know. You ought to have studied your arithmetic a year or two longer. If I don't get a check soon, I'm just gone have to start proceedings . . ."

"Listen, Mr. Redfield," cried Jerry, incensed: "We made every payment on that loan for the last three years—now we're a couple of weeks late and you're already talking about 'proceedings'? What kind of 'proceedings'? My granddaddy paid a mortgage on that place for thirty years, and when he died, my daddy finished paying it off. They never missed a payment. So why are you pushing this?" He looked about the bank in wonder, as if expecting someone to step forward to explain.

"Nathan Redfield!" gasped Evelyn at last: "Your daddy never spoke to me like this, and you shouldn't either! Your daddy never spoke to his customers this way!"

"My daddy is laid up in the bed, Miz Larkin, and he's not likely to get out of it to speak nice to you either. My daddy just don't have a thing in the world to do with it any more."

"Grandma, let's go," said Jerry, taking her by the arm, and pulling her up out of the chair. Casting angry agitated glances all around, they hurried out the door.

When Nathan returned to his desk behind the mahogany railing, a couple of the other officers came over to him, and leaning forward on their spread hands, said: "Hey, Nathan, what was all that about? Were you giving Evelyn Larkin a hard time, or were you just putting in your order for berries?"

Nathan tapped his desk blotter with the eraser of an unsharpened pencil. "She wanted to increase her loan, extend it three more years, and get five thousand dollars more. I told her we'd have to wait and see what this year's crop was going to be like. She didn't like that. She didn't want it for the farm, she just wanted to buy Jerry a new Oldsmobile Toronado. And what that kind of thing costs, you and me and the Cantonment track couldn't raise on July the Fourth weekend."

The officers laughed at Evelyn Larkin's impossible request, and returned to their desks, already embellishing the story that they would relate to all who might be interested.

Chapter 9

At ten o'clock that Friday morning, Jerry Larkin telephoned the sheriff's office, and left the message that Margaret had not returned, that they had received no news of her, and that Evelyn, in grievous disappointment, had taken to her bed. Jerry had called the doctor, and was awaiting him now.

When Ted Hale returned from watching Belinda practice cheerleading at the high school stadium, he took this information with displeasure. Hysterical women of an advanced age were a great nuisance. You had to deal with them carefully, and hope they didn't have heart attacks while you were just standing there.

Margaret Larkin, Hale believed firmly, was not missing, but had stayed over at someone's house because of the storm. If she had been a couple of years older, Hale would have suspected that she was simply shacked up with some boy in a fourteen-dollar-a-night motel on Pensacola Beach, with pink walls and concrete floors.

This kind of thing had happened before. It was his duty to search for the missing girl, but it would all be so much wasted effort. After the second full day of investigation he would hear, from somebody unconcerned, that the girl had come back for supper the previous night and the family had not bothered to call him up.

At any rate, he didn't intend to start knocking on doors, or posting the girl's photograph on telephone poles yet, though he wouldn't admit this to Evelyn Larkin. An easier and more promising course was to talk to Ed Geiger, who knew everything that went on in Babylon.

Geiger had been recently widowed and his new independence agreed with him. He went fishing every afternoon, leaving the store in the capable hands of Annie-Leigh Hooker, his late wife's young niece.

Geiger was almost bald, and his entire head was burnt bright red. His shape was irresistibly suggestive of a watermelon stood on end. At work he wore white short-sleeved shirts with a string tie, and dark striped pants from suits the jackets of which he had discarded. When he went fishing, Geiger changed his dark striped pants for khaki trousers with zippered pockets that he filled with live bait.

He was a pleasant, easygoing man, and considering that fishing was harmless, he had but one vice: gossip. He had stored more information on the inhabitants of Babylon and northern Escambia County than the welfare department, the Social Security Administration and the IRS put together. What he didn't know probably hadn't happened, and what he couldn't predict probably wouldn't come to pass. There was however nothing supernatural in his omniscience, for Geiger was reliant upon sources for his extensive knowledge: small, specialist, tributary gossips fed into him every day. He learned about the black population from his maid, who talked to him volubly over his lunchtime meal, standing cross-armed in the kitchen doorway while he bolted the food she had prepared for him. He knew about everyone under the age of twenty-one from Annie-Leigh Hooker, and via Ginny Darrish, principal of the high school, Geiger kept tabs on the intrigues among Babylon's "society." What these three females didn't know, the sheriff did.

Ted Hale trusted Geiger, and knew that if he prefaced his questions with the admonition to say nothing for a time, Geiger would respect it. The sheriff walked easily out of the town hall, and entered the sporting goods store. He nodded to Annie-Leigh, a scrawny girl with thick, short-cut black hair. She sat on a high stool behind the counter, playing with a jackknife, and doing the crossword in the Pensacola *News-Journal*.

"Hey, sheriff," she said in her drawling voice: "What can I do for you?"

"Is Ed around?"

"You come to arrest him for his evil ways?" she said slyly.

"Ed's got no evil ways, Annie-Leigh," laughed the sheriff. "Is he in back?" He nodded toward the closed door to the storeroom-and-office.

Annie's dull black eyes glistened suddenly; she closed them and sighed: "They didn't find Margaret, then?"

"How'd you know?!" cried the sheriff. He had spoken hardly two words, and the girl already knew why he was here.

"Easy. Jerry called this morning. I told him I hadn't seen Margaret. Jerry said they didn't know where she was. Their car was parked out front when I came to work, so I figured they must have gone to see you. Miz Larkin's the type to get upset, and of course," she added, "I don't blame her. Now you're here, not wanting to buy bait or anything, just wanting to see Ed, which leads me all to believe that Margaret hasn't made it home yet."

"You getting to be too much like Ed," said the sheriff in a low, awed voice. "I don't think I'm even gone be able to walk past your plate glass window no more without your being able to tell the whole town where I've been, where I'm going, and what I had for dinner three days ago."

"That's right," said Annie-Leigh, "you better go out the back way from now on." She hopped off the high stool, and opened the door into the back. "Ed!" she called briefly: "Sheriff's here to talk about Margaret Larkin. Come on out!"

Annie-Leigh turned back to Hale: "I'm worried." She raised her eyebrows impassively: "Margaret knows how Miz Larkin worries, and if she could get back, she would have. Hell and high water—'scuse my language—and all that. And she surely would have called. That's why I'm worried."

Ed Geiger appeared at the door, and nodded to the sheriff.

Hale returned the nod, but continued to speak to Annie-Leigh: "Let me ask you something—"

"No," said Annie-Leigh flatly, not allowing him to finish: "She wouldn't have. And it doesn't really matter whether she would have wanted to or not. Margaret loves her grandmother too much to worry her, and there's nobody like Evelyn Larkin when it comes to worry."

"You didn't even let me ask the question!" protested Hale.

"Ted," said Geiger, "Annie-Leigh is right. Margaret Larkin didn't go off with anybody at all, I mean, at least not of her own free will. Because if she had, she would have made up an excuse. Evelyn Larkin would have believed it, Jerry wouldn't have, but they wouldn't have been bothering you, in any case."

"Well," said the sheriff, reluctant to be convinced that the simplest explanation for Margaret's disappearance was impossible, "Who has she been seeing lately?"

"Margaret doesn't go out with boys," said Annie-Leigh. "She hasn't had but one date since Christmas, and that was with the Gillis boy, and the only reason she went out with him is because his daddy owns the garage where Jerry sometimes works, and Jerry asked her to do it for him. And she was in that night by ten o'clock, they couldn't even have seen a whole double feature out at the Starlite if she was home in bed by ten o'clock. But you know, sheriff," Annie-Leigh went on, with her head cocked to one side, "Jerry told me that she was supposed to be over at the school yesterday helping Mr. Perry with something or other. Mr. Perry's sort of cute, and I think Margaret has a little bit of a crush on him. She was his assistant when he directed the eighth grade graduation."

"I'd go talk to Warren Perry if I was you, sheriff," said Geiger.

"Ed," said the sheriff: "Margaret was supposed to be on her way home, on her bike, just about the time the rain started."

Geiger nodded: "I was out by the Styx bridge about that time. I felt three drops and packed up. I'm scared of lightning on that river, don't mind the rain, but it looked like lightning. I came back here, didn't see anybody on a bicycle. Up there at the red light, I pulled up aside of Ben Redfield with two six-packs on the front seat, but I didn't see anybody else. It was Coors that

Ben had, and I bet he drove all the way to Pensacola to get 'em. Nobody 'round here will carry Coors."

The sheriff nodded and turned to go. "Well thanks, ya'll. It's a good thing for the city budget that you two don't charge for your information."

He started out of the store, shaking his head, but was brought to a halt by Geiger's voice. It was the fisherman's habit to hold something back for the end, a last fillip of gossip to show that the extent of his knowledge had been underestimated: "Of course, I don't know how upset Evelyn Larkin really was this morning, if right after she goes in to report her own granddaughter missing, she runs direct across the street to the CP&M to take out a loan of six thousand six hundred and fifty dollars to buy Jerry a sky-blue Oldsmobile Cutlass Supreme to ride back and forth to Pensacola in."

Sheriff Hale looked questioningly at Ed Geiger and Annie-Leigh Hooker. "Is that true?"

"Probably not," said Annie-Leigh: "It sounds like Miz Larkin, 'cause there's nothing she wouldn't do for Jerry and Margaret, but she was upset—I talked to Jay Neal this morning—and it doesn't sound like Jerry either. He was with her, and he wouldn't have let her do it. Besides, an Oldsmobile Cutlass Supreme costs a lot more than that."

"Where'd you hear it?" demanded Hal of Geiger.

"Leilah Tompkins told me when I was over at the bank this morning. She didn't say where she got it. 'Course, Nathan turned Evelyn down flat for the loan."

"That don't make no sense at all," said Hale.

"I'm real worried," said Annie-Leigh. She and her uncle exchanged glances, but would say nothing more to the sheriff.

Chapter 10

Shortly before noon, Sheriff Hale drove around again to the high school. He was disappointed to find that Belinda had already finished with cheerleading. Only three cars remained in the parking lot: the aquamarine Vega belonging to the principal of the high

school, and two that he did not recognize. He had hoped to find
Warren Perry, in order to ask him about the previous afternoon.

Hale decided that as long as he was here at the high school,
he might as well talk to Ginny Darrish. It was possible she possessed information she had not yet turned over to Ed Geiger.

Ginny Darrish was the wife of the more prominent of Babylon's two lawyers, which is to say that Charles Darrish had secured the business of James Redfield and the CP&M bank. Ginny
was a good principal, not because she was anything like an ad-
ministrator, but because teachers and students alike were fond
and protective of her. She was a cheerful and pastel woman in her
late forties. Her fleshy skin was bright pink, her eyes a translucent
vivid blue, and her hair a shining silver. Everything about Ginny
Darrish—her makeup, her clothing, her automobile, her entire
house—was created, or bought, or painted, or redone in light soft
colors. A particular powder that she wore left in Ginny's wake a
scent as soft as her unwrinkled cheeks.

People in Babylon, who found fault with everyone, objected
to Ginny Darrish on three counts: She was an unrepentant
gossip, she didn't go to church, and she reveled in superstition.
Ed Geiger was a bigger gossip than Ginny, and other women in
Babylon had never seen the inside of a hymn book or the top-
side of a pew, but no one lived within such superstitious rigors
as did Ginny Darrish. She wouldn't drive on the night of a new
moon; she wouldn't open an umbrella indoors; she wouldn't kill
a spider; she wouldn't begin any project on a Friday; she crossed
her fingers whenever she went over a bridge. On a pantry shelf
she kept three decks of tarot cards, two Ouija boards, a magic
pendulum on a silver chain, and a stack of pamphlets that told
her how to read the future from tea leaves, cloud formations,
lines in the hand, and insect populations.

But on the whole, she was a kind and friendly woman, whose
only real enemy in Babylon was Nathan Redfield. James Redfield's first wife was Ginny's maternal aunt, and had she died
childless, and if James Redfield had not remarried, Ginny would
have stood to inherit the CP&M bank and all the old man's ac-
cumulated wealth. Her probable share was reduced to very little
after the birth of his two sons, and shortly after Nathan's return

from the Air Force, he and Ginny had a falling-out over even that promised little. Nathan swore he would see to it that Ginny received nothing at all. But Ginny knew that the size of her legacy expanded and contracted with the tenor of Nathan's relationship to his father; James Redfield, if he was displeased with his son, called in the lawyer—Ginny's husband—and upped Ginny's percentage of the take. She stayed out of the argument now, reckoning that Nathan's ill temper would do more than her own blandishments, but had reserved one of the three sets of tarot cards to predict how she would fare in the old man's will, as the sole living relative of his first wife.

The sheriff found Ginny in her office, just beyond the front door of the school. She motioned him inside, and he closed the door behind him. Briefly, he told Ginny about Margaret Larkin's disappearance. She listened silently, her pink brow furrowed beneath her silver hair.

"Well," she said at last, "Margaret *was* here yesterday afternoon, sitting at a table in Warren's room, helping him record supplies. He'd count and she'd write down. I saw 'em about three, when I went down the hall to the ladies' lounge. Warren's car was still here when I left about four. He'll be here today too, but not till one."

The sheriff nodded.

Ginny Darrish tapped a lavender fingernail against her coral lips. "Where you think Margaret is?" she said.

Hale shrugged. "Maybe she went to the beach. Maybe she just forgot to call her grandmother. Maybe she tried, and they weren't home, or the lines were still down."

"No," said Ginny shortly: "I don't know what happened, but it wasn't that. Margaret knows how her grandmother can worry. Margaret would have hired a troop of Girl Scouts to ford the Styx if the phones didn't work and the bridge was out, but she would have let Evelyn Larkin know where she was."

"You think?" asked the sheriff.

Ginny Darrish nodded cannily. "You think she went off with some boy, don't you?"

"Maybe," said the sheriff warily, "maybe that's what she did."

"Margaret Larkin is fourteen, Ted. She's just going into the ninth grade. If she's dating at all I don't even know about it. And in any case, I certainly don't think she went off with a boy."

"I sort of wish that was what happened though, Ginny, 'cause that would mean the girl is all right. Fourteen-year-old girls have run off before."

Ginny eyed the sheriff severely. "Not fourteen-year-old girls who had grandmas like Evelyn Larkin."

"Anyway," said the sheriff, after a moment, "I want to speak to Warren. Maybe he knows something. I imagine that girl's just sitting safe and dry somewhere, but we still got to find her."

"Listen, Ted," said Ginny, "as soon as I can leave here, I'm gone hightail it out to see Evelyn. She must be out of her mind."

"She's not in too good shape," said the sheriff, and shook his head.

Ginny nodded: "And I'm gone take my lucky sledgehammer out there, and hit her over the head with it, 'cause that's about the only thing that's gone calm her down if Margaret isn't back yet."

Chapter 11

After dismissing her cheerleaders at eleven-thirty, Belinda Hale had driven home, showered and changed. Then leaving a lengthy and complicated note for her father, which did not tell him where she was going nor when she would be back, Belinda drove to the Redfields.

She entered the house through the kitchen, where she cheerily greeted Nina at the stove. Belinda had seen, when she first came to the Redfield house, that it was essential that she be on Nina's good side. Nina's weak spot was Mr. Red, and when Belinda made it clear that her primary loyalty was to the old man, Nina extended her affection heartily to the young girl.

"Nina," Belinda cried, "with the smell of chicken blocking every one of my five senses, I don't know how I'm gone manage it, but I am gone leave this kitchen for five minutes, to say 'hi' to Mr. Red, and then I'm coming right back in here, and demand a piece of white meat off you."

"It's got your name on it, Belinda."

Belinda knocked softly at James Redfield's door, the same knock with which her father was familiar, and he called her inside.

She stuck her head into the room: "I am not here, Mr. Red, and you didn't see me!"

"Belinda," he said: "I do see you though." He was already pulling himself up in the bed, preparing for her company.

"No, you don't," she cried: "I got to go back in and sit with Nina for twenty minutes, and I want you to shoot me through the head if I'm fifteen seconds longer. She set me aside a breast of chicken, and I am just desperate to stick it between my teeth."

"Who's out there?" James Redfield demanded.

"I didn't see anybody but Nina. And you didn't see me!" she whispered, and pulled the door shut.

She wandered slowly back to the kitchen, and sat at the place Nina had set for her. "You already eaten?" she asked.

"'Fore you got here, Belinda."

"Then why don't you go on home? I'm gone be here the whole afternoon, not doing a thing but sitting and talking to Mr. Red, and trying to get some sun on this pale white body of mine that's going to flesh and fat."

"You not fat, Belinda, and you about as pale as I am. But you just let me wash these dishes up, and I'll go on," said Nina. "I 'preciate it, Belinda, and you tell Mr. Red I've gone home, and I'll see him in the morning."

"I don't want to hear it!" cried Belinda. "You fixed me this chicken that's fit to be served at the Married Feet of Canaan, and you think I'm not going to wash half a sink of dishes in return, why then you are crazy-out-of-your-mind-fit-to-be-sent-to-the-state-asylum-at-Winter-Haven!"

Nina clapped her pudgy hands together: "Belinda, I have never, I have *never* left a house where there was dirty dishes in the sink." She turned on the hot water.

Belinda sat at the table with her breast of chicken, her green salad, and her glass of iced tea, staring at Nina's back. Before Nina was finished, Ben came in from the pool, dripping water over the tiles. He threw himself into the chair next to Belinda's, and drummed his heels on the floor.

"You are splashing me, Ben," she said irritably: "You are getting my crust soggy."

"That's supposed to be *my* chicken," said Ben. "Nina said she was saving the breast for you, and she wasn't even sure you were coming! I had to make do with three drumsticks, but three drumsticks aren't worth one good breast . . ."

Belinda pulled at the gold chain around her neck, and made no reply.

Nina finished up, gathered her things quickly, and left the house by the back door. She said good-bye to Belinda but not to Ben.

"Well," said Ben, "I think that Nina would like to dip *me* in batter and stick me in a four hundred and fifty degree oven."

"I wish she would," cried Belinda vehemently. "You might be doing somebody some good then. It is something, I tell you, *something* for me to come over here in the middle of the day, about to start my nursing duties and I find you, a grown man with two shoulders and a head sticking on between 'em, in a chlorined swimming pool in a private backyard. It's amazing to me that you don't do something with yourself, Ben. I am liable to go in there this afternoon and tell Mr. Red to send you to El Paso, Texas, where they can stick you in a little concrete house on the Rio Grande River with a rifle, so that you can watch for Mexican families swimming over to the United States side. Then maybe you would be doing somebody some good. What good are you doing in the swimming pool?"

Ben waited patiently for the end of this tirade, then he said: "Hey, Belinda, why don't you go with me down to Cantonment this afternoon? We could have a real good time."

"Ben," cried Belinda, "I can't do that. I just sent Nina home, and I'm not gone leave Mr. Red all by himself."

"Well, wait'll Nathan gets back. Nathan can stay here with Daddy. Nathan usually gets home about now."

"Your daddy would have a apoplectic stroke if he thought he was here all by himself with Nathan."

"He's alone here with me and Nathan every night, and don't have a apoplectic stroke every night."

"That's night," argued Belinda, "this is the daytime."

"I don't see much difference," protested Ben sullenly.

"I'm not gone argue with you, Ben, I am gone go in there and sit with Mr. Red, and talk to him, 'cause he don't talk back to me the way you do. You wait for Nathan and go to the track with him like usual."

"You just don't want to go with me, that's all."

"You are right. I certainly do not."

Belinda had washed and put away her plate, cutlery, and glass. Without another word to Ben, she left the kitchen and returned to James Redfield's room.

A little later, she saw Nathan drive up to the house. In a while, he drove off again, with Ben.

"Mr. Red," she then said sweetly, "that was Ben and Nathan going off somewhere, and I don't know where they're going to, but I don't think they're gone be back 'fore suppertime. Would you mind if I took you around to the pool, so that I could get some diving practice in? I always carry a spare bathing suit in my glove compartment, you know, for emergencies."

Mr. Red agreed without hesitation. Belinda guided the wheel-chair through the house, and pushed it out onto the flagstone-paved poolside. She arranged the old man fussily in the blue shade of a large ornamental pine.

During the remaining hours of the afternoon James Redfield watched the young girl dive over and again from the supple board into the pool. Every fifteen minutes, Belinda, with red eyes and puckered skin, squatted at his side, wanting to know if she had improved with the last set of dives, and demanding whether, in truth, she were getting too broad in the behind.

Chapter 12

Warren Perry, of small stature and swarthy complexion, was only a few years older than the teenagers that he taught. He had grown up in Atmore, Alabama, only fifteen miles north of Babylon. In his senior year of high school he had been admitted to Vanderbilt University, but because of his father's bankruptcy that spring, he could not afford to attend. Even at the much less expensive and prestigious college at Troy, his funds were so curtailed that he worked to finish as quickly as he could, in just under three years. Directly after graduation, he had searched for a job as close to his mother as possible, and that position was in Babylon.

As much as was consistent with filial respect, Warren Perry disliked his mother. Mrs. Perry had affected emotional debility after her husband committed suicide in Warren's freshman year at Troy. She miserably and frequently declared to her son, over the telephone and on postal cards, that nothing but his constant attention could keep her out of the grave. Warren passed every weekend with his mother, and most of that time was unhappily consumed in resisting her woeful urgings for him to return permanently to Atmore. As it was, Babylon was a too-easy commute along the road that ran past the Larkin blueberry farm.

Because he spent a substantial portion of the week at his mother's house, Warren felt he did not need much of a place in Babylon. He was also obsessed with saving money, in order to stave off the bankruptcy that had driven his father to suicide. Warren didn't know that his father had lost all his money at the dog track in Cantonment. The widow had always represented the bankruptcy as a bolt from God, arbitrary, inexorable, fatal, and likely to recur in the next generation.

Above his garage, Ted Hale had a small apartment: living room, bedroom, kitchen, and bath. It had been set up for his mother-in-law the year before his wife ran away with the FBI agent. After her daughter bolted, the old woman had still wanted to move in, but Hale wouldn't allow her to do so. Since then the sheriff had rented it out for two- and three-year stretches to unmarried schoolteachers. Before Warren, this apartment had been taken by the female algebra teacher, who had moved to St. Petersburg with her sister—who the sheriff suspected was not related to her at all.

When Hale returned home shortly before noon on Friday, he found Warren backing out of the driveway in his beat-up green Rambler. Hale blocked his path with the cruiser.

"You in a hurry?" the sheriff called out.

"I got to be at the school at one," said Warren, surprised by the sheriff's guarded voice. "State Board is coming by, and Ginny asked me to help her out. D'you find Margaret yet?" he asked with averted eyes.

Without answering, Hale motioned for Warren to follow him into the house. They entered the kitchen through the back door, and while Warren stood impatiently by, the sheriff tried to interpret Belinda's lengthy but noncommittal message.

"No," said Hale at last, giving up on the note, "I haven't found her. I wanted to speak to you."

The schoolteacher looked away nervously. "I cain't imagine what happened to Margaret. She was helping me over at the school yesterday, and she left about five. It looked like rain, and I said I'd drive her back out to her place, we could put her bicycle in the back, but she said she had time to make it. It beats the life out of me what could have happened to her between the school and the farm out there . . ."

Hale looked closely at his lodger. Warren had never spoken so volubly nor so quickly. "And you didn't hear from her after that, you're sure?" said the sheriff at last.

Perry shook his head quickly. "No, no, and Miz Larkin sure must be worried. I know *I'm* worried. I cain't imagine what happened to her."

"What was she doing helping you, Warren?"

"She was helping me check in textbooks, you know, seeing how many had been marked up and so forth—"

"No," said Hale, "I mean *why* was she helping you?"

Warren shrugged easily. "'Cause she liked to help, I suppose. Margaret's a good girl, she—"

"She help the other teachers? She get paid for helping?"

"No," said Warren. "She just helped me, I guess. I'm real fond of Margaret. I sure do wish you'd find her, 'cause—" He glanced at his watch. "I got to get over to the school. Can you let me out?"

Hale nodded, and the two men left the kitchen. Slowly the sheriff pulled out of the drive, and the green Rambler scooted away.

Hale parked the cruiser beneath the water oaks in front of his house, and again examined the note his daughter had left him.

At one o'clock exactly, Hale crumpled the note in exasperation and got out of the car. He went cautiously around the side of his house to the garage in back. At the foot of the steps that led up to Warren's apartment, he sifted through his keys, and then walked slowly up. At the top, he hesitated with the key, but at last thrust it into the lock—and found that the door was unsecured. Hale stepped inside, and went hesitantly from room to room, not touching the furniture, opening the closet doors with his handkerchief.

He was relieved to find no evidence that Warren Perry had spent the night with a fourteen-year-old girl. In the drainboard of the sink was a single plate, and cutlery for one. Two old *Playboys* and the most recent *Penthouse* lay open on the rumpled bed.

But Hale was still at a loss to account for the schoolteacher's nervousness. He wished now that he had asked Perry exactly what his relationship to Margaret was. But it occurred to him also that this was a point which might be better cleared up by Ginny Darrish or Annie-Leigh Hooker, who would have no reason to lie about it—when Warren might.

Chapter 13

After the two tiresome representatives of the State Board of Education had left the high school, Ginny Darrish and Warren Perry climbed into Ginny's aquamarine Vega and drove out across the Styx to the Larkin farm. Warren knew the Larkins only slightly, but Ginny had insisted that he accompany her. It would doubtless reassure Evelyn to hear Warren say that Margaret had left the school safely the previous afternoon.

Jerry, sitting morose and unoccupied on the front porch, told them that his grandmother was in bed upstairs. He begged, however, that Ginny would go up and keep her company. "I'd stay with her every minute of the day," he said, "but sometimes she gets on my nerves. Sometimes I get short with her, when I don't mean to."

Ginny smiled sweetly at Jerry, and put by his offer to go with her into the house.

Fearful that their voices might carry from the porch to Evelyn's bedroom above, Jerry suggested that Warren walk with him through the blueberry patch. For the next half hour the two young men lost themselves among the enormous plants. As he walked, Warren gazed up at the sky, for the crowding luxuriant shrubs made him uneasy. From the midst of the patch where not even the farmhouse was visible, it seemed that all the earth was covered over in blueberries.

Jerry in contrast stared all the while at the ground. Frequently he would stop and miserably lift out of the mud the smashed lower branches. While he crushed the worthless berries in the palms of his hands, Jerry talked of his sister's unaccountable disappearance. He spoke haltingly and seemed near to tears, but Warren Perry was at a loss to determine whether Jerry was disturbed more by Margaret's failure to return or by the damage done to the crop by the previous night's storm.

Only for a few minutes each late afternoon did the declining sun shine directly on the Larkin farmhouse. Even at that, it illuminated no more than a portion of the papered wall opposite Evelyn Larkin's bed. All other times, in all other rooms, the surrounding pines deflected and broke apart the light.

Ginny Darrish wanted to close the curtains against the glaring hot light, but Evelyn Larkin wouldn't allow her. Confined to her bed by Dr. Everage, who had visited her at noon, Evelyn was irrationally convinced that Margaret was less likely to return if, from the Styx bridge, she saw her grandmother's drapes closed against her.

Evelyn lay on her side, facing away from the window. The sun, beating through the panes, was reflected off a glass-covered photograph of Margaret on the far wall, to shine golden but cold on the pillow behind Evelyn's head. Ginny Darrish sat in a rocker, with her rose-tinted sunglasses left on against the brightness in the room.

"Well," said Ginny, "I don't think you should worry, Evelyn, because Margaret has been up and down that highway, from here to Babylon and back, umpty-million times, and it doesn't seem likely from my point of view that she lost her way."

"Oh, Ginny," wailed Evelyn, her voice softened by tranquilizers, "that's just it! Margaret didn't get lost, she couldn't get lost, that's why something must have happened to her!"

"Nothing happened, Evelyn. Margaret is a good girl, she didn't run off with anybody."

"Who said that?"

"Well," replied Ginny, unperturbed: "When a girl doesn't come home for supper, that's what everybody's bound to say in Babylon. I've been principal too long not to know what people say about girls and boys, and I've been there long enough to know they don't deserve it."

"But what could be keeping her away, then?" demanded Evelyn.

Ginny flipped her aquamarine purse idly in her aquamarine lap. "I don't know, we'll just have to ask her when she gets back."

Evelyn turned wearily onto her back, and closed her eyes against the sun. "I wish I could get out of this bed."

"Don't you dare, Evelyn Larkin!"

"I feel like I ought to be up and about looking for Margaret. You know, Ginny, I would be up, I'd be combing the streets, if it weren't for Nathan Redfield . . ."

"Nathan!" cried Ginny: "What's Nathan got to do with this?"

Ginny listened with pink, pursed lips while Evelyn Larkin told what had happened in the bank that morning. "What can I do, Ginny? I can't think about Nathan Redfield and his old bank loan when Margaret is missing. Why does he keep on about this thing? We're behind, I know that, but it's the start of the season. The berries have always gotten us through, Nathan knows that, why doesn't he leave us alone? He's been pestering us till it seems like there's no end to it. I should have told him about Margaret, then maybe he would have left us alone. I cain't think about all this, you know how I am. Ginny, you couldn't be thinking about some old bank loan if you had a little girl and she was missing —could you?"

Ginny Darrish shook her silver head solemnly. "I could not, and that is a fact. It is a stinking shame what Nathan did to you this morning, even if he didn't know about Margaret, and I have a good mind to go straight to James Redfield, and tell him what Nathan did!"

"Oh!" cried Evelyn, "don't do that! Please don't do that! That might just get us in more trouble with Nathan. Nathan runs that bank now, his daddy doesn't have a thing to do with it. We're bad enough off, I don't want us to get in more trouble with Nathan. So please just forget I told you," pleaded Evelyn. "It's Jerry's business to handle all that kind of thing now. Nathan knows that—I don't know why he came up to me in the first place. But I don't want Jerry to know I've been talking about it, so please just don't say anything about it, promise me, will you, Ginny? I don't know *what* Jerry would say to me if he found out I told you that!"

"I promise," said Ginny, and clasped Evelyn's shaking hand tenderly in her own. "What's Margaret's sign?" she said.

"What do you mean?" said Evelyn: "What kind of sign?"

"When was she born? I'm gone look up her horoscope."

"Margaret was born on the twelfth of October. You don't think any horoscope is gone tell us where Margaret is, do you, Ginny? You cain't really believe that?" Evelyn's voice was guardedly hopeful.

"I do believe it, I believe every word of it. Margaret's a Libra just like my mama was. I know all about Libras." Ginny pulled out of her purse a small much-worn paperback book and skimmed expertly through it. "Where is Margaret's moon?" she demanded.

Evelyn shook her head bewildered.

"Well, I don't have time to figure that now. Let me see: for yesterday, it says: 'A journey postponed.' "

The two women looked at each other.

"You suppose that means she was on her way back here and she got delayed somewhere?" said Evelyn energetically.

"I don't see what else it could mean!" cried Ginny triumphantly.

"What does it say for today?" said Evelyn anxiously.

Ginny turned a page: " 'Time to settle old scores.' " She shrugged. "I don't know what that means. I cain't imagine that a fourteen-year-old girl has many old scores to settle." She raised her blue-penciled eyebrows in puzzlement.

She remained in the room until Evelyn had fallen asleep. Jerry had given his grandmother a sedative, telling her it was a new kind of aspirin.

"You call me if you need anything," Ginny said to Jerry when she came downstairs, "and I'll come right back out. Or call Warren, and he'll be glad to do whatever he can, won't you, Warren?"

Warren nodded solemnly. "I'm gone call my mama up in Atmore and tell her I'm not coming home this weekend. I'm gone stay in Babylon in case you need me, Jerry," the schoolteacher said: "If there's anything I can do to help, please just give me a call, because I'm just gone be sitting there on top of the garage, hoping that Margaret is all right."

"Now I don't want you to leave this house," said Ginny to Jerry: "Don't you leave your grandmama. She's not well now—"

Jerry knocked his wrists together violently: "She's not gone get well, either, till somebody finds Margaret."

It was five o'clock when Ginny Darrish and Warren Perry crossed the Styx River bridge on their way back to Babylon.

Jerry looked in again on his grandmother, and was relieved to find that she slept without stirring. He went down to the front porch with a bag of potato chips, and rocked in the swing, unconsciously keeping count of the vehicles that passed on the Babylon road. But these were so few that he took to numbering the fireflies that flittered among the pines in the yard instead.

It was dark at eight o'clock. No more cars passed, but the fireflies were multitudinous. Jerry walked to the highway to catch sight of the waning pale moon that had just risen, and then returned to the house to watch television.

Upstairs in her room, Evelyn Larkin slept badly, troubled by dreams of her granddaughter. Her gray hair matted against her brow, and the flowered pillowcase beneath her head was damp with cold perspiration.

Directly below, Jerry hunkered on a tattered ottoman, only a few feet in front of the television set. The volume was turned so low, for fear of disturbing his grandmother, that though he leaned crazily forward, he could barely make out the sound.

All around the house the pines swayed softly in the black night. Clouds had swirled up from the Gulf again, covering the moon. Beneath the high canopy of evergreen boughs, there was only the masked violet light of the television, and the erratic electricity of the fireflies.

A few dozen yards away, the Styx River moved muddy and silent beneath the black rotting bridge. Crayfish broke the surface of the shallow water between the sandbars and the banks, but otherwise there was no apparent movement in the river. Small animals skittered through the dense underbrush that skirted the Styx. Night birds called fitfully in the thick forest.

In all that long evening, a single automobile passed over the Styx River bridge, a beat-up green Rambler. Warren Perry was driving from Babylon to Atmore to explain in person to his mother why he would not be staying the weekend with her—she had refused to listen to his excuses over the telephone.

He slowed as he went across the bridge, and paused at the entrance to the Larkin driveway. Through the front window he could just make out the sterile glow of the television, and wondered if he shouldn't stop; but thinking that the sound of an approaching car would vainly raise Evelyn's hopes, he drove quickly on.

After the harsh flat glow of the Rambler's headlights breaking across all the vegetation around the Styx River bridge had faded and disappeared, and after the noise of its troubled motor was lost in the distance, the black waters of the Styx, in a place a little downstream of the bridge, began to churn in a way that could not have been caused by crayfish or bream.

The black water spiraled first in one direction, then in the other, but slowly, without agitation, methodically and calmly changing flow. At last the alteration ceased; in a slow deliberate fashion, the water swirled in a single direction, gradually forming a small downspout, a singular depression in the untroubled surface of the river. This black hole in the black shadow of the bridge reflected nothing at all.

But then there came a lightening of the spout, a dimness that wasn't black any longer, though it wasn't color either, but a rare gray paleness that was not so much illumination as simply a decreasing of the darkness, like the dawning of a day that will be broken by tornadoes.

That negative striated darkness turned also; it became larger, congealed in the center of the spout, and took on the form of a pale livid sphere, swimming with black impurities. As it turned, the sphere evolved lumps and creases and shadows that allowed it a grotesque resemblance to a human head.

The creases became fine and lengthy and swung part-free from the sphere, whipping ropelike in the spout. The soft lumps resolved haltingly into the features of a child's face. A second mouth moved slowly around the sphere, traveling like the eye of a flounder, and was transformed into an ear beneath the coils of rope. A gradual unhesitating refinement of the features on the water-born head reproduced the visage of Margaret Larkin, ashen and faintly luminous.

The small head fell back into the water. The Styx carefully parted the long fine colorless hair, and revealed a thin gray neck. The head and neck rose from the water, still turning softly in the same unvarying rhythm as before, but swaying gently now, as if in drug-induced reverie. Higher still, to display a garment that was as livid and pale as the neck and head and hair: all without color, a liquid, phosphorescent grayish-white. But while the hairs of the head could have been counted one by one, the garment was indistinct, of no particular cut, with hesitant suggestions of sleeves and gatherings and fastenings, shimmering and variable.

The slow spin, gentle sway, and smooth inexorable rise continued until the delicate bare feet skimmed the water. Gradually, then, the revolutions subsided and the figure hovered lightly on the surface of the river. It turned deliberately toward the Larkin farmhouse on the northern bank of the Styx. The eyes opened, but behind the gray lids was a flat infinite blackness, blacker far than the muddy Styx in the shadow of the rotting bridge. Those terrible eyes were without surface; the lids opened directly onto noisome void and nonentity, and the black holes were fixed on the darkened window of Evelyn Larkin's bedroom.

Later, when Warren Perry's green Rambler was driving back from Atmore, the headlamps flashed over that section of black water that earlier had swirled with such strange purpose; but there was nothing to differentiate it from any other place in the entire length of the river.

PART III

THE THING IN THE TREE

Chapter 14

Early Saturday morning, when Jerry brought his grandmother coffee, he found her sitting in a chair pulled up to the window that looked out over the Styx. She explained to him with a weak smile that she didn't want to miss seeing Margaret when she came sailing over the bridge on her wheel. Jerry made no reply to this, said only that he had to deliver a photograph of Margaret to Ted Hale, and that he would be back as soon as he could.

When he returned half an hour later, he found that his grandmother had not moved. When she saw him, she raised the cup of coffee to her lips, and tasted it for the first time.

Evelyn drank a little soup about noon, but remained at the window in her room, half the time staring intently at the bridge and starting up whenever a car came across it, but just as often remaining distracted and not even noticing when Jerry stood beneath her window and gazed up at her.

About three o'clock, Ed Geiger pulled his car off the side of the road, on the far side of the river, and Evelyn watched him make his way down to the river's edge. He waved to her hesitantly, and she waved back.

Ed Geiger had a favorite spot, as was common with many fishermen. A small sandbar that ran near the southern bank of the Styx, and underneath the bridge, terminated in a sharp spit. Just downstream from this gray tongue of sand and pebbles, the water went abruptly deep, and in this chasm Geiger was accustomed to dropping his line. He didn't catch as many fish here as he might have farther up or down the river, but since he gave away all that he caught anyway, the size of his catch didn't matter to him. The bank was grassy at that point and soft, and a large stand of pine was situated between him and the hot afternoon sun, so that he could move in and out of the shade without expending much energy. From this place too he could see who passed along the Babylon road, and was able to watch, in season, the work on the blueberry patch across the river. Today, knowing that Margaret Larkin had not returned home since Thursday, Geiger paid particular attention to the farm on the opposite bank. He was made a little uneasy by the old woman sitting motionless in her bedroom window.

Fish wouldn't bite before two o'clock; Geiger supposed they had their regular feeding times as well. Today, however, at four o'clock, they weren't even nibbling at the bait. When he raised his line from the water, the cricket hung on the hook limp and drowned, but otherwise intact. By four-thirty, even Geiger's well-practiced patience had been tried; he decided to reestablish a few hundred feet downstream.

When he tried to raise his line for the last time, he was surprised to find that it had caught on something, something that resisted as no trout or bream ever had. He supposed the hook had snagged on a ledge of rock at the bottom of the river. He let the line go slack, settle; then reeled in once more. Again caught; he decided that he might as well pull until he snapped the line.

He pulled harder. The rod bowed as much as if he were landing a shark, ten miles out in the Gulf.

Jerry Larkin, at the nearer edge of the patch, watched Geiger's struggle with interest; nothing that could pull a rod like that had ever been caught in the Styx. Evelyn Larkin too, from her window, stared fixedly at him.

The obstruction gave at last, but the line had not broken. Geiger began to reel in, but with difficulty; whatever heavy thing the hook had caught on was being dragged slowly up to the surface. The line pulled smooth, so the catch was not resisting.

On his feet, Geiger turned the reel slowly, and puffed with the exertion. He stopped momentarily, when a scrap of patterned cloth appeared on the surface of the water and then floated downstream.

"What you got, Mr. Geiger?" called Jerry from across the river.

Geiger shook his head slowly, then called out, as loudly as he could: "You come on over here, Jerry! Right now!"

Neither had heard the other's words, but the sense was amply conveyed.

Jerry, after a single moment's pause, hurried not toward the bridge, but downstream a hundred paces where a small boat was tethered. He hopped in, untied the rope, and rowed quickly upstream to the sandbar that ran beneath the bridge. Geiger was still reeling in slowly, but Jerry could see nothing in the water.

Movement across the river attracted Jerry's attention. His grandmother was hurrying across the lawn, catching at the trunks of trees in her breathlessness. He waved her back, but she continued heedless to the very bank of the river.

The hair of the corpse appeared first, floating like autumn water-weeds on the surface. Suddenly the head flopped back, and the sightless eyes stared directly up into the sun. The hook had caught in the roof of Margaret's open mouth. Just as the head was free of the water, and Evelyn had begun to scream, the line snapped, and the corpse sank.

Jerry stumbled into the boat and pushed off the dozen or so feet to Margaret. He leaned clumsily over the side and caught his sister by her hair, and tried to pull her up. The weight was greater than he expected, and the boat tipped, spilling him into the river.

He flailed—frigid with the shock of the water and the fright of trying to capture a floating corpse—but with a great effort toward forgetting just what it was he was doing, he caught the body by an arm, and pulled it into the shallower water near the sandbar. Beneath the surface of the Styx, Margaret's sightless eyes had stared at him through the muddy water; the mouth had gone slack again, reproachfully displaying the baited hook inside.

Jerry scrambled out of the water, shaking, and for the first time saw that the bicycle was caught around Margaret's legs. Weeping, and shouting incoherently at his grandmother to stop screaming, he pulled the corpse onto the sandbar. He untied the rope, and left the bicycle in the muddy water.

Geiger had waded a few steps into the river, caught the boat, and pulled it to shore. He righted it, then dragged it upstream to the sandbar. "I'll go get Hale," he said shortly, and hurried to his car.

Jerry knew that he ought to leave Margaret where she was for the sheriff to examine and photograph; but across the river, on her knees, at the very edge of the water, Evelyn Larkin wailed and caught her short breath in sobs.

Jerry cut loose the ropes that held the bicycle and gently lifted his sister's body. For the first time he saw the ghastly cuts in her skin where the clothes fell away from her; he placed her face downward in the prow of the small boat, then rowed slowly across the river, keeping in the shadow of the bridge.

Evelyn stumbled among the pebbles along the edge of the water, and called out for Margaret, but Jerry commanded her to get back. The old woman reluctantly climbed the bank up to the lawn, and held tightly to the resinous trunk of a pine while Jerry brought Margaret's body out of the boat, and laid her tenderly in the grass.

Jerry took off his shirt, and draped it over Margaret's face, but not before Evelyn had caught sight of the filmed eyes, the gray mottled brow, the livid lacerations made by Ed Geiger's hook, still with the cricket on it, that was caught in her mouth. She fell back silently, and Jerry drew her away to the house.

The same small green boat in which Jim and JoAnn Larkin had met their deaths had ferried their daughter's corpse across the Styx.

Chapter 15

Dr. Raymond Everage, who acted as coroner on the rare occasions Babylon needed one, was also the physician who had long taken care of Evelyn Larkin and her family. He rode out to the blueberry farm with the sheriff, took one look at Margaret's corpse, and then hurried into the house, and attended to the dead girl's grandmother.

Evelyn twisted, moaning on the bed and convulsively jerked her hand out of Jerry's grasp. He had tried to comfort her, although he knew there was no comfort to be had. The doctor's unexpected presence calmed her. She lay still enough to ask, "Is she dead? Is Margaret dead?"

Dr. Everage did not answer. He sat on the side of the bed, held two pills in his hand, and forced Evelyn to swallow them, handing her a glass of water to wash them down.

"Don't get out of this bed until I tell you to," he said sternly. "Jerry," he commanded: "Close the curtains."

Before Jerry had done so, the doctor was gone. Outside, the sheriff and two of his deputies stood around Margaret's body, not wanting to look, yet staring at the green-tinged joints, the drawn rubbered flesh, the strangely shredded clothing. Already the sheriff had taken an entire roll of film with a Polaroid camera, and was inwardly distressed that the color had reproduced true.

While Dr. Everage knelt in the grass beside Margaret, Ted Hale and his two deputies stood to one side, staring at the shrunken frail corpse.

"I don't imagine old Ed Geiger is gone be fishing in that spot any longer," said Jay Neal. The sheriff shook his head ruefully.

Everage looked up: "Those are rope burns on her legs," he said to Hale.

"She was tied to her bicycle, looks like. Tied to her bicycle and thrown off the bridge. Did she drown?"

"Probably," said Everage. "These bruises on her head couldn't have killed her. Knocked unconscious maybe and then drowned. Poor Margaret. She wasn't the prettiest little girl in town, but she didn't deserve this."

"Could she have been hit by a car?" asked the other deputy. "Out-of-state hit-and-run?"

Everage shook his head. "Car comes along and hits her in the head, but nowhere else?"

The deputy shrugged.

"These cuts aren't deep, didn't even bleed much, cut through her clothes. Why you suppose somebody did that?" asked Everage.

The sheriff shook his head: "None of it makes sense. She was two years younger than Belinda."

"Who you think did it?" said Everage.

The sheriff shook his head: "No idea, no idea why anybody'd

want to kill her. Listen Raymond, can we take her back to Babylon, back to your office now? Evelyn Larkin's bad enough off without seeing us out here in her side yard standing around Margaret like she was a dead rattler or something."

Everage nodded and rose from the ground. The two deputies carefully lifted Margaret's body onto a stretcher, and carried it to the driveway. Passing the house, Hale saw Jerry standing inside at the screen door.

Hale went over to the front steps. "Hey, Jerry, listen," he said in a low voice, "we ought to put Margaret in the back of your wagon, if you don't mind. The ambulance was being used to take Roland Phelps down to Pensacola this afternoon, and I think it would be better for your grandmama if we carried Margaret into Babylon right now."

Dr. Everage interrupted: "Jerry ought to stay here with his grandmother. She's probably asleep by now, but she ought not wake up in an empty house."

Jerry came out onto the front porch, and handed the keys of the car to the sheriff. "Have somebody bring it back out later," he said flatly.

The sheriff nodded and took the keys. Jay Neal lifted open the rear door of the station wagon.

Jerry went back inside, climbed the stairs quietly, and stood at the window of his own room, to watch the station wagon back slowly out of the driveway; he hurried to his grandmother's room, made sure that she was asleep, and then peered between the curtains to see Margaret cross the Styx for the last time.

Then he sat in the chair at the foot of his grandmother's bed, and rocked slowly for the better part of an hour. His grandmother slept soundly. Once when she turned suddenly, she knocked a pillow to the floor; when Jerry came around the bed to retrieve it, he found that it had fallen atop a small paperbound book, called *The True Believer's Guide to Dreams and Their Correct Interpretation*. It was printed on coarse porous paper and many passages had been underlined in violet ink.

This puzzled him until he recalled that Ginny Darrish had sat there the day before, and very probably it had dropped out of her purse.

He went back to his chair, turned on a small lamp on his grandmother's dresser. Hoping to forget for a few moments what had happened that afternoon, he began to read.

Somewhat later, Evelyn Larkin woke slowly. Jerry had dreaded this, and by her sudden choking whimper, he knew the moment she remembered that her granddaughter was dead. He said nothing while she wept, but continued to stare at the page, though tears in his own eyes blurred the small paragraphs.

After a while Evelyn left off, and drew up in the bed. In a shaking small voice, she said: "What are you reading, Jerry?"

He didn't look up from the book. "It's a book about dreams. It tells you what they mean. Ginny Darrish left it here yesterday I guess, by mistake."

"I had a dream just now," said Evelyn sadly. "I dreamed that Margaret got married. Even though she was still just a little girl, and fourteen's not old enough to get married."

Jerry looked up briefly at his grandmother but said nothing.

"Read me what it says in that book, Jerry. What does it mean when you dream about a wedding?"

Jerry flipped through quickly to the back of the book and found the correct entry. " 'Wedding—' " he read: " 'Dreaming of a wedding is very unlucky; it is a sure forerunner of grief and disappointment. Death and marriage represent one another. For the sick to dream they are married, or that they celebrate their weddings, is a sign of death, for it signifies separation from her or his companions . . .' " On the last sentence his voice cracked: " 'The dead do not keep company with the living.' "

"But Margaret's already dead," said Evelyn faintly, "so why would I dream about a wedding since she's already dead?"

Jerry made no reply.

"Somebody killed Margaret, didn't they, Jerry? Margaret didn't just fall off the bridge and drown, did she?"

"No, Grandma," said Jerry reluctantly, "somebody killed her. But we don't know *who*, and we don't know *why*." His voice was anguished.

"I know who did it," said Evelyn calmly.

Jerry looked up: "What?"

"I know who killed Margaret."

"Grandma—"

"When I dreamed that Margaret got married, I dreamed the whole ceremony, Jerry. I dreamed that you were up there at the altar giving her away, and I dreamed that Annie-Leigh Hooker and Belinda Hale were the two bridesmaids, and I was sitting there on the front row. But I couldn't see the man that Margaret was supposed to be marrying. He had his back to me, and I couldn't see his face. And then we all went out of the church, and we watched her get in the back of the car, but we didn't throw rice. We just watched Margaret climb in the back of the car all by herself, and then it drove away, and Margaret was beating on the back window trying to get out, and calling for me to come get her, and I wanted to go, Jerry, and I was about to go, but then I got stopped by the groom. He was standing right next to me, and it was Nathan Redfield. Margaret was marrying Nathan Redfield, and Ben Redfield was the best man, and Margaret got driven away in that big car of theirs. There wasn't anybody driving and Margaret was beating on the back window trying to get out. You don't have to look it up in that book to tell me what that dream means. It means that Nathan Redfield killed my little girl."

"Grandma," said Jerry softly, "I don't even know if he knew Margaret. I don't think that Nathan Redfield—" He broke off. "I mean we just don't know *who*—"

"I'll tell you how else I know," said Evelyn, interrupting her grandson. She sat straight up in the bed, resting against the headboard, with pillows to brace her: "Now listen, Jerry, Nathan's been on to us so much lately about that loan, and there's no call for it. I know we're behind a little, but he doesn't go after other people like that. He doesn't walk up to them every time they step foot in the front door of the CP&M. Then, right the day after Margaret disappears—and Margaret is lying face down at the bottom of the Styx—Nathan Redfield comes up to me and starts demanding payment and talking about proceedings. He ought to be writing us a letter or something, not badgering us like he is. So something's wrong, and what's wrong is that Nathan Redfield killed Margaret."

"Grandma, just because Nathan's on to us about that loan

—and it's not as if we weren't behind on it a little—that's no reason to go off saying that he's the one who killed Margaret."

"But that loan's not all, Jerry."

"What else is there?"

"Nathan Redfield used to look at Margaret . . . all the time. He thought I didn't notice it, but I did, every time Margaret and I went in the bank together. Oh, he never said anything to her when I was around, he leered at her and stared at her and his filthy thoughts were right there on his face for all the world to see. Margaret was only fourteen, Jerry, and Nathan Redfield was *staring* at her."

"But looking isn't . . . looking's not a crime, Grandma, and you were probably just imagining it anyway. I never noticed him . . . looking at her."

She ignored Jerry's objection: "He let it build up in him till he did something . . . till he killed her! Maybe she . . . said no to him. And he killed her, and threw her off the bridge into the river. And then the very next morning when I'm in the bank, he's practically on top of me demanding his money and trying to take this farm away from us. Because if he took this house away from us, where would we go? I'd be ashamed to show my face in Babylon. He knows that. He knows we'd go away somewhere before we went on welfare."

"Why would Nathan Redfield care where we went?"

" '*Cause he killed Margaret,*" cried Evelyn with exasperation: "As long as we're around here there'll be suspicion, because I know what he did. We go, and who cares what happened to Margaret, and who cares who did it? Jerry, there was a fishhook in my little girl's mouth. Your mama and daddy went out on that river and they never came back, and now Margaret's gone and drowned in it—I wish I could just roll over and die, and have done with it." Evelyn's feverishness had subsided into an exhausted whimper.

Jerry closed the book in his lap, and dropped it beneath the chair. He sat silent, thinking.

"I know I'm right," said Evelyn quietly, "and you will too, if you'll just stop and think about it. I know it and I feel it. When Nathan was still in high school, couldn't have been more than sixteen, he got those two girls in trouble up in Alabama, and they lost their jobs at that gun factory. There were probably others that I just didn't hear about. His daddy covered up for him till he just got disgusted, and then finally made Nathan go in the Air Force. And then there was the time he nearly beat the poor little Blaine girl to death in a ditch after a football game."

"Grandma, you just cain't go off and accuse a man of something like this without proof, and we don't have any proof." Jerry recalled the stories about Nathan with some discomfort.

"We'll get it! We'll talk to Ted Hale and he'll get proof. Police have ways of getting proof!"

Jerry had risen from his chair, and now sat at the foot of his grandmother's bed. She leaned forward precipitously, and grabbed his arm: "Don't you let this go, Jerry!" she hissed. "Margaret's dead, and there's no sense to it, and nobody cares but you and me. Nathan Redfield killed your sister and put her in the Styx and he wants us to get out of here so he can live with his conscience. But you and I won't let him. I want him locked up. I want to see that man as dead as Margaret was when you laid her on the riverbank. I would give every penny I had left in this world to see him out on that lawn with a fishhook caught in the roof of his bleeding mouth!"

On Saturday night, Dr. Everage examined Margaret's body thoroughly with the assistance of the county coroner, who drove up from Pensacola at Sheriff Hale's request. By midnight, the two physicians had agreed that Margaret Larkin was the victim of a homicide. The superficial cuts over her back and belly had been inflicted before her death. The bicycle to which her body had been secured had served to weight her down; the black impure water of the Styx had filled her lungs and Margaret Larkin had drowned.

"It's real nasty," said the county coroner: "I don't think I have *ever* seen a body tied to a bicycle and dumped in the river. You have any idea who did it, Sheriff?"

The sheriff shook his head no. "It's not the kind of crime we get a lot of around here. We get Saturday night poker murders on the north side of town, but you always know who did it, and nobody tries to keep it a secret. There's people screaming, and there's twenty-five witnesses, but I never got anything like this. And of course nobody's *ever* killed a fourteen-year-old girl before."

"Well," said the county coroner, "maybe you ought to have a little talk with the father."

"Jim Larkin's dead," said Hale, surprised: "He died in the Styx too, about fifteen years ago."

"No," said the county coroner, while Dr. Everage stood by tight-lipped, "the father of the baby that she was carrying. This girl was four months pregnant."

Chapter 16

After the county coroner had filed his report with the sheriff's office, Margaret's body was released. It was taken to the funeral parlor on the south side of town.

Ginny Darrish proved herself invaluable during this difficult time. Early Sunday morning, she drove out to the farm, and chose the clothing that Margaret would be buried in. At the funeral home she picked out a decent but inexpensive casket, and specified the minimum of services for the poor murdered girl. Later, when Margaret had been laid out, embalmed, cosmetized, and dressed, she returned to decide for a closed or open coffin.

"Well," said Ginny, staring down into the face of the corpse, billowed in blue satin: "She doesn't look bad, but she doesn't look like she died much of a natural death either. Maybe we just better keep the top down."

In the afternoon, Jerry drove his grandmother through town. Those passing on the sidewalk recognized the car, stared a moment at the weeping woman inside, and then turned away in sympathetic embarrassment. The morning edition of the Pensacola paper had carried notice of the murder, but the small article had none of the detail with which the gossip had already embellished it.

Ed Geiger as usual was the fount of much of the information, but he fairly gushed on this occasion. It was he, after all, who had discovered Margaret Larkin's corpse. He sat highly visible on his front porch all of Sunday. For many hours he entertained a fluctuating audience with a description, more detailed with each iteration, of how he had pulled Margaret Larkin up from the bottom of the Styx with a rod and reel. And all that sunny hot afternoon, the only time he paused in his storytelling was when the Larkins' station wagon passed the house. Geiger stood clumsily out of the swing and leaned over the front rail to wave mournfully at Jerry, who waved solemnly back. The half dozen persons on the porch were silent for a moment, and then Geiger continued: "I thought it had snagged on a shelf, a little shelf of rocks, so I jerked the line a couple times, to try and get it loose . . ."

At the other end of the porch, Annie-Leigh Hooker was installed in the glider, and after people were finished with Ed Geiger, they turned to his niece for the background of Margaret's strange disappearance on Thursday. Annie-Leigh knew the facts, and could recount the theories that had circulated. In her own way, Annie-Leigh was thought as reliable and important a witness as Geiger, for she was known to have been intimate with the dead girl. Her pronouncements were edged with melancholy, that her best friend in all the world had been mauled and ripped and drowned by a psychopathic killer who was very likely still walking among us.

In the dim, heavily air-conditioned chapel of the funeral home, where flowers for Margaret were already arriving, Evelyn Larkin sat and wept. She and Jerry huddled in the front row of folding gray chairs, while the coffin sat absurdly large and grandiose before them.

"I'm gone take you home now," said Jerry after a quarter of an hour.

"We're not going to leave Margaret here," Evelyn sobbed. "We cain't leave Margaret in here alone tonight."

"I'm taking you home," said Jerry soothingly. "Margaret's not gone be alone. I'm staying here till midnight—Ginny'll be at the house with you. Then Warren will be here from midnight on. He asked if he could. Margaret won't be left alone, Grandma. We'll take care of her."

Evelyn nodded. She stood, brushed her hand tenderly across

the lid of the closed coffin, and then turned away. Jerry led her from the room.

Ginny Darrish spent all that evening at the blueberry farm, receiving visitors in Evelyn's stead. Everyone expressed his astonishment and wonder at the manner of Margaret's death, and shook his head slowly over what must be Evelyn Larkin's condition upstairs.

When the last mourning guest had gone, Ginny went upstairs and sat by the side of Evelyn's bed. Margaret's grandmother was awake but dazed, and spoke incoherently. Ginny made her be quiet, and then began to talk softly of those who had been downstairs, and what they had said. She related all the stories that the condolence bearers had told of Margaret, and these inconsequential anecdotes did something to comfort Evelyn. Ginny sat and rocked in the darkness long after Evelyn had fallen asleep and refused Jerry's invitation to spend the night in Margaret's room.

"I'm gone stay here with your grandma, just in case she wakes up," whispered Ginny, "and besides, don't you know that it'd be bad luck to sleep in Margaret's bed before she's been buried?"

Jerry did not press, but returned to his own room, where he fell asleep heavily, and did not dream.

At the funeral home, Nina's eldest son kept night watch; he slept with his head on the reception desk. A transistor radio, at lowest volume, rested close to his ear.

In the chapel, Warren Perry remained alone with Margaret's coffin. He had pulled open the thickly lined nylon drapes so that the mercury lights in the parking lot shone on the lid of the coffin, making the powder blue shine a metallic silver. To keep awake, Warren played hymns on the small pipe organ in the corner; a small green-shaded lamp illumined the hymnal, and between verses he stared over at the silvered coffin. Not until dawn did he raise the lid.

In the harsh morning light, he was perplexed by the aspect of Margaret's body: It seemed smaller than he had remembered, shrunken though not shriveled, as if some of the essence had been evenly extracted from it during embálming. He was glad as he dropped the lid back that he had looked: The thing inside had seemed not Margaret at all, but a faulty replica, like a straw figure to be burnt at Halloween—there would be no regret at slipping that husk into the earth. The question remained however: Where was Margaret?

The funeral was held at nine. The Baptist preacher read a short sermon after a single hymn, and then Ginny Darrish spoke a few words about Margaret. Jerry and Evelyn sat in the front row, hardly a yard away from the coffin, and did not even look around to see who attended.

Ginny had made her husband come, and this large man twisted uncomfortably in the last row—Charles Darrish had no liking for funerals. The sheriff had sent Belinda to represent him, and she showed with five of her six cheerleaders, all in their black skirts and their black blazers—and they whispered to one another what a lucky thing it was that the school colors were gold and black. Other of Margaret's classmates were in attendance, friends of Evelyn's, and the man who owned the gas station where Jerry was occasionally employed. Annie-Leigh Hooker and Ed Geiger sat directly behind Jerry and Evelyn. Nina, the Redfields' maid, was the only black present. It was a respectable turnout, and though all admitted that they had wanted to have a look at Margaret, they agreed it was best, in the case of murder, to keep the coffin closed.

The Babylon municipal cemetery was located on an old street on the eastern edge of town. The houses nearby were dilapidated and inhabited by workers in the ribbon factory, Babylon's sole industry. The cemetery had been established about 1875, but none of the bodies interred dated from that time—all the cemetery's first-fruits had floated to the surface in the great flood of 1929. The grounds were wildly overgrown; massive cedars and live oaks had sprung up in the midst of family plots, and knocked tombstones awry; wild strawberries—nobody ate them —grew in the pathways. Honeysuckle and trumpet vines spread luxuriant along the rusting iron fences.

The Larkins had a family plot, bought many years before by Evelyn's husband in a time of relative prosperity. The place was marked by an ugly pink marble needle, inscribed with the family

name. There he was buried, and beside his grave was the cenotaph that mourned Margaret and Jerry's parents. Margaret was
to be laid immediately adjoining this, leaving room for only two
more graves within the low concrete curbing.

Those who were curious about the strange death of Margaret Larkin but who had not felt sufficiently close to the family to
appear at the funeral home were at the cemetery, half concealed
by the surrounding thick trees and foliage. Conspicuously present were the sheriff, his two deputies, and Dr. Everage.

The graveside service was short, with the Baptist minister
reading only the Twenty-third Psalm, and one more passage,
from First Corinthians:

> Behold, I shew you a mystery; We shall not all sleep, but we
> shall all be changed, in a moment, in the twinkling of an eye,
> at the last trump: for the trumpet shall sound, and the dead
> shall be raised incorruptible, and we shall all be changed.

Jerry held his grandmother's hand, and with a silver ladle, they
tossed clotted earth onto the coffin that rested on canvas straps
above the deep-dug grave.

With one motion, the crowd turned its face away from the
dead; and none of the mourners watched the coffin lowered into
the silty earth of the Babylon cemetery.

Chapter 17

The intense heat of that Monday morning broke as a surprise on
Evelyn and Jerry Larkin as they drove from the cemetery back
to the blueberry farm. Well before noon, the temperature was
above ninety; thick clouds hung oppressively just above the pine
trees. The Styx seemed barely to move, and vapor rose steaming
along its entire course.

On the way home, Evelyn and Jerry spoke not of Margaret,
but of the half dozen Boy Scouts who were expected at noon.
"I hope those boys like cake," sighed Evelyn, "because we've
sure got enough of it. People brought out enough food to raise
Cleopatra's army."

"They were just doing it because they were sorry about what happened," said Jerry cautiously. He hoped his grandmother had begun to view Margaret's death with the right and necessary acceptance.

"If they wanted to do what was right, they'd drag Nathan Redfield out of the bank and nail him to a tree."

Jerry was glad that there was work to do that day, for his grandmother's sake and his own. All afternoon Evelyn would sit at the rough deal table on the shaded back porch, keep count of the number of boxes each boy brought in, and put a cellophane wrapper around the top with a rubber band.

"We won't have enough to fill the car until Wednesday, I don't imagine," said Jerry, "so I won't have to make the trip into Pensacola before then."

"It's all right," said Evelyn, divining his meaning. "I'll be all right out here by myself."

At first, Jerry couldn't make out his grandmother's ease. She hadn't taken a tranquilizer at all that morning, and had wept hardly at all during either service.

He sat on the front porch, awaiting the arrival of the Boy Scouts. He read the accounts in the Mobile and Pensacola papers of Margaret's death. The Mobile paper said only that the body of a teenaged girl had been found in the Styx River only a few dozen yards from her home; homicide was suspected. The Pensacola paper, however, related many details of the wounds on Margaret's body, and the peculiar manner in which it had been discovered. Since it also mentioned Ed Geiger by name, Jerry suspected that it was the fisherman who had provided the information. The Mobile paper had probably called up Hale, who had told as little as possible.

The phone rang inside. Jerry wanted to run and answer it, but he decided he had better first hide the newspapers so that his grandmother would not be upset by the articles. When he reached the parlor, Evelyn had already hung up. "That was Jay Neal. He says the sheriff is on his way out here to talk to you."

"What about?" said Jerry.

"About Margaret," said Evelyn with small surprise: "What else would he want to talk to us about? Now Jerry, I want you to tell him about Nathan, that is, if he hasn't already figured it out for himself. He'll listen to you, he won't listen to me. He may be on his way out here to tell us that he's arrested Nathan already, maybe that's why he's coming."

Jerry suddenly understood why his grandmother had remained so calm: She had convinced herself that Nathan Redfield was guilty of murdering Margaret, and all her anxiety had been subsumed in the desire to be avenged on the man. Margaret would never return, Margaret was dead, and the only satisfaction that was left Evelyn in this world was to see Nathan Redfield punished for his crime.

"Grandma," said Jerry sadly, "I don't want you there. You stay in the kitchen, and see what you can do about putting up some food. We'll never eat all of it. We might as well throw half of it to the fish right now."

Their attention was drawn to the police car turning into the driveway from the Babylon road.

Evelyn nodded to Jerry significantly: "You remember what I told you," she said softly, and went towards the kitchen.

Jerry went out onto the porch, and sat in the swing, glancing over his shoulder at the police car that pulled up just beside the house. Hale had come alone.

"Is your grandmama inside?" the sheriff asked in a low voice as he approached the porch.

Jerry nodded, but said nothing.

"Nice service this morning," remarked Hale with tentative cheer, as he mounted the steps. "Your grandma seemed to take it not so bad."

Jerry paused before answering, but then plunged: "She wasn't feeling too bad because she thinks this afternoon you're going back into Babylon and arrest the man that killed Margaret. Jury's gone declare him guilty in two days, and she'll pull the switch on the chair. That's why she's not feeling too bad right now, when she's got all that excitement to look forward to."

"Well," said the sheriff with consternation: "Who does she think I'm gone arrest? Has she got anybody particular in mind?"

"Nathan Redfield."

Hale whistled.

Jerry recounted his grandmother's reasoning that led to so unexpected a conclusion, but he said nothing of her dreams.

"D'you try to talk her out of that? 'Cause that's just crazy, you know that, don't you, Jerry?"

"I know it, but that's what she believes, and right now, that's what's keeping her going. Now, I promised her that I would tell you that, and I did, but I don't know what I'm gone say to her when I have to go back in there and tell her that you are *not* gone go back into town and stick Nathan Redfield in the jail."

"You want me to talk to her?" Hale offered reluctantly.

Jerry shook his head. "No point in that. I'll tell her later. Why'd you want to talk to me?"

"I guess I just wanted to ask you if you had any ideas—any *other* ideas, I guess—about who would want to go and throw Margaret off the bridge with a bicycle tied to her feet?"

"I don't know," said Jerry simply. "I don't have any idea why anybody would want to kill Margaret."

Hale, who had seated himself beside Jerry on the swing, leaned forward and whispered: "Jerry, did you know that Margaret was pregnant?"

"No!" he cried aloud: "Margaret—" He lowered his voice abruptly: "No, I— How do you know that? Margaret was only fourteen!"

"Raymond Everage and the man from Pensacola, the county coroner, they found out when they examined her on Saturday night. It's in their report. She was in her fourth month."

Jerry shook his head: "Good Lord, just don't tell Grandma . . ."

"I've got to," said Hale, "or else you've got to, because there's going to be the inquest tomorrow, and it'll come out then."

"Does it have to? I mean, what does that have to do with Margaret getting killed?" Jerry shook in the swing; he had begun to perspire heavily.

"Maybe nothing, but Jerry, Margaret was only fourteen, like you say, and whoever got her pregnant was gone be in a lot of trouble. And since Margaret didn't have any enemies that anybody knew about, it seems like it might have been the father that did it."

Jerry shook his head in anguish.

"Listen Jerry, don't let your grandma come to the inquest to-morrow. You come. You have to testify that Margaret left home on Thursday, that she didn't come home, and then you have to tell about . . . finding the body, and bringing it across the river. Your grandma doesn't have to be there. But I still think it's gone come out about Margaret's being pregnant, and if you don't tell her, somebody else will and it's probably better if it comes from you."

Jerry nodded dismally. "Okay, I'll tell her later. Not now. Later. Maybe I'll tell her tonight."

"Who do you think the father was?"

Jerry opened his eyes wide. "I don't know!" he said, as if the question had not occurred to him before. "I don't know who it could have been. Margaret wasn't even dating yet! But maybe you're right, and it was the father who did it. But that's just hor-rible, for whoever it was to kill Margaret and the baby too."

"I was sorry to have to tell you this. I was hoping that you al-ready knew about it. You may be surprised: Maybe your grandma already knows. Maybe Margaret confided in her. Maybe Marga-ret told her who the father was," said Hale hopefully.

"I doubt it," said Jerry, "I really just doubt it." He paused. "What are you going to do now?"

Hale shrugged: "Start the investigation, I guess. Maybe some-thing will turn up. Maybe somebody'll confess."

"Somebody who gets a fourteen-year-old girl pregnant and then throws her in the river doesn't seem much like the type to get a guilty conscience all of a sudden," said Jerry ruefully.

Chapter 18

On Sunday, Ted Hale had begun his investigation into the murder of Margaret Larkin. He requestioned Geiger and Annie-Leigh, who had discovered nothing new in the meantime; he talked once more to Warren Perry, who declared himself mys-tified and sorrowful; he called up Ginny Darrish, who had no more ideas on the matter. He filled out reports to be sent to the county sheriff's office, and another to be filed with the state, in

Tallahassee. But beyond this, he wasn't sure how to proceed.

Hale was certain that Margaret Larkin's death was connected with her pregnancy. He had thought that possibly Margaret had been raped, then killed; but the two coroners said that there had been no sexual molestation, and Hale could see that her clothing had been ripped toward some other purpose.

Identifying the father was going to be a problem. Under the circumstances, the man was unlikely to step forward voluntarily. It was even possible that Margaret had told no one—or even did not know herself—that she was carrying a child.

The first new information concerning Margaret came on Sunday, the night before her funeral, by way of Belinda. "Daddy," the cheerleader said when they were halfway through supper, lightly, as if what she had to say was of no consequence: "You know what?"

"What, honey?"

"I was over at the Redfields' today, talking to Nina about poor old Margaret Larkin, and Nina said she *saw* Margaret Larkin that afternoon not five minutes 'fore the rain started."

"What!"

"That's right, Daddy! Nina was checking to see if the Mobile paper had got put in her mailbox yet, and up sails Margaret Larkin on her Schwinn, and she stops and talks to Nina for a couple of minutes, just chatting away. 'How's Miz Larkin?' Nina says, and all that—"

"Was Margaret upset? Did she act scared? What did Nina say, honey?"

"She said Margaret was just the same as she ever was, didn't even seem nervous about the rain, said she'd be home in five minutes. I guess she was wrong," added Belinda with raised eyebrows.

"Why the hell didn't Nina say anything about this to anybody?"

"Daddy, she didn't think it was important, or had anything to do with Margaret getting killed. It just came up in the conversation when I was over there, and I said, 'Nina, why didn't you tell my daddy this?' And she said she would have, if she had run into you on the street or something. But it's not important, is it? I mean, Margaret didn't talk about dying at the hands of a psychopath or anything, they just talked about the rain, and old Miz Larkin, and Nina didn't remember what all else."

"Well, honey, it is important though," said the sheriff, "I mean, now we know that Margaret was killed out there by the bridge. Before, all we knew was that she got thrown off the bridge there when she was probably unconscious, and drowned in the river. So far as I knew somebody could have knocked her out on the other side of town, and then thrown her in the trunk, already tied to the bicycle, and then chucked her off the bridge in two seconds flat. But now we know it came as a surprise, because if Margaret stopped to talk to Nina for a few minutes, then she didn't think that anybody was after her. I mean, she wasn't being chased. Did Nina say anything else?" begged Hale. "Did she see anything else that day?"

"No," said Belinda. "The only thing she said she saw was about ten minutes later, when she was standing out on her front porch, looking at the lightning, and she saw this hearse come barreling down the road with fishing poles stuck out the back."

"From the direction of the river?"

Belinda nodded: "It came from the other direction just when she was standing there talking to Margaret. She didn't know whose it was. She figured the man was going out fishing but changed his mind when the rain started."

"Did she see the tag?"

"I don't know. You'll have to ask her."

The sheriff did just that. Directly after dinner, he drove out to Nina's place, and talked with her at length. To his satisfaction Belinda had related the details correctly. Nina had not seen the tag, but knew that she had never seen that particular hearse pass the house before. It seemed possible, considering the timing of the vehicle's appearances, that the driver—if he was not the murderer himself—had seen or heard something near the Styx River bridge.

"So it wasn't the one that belongs to Mr. Cowles? His is painted green though. You sure this hearse wasn't green?"

"No," said Nina, "it was black. Half a dozen poles sticking out the back end."

Hale thought out the implication of this as he drove slowly around Babylon's dark streets—dark now as ever, beneath the new moon. His first conjecture was that a stranger in a fishing hearse, out by the Styx, had been in some way annoyed by Margaret to such a degree that he had killed her, secreted her body, and then driven like hell away from the place. Or perhaps he had seen something, and not wanted to get involved. But the sheriff concluded that it was most likely that the driver of the hearse had had nothing at all to do with Margaret's death. He had doubled back hastily on the Styx River road for some reason the sheriff would never learn.

In any case, since he had no other leads, the sheriff determined to find the driver of that fishing hearse, and in pursuance of that resolve, telephoned Ed Geiger. Geiger did not know who owned such a vehicle. The sheriff was discouraged, for if Geiger in his double capacity as town gossip and owner of the sporting goods store didn't know, then Hale doubted that the Bureau of Motor Vehicles could assist him.

For the time being then, Hale dismissed the hearse, and concentrated on Margaret's pregnancy. It was significant that Dr. Everage had known nothing of it until the body had been examined; either Margaret had gone out of town to a doctor, or she had simply handled the matter herself. Possibly she had been planning an abortion, though in that case it ought already to have been performed. She might have approached Jerry with her problem—for she'd have needed money—but she did not. But perhaps like most girls her age she was ignorant of these things, and imagined that abortions could be performed at any time up until the hour that labor commenced.

Jerry had told Hale that Margaret in the last month had seemed preoccupied, but that he and his grandmother had set this down to some adolescent trauma that all young girls went through. Hale could imagine that it was rather the monumental problem of her pregnancy that disturbed her. It was just possible that Margaret had intended running away, to give birth in some out-of-the-way place like Atlanta or Miami, and then return after she had given up the child for adoption, with some strained tale of six months spent waitressing in a chromium diner. Margaret was not the type to have critically distressed her grandmother with an unmarried pregnancy.

But simply the fact that Margaret had been killed pointed to the most likely sequence of events. The girl had found herself pregnant, had wondered for a time what to do, and had at last determined on confronting the father and demanding that he marry her, or pay for the abortion, or follow some strange alternative course her adolescent mind suggested. The man had been stunned, he had balked because he was afraid to have it known that he was the father—perhaps he had a reputation to uphold, or was already married. Perhaps he was himself only fourteen years old.

The likeliest in a townful of very unlikely suspects was Warren Perry. Hale had discovered from Annie-Leigh Hooker that Margaret Larkin had spent any number of afternoons in the schoolroom with Warren Perry, helping him to record grades and check homework and compile alternative seating arrangements for his classes. She had obviously had a crush on him, and he had done little to discourage her—if only because he did not realize that she was smitten. So far as Annie-Leigh knew, however, they had never seen one another outside of school.

Hale imagined that something like this had occurred: On Thursday afternoon, when they were alone in the school room together, Margaret had told Warren of her pregnancy. Warren had been upset, but at last had agreed to marry Margaret or take care of the abortion or whatever, and she left in relieved spirits. That explained the nonchalant way in which she had talked to Nina at her mailbox. But Warren Perry had then panicked. It would have been impossible for a high school teacher to marry a girl who hadn't yet entered the ninth grade. He would surely have lost his job, even though he was a favorite with Ginny Darrish, and would get another only with great difficulty and far away from Babylon. No one had sympathy for a man who seduced a fourteen-year-old girl.

He had driven out toward the farm, caught up with Margaret by the bridge, and then knocked her unconscious. He tied her to her bicycle, threw her off the bridge, and drove back into town. Maybe Nina had gone inside off her front porch for a few minutes, or she might simply not have noticed Perry's undistinguished automobile. Certainly it was easier to remember a fishing hearse than a beat-up ten-year-old Rambler.

The problem was to prove it, or alternatively, to force a confession from Warren Perry. Neither seemed an easy task, and the sheriff consoled himself with the observation that Perry was just the sort of man to suffer from a guilty conscience. If he only waited it out, the schoolteacher would slink across the driveway and give himself up in Hale's kitchen.

Therefore the sheriff didn't trouble himself much on Monday. He took the girl's photograph to the camera store to have copies made, prepared evidence for the following day's inquest, and spent the afternoon on the north side of town, questioning the impoverished inhabitants about Margaret Larkin and the fishing hearse that had gone by on the afternoon of her death. No one besides Nina had seen the girl or the vehicle. After four o'clock he sat at his kitchen table, leafing through the afternoon newspaper, wishing that Belinda would return from the Redfields', and half expecting Warren Perry to knock at the back door with a signed confession.

Chapter 19

Beyond the Larkin farm, there is not another dwelling, not another structure of any sort, until well after you pass the Alabama border. The road narrows and winds, and in all but the middle few hours of the day is shaded by the immensely tall pine trees that crowd in on either side. This is virgin timber, practically the only stand left in this vast area of pulp wood logging.

The land here is high and does not drain steeply into the Styx, but rather falls slowly westward into the Perdido, miles distant. The floor of the forest is soft and spongy in centuries of undisturbed pine needles. Stunted wild dogwood alone survive, in scattered specimens, beneath the high shading canopy of evergreen boughs. Here and there, where small fires set by lightning have burnt off a few acres, trees of other species have grown up, only just managing to establish themselves before the pines encroach once more.

Three miles from the Larkin house is a particularly splendid live oak, set in the midst of this pine forest. Its circumference is more than two hundred feet, and its height nearly fifty. The lower branches on the trunk are so massive that the extremities drag the earth, forming a protective lush umbrella. Even on hottest days this interior space around the black trunk is cool. In all the panhandle of Florida no place is more remote and sheltered than this green hovel beneath the curving dank moss-strewn branches of this tremendous oak.

The tree is known, however, for a small massacre took place there in 1809. The county historical commission has wanted to erect a plaque there, but no one can decide whether it was the Indians who killed the Spanish settlers, or Spanish who killed the Americans, or Americans who killed the Indians. In dry weather, an old trace can be discerned which leads meanderingly from the highway to the live oak.

In this green-lighted space, late in the afternoon following Margaret Larkin's funeral, and while the sheriff sat at his kitchen table wondering where his daughter might be, Belinda Hale rolled naked on a lime-colored blanket. Her cheerleader outfit lay neatly folded atop her shoes a few feet away.

Silent, sitting with his knees tucked up beneath his chin, smoking a cigarette, and also naked, was Nathan Redfield.

Belinda sat up suddenly, twisted her neck around and tried to examine her shoulder blade. "Nathan!" she said petulantly: "I do believe your teeth met under my collarbone! You bit me all over! This time tomorrow, I am gone look like a road map. I'm gone have to tell Daddy that I got trapped at the bottom of a ten-girl pyramid at cheerleader practice."

"Your daddy is not gone see all those bruises," said Nathan. He stared directly ahead of him, at the vast black trunk of the tree.

"Well," said Belinda, pouting to get his attention: "Somebody else might."

Nathan stubbed out his cigarette by the side of the blanket. In a voice so low Belinda had trouble making out the words, he said:

"You better be making a joke, girl. I ever find that's true, and the headlines are gone read: 'Cheerleader smothered to death with her own pompoms.'"

"Nathan," she said: "I was only kidding, it's just that I'm not gone be able to wear a bathing suit for the next five days and four nights."

They said nothing for the next few moments. Belinda stretched lazily on the blanket, staring upward into the black branches, the green coarse leaves, the hoary Spanish moss.

"What time you suppose it's getting to be?" said Nathan. He had pulled a small bottle of bourbon from the pocket of his discarded jacket, and was now and then sipping at it.

"I don't know," said Belinda, her eyes closed, "I suppose— Hey!"

Nathan looked slowly over. "What is it?"

Belinda sat up hastily. "Something dripped on me." She brushed liquid from her lashes, and smelled gingerly the fingers that had been stained black. "Just water, I guess, I didn't know that moss—" She lifted her head back to stare up into the branches of the tree, no more then ten feet above her, and gently curving toward the ground.

"God, Nathan!" she shouted, and jumped toward him with such force that she knocked him off the blanket onto the soft earth. He slapped at her, and cried "Goddamn it, Be—"

"Nathan!" she cried: "Somebody's up there in that tree. I saw somebody looking down at me. There's somebody right up on that big branch!"

She clung to him.

He brushed her off, stood, and staggered backward. He stared upward at the large limb above them. He moved quickly around trying to see along its whole moss-shrouded length.

"Belinda," he said after a moment: "I don't see anything. What'd you see? You didn't see anybody. You—"

"Nathan!" she interrupted him: "Somebody was looking down from that branch. Somebody was up there on it. There was this face looking down."

"Well, who was it then? I mean, what'd he look like?"

Nathan continued to dance around naked, staring up into the

mass of rotting wood and dank foliage. Belinda struggled into her clothing, but her shaking fear made this a difficult operation.

"It wasn't a man," she said, "it looked like a woman—"

Nathan stopped dead at this. He looked at Belinda caustically. "Belinda, there's no woman in that tree," he said quietly. "There's nobody in that tree at all, and there's for sure no woman up there. You saw something. The moss probably, the light's so dim under here, the moss can look like just about anything you want it to."

"Nathan," she squealed: "I saw something up in that tree. Somebody up in that tree dripped water on me, and then I looked up and I saw her staring down at me and I don't care if you believe me or not, I just want to get the hell out of here, and I would appreciate it to no end if you would put down that bottle of bourbon and put your clothes back on." Already she was folding the blanket up, and pointedly did not look up into the space above her head.

Nathan, with nervous haste that belied his assertion that Belinda's imagination alone had been at work, stepped into his clothes. Less than a minute later, they pushed through the screen of leaves into the pine forest proper, and breathed more freely.

On her own, Belinda would have run toward her car, parked a hundred or so yards from the road, next to Nathan's International Scout; but Nathan, to show his fearlessness, insisted on walking an unnatural leisurely pace toward the highway.

They moved across the carpet of pine needles without speaking; Belinda pressed herself against Nathan's side and glanced warily behind her at the great live oak they had just left. It stood grotesquely vast and darkly gleaming in the small clearing among the pines. She had been beneath it before, but for the first time understood why it was rumored to be haunted.

They followed the track, which was plain enough, but the cars seemed farther away; both expected them to come into view with every step forward. But five paces ahead, ten, it was still only darkening forest around them.

Gradually, Belinda became aware of a sound that grew beneath the slight noise of their shoes on the soft earth; a melodious swish, low pitched and only slightly varying in intensity, as of an oar turned idly in the calm surface of a sheltered lake. The noise was, if nothing else, decidedly liquid.

"Nathan," she whispered: "What's that?"

Nathan didn't answer, but Belinda felt cold perspiration on his forearm. She glanced up at his face, found it set and troubled. He said nothing.

The noise grew louder, and Belinda tried to think what could create the sound of water being whipped among the trees. It seemed to come closer; she stared wildly to the right of her, and abruptly changed her position, stumbling, to put Nathan between herself and the sound.

"Goddamn it," hissed Nathan, "where the hell is the Scout?"

"We're not going the wrong way, are we?" demanded Belinda in a faltering voice: "We didn't go the wrong way from the tree, did we?"

"No, we're right," he growled, "but where the hell is the Scout?"

It was dusk in the forest; now Nathan hurried along with ample strides, and Belinda had almost to run to keep up with him. "Nathan," she whispered, "I am just about out of my wits. What is making that sound?"

Now the noise was directly behind them, low but unfaltering, slightly pulsating with a rhythm that seemed to match their fear. Belinda skipped forward ahead of Nathan, letting go his arm.

"Hey, wait up!" he called hoarsely and pushed on. He tripped over an exposed root and fell, spilling the loose clothing and blanket that he had been carrying.

Belinda looked around in terror; the sound had suddenly decreased but hovered among the tree trunks, in the thick green air twenty perhaps thirty feet back. She glanced that way wildly, but saw nothing. She felt that something hid behind one of the slender pine trunks—but what could be that thin? She lurched back to Nathan, dragged him to his feet, and gathered what had been dropped. "God," she cried: "Nathan, let's get the hell out of this place!"

Nathan broke into a run down the path, but he could hear that terrible wet swishing move forward too, volume increasing with speed. Belinda staggered behind.

He stopped short, and she collided with him. "Nathan—"

He pointed ahead: A hundred feet away were the Scout and the powder-blue Volkswagen. The glistening metallic colors were oddly reassuring in this dim forest of muted green and brown. "Thank God!" cried Belinda, and they hurried forward.

They fell panting against the high hood of the Scout. Belinda glanced around. "It stopped following us. After we saw the cars, the sound stopped. Nathan, what was it?"

"It wasn't anything," he said harshly. "You just got scared, that's all, because you're afraid of the woods when it's getting dark."

"Listen, Nathan Redfield, back there you were so scared your drawers were drooping—now let's get out of here!"

He nodded: "You go first, I'll be right behind you. But don't you start off till I get in the Scout, and get it started, you hear me?"

Belinda climbed into the front seat of the VW; but suddenly she jumped back out. "Nathan!" she cried again: "This seat is soaking!"

"What!" he cried in irritation at this delay. He leaned into the car, and felt the seat. Belinda was right: when he pressed his hand against the fabric, water squeezed up and wet his fingers. They came away black and smudged.

"Goddamn, Belinda," he said in exasperation: "I don't know what it is, just put something down on it, and get in, and let's get out of here. You be careful turning, I don't want to have to stick around trying to unlock your bumper."

Belinda threw the lime-colored blanket over the seat, and got in. She turned the key in the ignition, sighed when it started at once, and pulled on her lights. She turned to smile wanly at Nathan, but he was already in the Scout. He quickly turned it around on the light forest track, skinning bark from a pine with his bumper. He flashed his lights twice as a signal that she should drive on back to the highway.

Belinda moved forward slowly through the trees until she came within sight of the Babylon road; she wheeled out onto the pavement without looking for oncoming cars. Nathan was less than twenty feet behind her, desperately guzzling the last of the bourbon—for even as he had put the vehicle into forward gear after turning around, he had heard and felt that liquid swish against the side of the Scout. Something had tried the handle of the locked door across from him, something that could not be seen when he stared wildly through the passenger window.

PART IV

OUT OF BLACK WATER

Chapter 20

The inquest into the death of Margaret Larkin went off easily enough. Jerry testified, and was followed by Warren Perry, who bore the hard gaze of Ted Hale throughout his evidence. Ed Geiger, Hale, and, at the last, Dr. Everage went to the stand. There was commotion throughout the courtroom when Everage testified that the victim had been pregnant at the time of her death. Jerry blushed and stared down into his lap; Warren's mouth fell open, and would not shut.

In ten minutes, the jury brought in a verdict of homicide by person or persons unknown.

Afterward, Jerry accompanied the sheriff back to the town hall and sat alone with him in his office.

"How's your grandmother?" said Hale.

Jerry paused before answering: "All right, I guess. About as well as can be expected right now. She's out at the house with the Scouts. Picking's just begun."

"Did you tell her about Margaret's being pregnant?"

Jerry nodded: "She didn't believe me though, and I didn't push it. It's just as well that she doesn't. She probably realizes it's true, but it's easier for her if she denies it to herself for a while."

Hale nodded sympathetically.

"But I tell you something, sheriff—"

"What?"

"She's still mad at you for not arresting Nathan Redfield. She's still convinced that Nathan killed Margaret, and that he's trying to get us out of town. Somebody from the bank called up at the house this morning and asked about the loan payments again."

"It wasn't Nathan, though?"

Jerry shook his head: "No, but it's Nathan's bank, and they wouldn't have called without him telling them to."

"You don't know that. Listen, Jerry, you tell me straight out now: What is it that *you* think about all this?"

Jerry paused, then he shrugged: "I don't know. Grandma and I just want the same thing. We want to know who it was that murdered Margaret on the bridge, and then threw her in the river."

"So do I!" cried Hale: "But you're not going to tell me that you're starting to believe what your grandmama's been saying about Nathan Redfield, are you?"

"Nathan Redfield nearly beat Shirley Blaine to death in a drainage ditch. She's still got one leg that's shorter than the other."

The sheriff looked disconcerted. "That was fifteen years ago. You were too young to remember that right. Besides, he didn't beat her 'nearly to death.' They were drunk, both of 'em, and he fell on top of her in the ditch, that's all."

"I don't know what to think, then," said Jerry miserably.

Hale sighed. "All right, listen, you go on home now, tend to your berries. I'll be out there directly, and talk to your grandmother."

Less than an hour later, Hale was out at the blueberry farm, sitting on the front porch at the opposite end of the swing from Evelyn Larkin.

"You're no sheriff," she accused him, "if you are letting Nathan Redfield prowl the streets of Babylon, after he went and murdered my little girl."

"Miz Larkin," Hale protested lamely, "you are in no condition—"

"Neither is Margaret. Margaret would have to claw through six feet of earth if she wanted to do something about it, and I just don't think she's capable of it right now. But I'm still here, and I don't intend to let you forget about her just because it's more convenient!"

"Nobody's forgetting about Margaret, Miz Larkin, it's just that right now we don't have any idea who could have killed her."

"Nathan Redfield killed her!"

Hale ignored this, and waved away a curious Boy Scout who had come to the front of the house. He scampered off.

"Listen, Miz Larkin, I know that Jerry told you, and it came out today in the inquest, that Margaret was—going to have a baby."

Evelyn looked away; her face had reddened.

"Well," Hale went on uncomfortably, "I just wanted to know if you had any idea who the father might be."

"There wasn't any father, because there wasn't going to be any baby," said Evelyn: "Fourteen-year-old girls don't get pregnant."

"Do you think it could have been Warren Perry?"

Evelyn's eyes widened, and her voice went hard: "You think it was Warren Perry that killed Margaret. Jerry said you were asking about him the other day. Warren Perry is the sweetest boy in the world outside of Jerry, and you are a despicable man to try to pin this on him, when if you would sit still for five minutes, you'd know it was Nathan Redfield that did it. Warren Perry wouldn't squash a boll weevil, and Margaret thought the world of him. It's just because Warren is so good to his mother that you're on to him like this; and it's because Nathan Redfield is your friend—and because he's got all the money in the world —that you won't do anything about it!"

"Miz Larkin—" Hale protested in a low voice.

Evelyn rose from the swing. Her eyes glistened with hot tears: "Nathan Redfield is not gone get away with this, so when you go to report to him, as I am sure you'll do as soon as you leave here, you tell him that I am hiring a lawyer to charge him with murder. You won't look for proof, but our lawyer will. And if he won't, I'll do it myself. If it comes to it, Jerry will tie a rope to my waist, and sink me in that river, and leave me there till I bring up the evidence that will prove that Nathan Redfield caused my little girl to die."

Chapter 21

The following morning, after running errands in town, Ginny Darrish drove out across the Styx River to the blueberry farm. She found Evelyn, pale and red-eyed, on the back latticed porch among the boxes of blueberries. Ginny sat down cheerfully beside her friend.

Jerry, who had seen the car approach, came up to speak; but just after he had done so, Evelyn turned to him, and said: "I'm going to tell her . . ."

"I wish you wouldn't," said Jerry, tight-lipped.

"I have to," said Evelyn.

"Tell me what?" cried Ginny happily. The mystery excited her.

"I won't be here, then," said Jerry, and nodding once more to Ginny, he returned to the supervision of the Boy Scouts in the patch.

Then, pausing only when a Scout entered briefly with his several boxes of berries, Evelyn told Ginny her suspicions about Nathan Redfield. Ginny heard all of this with wide eyes beneath her silver hair, but made no protest of disbelief.

"The sheriff was out here yesterday," concluded Evelyn, "and Jerry told him this too, but he wouldn't listen. He knows it's true, but he doesn't want to go against the Redfields; or else he's out there protecting Nathan for all he's worth."

"Well," said Ginny cautiously: "I just saw Nathan and Ted together this morning at the drugstore, sitting in the next booth like they were a couple of junior girls talking about their Friday night dates, and they didn't say a word after I came in, I can tell you."

Evelyn shook her head significantly, and with some distress: "That means that the sheriff *is* in on this."

"It's possible, I guess," said Ginny cautiously. "But you know, Evelyn, don't you, that those two have been close for a long while. It's not the first time that I've seen them there in the drugstore booth together."

"Ginny, listen—"

"What?"

"Do you think Charles would take us on as his clients in this? Ted Hale's not going to shake a finger to arrest Nathan Redfield, and so I've got to get at him some other way. I don't know what Charles can do, but he's a lawyer, and he ought to have some ideas—"

"Well, I think he just might. There's no love lost between Charles and Nathan. And he certainly will if I talk to him about it."

"Would you?"

Ginny nodded, and placed a pink hand atop Evelyn's blue-stained fingers. She dug her lavender fingernails affectionately into the bereaved woman's wrist.

"I don't know what we could afford to pay him right now," said Evelyn hesitantly.

Ginny threw her hands up over her ears. "Evelyn Larkin!" she cried: "I'm not going to listen to you talk about money! It makes me giddy, I tell you, it just makes me giddy to hear it!"

Evelyn smiled weakly: "Thank you, Ginny," she whispered. "Jerry doesn't want me to do this, but"—she faltered, then picked up again bravely—"but my little girl was murdered, and I'd like to take the man who did it and split him open from top to bottom, then sew him back up with barbed wire."

Leaning forward to kiss Evelyn on the cheek, Ginny whispered: "If Nathan Redfield did this, you and I will see to it that there's not enough left of him to get tied to a bicycle."

Chapter 22

Charles Darrish occupied the offices that his father had had before him. These were five rooms on the second floor of a brick building only several doors down from the town hall, and on the same side of the street Florida lawbooks dating from the 1830's and containing countless decisions handed down in the cases of runaway slaves, lined the walls in glass bookshelves. These had not been disturbed in sixty years. Newer lawbooks, which Darrish never looked at either, lay stacked in piles in all the corners. The rooms were dark and dusty, and wasps that had constructed nests at the top of the high paper-shaded windows, flew lazily about the hot airless rooms. The furniture for clients in the waiting room was of green-painted wicker with light green cushions that Ginny had made in the first years of their marriage. The walls were of dark-stained pine that after a century still bled sap in hot weather.

Charles Darrish, a bulky awkward man with a perpetual squint, sat at a large table in the innermost of the rooms; it was piled high with briefs, and file folders, and summonses, and legal documents, unanswered letters, thin journals five years old that hadn't yet been taken out of their brown paper wrappers. A large floor fan underneath the table cooled his ankles and peri-odically sucked in the cuffs of his pants, but otherwise had no effect in the stifling chamber.

In large chairs on the other side of the table sat Evelyn Larkin and Jerry. Squinting at them over the high piles of dusty papers, Darrish had listened intently while Evelyn explained why she was convinced that Nathan Redfield had murdered her grand-daughter. Then he had refused to take the case.

"There isn't any case, Miz Larkin, there's just no case at all. Jerry," he said, squinting in a slightly different direction: "You can see there's no case, cain't you?"

"But he did it!" cried Evelyn: "We know that he did it!"

"You may know it," said Darrish, "or you may think that you know it, but you just cain't prove it. And, Miz Larkin, even if I was to take it on, I couldn't prove it either. There's no proof, and right now, it don't look like there's going to be any. Nathan Redfield's not going to jail for murdering Margaret unless some-body comes up with five white witnesses and a Polaroid of him tying the bicycle to her ankles—and that don't seem likely to be forthcoming."

Jerry gazed at his grandmother pleadingly, wanting them very much to leave. He could not look at Darrish for his embar-rassment.

"Did you talk to Ginny today?" asked Evelyn sharply.

"Ginny called," Darrish admitted: "And she told me you were coming. I wasn't surprised to see you here when I got back from lunch and I knew what you were here for. If you could have brought me some proof, just a little bit of something that I could have tagged in the courtroom, then I might have considered it, Miz Larkin, but if I took you on, I'd be making a fool of you, and a fool of myself to boot."

"Nathan Redfield got to you first!" Evelyn cried.

Darrish looked up sharply, and for the first time, Jerry made out the pupils of his eyes. "Miz Larkin, you know about how well Ginny and Nathan get on. I handle the CP&M, but Nathan don't even speak to me on the street. Besides, how would Nathan know that you were coming here?"

"Ted Hale told him."

"Grandma—" protested Jerry.

"Miz Larkin," said Darrish quietly: "I'd love to help you, I'd like nothing more in the world than to go and fight for you in the court, and string up the man who killed Margaret. But whoever it is, I don't think it's Nathan Redfield, and even if it is, right now, with what we have, with what the sheriff has, we couldn't convict him."

"Ginny told me you would help us!" charged Evelyn.

"Miz Larkin, if I could—"

"Grandma," said Jerry in a low voice: "Mr. Darrish was real nice in listening to us, but he cain't help us, and I knew he couldn't, and I told you he couldn't. Now we ought to go right now, and not take up any more of his time."

Charles leaned back in his swivel chair, and peered blankly at the bookcase behind Evelyn and Jerry, as if the conversation did not concern him.

Evelyn rose precipitately, and hurried out of the office into the long dark hallway. Jerry remained behind a moment longer: "Thank you, Mr. Darrish, we really appreciate you listening to us. Grandma wants to do something about Margaret, and she just cain't accept it yet that there's nothing to be done."

"I know, Jerry," said Darrish, blinking rapidly in apparent compassion. "You did right in coming here, because sooner or later Evelyn'll come out of this, and she'll realize that it wasn't Nathan that killed Margaret, but it may be she'll have to hear everybody in town tell it to her before she does accept it."

"I got to go," said Jerry apologetically. He had glanced out into the hallway, where Evelyn stood impatiently awaiting him. He eased out the door, and closed it softly.

Chapter 23

"Charles!" cried Ginny Darrish to her husband less than an hour later, "I *do* wish you'd let me call the exterminator! These wasps get bigger every year—I'm surprised you don't give 'em names!" Ginny closed the door behind her. "You know why I'm here," she said then in a low and accusing voice.

"About Jerry and Evelyn," her husband said, without discernible emotion.

Ginny nodded: "Charles, what did you do to them? Not ten minutes ago Evelyn was out at the school, all but accusing me of having put my finger to the knots that tied poor Margaret to her bicycle!"

Charles nodded, raising his eyebrows and shutting his eyes altogether. "She was already real upset when she came in here, and I know I told you I'd take her on, but Ginny, I cain't afford to represent a crazy woman—"

"Evelyn Larkin is not crazy, and besides, you wouldn't have had to do anything! It's just to reassure her till she comes out of this—that's all."

"I wouldn't have to do a blessed thing," said Charles, "except to apologize to half the town every other day, and try to explain why Evelyn Larkin had accused them of murder, and I don't know what all else. It would be all right if I could count on her just staying out at the farm, and keeping quiet in the bed, but I cain't count on that, Ginny. You saw how she was, just itching to get her nails into Nathan Redfield's neck. She accused me of being in on it too. I cain't just up and represent somebody who's not in control. When they got here—they were sitting in the waiting room when I got back from having a plate of catfish at the White Horse—I was all ready to sign her on, but she got to talking, and I was looking at poor old Jerry out of the corner of my eye, how he was so red and sweaty, and I felt so sorry for him

I didn't know what to do! And Evelyn went on and wouldn't stop going on about Nathan, and by the time I finally got her out of here, she had the whole town behind bars, and that was including you and me and Ted Hale. She had dragged poor Margaret up out of her grave, and stuck Nathan Redfield down there in her place."

Ginny patted her powdered cheeks lightly in thought. "She's upset, Charles, and I just cain't say that I blame her."

"Sure! And she's got a right to be, but she ought to leave this to Ted Hale. Besides," he whispered, and leaned forward, toppling a sheaf of dusty papers in his wife's direction: "You know and I know that Ted is not gone find anybody to put this on. Nobody's gone come forward saying he murdered Margaret Larkin, nobody's gone come forward and say that he was the one who got a fourteen-year-old girl pregnant. You think I want to look like a fool, representing a crazy woman?"

Ginny nodded, defeated. "I just feel so sorry for her . . ."

"So do I," said Charles energetically.

"And I feel bad that she's just gone be disappointed again, if she talks to that lawyer in Pensacola."

"What lawyer?" demanded Charles. His eyes opened wide for half a second.

"Well, after she got through blessing me out, she went in to see Warren Perry, and told him the same story, about how you wouldn't take her on. And Warren told her about this lawyer in Pensacola. This lawyer is Warren's mama's cousin, and he lives right on Palafox, and Evelyn made Warren go in the teachers' lounge and call the man up, and now Evelyn and Jerry are going down there tonight to see him. Well, when Warren told me that, I hit the ceiling! I sent Warren out to the farm to call it off, to make up some excuse, because if Evelyn talks to that man, she's just gone get upset again. Of course he's not gone take her on either. She ought not be making that trip down to Pensacola, just to be disappointed all over again."

Charles nodded thoughtfully. "You're right," he said: "I let her down easy, but you get some lawyer from Pensacola, you just don't know what he's gone say to her. What was his name—the lawyer in Pensacola, I mean?"

"I don't know," said Ginny, looking up: "Why? What does it matter?"

"It doesn't—I just—"

"You know what else?" cried Ginny, interrupting her husband. "Evelyn told Warren that Ted Hale suspected—"

The telephone rang, and Ginny broke off.

"Hello?" said Charles, and after a moment, he handed the receiver across the desk to his wife. "It's Warren," he said.

Ginny took the receiver: "Warren, where are you?" she cried.

"I'm at home. I—"

"Warren, hold the phone up to your mouth. I can hardly hear you speak. Did you find Evelyn and Jerry? D'you talk her out of it?"

"No. When I got out to the farm, they had already left. A couple of little boys were out in the patch, and they told me that Jerry and Miz Larkin went to put flowers on Margaret's grave and then they were going to Pensacola."

"Well, why didn't you go to the cemetery then, and try to stop them?"

"I did. They left a nice little pot of yellow zinnias on the grave, but they had already left. I thought about following them to Pensacola, but I didn't know where Jerry was going with the berries. It wouldn't have done me any good."

"Why don't you call your mama's cousin, that lawyer you sent them to? You told me his name and I forgot it."

"What for? That wouldn't serve, Ginny. You don't want him to turn 'em away at the door. He'll listen to Miz Larkin, and maybe he can do some good talking to her, because he's not from Babylon. Maybe she'll listen to him."

"Maybe," said Ginny doubtfully. "What was his name?"

"Henry Harp."

"Henry Harp," Ginny repeated the name carefully, and her husband wrote it down. "Warren," Ginny went on, "are you gone be home this afternoon, just in case I need you?"

"I'll be here. I was supposed to take the car up to Atmore but I've decided to put that off for a while."

"Bye then. I'm just sorry all this happened," she added, and hung up the phone.

"This is a bad business," said Ginny to her husband, "and I don't rightly see how any good is going to come out of it." She stared at Charles across the desk for a few moments. "Charles, listen," she said, "you don't think that Nathan had anything to do with this, do you? Margaret's death, I mean."

Charles covered his closed eyes with his hand. "No, of course not, he didn't any more murder Margaret than Warren did. And Warren Perry wouldn't tear the wings off a butterfly."

"Who you suppose did it?"

He splayed his hands, and looked away. "Who knows? I don't imagine we'll ever know. I suppose we'll be lucky enough if it doesn't happen to any other young girl out there on that bridge."

"I wouldn't like to think that Nathan had anything to do with it. I don't care anything for him, heaven knows, but he's sort of family, and it doesn't do to have family in the pen, especially with you being a lawyer and all."

"No," said Charles, "it wouldn't do this practice any good if Nathan Redfield went to the pen for murdering Margaret Larkin. And she was one of his customers, too."

It was past three when Charles Darrish at last persuaded his wife to leave, and at that, he had to bribe her with two twenties for a new dress.

Chapter 24

After Ginny Darrish had talked to her husband on Wednesday morning, warning him that Evelyn Larkin and Jerry would be coming by his office, the lawyer had met Nathan Redfield at a restaurant on the Pensacola highway. Nathan's invitation had come as a surprise to the lawyer, for on most occasions the banker could barely be brought to speak five consecutive words to Charles Darrish. Darrish had accepted as much out of curiosity as anything else.

There Nathan talked to the lawyer, until recently estranged, not of the death of Margaret Larkin, but rather of the land that Evelyn Larkin owned, stretching along the bank of the Styx. Nathan confided to the lawyer that the old woman was far behind on her payments on the substantial bank loan, and would doubtless lose the farm within the next couple of years. This would be a matter of no consequence, smiled Nathan, except that it appeared likely that a great pool of oil underlay the whole of the property. Nathan said that he had some time ago decided that Evelyn Larkin and her grandson ought to be made to relinquish that land before the representative of Texaco showed up in Babylon, waving his checkbook.

"Charles, listen," said Nathan earnestly: "I've been having dealings with those oil people for the past year, because they've been after Daddy to let 'em drill some test rigs on the land that we own between the house and the Perdido, but Daddy's holding 'em off, just to spite me. I think they're getting put off about that, and they don't want to put up with Daddy any more, and it's starting to look like we're gone get passed by because Daddy's being so stubborn about it. And I cain't talk to him, he won't listen to me on something like this, and if I was to try to talk to him, it'd only make things worse. Now I was down there in Mobile having supper with two of these men, and they were staying at the Government House, and they took me up to their room for a couple of drinks, and they had all these maps spread out on the bed, and I think I saw a couple of 'em that I wasn't supposed to see, 'cause I saw where they had marked the land that's all along the Styx as the most likely place for oil. Now we own gosh knows how many thousand acres between the house and the Perdido, but they're actually more interested in the land that's right along the Styx, and on the other side. Different kind of rock formation or something, I guess."

"They tell you that?" said Darrish suspiciously.

"Not exactly. But they asked me who owned that land up there, all that land north of town and on this side of the Alabama line. I said most of it belonged to some man up in Boston who's not ever down here, and that the rest of it belonged to the Larkins. Then they asked who the Larkins were, and I knew something was up."

"Have they gone to the Larkins yet?"

Nathan shook his head. "No," said Nathan: "I put 'em off that. I told 'em I was the Larkins' investment counselor and that

I would approach 'em. They called back a couple of times, called me, and I told 'em I had spoken to old Evelyn Larkin and that she wasn't interested in even talking about selling until the berry season was over."

"They really believe that?"

"I guess so. 'Cause they haven't been down here yet. But they're working their way west from Jay and south from Atmore and it looks like they're gone be here any minute. Now," said Nathan, and leaned forward across the table, littered with plates of half-eaten catfish, plastic baskets of white rolls, and dishes of creamed corn: "I don't think that you and I ought to let 'em get out of this cheap—the oil companies, I mean."

"No-siree-bob," said Darrish earnestly: "I don't think we *had* ought to let 'em do that!"

"Evelyn Larkin is gone lose that farm right soon, if not this summer, then next, or sometime in between. I want to make sure it comes to the bank, and if we can manage—you and I that is—" He smiled expansively. "Then I want that land to come to me."

Darrish nodded, but the smile on his face had fled.

Nathan paused, then said: "I'm not smart enough to do all this on my own. I got to have somebody to advise me, somebody to help me. It's the kind of thing that's got to be done careful and done right. I've handled it all right up till now, but I was thinking that maybe you and I could go into a partnership on this land, we'd buy it from the bank, put it in a dummy corporation or something. Maybe that could be arranged through somebody you know in Pensacola—"

"No," said Darrish—and Nathan knew that he had the lawyer. "Somebody in Mobile. Have the corporation set up in Mobile, it's best to have it all out of Florida. Not as easy for them to check."

"Mobile then," agreed Nathan: "Mobile would be just fine. You think that can be done?"

Darrish nodded confidently: "But I'd better get on it soon, just so that it will all be ready when we are, when . . ." He twisted his head inquiringly, but it was not possible for Nathan to read his narrowed gaze.

"I'm getting on this now. I've been pushing 'em a little on the loan, and why not? They're behind, they're well behind, and that storm we had last week—I heard Jerry say that storm did them in."

"Jerry told you that?"

"He told Ted Hale. Ted told me."

"Margaret Larkin died during that storm," said Darrish.

"Well," said Nathan after a pause, "that's all the more reason for them to want to be out of that place."

"You know," said Darrish carefully: "Evelyn Larkin is coming to see me this afternoon, and try and get me to prosecute you for that murder. I—"

"I know," said Nathan quickly: "Hale told me that too. Now listen, because that's why we've got to be double careful. She's got it in for me, and we cain't let her know that I—the bank, I should say—is after the land. I mean, I don't take it personal that she's saying I killed that girl, because I realize that she is under strain. She's not responsible, and that's all the more reason to get her out of the house. They have no business there. The girl died within sight of the house, and that farm is no good any more. I don't know why they would want to stay around anyway. Nobody's gone be real surprised when she loses the farm on top of everything else. A hysterical woman ought not be worried with a blueberry farm, and everybody in town knows it. I've heard people say they wonder why she didn't sell out long time ago, when Jim and JoAnn died. I just want to give 'em a little push to be on their way far away from Babylon, where they'll be a lot happier."

"A little push," echoed Darrish without expression.

Chapter 25

Nathan Redfield was genuinely disturbed by Charles Darrish's phone call late Wednesday afternoon, telling him of Evelyn Larkin's resolve to visit the lawyer in Pensacola. Charles had assured him over lunch that there would be no difficulty in putting Evelyn off when she came by the office, but neither of them had expected that she would be so energetic in prosecuting her strange belief. Also, they didn't like the idea that she was going out of town to find someone to represent her. The man might smell green blood around Nathan's banker carcass, and come up to make trouble.

Nathan cursed Warren Perry for having told Evelyn Larkin about his mama's cousin Henry Harp.

After Darrish called, Nathan lay disconsolately in a chaise by the side of the pool. His father was a dozen feet away, in the shade of some ornamental pines, watching Belinda and Ben in the swimming pool. James Redfield spoke only to Belinda, and addressed not a word to either of his sons.

Sipping at a scotch, because there was no more bourbon, Nathan tried to reassure himself that all would go well, that it was only necessary to wait things out. In another month, two at the most, Evelyn Larkin and Jerry would have gone off wherever it was that homeless impoverished persons went; he would, by proxy, own the blueberry farm, and would be in close expectation of large sums of money rolling in from oil exploration leases.

By five o'clock Nathan was drunk, and dozing with hot amorphous nightmares in the chaise. Awakened by Ben a couple of hours later, Nathan was disconcerted to find that it was nearly dark. His father had been taken back to his room, and Belinda had gone home.

"Nina made supper, Nathan, it's already on the table. Come on inside now."

Nathan wouldn't speak during the meal. He was angry with himself for sleeping in the middle of the day, when he ought to have been working on the best way to get Evelyn Larkin and her grandson out of Babylon.

There was something beyond this, however; another fear, less defined but just as strong, and one moreover that Nathan didn't dare admit to himself. He had awakened frightened on the chaise. The atmosphere around the familiar pool, when he opened his eyes, was threatening—identical in texture and color and smell to the forest north of the Styx River. He smelled, heard, and tasted the fear he had experienced with Belinda in Monday afternoon's dusk. The quality of the air was the same, the light altered to just such a point in the gathering evening. When he craned his head upward, the pines about the house were identical to those in the forest northward. He stared around the pool and looked into the black corners of shrubbery. But fearful of seeing something there that had not been present when he fell asleep, he hurried into the house after Ben, ashamed of his own skittishness.

When they finished supper, Ben piled the dishes in the sink for Nina to wash the next morning, and then went into the den to watch television. Nathan sat with him through the national news, but did not respond to any of his comments.

"Ben," he said, "why don't you go turn on the patio lights. It's so dark out there, I don't like it."

Surprised, Ben got up and flicked the switches next to the glass doors to the patio. Bright mercury lights suddenly broke against the night.

"Nathan," said Ben timorously: "Liquor store closes at nine. You want me to go? 'Cause you just finished off the scotch and there's no more bourbon."

Nathan at first made no reply. Then he rose with sudden resolution. "No," he said: "I ought to go. I want to get out for a few minutes anyway."

Ben pulled open the glass door for his brother.

Nathan walked quickly across the patio, nervously glancing over the shrubbery. The interior of the garage was brightly lighted, but the floodlamps reached only a few feet into the expansive driveway behind. Beyond was uninterrupted blackness.

Nathan climbed into the Continental, and turned the key in the ignition. As he put the car into reverse, he automatically glanced into the rearview mirror. There, just outside the perimeter of light on the driveway, stood a young girl, dressed in a colorless textured shift. Her face, its features obscured by shadow, was as grainy and dim as her garment. Only the mouth, widening slowly as if in careful speech or a labored scream, could Nathan make out: a perfect expanding black circle.

The sudden apparition in the mirror frightened Nathan, but he immediately assumed that it was Belinda, inexplicably in a nightgown, and appearing strangely small. He thrust his head out the window to yell at her for startling him so, but when he looked back, no one was there. The blackness beyond the reach of the flood-lamps was solid and undisturbed. He had the distinct feeling that the girl behind the car had not fled either to the left or to the right, had not retreated into the black forest, but rather had simply vanished.

He called Belinda's name a couple of times, and waited for a reply. None came. Watching nervously in the mirror, he shivered with a sense of vulnerability, which prompted him to push the buttons that raised the windows of the car and locked all the doors.

Nathan wanted to lift the door handle, leap out, and flee into the house, but this trip was being made precisely to show himself there was nothing to fear. He took his foot from the brake, and backed screeching into the driveway. He braced himself for the satisfying thump that shuddered the Lincoln when it ran over a large dog. It did not come. His lights flashed along the black hedges that bordered the drive, but he saw nothing. To his right were the high mercury lights over the swimming pool, masked by a row of planted specimen pines.

He sped away from the house, trying to convince himself that the figure in the driveway had been a trick of the harsh lights and the scotch he had drunk with dinner. He conjured the figure in his mind, tried to make it grow taller and older, tried to make the features conform to Belinda's. To some extent he succeeded, and with relief, began to curse the cheerleader for raising such fear in him.

At the liquor store on the south side of town, he took his time about buying the bourbon and scotch he wanted, talked for a few minutes to the proprietor, and only then headed slowly, cautiously back home.

At nine o'clock, downtown Babylon was deserted. The convenience stores and fast-food restaurants were all farther to the south, on the roads leading away, while the shops on John Glenn Avenue had closed at six or earlier. Even the two stoplights that regulated traffic during the commercial day had been disconnected for the night. There was not even the usual patrol car in front of town hall, and Nathan supposed the officer on duty must have gone out for an ice cream cone, or a drink. No vehicle moved on the street but the Lincoln.

Nathan had just passed the bank, going north on John Glenn, when the second traffic light was unexpectedly activated at the intersection just ahead. The red light popped on.

Nathan stopped the car, smiling wryly at the peculiar circumstance. He was thinking he might twit Hale on the unreliability of his traffic equipment, when he noticed that the sides of the signal were unlighted—they did not show green.

Imagining then that there was an electrical mishap with the system, he lifted his foot from the brake—but immediately he stamped down again, for just beyond the reach of his headlights, stood the same figure that had appeared in his driveway. It was not Belinda. This girl was younger, not as pretty, with a figure that was more like that of a child than a young woman. He stared harder this time, and inched the car forward a few feet for a better look. The dress, or whatever it was the girl wore, seemed somehow different, though Nathan could not think exactly how—but the singular reflective coarseness of the garment was the same. It appeared that the flesh and the clothing of the girl were of identical substance. She looked like a cheap funerary statue, sandstone flecked with mica, even a tiny figure lurking in the background of an old photograph, grainy and suggestive and unidentifiable.

The Lincoln crawled forward. The figure retreated gravely, but, astonishingly, preserved the appearance of motionlessness.

The red stoplight glowed directly above, reflecting off the hood of the car into Nathan's eyes. It changed color suddenly, to a light metallic blue—the color of no traffic light that Nathan had ever seen. He craned his head but could not glimpse the signal at that angle.

In the road ahead, the girl was gone. She had fled backward into the darkness, or snapped off to the side of the road. Perhaps she sheltered herself in the darkness of a recessed doorway, or had slipped into the foot passage between two buildings. The Lincoln lurched forward, beyond the stoplight. Nathan stared into the rearview mirror, trying to see what had caused the signal to turn that frigid blue; but behind him the street was obscure. He was certain that when he had passed the bank and town hall, the streetlamps and several neon shop signs had been burning, but downtown Babylon was now as black and lightless as the pine forest at night. In the forest, however, there was the incessant clamor of insects, animals, birds, and wind-blown foliage, and here all was silent. Nathan heard the blood rushing in his ears.

He took a sharp left onto the street that half a mile away terminated in the cul-de-sac by his home. Houses in this part of town were built far back from the road. Streetlamps set equidistant on alternate sides of the street were gently masked by the thick foliage of oak and pine. Nathan was reassured as he turned onto this familiar course, but that relief deserted him when the first street-lamp, ten yards ahead, winked out, as if his approach triggered the darkness.

He drove on. One by one, the lights failed as he neared. The darkness behind the car was absolute. The road itself seemed longer, straighter than before. He ought to have reached the cul-de-sac, but two lines of lights stretched before him.

Nathan pushed the car up to fifty. His mind had distorted distance, but speed would get him there despite the tricks of his brain. As he drove faster, the lamps went out more quickly, but their number rising out of the darkness ahead did not diminish. And worse, much worse, was that Nathan now saw the pale gray girl standing beneath each lamp, still and stately. Just before he was close enough to see her face, the light was extinguished, and she was at the next, on the opposite side of the street. He increased his speed, trying to overtake the retreating figure, throwing his gaze from one side of the road to the other, his foot ever heavier on the gas pedal.

The streetlamps all came on at once, with an intensity three or four times greater than normal. He was blinded ahead, and the rearview mirror exploded in light from behind. He closed his eyes in pain, opened them on the figure in the middle of the street. The girl reflected the white light of the lamps and of the headlights, shadowless, like the surface of a pond, with the moon glancing off it at an angle. But the eyes, turned directly on Nathan, opened on a featureless expressionless void. He was going seventy.

Swerving, but not in time, Nathan hit the girl solidly. She exploded, covering the windshield with a viscous black liquid. It was thick and opaque, and Nathan could see nothing ahead.

He slammed on the brakes, and ran up over the curb, stopping only half a dozen feet from the massive trunk of a live oak. He turned on the windshield wipers to sweep away the liquid. He grabbed a cloth from the glove compartment and feverishly blotted the filth that oozed through the tight-closed windows at his side. When the windshield was cleared, and the last of the black water was seeping through the vents in the hood, Nathan saw that the streetlamps, before and behind, were all lighted to their accustomed brightness. The road was familiar once more.

Nathan drove cautiously the remainder of the hundred yards home, but once safely inside the garage, he jumped out of the Lincoln and ran gasping into the house.

Ben stood out of his chair, amazed. "Nathan—"

"Ben," Nathan cried, "go on out to the garage. I left the lights on in the Lincoln, turn 'em off. Close the doors, lock 'em!"

Ben moved hesitantly, pausing in concern, but Nathan shouted: "Now! Ben, do it now!" Ben hurried off, and Nathan stood at the glass doors, both hands held tight over the lock.

In a few moments Ben came back in from the garage, swinging the two bottles of liquor Nathan had purchased.

Nathan cautiously opened the glass doors. "D'you see anything out there?"

Ben smiled: "Looks like you run through every mud puddle in town, blackest mud I ever saw—"

Smiling, he held up his finger; it was smudged black with a fine grainy soil.

Nathan slapped away his brother's hand.

"What it looks like," continued Ben, desperate to reassure his brother, and having no idea in the world how, "is, it looks like they just dragged the Lincoln up from the bottom of the Styx, more like river silt, don't look like mud at all. What happened?"

Nathan dropped shakily into his chair: "Some girl on the street some goddamn girl . . . she threw something at the car—"

"Maybe it was a water balloon—maybe that's what scared you. I bet it was a water balloon that somebody threw at the car, Nathan."

Nodding slowly, Nathan turned and stared at the black shadows cast across the drapes by the pale rising sliver of a moon.

PART V

WAXING MOON

Chapter 26

Nathan Redfield knew it was no water balloon that had burst against the windshield of the Lincoln. Something had just tried to kill him—the same thing that had dripped on Belinda from the branch of the live oak in the forest, had hid among the leaves and the moss while he had lain with the girl, had stared down at them out of those black holes it had instead of eyes. It had whipped along the forest, tree to tree, keeping close beside them, toying and whistling wetly. It had sat in the front seat of Belinda's Volkswagen. It had pressed its liquid fingers around the handle of the Scout, and tried to get in.

And what Nathan Redfield also knew, as he shakily poured out bourbon into a tall glass, was that whatever that monstrosity was, it had taken the form and the aspect of Margaret Larkin.

"Ben," he said: "Close the curtains." His voice was so low that Ben did not hear him. Nathan turned savagely: "Close the goddamn curtains, Ben!"

Ben leapt up and pulled them to. At the same time he flicked the switch that killed the lights around the patio.

"No!" cried Nathan: "Those you leave on! Leave those lights on!"

Ben shrugged fearfully, not daring to ask the cause of his brother's anxiety.

Nathan sat, commanded that the television be turned off, and then he drank swiftly, not taking his eyes from the sheer white curtains. The mercury lights outside cast strong black shadows on the drapes, shadows of the frames of the sliding doors, of the plants in pots that stood in the corners, even of the pine straw that occasionally blew against the glass. Nathan waited, watching for Margaret Larkin to appear, outlined in black across the white material.

Nathan's single hope was that he had destroyed her, that the ghost—was there any other word?—had sacrificed itself in the attempt to make him wreck the Lincoln. He concentrated on this comforting thought.

"Nathan . . ." said Ben tentatively. His brother didn't answer.

"Nathan, what happened? Why don't—why don't you let me turn the TV back on?"

"No!"

Nathan glanced above the brick fireplace at the portrait of his great-grandfather, an old decrepit man with senile eyes, dressed in a Civil War uniform. He had been a lieutenant colonel in the Confederate Army, in charge of the defense of Fort Pickens, at the western tip of Santa Rosa Island. The star-shaped fortification had never been attacked, and the soldier's sword never saw action. This fine weapon hung now beneath the portrait; at James Redfield's direction, it was kept polished and sharp by Nina.

"Ben," said Nathan in a low voice.

"What?"

Nathan covered his eyes with his hand, and bowed his head. "Turn out the lights on the patio. Lock the doors. Go check on Daddy too. Make sure his patio door is closed and locked."

Nathan didn't raise his head until Ben had returned.

"Daddy was already asleep but I snuck in and pulled the door to. Everything else was already locked."

"Listen, Ben," said Nathan quietly: "You gone help me do something?"

"What is it?" said Ben reluctantly. The way that Nathan glanced toward the glass doors every few seconds made him uneasy. "Is somebody out there?" He got up and made his way to the curtains, reaching out to pull them back.

"No!" cried Nathan with fear greater than his anger: "Don't touch 'em!"

"Somebody's out there then!" cried Ben nervously.

"No," shouted Nathan: "there's nobody out there! You got to help me—" He broke off, then resumed calmly: "We're gone put a little scare into Evelyn Larkin and Jerry tonight."

"A scare?"

"You know," said Nathan evenly: "Scare 'em a little. That's all."

"Why?" said Ben.

"Cain't you think of five reasons while you're just standing there? They're behind on their payments, so we're just gone scare 'em into making their payments, that's all."

"Nathan," said Ben carefully: "That don't make much sense to me. How is scaring 'em gone make 'em pay up on a loan? And why are we supposed to care about it anyway?"

"All right," said Nathan with a wave of his hand: "The truth is, I want 'em to leave Babylon. I want 'em both out of town. I have gotten fed up with Evelyn Larkin riding down the street and yelling out the passenger window that I was the one that killed Margaret. I want her to stop it. She is in Pensacola this very minute talking to a lawyer about how to get me in jail, and when she comes back I want to scare her a little, that's all. So she'll shut up."

"How will scaring her make her shut up? Won't that just make her all the worse?"

"Look Ben, I'm gone go out to the river, and I'm gone scare her, right now, tonight, I'm going out there and wait by the bridge, until they come back from Pensacola, and then I'm gone scare 'em a little. You don't have to do a goddamn thing. I just want you out there, to drive me out there in the Scout, and keep me company while I'm waiting, that's all. I don't want to be out there by myself, I might fall asleep or something, and miss 'em. That's all. You don't have to do a thing."

He lurched drunkenly out of the chair, staggered over to the mantel, and pulled his great-grandfather's sword from its scabbard. He drew the blade between his fingers. The dim light of the single lamp in the room glinted dully on the metal.

"Is that what you gone scare 'em with?" said Ben doubtfully.

Nathan nodded. "See? You're scared, aren't you? Well then, it'll probably scare that old woman too, won't it? And Jerry? Jerry doesn't look much like the type to run up against somebody with a sword, does he? We'll just scare 'em!" Nathan laughed.

"How are you gone do it though?" cried Ben. "I mean, they're gone know it's you, and then tomorrow they'll go running right to Ted Hale."

Nathan laughed again, brutally. "They're not gone know it's me, that's how. You wait here, I'll be right back."

Nathan dropped the sword onto the couch, and hurried out of the room. Ben made a couple of steps toward the gleaming blade, but stopped and turned his back. For several seconds he stared unseeing at the cypress-paneled wall that was covered with the annual photographs of the employees of the CP&M bank.

Behind the curtains drawn across the patio windows, there was a sudden soft tap, an unrepeated muffled slap against the glass. Ben whirled around, and automatically moved forward. It could have been pine straw falling against the window, it could have been only his imagination, or it could have been whatever it was that had so frightened Nathan.

Ben was fearful, but didn't dare call out. Because he had turned out the patio lights, he could see nothing outside, but whoever was out by the pool would be able to see his shadow inside, if he moved between the lamp and the drapes. He reached over, and carefully switched out the lamp. The room became dark, but no shadows from outside appeared against the folded drapes. The moon, a waxing crescent, cast but feeble light.

He moved cautiously around the sofa, glancing down at the sword, so disturbingly out of place, and edged up to the light panel. He flicked on all three switches that controlled the outside lights. The mercury lamps tore on after a half-second hesitation, and densely pallid light flooded through the drapes into the room.

Out of the corner of his eye, looking sideways along the bank of curtained windows, he glimpsed an amorphous but definitely upright shadow. It retreated without sound.

Ben pulled aside one corner of the curtains, peered out but saw nothing, no one fleeing toward the garage, no one trying to scale the outside wall. He let the curtain drop, and then was startled by a soft splash in the pool.

Courageously, Ben snapped open the curtains, went to the door, and stepped out onto the patio. He moved cautiously up to the edge of the pool, not knowing what to expect. No person certainly: The splash had not been loud enough, and it wasn't the sound made by anyone easing into the water either—it was the sound, oddly, of someone pouring a bucket of some dense liquid into the pool.

He glanced over the edge and looked all around in the pool. Nothing appeared to have fallen into the water. The lights shone so brightly that he could have seen a half-dollar on the bottom. He suddenly became nervous that he was being watched, that someone crouched behind the dense black shrubbery and peered out at him. He turned quickly—but in so turning, he saw a little movement in the shadow of the diving board, on the surface of the water.

He stared a few seconds, and realized that it was the shadow itself—something was wrong about it. It wasn't as sharp as it should have been; it was unequal in intensity. As he gazed, it shifted slightly, though the light above did not flicker, though the water was motionless.

He balled his hand into a fist and knocked it against his tight-shut mouth. He moved a little, to catch the shadow from a different angle, and to his horror, the shadow turned, slowly, with a certain deliberate grace, and floated out toward the middle of the pool. It was in the form of a human figure, a loose black form, with its legs together, but the arms gently waving close at its side. Sometimes it had fingers, sometimes those fingers melted into the water. Hair floated indistinctly about the very darkly shadowed head, the most intense part of the figure, almost black. Certainly the eyes were pitch, perfectly formed and unambiguous—though entirely too large—in the gently shaped face.

Ben knew it wasn't his imagination, for the shadow possessed a shadow of its own on the bottom of the pool, gray and quivering. He turned back to flee to the house. Glancing over his shoulder, he saw that the figure had moved around, ninety degrees, and was floating toward the side of the pool, in his direction. He stopped, stared wildly about, and ran toward the small flower bed set at the inside corner of the house. He dislodged one of the large white stones that formed the border of the bed, and turned with it. He could see the black silhouette already at the near edge of the pool. One of the arms had crept out of the water, but not as a shadow. A glistening fat hand, liquid but substantial, clawed at the tiles. The same substance that formed the shadow in the pool swam over the surface of the hand and wrist, like the impurities in a soap bubble.

With a strangled yell, Ben heaved the stone. It fell directly atop the hand, and the thing burst silently. It left a dark puddle by the edge of the pool. The large rock skidded over into the water, smashing through the breast of the shadow. The rock dragged that blackness down with it; below the surface, the form disintegrated, murkily dissipating like fine sand. After only a few seconds nothing was left but the black eyes that drifted down slowly, maintaining their distance apart, and faded only just before they touched bottom.

Ben staggered back into the unlighted living room, and was calling for his brother, when another shadow, its face as black and featureless as whatever had groped to climb from the swimming pool, suddenly leapt in front of him. The sword was in its upraised arms, and it swung the blade in quick circles about its voidous head.

Ben fell to the floor, screaming for Nathan.

His brother laughed loudly.

Ben looked up, and in the light spilling in from the patio, he saw that Nathan had covered his head in a tight-fitting leather mask, seamed and zippered. He wore black pants but his dark, heavily haired chest was bare.

Nathan pulled the zipper over his mouth, choking off his own laugh, leapt to the couch, and swung the sword above his head. His chest heaved in unrhythmic spasms.

"Nathan, Nathan!" pleaded Ben: "Put it down! Put it down!"

Nathan swung the sword more quickly still.

Chapter 27

An hour later the International Scout was parked on a disused logging track north of Babylon, just at the point where the dim trace turned to run parallel to the Styx. The bridge and the

Larkin blueberry farm were only several hundred yards downstream, though out of sight around a bend in the river. Ben Redfield was so distressed by his brother's conduct that, despite his
fear, he had not told him what he had seen in the swimming pool.
He accompanied Nathan with ill-concealed agitation through the
dark forest to the highway. The crescent moon was sometimes
visible ahead of them, when the track straightened for a few
dozen yards, but otherwise there was no light.

"How we gone arrange this, Nathan? I mean, how you gone
know if it's the Larkins that are coming along, and not somebody
else? You don't want to jump out in front of the wrong car, you
know what I mean?"

"Well, first," said Nathan, in a deliberate voice that did a little
to calm his brother, "we time it. They're meeting the lawyer at
nine, figure on half an hour, forty-five minutes for that, and then
forty-five minutes to get from Pensacola back to Babylon, and
you're putting it at ten-fifteen, ten-thirty. It's a little after ten now,
we're not gone have long to wait. And Ben," he added, *"you're* the
one that's gone be jumping in front of the car."

Ben digested this information with misgiving, but dared not
refuse his brother, who swung the sword jauntily at his side.

"Maybe they're already at home," Ben suggested with undis-
guised hopefulness.

"They'd have lights on in the house," said Nathan. "The house
is dark, that's why we drove by."

"Well, why the bridge? I mean, out here in the open? Wouldn't
it be better to scare 'em in the house when there's not likely to
be people passing?"

"People don't pass much on this road at night. At least not
after nine when the liquor stores have closed. That's how we're
gone know it's them. Besides, you know how much noise that
wagon makes. They ought to have dumped it three years ago."

Ben shrugged unhappily; Nathan had not answered his question.

In the dark, Nathan glanced at his brother, and said slowly:
"It's not the same thing, scaring them in the house. They can feel
protected in the house. They've got the telephone. They've got
lights, and for all I know, they've got a gun. Out on the road, on

this bridge, they're not expecting anything. There's no defense."

"Nathan," said Ben carefully. "What are you planning on doing?"

"Scare 'em," smiled Nathan: "That's all, just scare 'em."

They said nothing for a few moments, while they arranged themselves behind a large clump of shrubbery. It was dense enough to conceal them, especially in their black clothing, but of a sufficiently loose texture to allow a view of the road into Babylon that curved off fifty yards down. Nathan once more secured the mask over his head, and then pulled on a pair of blood-stained motoring gloves.

The black night closed in. This was the seventh year for cicadas, and thousands of the insects clicked on the trees around them, so that the slender trunks of the pines jabbered in shrill staccato. Colonies of fireflies flashed in the forest behind them and across the road. Twenty feet away the Styx flowed black and silent beneath the wooden bridge, and only the occasional plop of a fish, a falling branch, or a loose rock tumbling into the water reminded them that the river was there.

Above, the sharp livid moon shone behind a caul of thin white clouds that overspread the sky. No star shone through.

Ben, on his haunches, grew weary. Ten-fifteen had passed. A vehicle approached at ten-nineteen—Ben first heard it while looking at his watch—and he raised himself in anticipation. Nathan clapped his hand sternly on his brother's thigh: "That's not them, you idiot! Listen how that motor runs—too smooth!"

They peered out of the bush, both nervously, but then with relief as a large silver Cadillac passed with Alabama plates.

"Nathan," said Ben miserably: "Why don't you just foreclose? Then they'll have to leave town."

"They may stay and fight," said Nathan. He paused: "We couldn't count on them leaving just because they lost the farm, and I want them out of Babylon. There's something you don't know, Ben. There's probably oil under their land, and there's probably not any oil under ours. I want this land for us."

Ben whistled.

Nathan rubbed his sweating hand over the black hair of his belly, and turned the black mask toward his brother. Ben looked away slightly, for in the dark, the mask was inhuman and ghastly. The zipper over Nathan's mouth grinned like the teeth of a fun-house skull.

"Besides, Ben," said Nathan slowly. "You remember what happened last time—"

"Last time?" said Ben confused.

"When Jim and JoAnn Larkin died in the river, you'd have thought that Evelyn Larkin, that old bitch, would have packed up with those two children, and moved out then. That's what you would have thought—but they didn't. They stayed, and now they've made a goddamn nuisance of themselves."

"Nathan," whispered Ben, and wished he could stop himself from saying anything more: "Listen, you're not doing this be-cause it was you and me who threw those snakes in the river that day, is it? I mean, we didn't mean to, and it was so long ago, and you wouldn't have done it if you had known what was gone happen, and of course nobody ever found out . . ."

In July of 1965, a week after Nathan Redfield had been honor-ably discharged from the Air Force, he had gone with eleven-year-old Benjamin to hunt rattlesnakes for the rodeo on Jim Lar-kin's blueberry farm. They had in fact been trespassing, but no place near Babylon bred more rattlesnakes than the pine forest surrounding the Larkin property.

Luck had not been with them that day however, and Nathan had managed to catch only five small specimens, which were thrown into the nested croker sacks that Benjamin nervously dragged along. Not wanting to return to Babylon and Sheriff Hale with so poor a showing—fewer than half a dozen snakes and not one of them over eighteen inches long—Nathan insisted that they drown the snakes, and pretend they had never gone out.

Ben had watched with relief as the sack was heaved into the black water of the Styx. It hadn't sunk at first, but a large stone, accurately tossed, carried it to the bottom. Nathan drove home, and casually explained to his father that he and Benjamin had been out south of town looking at a new litter of bird-dog pup-pies.

Benjamin Redfield, when he heard of the croker sacks and the drowned rattlesnakes found beneath the Larkins' overturned boat, had been sick with fear; but beneath Nathan's threats he had remained silent.

And now, as he crouched behind the shrubbery at the side of the highway that sickening fear came upon him again. He couldn't remove his gaze from the stupefying reflection of the sickly moon, pale and cold, in each lashless eye behind the sharp leather slits of the black mask that covered his brother's face. "Is that it?" Ben stammered: "Di . . . did Evelyn Larkin find out it was you and me that was out there that day, hunting the snakes, and we threw 'em in the water?"

"Shut up, Ben," said Nathan quietly: "Nobody knows about that. How could Evelyn Larkin find out anything 'bout it after all these years? They cain't even find out who killed Margaret, and that was just last Thursday night."

"Nathan," said Ben tremulously: "You never said the other night when I asked you—were you the one who—"

"Shhhh!" Nathan cautioned: "Get ready! I hear a car coming, and it's probably them!" He nodded down the road. A faint troubled engine could be heard in the distance, and quite suddenly, harsh white light broke on a stand of trees a few dozen yards down the road—the car would be coming around the bend any moment.

Ben rose on his haunches to make sure his cramped legs were sufficiently limber for what he had to do. He gazed down the road, waiting for the automobile to appear. But Ben lost all sense of where he was and what his brother expected of him, when the lights of the Larkin station wagon turning in the bend picked out the quivering gray figure of a young girl, pressed against the trunk of a tree at the edge of the forest. Ben was shocked immobile by her face—grave and unshadowed and the color of the cold moon above them.

Chapter 28

Henry Harp, the cousin of Warren Perry's mother, listened politely to Evelyn Larkin and even with some interest, since her story came new to him. He was a thin, rich, white-haired widower who had suffered a heart attack at his wife's funeral. Since that unhappy day, two years before, he had never gone to bed at night with the full expectation of waking in the morning. He had shown Evelyn and Jerry to the back of the house, a dense fragrant garden of camellias and azaleas and oleander, where they sat in the warm early evening on wooden lawn furniture beneath the pale moon.

He told Evelyn afterward, quietly, that there did not appear to be much of a case against this young banker, but that he would be happy to drive up to Babylon and talk to the sheriff for a few minutes and see what he had to say about it all.

"Don't bother doing that," said Evelyn.

"Why not?" asked the lawyer.

"Because Ted Hale has been in on this from the beginning."

"Is that right?" said Henry Harp tonelessly. "I tell you what then: You think it through tonight, and you talk it over with Warren tomorrow. If you're still interested in making some sort of formal accusation, you give me a call. I'll drive up, and we'll see what's what. I might come up day after tomorrow. I'm free that afternoon. I don't think I've been to Babylon in fifteen years. Babylon's out of the way. I could even visit a little with Warren. I haven't seen that boy since his daddy's funeral."

Evelyn and Jerry thanked the lawyer, and accepted his escort back to the front of the house. They drove off toward Babylon, with the station wagon considerably lightened now that all the blueberries had been delivered to the wholesale market down by the old cemetery.

"I feel so much better," said Evelyn, as they drove out of town. She gazed out the side windows at the moonlit waters of Pensacola Bay, silver-blue and calm.

"I'm glad of that," said Jerry shortly.

"What's the matter now!" Evelyn demanded, for she sensed the grudging disbelief in her grandson's voice. "That man is coming up on Friday afternoon, and maybe then something'll start to be done about all of this."

"Grandma, Mr. Harp was real nice, but there's nothing he can do, just like there was nothing that Charles Darrish could do. There's no clues, and there's nobody in town that thinks Nathan Redfield killed Margaret except you. Even if it's true, and I still don't see much reason to believe it is, there's no way in this world to prove it. There's no way in this world to get back at him for it."

"Jerry," said Evelyn sternly, "Mr. Harp wouldn't have said he would come up to see us if he didn't think he could do something."

"He's doing it as a favor to Warren Perry, or Warren's mama, and that's all. Or hell come up, look around for ten minutes, talk to the sheriff, talk to Charles Darrish, and then go away and mail us a bill for seventy-five dollars that we cain't even begin to pay."

"He didn't say anything about money!"

"Well, Grandma, you didn't really think he would come up from Pensacola to Babylon for free?"

"But Warren talked to him . . ."

"Did Warren talk to him about money?"

"I don't know," admitted Evelyn reluctantly. "Maybe not."

"Grandma," said Jerry in a low sad voice, "even if there was a possibility of Mr. Harp finding out something on Nathan Redfield, where would we get the money to prosecute? If Nathan Redfield saw something coming, he would foreclose on us faster than it takes to roll down the stairs. We'd have no money, no place to go."

"Jerry—" his grandmother protested weakly, and turned to stare out the window at the gently rolling pine forest, black beneath the night sky. The road from Pensacola to Babylon was forty-five miles long, but with perhaps no more than two dozen houses along it. Half of these were unlighted even as early as ten o'clock. Absurdly, this little-traveled road was four lanes wide, a pork-barrel project initiated by the Florida congressional representative for the benefit of a contractor who made large contributions to his campaign funds. The pine forest closely encroached on the two black ribbons of asphalt, and the median strip had grown over in thick scrub. The station wagon rattled along this deserted unlighted highway, its headlights fading and shaky because of the battery that wanted replacing, with the desperately unhappy old woman and young man inside.

Evelyn and Jerry talked little more on the journey home. Evelyn's hopefulness directly after speaking with Henry Harp had faded beneath Jerry's weary logic. Jerry was disgusted with himself for having so quickly and sternly drained his grandmother's temporarily suffused spirit. And there was nothing to say now that had not been said before.

The route was familiar, even in the dark. A slight rise in the road gave expected way to a familiar depression; a certain bend turned to an aluminum bridge over an unnamed but well-remembered creek. Evelyn and Jerry looked automatically at the brightly lighted parking lot of the Tastee-Freeze on the south side of Babylon, filled with those teenagers who had cars but no curfews. Downtown was deserted except for a man Jerry did not recognize making a night deposit at the CP&M. Jerry did not pause beneath the unlighted traffic signals, and was quickly on the road that led out of town toward the Styx River.

Here every tree was anticipated, every rusted advertising sign predicted and read out in his mind before the lights of the car flashed over it. Evelyn sighed heavily, thinking, Jerry knew, of Margaret, and her last trip out this road; but the boy said nothing to his grandmother.

He sighed also just before the last bend in the road, that would bring them within sight of the bridge, and the second story of the house on the other side of the river.

Evelyn Larkin, miserably depressed and nearly asleep from the silent ride, sat turned slightly, with her chin resting on her hand, gazing out the side window into the black forest. Suddenly, when the car made the turn on that final bend, the headlights, rushing ahead along the fanning circle of trees, caught on a figure, white and unmoving, against the trunk of a diseased pine.

"Jerry!" she cried: "Margaret's there!"

He had seen the figure too, but it fell away the moment he set eyes on it, a chalk-white evanescence that had simply lost its solidity and flowed into the black waving grass.

"No!" he cried desperately: "It's nothing!" But he was already and instinctively applying the brakes.

"Stop! It was Margaret! Margaret's in the woods!"

Jerry took his foot from the brake, and stamped on the accelerator. Margaret was dead, he had seen nothing—or whatever it was he had seen had been a trick of his eyes, his weariness, the dark night. Sap running on the side of a tree had caught and twisted the light and thrown it back at them in the form of his dead sister.

"It's wasn't anything!" cried Jerry, with determination. "There was nothing there!"

"Go back!" cried Evelyn, but then she screamed, for another figure, this one as black as the other had been white, reared up in the middle of the road, and waved its long arms wildly.

Chapter 29

The figure standing against the tree faded suddenly; Ben was pushed by his brother out into the road. He jumped up and down, as if to flag down the station wagon for assistance. But he felt suddenly frightened, not only of the probable repercussions of Nathan's strange actions but of the actual possibility of being run down by Jerry, which he had not really considered before. It seemed now an insanity—to run out in front of a moving automobile, dressed in black clothing, on a dark night. He flailed wildly, leaping like a bizarre jumping jack, and knew that he did not at all appear a man who had suffered trouble with his car.

The station wagon screeched to a halt thirty feet away. The headlights shone on his pants, but Ben knew that his face was in shadow. Looking through the windshield, he caught Jerry's face frozen in stupid terror, and Evelyn Larkin pulling back weakly after having been thrust forward with the violent braking.

"Help!" Ben shouted, at an abnormally high pitch, attempting to disguise his voice: "Please come help me!"

He then ran toward the side of the road, and stood wavering there for a few moments, out of the range of the headlights.

The station wagon lurched forward a few feet, and then was jerked to a halt. Ben sensed that it had been thrown into park; and this was confirmed when he heard one of the car doors open. Behind the headlights he could make out Jerry's hesitant figure, standing by the front fender. He heard Evelyn Larkin say feebly: "Jerry, what is it? Who is that out there?"

"I don't know," replied Jerry, in a loud worried voice.

"Jerry, please don't go out there! Jerry, Margaret's back there, I saw—"

Ignoring his grandmother, Jerry moved cautiously forward into the light of the headlamps. "Hey, who is it? What's wrong?" he called.

Ben backed slowly to the bush that had secreted him before, and whispered: "Nathan! Nathan! Where—"

He gasped in terror, for Nathan was not behind the shrubbery. He had moved on, in some grotesque joke, leaving Ben to explain to Jerry Larkin why he had jumped out in front of the car. In a slightly louder voice, he began to curse his brother, in a high-pitched unnatural whine: "Nathan, goddamn it, why the hell—"

A man suddenly appeared in the wavering triangle of illumination before the station wagon. He had planted himself six feet in front of Jerry and was swinging something forcefully above his head; whatever it was shone brightly when it came within the range of the lights, and disappeared altogether when it was raised high. Both Jerry and Evelyn in the front seat of the car were mesmerized by his face, a black skull with a silver mouth and gleaming eyes.

He moved a step closer to Jerry.

"No, no!" cried Evelyn, fumbling with the handle of the door.

"Nathan, Nathan!" a voice cried from the side of the road.

"Nathan . . ." she whispered, and then called loudly for Jerry, many times over.

Nathan suddenly moved three steps closer, and brought the sharp edge of the sword down at an angle across Jerry Larkin's neck. A stream of black liquid shot out in a high arc through the air, but it turned gleaming red when it fell to the pavement in the light of the headlamps.

Jerry's body collapsed on the asphalt, neatly between two painted white stripes. Blood poured from the severed neck, and the head lolled at a severe angle from the trunk, as if it were opened on a hinge.

"Nathan!" cried the voice from the edge of the road.

Nathan stepped over the body, and thrust the sword in the empty space between the head and the trunk. With some difficulty, he sawed the head loose.

Evelyn Larkin, screaming without even knowing that she screamed, fell out of the station wagon onto the hard pavement, when the door suddenly opened. She scraped her legs badly, and damaged something along her side, but rose without feeling pain, and staggered to the front of the car, still calling out and crying for Jerry.

She thrust her hands over her eyes when she saw her grandson's head wobble over the rough asphalt, several feet away from his bloody body. The eyes were still open, and it came to rest on the left cheek, staring down the unlighted road that took you to Babylon.

The hysterical woman turned to the man in the black mask. "Who—" Her attention was for a second distracted by another figure that stepped out of the darkness at the side of the road. She turned for his help.

Nathan leveled the sword and ran it through the old woman's back. She groaned, stiffened, and went limp. She would have fallen but the sword supported her; the sharp edge of the blade was turned up, and began to cut through the flesh of her lower back and abdomen as she sank. Nathan raised one foot, and placed it against Evelyn's backside; he pushed, and the old woman slid forward off the sword, dropping heavily and face down on the pavement. Her head crushed against the rocks between Ben's feet. He jumped back.

"Good Christ!" he whispered: "Nathan, I thought we were gone scare 'em."

"Yes, well," said Nathan after he had pulled the zipper across his mouth open, "they were scared all right—I never heard any-body scream like that in my life."

"The whole county probably heard it! Why—"

"Shut up, Ben," said Nathan, "we got to get rid of 'em."

Ben shuddered. Blood oozed and soaked through Evelyn Lar-kin's pink print dress, and he didn't dare look across to the de-capitated corpse behind his brother.

"Throw 'em in the car. Go 'round and open the back. We got to hurry, Ben!" Nathan shouted, when Ben made no move at all: "Hurry! 'Fore somebody comes by!"

Nathan had turned off the ignition of the station wagon, and extracted the keys. He tossed them through the dark air to his brother. Ben hurried to the back murmuring, "Oh Nathan, why you want to make me do this?" He unlocked the rear and lifted the door with a shaking arm.

Nathan had picked up Evelyn's body beneath the arms, and dragged it backward along the side of the car. "Help me lift her, goddamn it," he hissed, and Ben ran quickly around, and lifted her feet from the pavement.

Blood poured thickly onto his fingers, and he dropped the burden. In exasperation, Nathan did also: Evelyn's corpse fell heavily against the pavement. Fragile bones in the thin wom-an's arm cracked sickeningly. "Ben," said Nathan in a low, con-trolled voice: "Pick her up, because if you don't, I'm gone have to get rid of *three* bodies, all by myself. Now you understand me?"

Ben nodded, and lifted the feet, never minding the blood. In another few seconds, they had thrust Evelyn into the back of the car, and shoved her to one side, so that there would be room for Jerry as well.

"Nathan," whispered Ben, as he followed his brother to the other side: "Please just don't make me touch that head."

Nathan laughed. He picked up Jerry's head by the hair, and tossed it through the window. It flew across the front seat, struck Evelyn's corpse, and then rolled slowly to rest.

"Pick up the feet again, fraidycat," said Nathan, and lifted the headless corpse by the arms. More blood spilled out of the severed neck, and splashed over Nathan's shoes. With his head turned aside, Ben lifted the feet and skipped backward to the rear of the car. They shoved the body inside.

Nathan slammed the rear door shut, and flew to the driver's seat. Ben climbed in beside him, trembling, and handed Nathan the keys. Nathan backed the car quickly down the road, and turned it sharply right onto the disused logging track. The weak wavering lights of the station wagon ricocheted from tree to tree nightmarishly as they pushed forward into the forest.

Ben lowered the window, for he was sickened by the stink of blood and fear. Not wanting to look at his brother, not daring to look into the back, Ben stared only into the black forest. The cicadas clamored deafeningly, over the sound of the troubled engine and the unrhythmic thump of the bodies of the grandmother and her grandson.

Nathan had passed the Scout, and was following the road as it went upstream along the riverbank, into the uninhabited forest drained by the Styx. About a mile from the Styx bridge, the track rose onto a small bluff, and at the top of this, Nathan halted. He punched out the car lights, and they were in darkness. The moon was masked by the trees.

"What are we gone do?" demanded Ben. "Nathan, I don't like any of this. You didn't tell me—" He almost wept.

"Get out, Ben, or stay in, I don't care, but in ten seconds this car goes over the bluff and into the river, whether you're in it or not."

Ben jumped out of the car, and ran to Nathan's side.

"Move away, Ben!"

Ben pulled back a couple of steps. Nathan edged the car up to the edge of the precipice, then jerked on the emergency brake.

He got out, went to the back of the car, and braced himself against the rear door. "Ben, you release that brake when I tell you to, then come back 'round here, and help me push it off. And lower that front window so it'll fill up."

"All right," said Ben, "I'm ready."

Nathan nodded, and Ben released the brake, slammed the door, and ran to the back. With only two small heaves, they managed to get the front wheel over the edge, but then the automobile collapsed on its chassis, only six feet over the edge.

"It's stuck!" cried Ben.

"Push!" cried Nathan, then: "Wait! We got to get the god-damn sword out!" He ran then to the other side, and gingerly pulled open the front door. It swung free out into the air, thirty feet above the Styx. "Ben, don't touch that car till I get this damn thing out." Ben backed away from the car, and went around to stand just behind his brother. Nathan knelt on the crumbling edge of the bluff, and reached inside the car for the sword, which had rolled beneath the front seat.

"Ben, you come hold onto my feet! I don't want to go flipping over in the water!"

Ben knelt and grabbed his brother's ankles tightly. Nathan leaned farther forward, out over the drop, and into the front seat. He had just grasped the sword, when the car tipped forward. "Goddamn!" he whispered, "Ben, pull me back!"

Ben jerked heartily. Nathan was drawn out of the car, which was rolling forward. Unaccountably the passenger door swung shut, narrowly missing Nathan's head, but slamming closed on the sword blade. It snapped, leaving the last foot of bloodied metal inside the automobile.

Nathan and Ben scrambled out of the way, and the car was precipitated forward, its bottom scraping harshly against the graveled earth. It moved not at all in the manner of a vehicle roll-ing down an incline, following gravity and momentum, but as if laboriously pulled with chains. The station wagon dropped nose-first into the Styx. It righted and sank after only a few moments.

Nathan stared at the water until the last of the air bubbles had broken blackly on the surface of the river. He smiled then and said: "Let's get back." He ran down the bluff, and hurried along the level track, not once glancing behind.

"Nathan," cried Ben, hastening to catch up. "Nathan, please take that mask off. You don't need it any more."

"I'm just filthy!" cried Nathan, and reached up to unzip the hood at his neck. After removing and thrusting it into his back pocket, he wiped the sweat from his brow. "Good," he said easily: "That's all taken care of."

Ben shook his head miserably: "Hey, Nathan, what we gone do now?"

"Nothing," replied Nathan: "We don't have to do anything. Everything is fine now. They're not gone find that car where it is—the river runs deep there, nobody ever comes up to this part of the river. And even if they do find it in about a million years, they're not gone know we had anything to do with it."

"But everybody in town knows Evelyn Larkin thought you were the one who murdered Margaret."

"And everybody in town thinks she was crazy to say that," argued Nathan with a ghastly smile.

"But," said Ben cautiously, "you did kill her, didn't you?"

"Yes," said Nathan calmly: "But nobody knows that. And nobody's gone find out. Not unless you tell somebody, that is," he added lightly.

Ben shrugged and bit his lip; he took the implied threat seriously. "I'm not saying anything about it. I never said anything about those rattlesnakes, and I wasn't hardly ten years old. If I could keep a secret then, I guess I can keep a secret now."

"I guess you can," said Nathan meaningfully.

"Nathan—"

"What?"

"Let me ask you though: Why did you kill Margaret Larkin?" Though they were alone in the forest, Ben whispered.

"Oh," smiled Nathan, "just because . . ."

PART VI
THE COFFINLESS DEAD
Chapter 30

Ted Hale woke on Thursday morning, the eighth of June, oppressed with the knowledge that Margaret Larkin had been murdered exactly one week before, and that he had no idea who her killer was. The two suspects hardly deserved his consideration. Warren Perry was a small dark pusillanimous thing, always nervous about the pistol in Hale's holster, even after the sheriff had assured him that it was unloaded. And Nathan Redfield was under the most cursory suspicion only because Evelyn Larkin was so adamant in her accusations of the banker, not because there was any possibility of his being the murderer.

The sheriff had not seen the Larkins since Tuesday, and he was conscience-pricked for that. This was, after all, an important case. It had been picked up by the Pensacola and Mobile papers, and he had heard that it had been written up in Sunday's Tallahassee *Daily Democrat*. Unsolved murders were rare in Babylon. In the past ten years, several homicides had gone unpunished, it was true, but in each case, Hale had known the identity of the murderer and the all too justifiable motive. But Margaret Larkin had perished cruelly by vicious hands, and without sure reason. Hale didn't at all care for the uncertainties of the case, and he wished that it would solve itself or go away.

Shortly after eight o'clock, while Belinda was still blearily wandering about the house, unable to decide whether to drink a glass of milk and coffee or take a bath first, Hale got into the patrol car, and drove out to the Larkin blueberry farm. The morning was wet and warm, and the already high sun promised a sultry uncomfortable day. He raised the windows and turned on the air conditioner.

He noted the place, just before the Styx River bridge, where some animal had died bloodily, but the carcass had been dragged off into the highway grass by scavenging animals. From the amount of blood, Hale assumed it had been at least a very large raccoon.

Turning into the Larkin driveway, Hale drove slowly up to the house, surprised not to see the station wagon there. He got out of the cruiser, walked first to the back, to make sure that the vehicle was not simply parked out of the sight of the driveway, and then he knocked on the back porch. No one came. The door was hooked, and he peered between the latticed boards. Evelyn's chair was pushed beneath the deal table, on which several hundred empty green cartons were neatly stacked. The morning light filtered unsteadily over the porch, and gleamed softly on a small puddle of water beneath Evelyn's chair. This only caught Hale's eye when the liquid suddenly drained away through crevices in the painted floor, leaving a black and grainy residue.

Hale turned thoughtfully down the back steps. He moved slowly around the far side of the house, glancing apprehensively at the curtained windows. Obviously that water had only just been spilled or it would have drained away before. Who was inside? And why did no one come to the door?

At every window, Hale paused, watching to see if the curtains moved. He had the uneasy feeling that someone stood concealed behind each set of drapes, but the intuition was just as strong that it was neither Jerry Larkin nor his grandmother that moved inside the house, window to window, matching his progress around the house.

Hale mounted the front steps with every appearance of courage, and had raised his hand to knock, when his motion was arrested by a small sturdy click in the lock of the house door, as if the key had been turned. Someone was on the other side, but Hale could see nothing through the rusting screen and the white-curtained panes.

A trickle of black water, abruptly commencing, flowed out from underneath the door. Hale leapt backward, instinctively avoiding it. The water formed a small shallow pool with a vibrating surface, and then began to seep down between the floor boards to the sandy ground beneath the porch.

The sheriff watched nervously for a full minute as the water poured out beneath the door, slowly, deliberately, a gallon or more of the black impure liquid. Its odor was slight but noxious.

He balled his fists, uncurled them, then drew out his unloaded pistol, but was too frightened to call out.

The last of the water drained away, and he didn't dare look up at the small curtained panes in the wooden door behind the screen.

Hale waited for about fifteen seconds for the flow of water to begin anew, but it did not. He pulled open the screen, and with some trepidation, turned the knob of the wooden door. It was unlocked—whoever was inside the house had wanted him to enter. The realization was not reassuring. Hale's great desire was to turn and scurry to the patrol car. He could return later with his deputies, he could satisfy himself with telephoning. Jerry would answer, and all would be in order.

Hale cautiously pushed the door open with the barrel of his pistol. On the small blue rug before the door was a damp black stain. Hale stepped carefully over it. He eased the door shut behind him, found that the key was in the lock. He touched it, and his fingers came away with a black stain that he wiped with distaste on his trousers.

Hale paused, listened intently, heard nothing but the floor creaking beneath his shifting weight.

"Miz Larkin! Jerry!" he called weakly, and glanced into the two dimly illumined rooms on either side of the tiny entrance hall.

Hale flicked the overhead light in the parlor, and planting himself in the middle of the room, turned in a slow circle. Nothing appeared out of place. He moved to the window that looked toward the Styx River, and pulled the curtain aside slightly; beneath his fingers, the edge of the material was stained with the same black silt that he had found on the key. He drew his hand quickly away; whoever had turned the key in the door had also pulled back the drapes.

Looking around more carefully now, Hale found the stain everywhere: on the cushions of the couch, on the mantel, on the walls beneath a framed photograph of Margaret. He hurried across the entrance hall to the dining room, ashamed of his own fearful haste.

A single chair had been pulled out from the head of the table, and the black damp stain covered the seat. Hale didn't look for more, but stumbled toward the kitchen.

Here the white tile floor, the white metal cabinets, the white linoleum counter tops, all the white porcelain appliances bore the black amorphous stains, finely grained black dirt, damp and faintly gleaming. The light noxious odor that he had caught on the front porch was stronger here.

The door onto the back porch was open, and he staggered out there, reaching for the latch. Something had been in the house, was still perhaps inside with him. He had to get out. Certainly Jerry and Evelyn weren't there, and in any case he wasn't going upstairs to look for them. He had caught sight of the black stains on the stairs leading to the second floor.

He could come out later with his deputies. He could send his deputies out alone. He—

There was a noise behind him, in the kitchen—a soft wet slap, as of a sodden sponge falling to the floor. Hale had already unlatched the back door, but he turned instinctively and stared into the kitchen. A tiny naked arm, gray and wet, dangled over the edge of the sink. The slender fingers unclutched slowly out of a fist as it slowly drew back into the basin.

Without thinking, Hale rushed back into the room. He reached out for the hand as it slipped over the edge and flopped wetly against the porcelain. The forearm withdrew easily into the drain, but the hand from the wrist down was still visible.

Hale picked something up out of the drain—a fork as it turned out—and stabbed at the gray hand, that looked small and bloated. It broke loathsomely open like a jellyfish, and the liquid drained away immediately, leaving behind a black stain on the porcelain. Hale fled the house.

Chapter 31

"Insects!" cried Ted Hale to himself as he drove away from the Larkin blueberry farm. His sweaty hands slipped on the steering wheel, and over and again he told himself that all he had seen in the house was due to "insects!"

He had seen nothing, he told himself, nothing but mildew on the furniture and on the walls. That was because of the house's proximity to the Styx coupled with the recent heat. It probably happened out there every year, and no matter how good a house-keeper Evelyn Larkin was, she couldn't keep out the mildew. A house damaged by flood, as the Larkin house had been, could never be set entirely back to rights.

What he had seen in the sink, however, was insects. How one insect, how a thousand insects moving in concert could form the likeness of a human arm and hand Hale couldn't determine. How they could explode into brackish water, Hale had no idea. But these questions the sheriff set conveniently aside. It was a comfort—more than that, it was a psychological necessity, that he believed that whatever he had seen in the kitchen was only in-sects. It wouldn't have happened if the Larkins had good screens.

Hale did not return directly to the station, but went home first, to change his clothing, which was soaked through with nervous perspiration. From the kitchen, where Belinda sat grog-gily nursing her milk and coffee and leafing through an old copy of *Glamour*, Hale dialed the Larkins' number, and allowed the telephone to ring twenty times before he gave up.

"Who you calling like that, Daddy?" said Belinda.

"Old Miz Larkin . . ."

"Don't sound like she's there."

Hale shook his head sadly, but did not tell his daughter that he had already been out to the farm.

Hale realized now that he must return to search the second floor of the house. He could think of no reason why the Lar-kins would not be home early in the morning at the first peak of the blueberry season. The car was gone, so they were off somewhere, but perhaps it was only to put flowers on Margaret's grave, a week's anniversary of flowers.

He dialed the number again; still no answer. He determined to drive by the cemetery to see how recently the flowers had been laid on the grave. If they were not fresh, he would send his deputies out to the house, and let *them* go up the stairs. Maybe his deputies weren't susceptible to mildew; maybe the insects in the sink would have dispersed by that time. Perhaps Evelyn and Jerry Larkin would have returned.

Hale kissed his daughter, returned to the cruiser, and drove eastward through town to the cemetery where Margaret Larkin was buried. The flowers on her grave were wilted; they had not been placed there that morning. Preoccupied, he drove then to town hall, but on impulse, went first into Ed Geiger's store, and asked him if he knew any reason Evelyn and Jerry might not be at home this morning.

Geiger shook his head. He was troubled that he did not know, for it seemed a peculiar thing that wanted explanation. Reluctantly, he referred the sheriff to Ginny Darrish. "She's keeping close with Evelyn Larkin these days, and she might know. I haven't heard a thing, not a thing about the Larkins since day before yesterday."

Hale went to his office and made several telephone calls, the first to the high school, though he doubted that, in the summer, Ginny Darrish would be in her office so early. The second was to the Darrish home, where there was no answer either. He called Charles Darrish in his office, and asked the lawyer if he knew where his wife could be reached.

"Ted," said Darrish: "I would suppose now that she's well on her way to Tallahassee. There's a meeting of some kind with the State Board, and she said she doesn't think that she'll be back until late tomorrow night. I don't expect her before then, because I imagine she'll stop in Pensacola on her way back. You know that steak-and-seafood place out by—"

"She wouldn't have taken Evelyn Larkin with her, would she?" Hale asked cautiously.

Darrish laughed. "No, she didn't say anything about it, and I don't imagine she would have. I mean, if it was just a day trip, maybe she would have taken Evelyn along, to get her mind off things and all, but Ginny's staying at the Ramada tonight with a woman from over at Jay, so I don't much imagine that Evelyn is with her. Why?"

"Well," said Hale: "I was out there this morning, and there was nobody around. It seemed funny, that's all. Car's gone. It seemed funny that both Jerry and Evelyn were gone, at this time of year I mean. I was just thinking that Ginny might have some kind of idea where they might be."

"You make a breakthrough on this case? You find out who killed Margaret?"

"No," said Hale: "I just wanted to make sure they were all right, that's all."

"Why shouldn't they be?"

"No reason," said Hale: "It just seemed funny that they weren't there."

"Well, I tell you," said Darrish, after a small pause: "I tell you where they might be, now."

"Where?" said Hale quickly.

"Now I don't know if you knew it, you might have heard it from Ed Geiger, because I know Ginny sometimes tells him things, but yesterday Evelyn and Jerry came by here, asking me to represent them against Nathan Redfield, and of course I was nice to 'em and all, but there was nothing I could say but no. Now Evelyn got all heated up and upset about it, and said she was going to Pensacola to see some other lawyer about it, and find somebody who *would* represent her."

Hale considered this, and then asked: "Did she say who it was she was going to see?"

"No. I asked her, just curious and all, but she wouldn't say. I don't know who she was going to try to get. I guess she could just go through the yellow pages under 'Lawyer,' but I don't know where they were going to get the money for a retainer. I mean, if I had taken 'em on, I wouldn't have charged—Ginny wouldn't have let me—but I wasn't about to start proceedings against Nathan Redfield for murdering Margaret Larkin."

"No," agreed Hale, "of course not. But if they went down to Pensacola yesterday, they ought to be back by now."

"Well maybe," said Darrish: "But maybe not."

"How do you mean?"

"Well, Jerry was saying something about relatives in Pensacola, and staying there for a few days, keeping Evelyn away from the house and so forth until she gets over Margaret a little. I hope he *can* keep her down there, being away from the house will do her more good than anything else right now."

"You think Jerry'd stay away during the berry season?" asked Hale.

"Well," said Darrish, "I think he'd do just about anything for his grandmother. She was out in the hall for a few minutes, and he said something to me about arranging for the place to be sold. It doesn't make any money any more, he said, and every season they were going deeper in debt. I told him he ought to give me a call from Pensacola if he wants to sell the place, and I'd put it up."

"I see," said Hale, after a moment. "Listen, Charles, if Jerry does call, you tell him to give me a call too, at the station, at home, it doesn't matter. I want to talk to him for a minute . . ."

"I'll do that."

"And listen, Charles—"

"What?"

"You might not have such an easy time unloading that place."

"Why not?"

"That house is not in such good condition as I thought. The time the Styx rose a few years back, I think it did something to the place—"

"Did what?"

"Damp rot," said Hale slowly: "That's all, I guess, just damp rot."

Chapter 32

Charles Darrish was not so instinctual a liar as to be able to fashion extemporaneously the story that he had told Ted Hale of the probable whereabouts of Evelyn and Jerry Larkin. He only repeated what Nathan Redfield had told him to say in case anyone

asked. Darrish had without much difficulty convinced Hale of
the plausibility of the fabrication, but Darrish didn't know how
he was to explain it to his wife when she returned from Tallahassee the following night. Ginny Darrish would know that the
Larkins had no relatives in Pensacola, and would not accept the
tale that Darrish had told the sheriff.

The lawyer didn't know why Nathan had insisted on the story
when he telephoned late the night before. Nathan had claimed
that it was the truth, that he had found out from somebody or
other that Jerry and Evelyn Larkin were planning to stay away
from Babylon for a bit, and that this absence fit in well with the
plans for procuring the blueberry farm. Darrish, who had taken
the call in the den, desperately hoping that Ginny would not surreptitiously lift the line in the bedroom, didn't believe Nathan,
but did not dispute the veracity of the story. If there was something peculiar about it all, and it looked as if there were, he
would just as soon not know the truth. He refused to speculate,
even to himself.

But without knowing or wanting to know what had become
of the Larkins, Darrish knew enough to call up Nathan at the
bank, as soon as the sheriff had rung off. He repeated the conversation at length, and appended the judgment that the sheriff
had believed the story.

"Why shouldn't he?" demanded Nathan: "It's the truth."

"Oh," said Darrish easily, "just because he was getting it sec-
ondhand, that's all."

"All right," said Nathan, "you let me know if he calls again.
Did you say anything to Ginny last night about this?"

"No. I knew if I did, she'd call 'em up, and if they weren't
there, she might go out there or something. Who knows what
Ginny would do? I'll tell her when she gets back tomorrow
night. Maybe—what do you think?—I should tell her that I heard
from 'em, they called the house from Pensacola, saying they'd
be there for a while. Evelyn didn't leave a number, but said she'd
call back in a few days. I could say that—"

"Good," said Nathan: "Say that. I don't want anybody looking into this—I mean, you and I could use a few days to clear this
thing up, get everything ready, while they're still out of town."

"Good idea," concurred Darrish: "How long you suppose they're gone be gone?" he asked, without any expression that Nathan could interpret over the telephone.

"Oh," replied Nathan: "At least a week, I'd say. At least a week."

By eleven o'clock the next morning, the clock-thermometer in front of the CP&M bank read 101°. The sky to the south was crowded with gray clouds that filled the air with moisture but did not mask the sun. There was but one car in the parking lot in front of the high school, Warren Perry's beat-up Rambler, set far off to one side, in the dense shade beneath the outermost row of pecan trees in the neighboring orchard. The young man had agreed, for the two days of Ginny's absence, to sit for a few hours in the principal's office.

Warren sat hunched over Ginny's desk, working in a paper-bound book of crossword puzzles. He had finished all the easy ones first, and had started in on the second grade of difficulty; he was having trouble. The shade of the window that looked out onto the parking lot had been lowered against the sun; but it penetrated the dark paper and filled the room with hot green light. A rent in the shade focused a brilliant white spot on the desk. Perry stared at it while trying to think of short unfamiliar words that fit the incomprehensible definitions.

A large floor fan in the doorway was turned to highest speed. Over its noise, Warren did not hear the International Scout as it passed outside the window.

Ben Redfield was driving, and despite the heat, wore close-fitting leather motoring gloves that snapped at the wrist. He drew up also beneath the shade of the pecan trees, and parked so that the Scout obscured the back of the Rambler from anyone passing.

With his hand on the door, Nathan turned to his brother and said: "Wait till I get inside, then count thirty. If I haven't come back out, go to work. There's nobody around. Nobody in his right mind is out today."

Ben nodded but said nothing. He mopped the sweat from his forehead with his arm, to avoid staining the leather gloves that he had carefully wiped of the Larkins' blood. Nathan got out of the car and walked toward the portico of the building. Ben watched his progress in the rearview mirror, and as soon as Nathan reached the top of the stairs, he began to count slowly, aloud: "One. Two. Three. . . ."

Nathan entered the building and knocked loudly on the door-jamb of the principal's office. Warren jerked his head up. For a moment he stared stupidly at Nathan.

Nathan smiled pleasantly.

"Hey, Warren, how you?"

Warren nodded, but found he couldn't produce a smile. He motioned to the fan: "Turn that off, if you want. . . ."

Nathan shook his head no, and stepped carefully over the machine. "Is Ginny around?" he asked.

Warren shook his head. "Ginny's in Tallahassee."

"Oh," said Nathan, "that's too bad, I had to talk to her for a few minutes . . ."

Warren distrusted Nathan's pleasant untroubled demeanor, but out of automatic and irresistible politeness, he asked: "Is there something I can do for you?"

"No, not really," said Nathan, "I really came by to talk to her about Evelyn Larkin. . . ." He trailed off in apparent sympathy with the Larkins' misery, then picked up again: "I just wanted to tell Ginny that we weren't going to do any more about that loan for the time being."

"Well," said Warren quietly, "I'm sure Miz Larkin and Jerry will be glad to hear it."

Nathan smiled then. "Yes, but why don't you let Ginny tell them? I think it'll be better coming from her. You understand, don't you?"

Warren nodded yes, but in fact he didn't understand at all. "It would be a load off their minds if I could go out and tell 'em today, though. Ginny won't be back till late tonight, so she couldn't get out there till Saturday. I know they're worried about paying you back. They want to of course, and I know they'll be able to once they get a little deeper in the season. I know Jerry went down to Pensacola to deliver a whole carload of berries, so there'll be money off that—" He spoke quickly, without think-ing—Nathan Redfield made him that nervous.

But he broke off, remembering for what other reason Jerry had driven to Pensacola. He supposed that Nathan knew that Evelyn had accused him publicly of murdering Margaret, but he was glad that the man held no apparent grudge against her.

"Let Ginny tell them," said Nathan again. "They're not out at the house now anyway . . ."

Warren looked up curiously. Nathan had taken the chair between him and the shaded window. It was impossible to make out his eyes in the thick green light, and difficult to hear his voice beneath the low-pitched roar of the fan.

"Where are they?" Warren asked.

"Pensacola, I hear," smiled Nathan. "I don't really know though, I've just heard. I heard they went to Pensacola, and were going to stay with relatives for a few days, try to get Miz Larkin's mind off things. It's a good idea if you ask me."

"I'm surprised," said Warren, "real surprised to hear it. It's hard to imagine that Jerry would leave in the season. It's all he talks about, the season, and what it means to all of them."

"Well," said Nathan with a curious smile, "I guess his grandmother means more to him than the blueberries. Besides, as far as I know, he may have somebody out there taking care of it for him."

"Who?"

"I don't know who. I haven't been exactly intimate with Jerry and Miz Larkin lately—though I don't bear 'em any ill will now, and I'm just real sorry for what happened to that poor girl—but it doesn't seem unlikely that there might be somebody out there looking after the farm."

"Maybe I'll go out there this afternoon," said Warren thoughtfully.

"You do that. I heard you've been real good to them, and God knows, they need some help right about now. Anybody would, in their fix."

Nathan stood, and walked casually to the window, and peered out behind one corner of the shade into the parking lot. "Too bad you don't have air conditioning in here. This side really gets the sun." He turned to Warren with a broad smile. "I ought to run on now. You tell Ginny I stopped by."

"I will," said Warren, with a trembling smile.

"Bye now," said Nathan, and stepped over the fan. Warren stood, and made steps toward the door, but Nathan waved him back. "Don't bother. Go back to your puzzle. It was nice talking to you."

Warren dropped into his chair. He was at a loss to account for Nathan Redfield's altered behavior, his affability, his ungrudging leniency toward Evelyn Larkin. But it was difficult to think in the heat, and he put aside those questions until it was cooler, until Ginny Darrish had returned from her meetings in Tallahassee.

He telephoned the Larkins, but there was no answer. Maybe he wouldn't drive out there this afternoon after all; tomorrow he could stop by on his way to Atmore. If they weren't there by then, he would leave a note. He wanted for himself the pleasure of telling Evelyn and Jerry that Nathan Redfield had decided not to push them on the loan. Perhaps then, Evelyn would realize that the man could not possibly have murdered her granddaughter.

He sighed heavily. His great unselfish wish was for the old woman to be able to mourn her grandchild in peace. There was so little left to her and Jerry, they ought to be allowed at least that. Warren returned to his puzzles.

Meanwhile, Ben had got out of the Scout with a long screwdriver clutched in his gloved hand. He squatted on the hot asphalt behind Warren's Rambler, and thrust the screwdriver into the hole in the trunk, from which the lock had long ago fallen out. After fifteen seconds or so of jiggling, he pressed against the latch, and the trunk jarred open. Holding it down, he reached through the open door of the Scout, and pulled from beneath the front seat the broken sword, by which Evelyn and Jerry Larkin had perished. Blood had dried dark brown along its length and was spattered on the golden hilt.

Quickly Ben slipped the sword along one side of the trunk, among the greasy tools there, and covered them all with one of the large dirty beach towels that lay folded beneath the jack. He brought down the lid of the trunk quietly, tested it twice to make sure that it had latched, then quickly got back into the Scout. Until Nathan returned, he kept a feverish watch for anyone passing by, but in the scarce five minutes his brother was absent not a single vehicle passed on the steaming road, not a soul crossed the baking lot, or took refuge beneath the drooping foliage of the pecan trees.

Chapter 33

That same morning, shortly before noon, Nathan Redfield crossed John Glenn Avenue, from the bank to town hall, and stuck his head in the sheriff's office.

Hale motioned him inside, but Nathan shook his head grinning no.

"I just came by, cain't stay, to ask you to come over to the house for a drink after you're through here. I got something I want to talk over with you."

"What's that?" said Hale.

"Nothing, nothing much," said Nathan: "You just come on over to the house, okay?"

Hale nodded yes, and Nathan disappeared.

When the sheriff arrived at the Redfields' that afternoon, he was not surprised to find his daughter's car parked in the knob of the cul-de-sac.

Nina opened the front door to the sheriff, and showed him into the den. The curtains had been opened onto the patio, and Hale paused to watch Belinda perform an excellent jackknife. He liked the sound of the splash and the reverberating board.

"I'll go get Mr. Nathan," said Nina, and left the room.

Hale stepped out onto the patio.

"Oh hey, Daddy!" cried Belinda, when she shot up out of the water, shaking her head. She stroked to the side of the pool. "What are you doing here?" She crossed her arms on the tiles, and raised herself a little in the water. "We sure are lucky to know rich people with a private pool, aren't we?" She smiled. "Aren't you gone speak to Mr. Red, Daddy?" Belinda nodded in the direction of the high shading ornamental pines.

James Redfield, pale and wasted, slouched in a painted metal rocker. He squinted and nodded to Hale. "Hey, Ted," he said briefly, "I hope you didn't come over here to take Miss Pie away."

"No," said Hale affably, "I just came by to see if you were taking good care of her."

"I keep her out of trouble," the old man wheezed, and chuckled hoarsely. "She doesn't get in trouble when I keep her round me. That's more than I can say for other people in this town. That's more than I can say for that Larkin girl. I hope you're not letting Miss Pie ride her wheel out toward the Styx River bridge, are you, Ted?"

"Mr. Redfield, I don't think Belinda has a bicycle to her name, but if she did, I wouldn't let her be riding it out that way, I can tell you."

Belinda climbed from the pool. "Daddy," she said, approaching him, "why you here? You couldn't do without me for five minutes?"

Hale thought he could detect a little nervousness to her question, but he pretended not to have caught it. "Honey, I just came out to talk to Nathan for a few minutes. He said he wanted to talk to me."

"What about?" demanded Belinda in a sharp low voice, turning her head so that Mr. Red could not hear her.

"Honey, I don't know," said her father, "and—"

Nathan appeared in the doorway, and motioned Hale inside. Belinda started to follow, but Nathan said to her: "Belinda, you let me talk to your daddy alone, you hear me? You take care of Daddy for a while, you make sure he's not getting burnt."

Belinda looked at Nathan quizzically, but said nothing. She didn't like to speak to him in the presence of her father, fearing that she might betray their intimacy by her too-easy manner. She moved to Mr. Red, and sat cross-legged by the side of his chair.

Inside, Nathan led Hale to the couch before the fireplace. The sheriff sat and Nathan brought bourbons and water that he had already prepared.

"What'd you want to talk to me about?" said Hale. He suspected that it had something to do with the Larkins. It wasn't unlikely that Nathan had heard of Evelyn Larkin's search for a sympathetic lawyer in Pensacola. Since his experience the morning before, which the sheriff had tried without complete success to attribute to mildew, insects, and the early morning heat, Hale was more and more uneasy with the case.

"Not much," said Nathan: "Not much really: I just wanted to talk to you about Belinda."

"Belinda!" cried Hale. "What about Belinda!"

"Nothing," said Nathan, in a tone to reassure Hale: "Nothing about her directly. I just wanted to tell you something that you might not have known about, something I just found out myself."

"What?" demanded Hale.

"Shhhh!" said Nathan. "Belinda doesn't know anything about this now, and Daddy and Ben and I just love the daylights out of her, but you know and I know that she is capable of listening in at the door, so you just keep your voice down."

"What about Belinda?" whispered the sheriff desperately.

"Not really about Belinda," said Nathan, in a low considered voice, "it's about Warren Perry."

Hale looked up sharply, with narrowing eyes, but Nathan either did not or pretended not to notice this.

"Perry's been hanging around the house," said Nathan carefully.

"Hell," said Ted Hale, "the man lives on top of the garage. Of course he—"

"Not *your* house," explained Nathan, "*this* house."

Hale considered this over a sip of bourbon.

"He drives by," said Nathan: "And turns round in the cul-de-sac, and I don't know if he thinks we cain't recognize a ten-year-old green Rambler when we've seen it about two hundred times. He drives by—but only when Belinda's here. Like he was keeping an eye on her or something . . ."

"Well, that's not much . . ." said Hale, but was apparently disturbed.

"No," said Nathan: "It's not much, you're right. But it's not all either. Ben and I have caught sight of him in the woods. Sometimes in the evening, we see him down by that little stream. Ben's got good eyes, Ben's got night eyes, and he can see Warren when he's down there. That's our property, and I'm not gone prosecute him for trespassing or anything like that, but he doesn't have any business down there. The only time we see him is when Belinda's in the house. I just thought you'd like to know, keep an eye on him and everything. You know how much we all think of Belinda, especially Daddy, and I think we couldn't go on like we are if anything happened to her, like for instance the way it happened to poor old Margaret Larkin."

Hale nodded solemnly, troubled. "Anything else?" he asked quietly.

Nathan looked up at the portrait above the fireplace for a few seconds before answering. "No," he said: "Just one other thing. *Somebody* broke in the house—"

"What?!"

"—and took the sword that was hanging down right under that picture."

Hale spluttered. "Somebody broke in! When? Why didn't you tell me before?"

"Listen," said Nathan, holding up a cautionary hand: "We don't know when it happened. Last night, Ben noticed that the sword was gone. The scabbard was still up there, and we just hadn't noticed it before. I don't think it had been gone long, but we just cain't be sure, 'cause we don't go looking at it every day."

"What else is gone?"

"Nothing," said Nathan: "That's what was funny about it. Nothing else was gone, that we can think of. Now, I didn't want to report this, because I didn't want to get Daddy upset by telling him that there had been a robber in the house. We don't know who took it, and even if we did, I don't think there's much chance of getting the sword back, and to tell you the truth, I don't care much whether I ever see it again or not." What Nathan did not say, but what Hale understood perfectly, was that Nathan suspected that Warren Perry had taken the sword from the house.

Hale swallowed the rest of his drink in one gulp, and declined Nathan's offer of another.

"Stay for supper," Nathan suggested as well, but Hale refused out of hand. "No," he said, "you let me go home and think about this. Ben was sure now that it was Warren Perry that he saw in the woods? And it was when Belinda was here?"

Nathan nodded.

"All right," said Hale: "Don't say anything about any of this to anybody, okay? I don't imagine, at least I hope that there's nothing in it, and probably there's not—"

"Probably not—" said Nathan.

"—so we don't want to go starting trouble for Warren when there's no need to. I'll talk to him maybe, but I guarantee you that I'll keep an eye on him."

Nathan smiled and rose. "I didn't want to upset you, Ted," he said: "But I just thought that you ought to know. If anything did happen, and of course it won't, I wouldn't have been able to face you, knowing that I hadn't told you what I knew."

The two men shook hands warmly, and Hale went to the door to call Belinda over. Father and daughter stood on opposite sides of the screen, one baking with the sun at her back and the other shivering with air-conditioned drafts. They spoke in low voices.

"Listen, honey—"

"What, Daddy?" Belinda appeared nervous.

"When you get ready to leave here tonight, you call me up at home, and tell me that you're on your way, okay?"

Belinda glanced at her father warily. "Okay," she said slowly. "Sure. Why, though?"

"Just because. And I want you to get Nathan or Ben to walk you out to the car, okay?"

"Daddy," Belinda said doubtfully: "That car is parked about five inches from the front door, I don't need anybody to walk me—"

"Do it for me, honey, will you please? And please don't ask me why, either."

Belinda had feared that Nathan was saying something to her father regarding their carrying-on; but he evidently had told Hale something quite different.

"Daddy," she said: "Of course, if you want me to do it, I will do it. If you had told me, I'd get down on my hands and knees and empty that swimming pool with a 'luminum strainer."

Hale smiled and turned away. Nathan walked him to the front door. "You haven't said anything to Belinda?" asked the sheriff.

Nathan shook his head. "She's got a mouth, your little girl, and I'm not really accusing Warren Perry of anything except driving around in the cul-de-sac and wading through the creek down in the back of the house. Besides, she might have gotten scared. There was no reason I could see for telling her."

Hale nodded: "Don't do it now, either. She's gone try and worm it out of you when you get back in there, she's gone try to get you to tell her what it was that we talked about. Don't tell her."

"I won't," Nathan promised, and closed the door.

Hale regarded Nathan's information in troubling relation to the case of Margaret Larkin's death. Nathan evidently hadn't made the connection, but Hale saw now that if his first conjecture was correct, and Warren Perry had indeed murdered the girl, then Belinda herself might be in danger. Maybe Warren Perry had Belinda in mind for number two in the series.

This possible danger to his daughter prodded him in a way that none of Evelyn Larkin's hysterical remonstrances could. It was necessary, if Warren Perry was the murderer, to prove that fact directly, before he really got going on his second victim; but Hale realized with despair that he was no nearer obtaining proof than before.

Hale resolved that he would keep Belinda well out of Warren's path, until he was certain of the man's innocence. He knew that the schoolteacher was spending the weekend with his mother in Atmore, so all was well for the time being; but he would return on Sunday night or Monday morning, and then it might be necessary to warn Belinda to remain out of his way.

This most important question set aside, Hale, as he drove back toward his house, tried to think what on earth Warren Perry could want with a Civil War sword.

Chapter 34

The Boy Scouts, the Cub Scouts, the Girl Scouts, and the Brownies of Babylon were beside themselves with frustration and disappointment because Evelyn and Jerry Larkin had deserted their farmstead without notice, at the height of the blueberry season. Several days of promised lucrative employment had not materialized. Each morning a few of the older boys and girls rode their bicycles out across the Styx, trembling exquisitely as they crossed the bridge. They knocked on the front and back doors of the farmhouse, prowled through the patch, grabbed handfuls of the ripest berries for their own throats, and wondered aloud what could have become of their seasonal employers. Two twelve-year-old girls, twins called Nadine and Nerlene Comer, rode out to the blueberry farm shortly before noon on Saturday. They pulled open the back door which had remained unlocked since the sheriff had fled the house, and stepped onto the dappled latticed porch. Nadine called hesitantly for the old woman. From the smell, Nerlene declared herself certain that seven rats had perished beneath the kitchen sink. They hurried nervously down the back steps, having decided against exploring the house.

But once outside, Nadine and Nerlene were reassured by the warm fresh air; they considered that they had the run of the place in the absence of the owners. Both had attended vacation bible school with Margaret the previous summer, and felt keenest interest in her death. On this partially cloudy morning they walked among the blueberry bushes, deliciously losing themselves, pretending there was no way out of the lush green maze.

A series of giggling right-angled turnings brought them suddenly upon the eroding bank of the Styx. A couple of large bushes had recently tumbled into the water, and washed down to the junction of the Perdido. Their root systems lay exposed in a yard-high declivity over the whirling black water. Here, tied to a stake set not very firmly into the ground, was Jerry's small green rowboat.

The girls decided there was no reason they should not get in, and row across to the sandbar where Margaret Larkin had been killed. They'd look for bloodstains and some clue that Sheriff Hale might have missed. They'd come back to Babylon in triumph, bearing the solution to the crime.

The twins rowed sturdily upstream along the north shore of the river, where the current was not so strong. Gliding under the bridge, they shivered; it was unexpectedly chill and damp beneath, and the unreflecting black water seemed abysmally deep and lifeless. No fish swam there, and dead things swilled along a few inches below the surface of the water.

During the few seconds they were under the bridge, the sun went behind a bank of clouds that looked to hide it for the remainder of the day. The upstream side of the Styx, above the bridge, was wild, cold, and dark, and the two girls thought they had passed onto a different river altogether.

Above the bridge, the course of the stream was tortured, and narrow, and its banks uninhabited. Abundant shallows and numerous snags made the going difficult, and the water rushed headlong in those narrow channels where it ran deep. Nadine and Nerlene had heard of canoes and small boats overturned inexplicably on this portion of the Styx, and of young divers, no older than themselves, whose heads had broken open on submerged tree trunks.

The two young girls, no longer giggling, rowed carefully across the river, along the pilings of the bridge. The water knocked the boat harshly against the rotting wooden posts, and the jarring was so great, so seemingly deliberate, that they cried out a little with each accident. Finally they reached the upper end of the narrow sandbar that ran beneath the bridge, at the other end of which Margaret had been murdered. Nadine jumped out, and then dragged the boat onto the gravel, so that Nerlene would not ruin her new shoes.

They then proceeded slowly along the length of the sandbar, staring nervously at the gravel and sand and small dank weeds, now very much afraid of finding anything like blood, or pieces of torn clothing, or an identification bracelet that had belonged to the murderer.

That portion of the sandbar directly under the bridge was dark, almost as black as the Styx itself. It stank of rot and damp, and was unnaturally cool. The girls whisperingly decided that they would hurry to the end, proving their courage, and then ran back to the boat, paddle swiftly back across the river, race through the patch, and then pedal home to Babylon as quickly as they could.

Holding hands then, Nadine and Nerlene raced across that little black space, emerged gasping into the clouded light, and moved quickly to the end of the bar. Here they were unnerved by the indistinct impressions made in the sand, most recently by the sheriff and his deputies, before that by Ed Geiger and Jerry Larkin, and in the beginning by Margaret and the man who murdered her. The gravel had been disturbed; clods of low-lying red clay had been thrown up to the surface. A small depression was filled with stagnant water and leeches.

"All right," said Nadine, in a low measured voice: "We can go back now." They turned.

Just within the shadow of the bridge, propped against a little mound of pebbles and palely gleaming, was the severed head of Jerry Larkin. Light bouncing off the white gravel illumined his filmed eyes. Large black ants trailed in and out of the slack mouth.

The head blocked the twins' path back to the boat. Nerlene pushed Nadine into the water on the shore side of the bar, then, never minding her new shoes, jumped in after. The girls waded through the waist-deep water, and clambered up the muddy bank opposite from where they'd set out.

They looked back once at Jerry's head, screamed in unison, and then, abandoning their bicycles that were on the other side of the bridge, ran all the way back to Babylon.

Chapter 35

The bodies of Jerry and Evelyn Larkin were not recovered before the following morning. On Saturday afternoon, the sheriff, his deputies, and several state highway patrolmen started out in

boats from the bridge, moving slowly upstream, carefully prod-
ding the riverbed with long cane poles. They located the station
wagon in only an hour and a half. A diver dispatched from Pensacola arrived at five, and ascertained that the bodies were in
the back. The driver's window was open, and it was assumed
that Jerry's head had floated out of the automobile sometime
during the night, tumbled downstream, and come to rest on the
sandbar beneath the bridge.

Hale decided to leave the bodies as they were until the automobile itself could be raised. It was possible that some clues
might be disturbed if the attempt were made to pull the corpses
from the car now; the doors were stuck and could not be opened
without torches, which weren't available anyway. The county
coroner, called back up from Pensacola, assured the sheriff that
the two bodies would not appreciably deteriorate before dawn.

The Sunday morning papers made but brief mention of the
discovery of the bodies, for Hale had not released the information until late on Saturday night. He had tried to think of some
way to disguise the obvious fact that an entire family under his
jurisdiction had been wiped out in a peculiarly bloody and disgusting fashion. A young girl had been murdered brutally; he
had failed to discover her killer, and the man had returned now
to do away with her brother and her grandmother. Hale knew
nothing like it had occurred in all of Florida for years, and he
soon realized as well that there was no way to soften the tale.

The sheriff sat up late Saturday night with the county coroner and the two state patrolmen who had assisted on the river;
and with them he went over the entire case in great detail. The
strained consensus of their opinions was that Warren Perry
had killed all three, but once this conclusion was grasped at, the
county coroner and the state highway patrolmen declared themselves astounded first that Hale hadn't seen it before, whereby he
might have avoided these horrible double deaths of the grandmother and her grandson, and second, that he had allowed the
man to leave the state without even a warning.

"Well," said Hale defensively: "Warren's not exactly out-of-
state, I wouldn't call it. He's up at his mama's in Atmore, that's
all. And he's not exactly fleeing, because all his stuff's out there,

and he's not the type of boy to go off without saying anything about it. I mean, the rent's due on Tuesday, and Warren's always on time with the rent."

The county coroner and the patrolmen were unconvinced, pointing out sensibly that if the boy were the murderer, he would hardly let himself be caught because of financial obligations to his landlord.

At their urging, Hale telephoned Warren in Atmore and asked him to come back to Babylon directly. Hale said he needed Warren's help to assess some vandalism that had occurred at the high school.

"You're at the school?" said Warren.

"No," said the sheriff: "You come by the house first."

Warren arrived shortly before dawn, and went directly into the kitchen, where he found the men gathered at the table, drinking black coffee, eating frozen coffee cake, and staring him down with dreadful countenances.

Hale, in short order, told Warren what had happened. Warren declared himself distracted with amazement and grief.

"Warren," said Hale, with some embarrassment, for though the little evidence there was all pointed to the schoolteacher, he could not readily imagine that the small quaking boy in front of him had cut off Jerry Larkin's head, or had pushed the station wagon, with two corpses in the back, over a bluff into the Styx —"Warren, what do you know about all of this?"

"Know?" echoed Warren: "I know what you just told me. I just came over that bridge. You told me somebody had broken into the school. You—"

"I just didn't want you going off—"

"Going off?"

The county coroner and the patrolmen stared hard at Warren.

"I—I thought Jerry and Miz Larkin were in Pensacola. I thought they were staying with relatives in Pensacola."

"They were in the back of their station wagon, under twelve feet of water," said one of the patrolmen. "D'you put 'em there?"

Warren stared wide-eyed at the officer, then at Hale. "Me? I—"

"Warren," said Hale earnestly, "d'you have anything to do with this?"

Dumbfounded, Warren shook his head no. He leaned trembling against the sink.

"Would you have any objection if we searched your place?" asked Hale.

Warren shook his head distractedly.

"You sit here, then," said Hale: "Have a cup of coffee, and keep Dr. Dickinson company."

Warren sat without a word. He had been awakened by Hale's phone call, and still wore the tops of his pajamas, tucked into a pair of old corduroy pants. He shakingly poured a cup of coffee, and stared at the county coroner, who turned away.

Hale and the two patrolmen got up and went out into the driveway. Above, in the east, the sky was pink and eggshell blue. The green Rambler still ticked after the rapid drive back to Babylon from Atmore.

"We might as well look in the car first," said one of the patrolmen. He climbed into the front seat; Hale got into the back, and leaned down and thrust his hand beneath the springs.

The second patrolman asked for the keys to the trunk, but Hale looked up and said: "Lock's gone. You'll have to fiddle with it. Wait, look in the glove compartment, he keeps a screwdriver up there, I think, to open it with."

The first patrolman, a little surprised at Hale's knowledge of the suspect and his ways, retrieved the screwdriver, and handed it to his partner.

After only a few moments, full of low curses, the officer was able to open the trunk, and he made a quick search of the junk in the back. With the end of the screwdriver he tenderly lifted the tools, the miscellaneous bits of clothing, the soiled beach towels.

"I found something," he cried with soft triumph.

"What?" demanded Hale, and quickly backed out of the car.

"Come look," said the man.

Hale and the other officer went around to the trunk, and he pointed out the bloodied sword.

"It looks like that's what took that boy's head off, don't it just?" said the officer who found it.

"Why'd he leave it here though?" asked Hale. "Why didn't he just throw it away somewhere?"

"If he was dumb enough to use something like that to try to kill somebody, then he's dumb enough to keep it in the back of his car."

"Where'd he get something like that?" said the first officer.

Hale looked between the two men, then said softly: "He stole it. He stole it from Nathan Redfield not long ago. Nathan said the sword was missing, and he said he had seen Warren hanging about the house of late. That's probably where it came from."

"I think you got a case," smiled the second officer.

"I guess I do," sighed Hale, and glanced toward the kitchen windows; the dawn was not yet strong enough to block the light from inside, and he could see the top of the coroner's immobile head.

"I think," said the first officer: "That we had best go back inside before something just perfectly awful happens to Dr. Dickinson."

Warren Perry was duly arrested and taken to town hall, where he was placed in the best cell, a young thief having been moved to a windowless cubicle because he was not, after all, a local boy. The schoolteacher did not even protest to Hale, except to say in a low and wondering voice that he was innocent. He begged Hale to make sure that it was Evelyn and Jerry who had been killed—he was almost certain that they were still in Pensacola. He looked at the sword dumbly, and avowed that he had never seen it before.

Hale promised that he would call Charles Darrish, who because of his friendship with Ginny, would no doubt be happy to represent Warren.

Hale was more troubled by these proceedings than Warren himself. The schoolteacher was in shock, as much astounded by the deaths of his newfound friends as by the accusation against him. But the sheriff was disturbed by the incongruity of the evidence; it pointed easily enough to Warren, and the only point in his defense was his character. Yet the balance was in Warren's favor: Hale knew it was impossible that Warren had committed any of the three killings. The man didn't have it in him. Though Hale had suspected Perry before, he realized that this was mere laziness on his part, and a desire to have some explanation for the inexplicable. Now that the evidence had presented itself in fine incontrovertible fashion, he was inclined to disbelieve it. But it was impossible to explain how a bloody sword had found its way into the trunk of Warren's Rambler.

After the station wagon was raised and drained, and the two corpses had been removed to the funeral home on the south side of town, an examination of the wounds and an analysis of the dried blood on the sword proved that it had been the murder weapon, had killed both Evelyn and Jerry Larkin. Moreover, that portion of steel found beneath the front seat of the station wagon matched perfectly the broken blade discovered in the trunk of Warren's car. Fingerprints were unfortunately lacking.

The news spread widely in Babylon that next day, and before Sunday school and after church, no one talked of anything else.

Early that morning, Ginny visited Warren in jail. She brought with her the assurance that her husband was willing and anxious to represent him in this case, and they wouldn't even mention fees until it was all over and done with. And, just as his wife had promised, Charles Darrish showed up just at eleven, and conferred with his client at some length, making a few notes on Warren's movements since Wednesday night.

His one telephone call—Hale would have allowed him as many as he liked, but Warren had no one else he wanted to talk to—was to his mother in Atmore. She was inexpressibly shocked by what had happened, and declared she was sure that Warren hadn't done it, but that she couldn't possibly bring herself to visit him in jail, that she had never been in a jail before in her life, that her husband had committed suicide before *he* was carried off to jail, and that she felt it would be harmful to her fragile emotional and physical condition if she were to make the trip to the Babylon town hall. Warren said that he understood, that he had not for a moment expected that she would come down to see him, and that if she liked, he would call again, sometime before the trial, to let her know how things progressed.

Hale heard Warren's end of this call, and looked with pity on the accused boy. It was an odd thing that only two days before he had resolved to keep Belinda away from the man, fearing for her safety. But now he called Belinda at home, and asked her to go out and buy some barbecue for Warren and bring it to the office, and in fact, to bring enough for the three of them. They would take a little supper together, in hopes of cheering Warren up.

"Daddy," said Belinda doubtfully: "But you think he did it, don't you? I mean, everybody in town says that they were surprised he hadn't cut somebody's head off before this, and don't know why he waited so long to start tying high school girls to their bicycles and throwing 'em off of every bridge in the north part of the county, and I don't know what all else."

"Honey," said Hale softly: "I really don't think that Warren did do it. And even if he did, that's no reason why we cain't bring him a little barbecue, and share it with him."

"I guess not, Daddy," said the cheerleader, even more doubtfully; but half an hour later, she showed up smiling at town hall with boxes of barbecued chicken, a carton of French-fried onion rings, and two quarts of Dr Pepper.

Warren was touched by the simple meal eaten around Hale's desk. They did not talk of the deaths of Margaret, Evelyn, and Jerry Larkin at all, but of Belinda's plans for the coming school year, and of the Rattlesnake Rodeo, which would begin in another couple of weeks.

Dr. Dickinson, the county coroner, completed his investigation late Sunday afternoon, and turned the bodies over to the undertaker. Because the Larkins, despite what Hale had heard from Charles Darrish, proved to have no family that could be located readily, it was decided to proceed with the funeral as soon as possible. Evelyn Larkin had a burial policy, which in this case was stretched to cover two. This was possible, the undertaker agreed, because it was a double closed-casket ceremony, and he could supply both coffins, with only slight interior damage, at a much reduced rate. It would not be possible however to have concrete vaults in the cemetery.

The small embarrassed funeral was held Monday morning, with services only at graveside. The sheriff showed up with Belinda beside him, Ginny and Charles Darrish were chief mourners, and behind them were the multitudinous curious of Babylon, who were disappointed that the Baptist minister made no reference, in his brief eulogy that served to commemorate both grandmother and grandson, to the manner of their deaths.

The common remark that morning was that no one had seen a family plot fill up as fast as the Larkins' had.

Standing distant among the evergreens were reporters from the Mobile *Press-Register* and the Pensacola *News-Journal*. The *Press-Register* called Ted Hale aside, and demanded confirmation of the rumor that he had sheltered the maniac for the past twelve months above his garage, when the man was wanted in three states of the Southeast for similar crimes.

While the sheriff was reluctantly admitting it was true that Warren Perry had signed a lease that many months in the past, the Pensacola *News-Journal* persuaded Belinda to return to the graveside, where she posed with a sorrowful face beside the two open graves. The two black cemetery workers flanked her, their upraised spades dramatically filled with soil about to be tossed atop the coffins below. The photograph appeared in the later afternoon edition, and Belinda bought fifteen copies of the paper, one of which she proudly carried to Warren Perry in his cell.

Chapter 36

While the coffins of Jerry and Evelyn Larkin were being lowered into the single wide-dug grave in the Babylon cemetery, Nathan Redfield was collecting winnings of $163 at the racetrack in Cantonment. He didn't often recover money that he had bet, but today he wasn't surprised that luck had fallen his way. With all that had gone right for him, it seemed improbable that anything so small as the picking of Mr. Pudding as the winning dog in the third race, would go wrong—and it had not.

He was returning to Babylon now after a leisurely oyster supper on the municipal pier in Pensacola. The moon was within four days of waxing full; and on this cloudless warm night it shone feverishly across the tops of the trees in the dense pine forest, shimmered over the tin roofs of the few houses on this road, held distractingly in Nathan's eyes all the way back. Though he turned sharp curves in the road, the moon cast implacably through the same spot in the windshield.

Nathan was pleased with the events of the last few days, and as he drove through the silent forest, beneath the waxing moon, mused contentedly, certain that at last, he was coming into his own.

Nathan had been born a rich man's son—though James Redfield's fortune at the end of World War II was actually rather modest, in so small and poor a place as Babylon it seemed substantial indeed. Nathan's early life had been predictable: He grew up proud and recalcitrant, was sullen with his father and impatient with his mother while she lived. When James Redfield remarried, Nathan did his best to irritate his stepmother, but this imperious woman didn't brook interference from an adolescent, and she had Nathan packed off to a military school in Ohio. Ben, because he was more docile, was not required to accompany his brother. When his stepmother died, Nathan Redfield came back to Babylon for the funeral—and he never returned to the military school.

He took at once to himself the title of "rich man's son," and set about to enjoy himself as much as was possible with his father not yet dead. He attended the University of West Florida for a year, while living at home, but after an argument with his father, he left school and joined the Air Force.

Things were never the same after this in the small family; the rift between the father and his two sons only widened. Ben completed high school, speaking to his father only every three days or so; and when Nathan returned from his stint in the Air Force, he was given a job at the CP&M, though he sat at a desk as far removed from his father's as possible. Nathan sought advancement not because he was ambitious, but rather because he knew it would irritate his father, who liked to regard him as a disappointing self-willed offspring. During the period of convalescence following James Redfield's first automobile accident, in which a senior vice-president of the bank had been killed, Nathan rose to be acting manager of the CP&M; he relinquished this to his father a few months later. But shortly thereafter came the second accident, which completely incapacitated James Redfield, and Nathan took over the bank entirely.

Still, although this succession seemed easy enough and only right in the critical eyes of Babylon, it was not an easy inheritance. James Redfield was ill-disposed toward his sons; his was a bitterness that could not be dispelled by any number of years of good behavior on the parts of Nathan and Benjamin. He had a general mistrust of their ways and motives. Nathan knew that just some small, arbitrary thing could cause his father to change his will in favor of Ginny Darrish, leaving him and Ben with insultingly small trust funds and possibly not even control of the bank.

Nathan had no desire to give up his present comfortable life, and he had some time ago begun to make plans to get money on his own, money over which his father had no control. He knew he hadn't the instinct for good investments, and he hadn't the energy for entrepreneurship, and so he had determined to wait patiently until something showed itself.

He had discovered his chance in the first visits of the Texaco representatives to his father. James Redfield had wanted to keep these secret, but Ben had informed his brother of the unexpected appearance of the yankees at the house. Nathan had demanded the full facts of his father. But James Redfield had unconscionably delayed the signing of the exploration leases, only to irritate him, Nathan was certain. They might already have been a couple of hundred thousand dollars richer.

Because he didn't know what else to do, Nathan began to buy up small plots of land south of Babylon, five- and ten-acre farmsteads, and twenty-acre tracts of scrub woodland. But these tiny parcels of land were scattered, and even when colored in on a map that he kept hidden in his chest of drawers they seemed insignificant; it was unlikely that the oil companies would decide to drill twenty wells on just those morsels of land that he had purchased at random. Moreover, Nathan hadn't the liquid capital to purchase much more; his income was only a little more than moderate, but he gambled and he spent money in Mobile, and his savings account was embarrassingly small for a banker —he would be able to afford little more land.

Then had come the discovery in the oil representatives' hotel room in Mobile—that Texaco was interested in the land north of the Styx. Nathan had surreptitiously written to the lawyers of the man in Boston who owned most of that property, but he was not interested in selling. He turned his attention to the Larkin blueberry farm, and wondered how he might secure it for himself.

Nathan remembered Jim and JoAnn Larkin's disappearances and he more than anyone else in town had a good idea of what had happened to them; it seemed all the more fitting then that he should try to wrest the blueberry farm from Evelyn Larkin's hands. A few times he had spoken to the old woman, casually, of the possibility of selling the farm if circumstances required and the right buyer presented himself; but Evelyn Larkin had said that she would never sell, that the farm was all she had ever known, and that she would have nowhere else to go. The blueberries supported both her and her grandchildren and if only just for their sakes, she would remain.

It was shortly after this that Nathan Redfield had first taken serious note of Margaret Larkin, not only because she was a young, lithe, handsome girl, but also because she was Evelyn Larkin's granddaughter. Nathan had contrived to sit next to Margaret at two football games, since her place on the North Escambia High School Typhoons pep squad was at the end of the top row. She had shyly accepted his interest, without really understanding it, and had nodded and spoken to him whenever they passed on the street or saw one another in the CP&M.

Once, on driving home from the bank, he had passed her on the street; he turned the car around, and offered her a ride out to the blueberry farm. She accepted, but insisted that he let her out just at the bend before the river, so that her grandmother might not see her approach in his car. Margaret's willingness to engineer this small deception led Nathan to believe that the girl could be coaxed into greater concessions. Nathan liked young women, especially those still in high school; in fact, he hadn't any use at all for females who had passed the age of seventeen.

After that, whenever he saw Margaret on the street, he would drive her out to the farm; he mentioned this to no one, and was certain that she never said anything of it. If they had been seen together in so small a town as Babylon the word would have got back to him in the form of lighthearted ribbing. But he had never been accused of having a romance with the adolescent blueberry heiress, and so was certain that no one knew of their casual meetings.

One day early in February, instead of letting Margaret out at the bend before the river, he turned the Scout onto the disused logging track, and drove up to the bluff above the Styx. He pulled a blanket out of the back, and spread it beneath the pines. He poured out bourbon into Dixie cups. The young girl was excited by the illicitness of the impromptu picnic with the older man, and unused to the liquor, became quickly drunk. In time, Nathan pinned Margaret beneath him and raped her. Afterward, she crawled off a few feet and threw up.

He drove her back to the Babylon highway and pushed open the door for her. She climbed silently out. "Just give me the high sign when you're ready to do it again," he laughed, and drove off. In the rearview mirror, he saw that she had not turned toward her house, but stood unmoving in the middle of the road, pale and gray, staring vacantly after him.

Now, recalling that moment, Nathan glanced in the mirror. A dozen yards behind the car stood Margaret Larkin, gray and still. But the car moved forward so quickly, and the forest was so dark, that she was gone before Nathan's brain had even registered his fear. He shuddered, stamped down on the accelerator and drove faster, to flee the vision. The moon shone down through the windshield and seemed almost to blind him.

She appeared again on the road ahead. He immediately took his foot off the accelerator and was about to apply the brakes, when the gray figure suddenly shifted into a wisp of fog, so common on Escambia County roads on warm humid nights. The thin cloud swirled and dissipated when the Lincoln swept through it. Nathan breathed more easily—what he had seen in the mirror was no more than just another column of fog, altered by the moonlight, the distorting mirror, and his own imagination. Margaret Larkin lay very still and quiet in her grave, slowly liquefying.

Nathan tried very hard not to look again at the dark silent road that so quickly retreated behind the Lincoln, but every ten seconds or so, his glance would dart to the mirror; he would fear to see something, see nothing, and breathe deeply in relief.

He wished for other patches of fog, to reassure himself of his mistake; yet began to fear that the clouds would take on other shapes as well, and so dreaded to find them.

He tried to think of something else, but could not rid himself of thoughts of Margaret Larkin.

After the incident in the woods, the girl had not spoken again to Nathan, until she had called him up at home to tell him that she was pregnant, and that it was up to him to do something about it.

Nathan's first reaction was to accuse Margaret of having mistaken the symptoms—fourteen-year-old girls, he told her, didn't get pregnant. He had never even heard of such a thing. With adolescent embarrassment, Margaret recounted the signs. Nathan said nothing for a few moments, certain now that he was in great trouble.

Then he denied that the child was his, but Margaret stated simply that she had never had sexual intercourse with any other man, and that further, she did not intend to have an abortion. He could marry her, or he could not marry her, as he preferred, but he must acknowledge and provide for the child. No one else, neither her grandmother nor her brother, knew of it.

He tried then to reason with her, pointing out that a marriage between them would be wrong, ludicrous, and unhappy; but Margaret only stubbornly repeated her belief that if he was capable of getting her pregnant, he was capable of marrying her. The question was, she said, was he ready to have it known that he had slept with a girl not yet even in the ninth grade?

Nathan at last acquiesced to her demand, and only begged that she give him a few days in which to break this news to his father. At the end of that time, she would be free to tell her brother and her grandmother, to order the invitations for the wedding, to choose the place where they would honeymoon.

It was while he spoke these comforting words that Nathan decided that he would kill Margaret Larkin. Certainly, he would never marry her: Her grandmother—and probably the laws of the state—would not allow that. Even if she could be persuaded to have an abortion, the news would probably leak out, get back to his father, and destroy that already tenuous relationship. James

Redfield had declared that if either of his sons did anything that shamed his name, he wouldn't hesitate a moment to call in Charles Darrish to change the will, cutting out *both* Nathan and Ben. Nathan had the idea that James Redfield expected that he and Ben would fake a robbery of the daily cash run from Pensacola to Babylon. But impregnating a fourteen-year-old girl would probably do just as well.

Nathan was certain that Margaret had told no one yet; she was too earnest a child to have lied about that. Within a few days he had laid his plans carefully; he had seen her in the bank once and whisperingly reassured her that all would go through, and they would be married in only a few weeks' time. Marveling that she accepted this, he cautioned her to say nothing yet of it to anyone. She nodded gravely.

On Thursday, the first of June, he discovered by anonymously telephoning her grandmother, that Margaret was spending the afternoon with Warren Perry at the high school. He drove to the school in a vehicle that could not be identified as his own. The week before, the CP&M had foreclosed on a ribbon mill worker who lived well south of town. This man had given up the large black fishing hearse that he and his two sons used for weekend trips to the Gulf of Mexico. Nathan, who had access to the keys, had brought the vehicle up to Babylon, and parked it behind the football stadium.

He hung about in the shade of the pecan trees until Margaret appeared at the front door of the school. While she made her way down to the bicycle rack, Nathan hurried toward the hearse. At a distance, he followed Margaret through town, and overtook her only when she paused to speak to Nina at her mailbox. He turned his head aside so that they would not recognize him, and drove quickly out the Styx River road. He parked the vehicle just out of sight on the disused logging track, pulled on the leather motoring gloves, drew the black leather mask over his head, and then lay in wait for Margaret by the side of the road.

At first Nathan had regretted the murder of Margaret Larkin. It had been certainly the most radical—though probably also the safest—solution to the problem of her pregnancy and absurd demands of marriage. He had feared that her death would adversely affect his chances of getting the Larkin property; but before that really came of issue, he had been put to the necessity of murdering the girl's brother and grandmother as well. This exigency he had not foreseen, but now that it was accomplished, Nathan saw that it was perhaps all for the best, and the blueberry farm would more easily be his. The idea of bringing Charles Darrish into the plot was so clever that he wondered he had not thought of it before. Darrish would see to it that their legal trail was covered, a partnership with the lawyer would serve to keep Ginny at bay, and Charles might even be able to mishandle Warren Perry's defense so that the man would be convicted. Nathan complacently considered that though he had acted mostly by impulse in these three murders, no long-considered plan would have produced such salutary effects. One way or another, Nathan laughed aloud, he had got rid of the entire Larkin clan.

The laugh seemed to bring him to his senses. He wondered how long his attention had been centered on Margaret Larkin, for staring at the highway, Nathan realized that he did not know where he was.

The road was familiar, he knew he had traveled it before, but he was certain that it was not the way that led from Pensacola to Babylon. The forest was thick but the grassy shoulders were too narrow. The bed was the same width, but the gravel in the pavement was coarser. Only the moon was where he had left it. The road curved slightly; Nathan took the turn carefully, staring all the while at the moon. It seemed to move with the Lincoln, and shone through the same spot on the windshield.

Behind and ahead were no lights from other cars, and the encroaching forest was uniformly black. The other half of the four-lane highway was masked by large stands of pine on the median, and he could not see it. That meant—if he were on the right road at all—that he was only a few miles from town. He stared ahead hoping for the marker that read BABYLON 5 MILES but knew, in spite of his hope, that the familiar sign would not appear.

Nathan's heart broke and skipped. Directly in front of him were headlights. Nathan, who was in the left lane, swerved into the right, and narrowly missed a collision with the other vehicle. Its horn, blown continuously, rose in pitch as it approached, swelled, and died quickly behind him.

Nathan was sweating. He slowed to no more than fifteen miles an hour, and swore in a low voice at the driver of the other car, who had through drunkenness or stupidity driven the wrong way on a four-lane highway. Nathan hoped the man would be killed.

It was then he first noticed the yellow stripe in the middle of the road, to warn against passing. The other car had blown its horn adamantly because *he*, Nathan, had been in the wrong lane. He was not on the Babylon road at all. He was somewhere else, perhaps not even in Escambia County; he hadn't even the confidence that if he reversed direction, he would end up in Pensacola.

Where had he turned off the highway? The road still was familiar, and he had the uneasy feeling that he could identify it, if only it were day. He proceeded cautiously, scanning the black landscape for a sign or a familiar building that would identify the route. At the beginning of every turn he would hope that the moon would disappear behind the high trees of the surrounding forest, but it maintained its position, always directly ahead on the highway, leading him forward.

He pushed the buttons that raised the windows of the car and locked the doors, and turned on the radio softly to the Pensacola country-and-western station. He marked time by the progression of the songs, of which he heard only the beginning notes. The rest was lost beneath his attention to the road.

He had counted off six songs when he saw, around a small sharp curve, the white fervid light of a mercury lamp. A hundred yards further on, he came upon it, in the paved yard behind a low long brick building. This he recognized, after just a moment, as the Babylon ribbon factory. He was on the uninhabited secondary road that ran not anywhere near Pensacola, but rather from Jay, directly east of Babylon. He had not been through Jay. He tried to visualize a map of Escambia County, but could not recall any sequence of turns that would have taken him off the main Babylon highway that went south-to-north, and onto this one, that traveled east-to-west.

At any rate, he was back, and must ascribe his perplexing wandering to a fit of distraction, occasioned by a dozen oysters too many, the unaccustomed winnings at Cantonment, the discovery of the corpses of Jerry and Evelyn Larkin over the weekend. He imagined that he had been hypnotized by the moon, thrown into one of those trances that were common enough at night, on lonely stretches of road, to solitary drivers. "That's it," he whispered to himself, "I was led astray by the moon. But now the moon's brought me home safe again . . ."

Chapter 37

Nathan drove slowly along the dark deserted streets of Babylon. It was close to midnight by his watch. He had lost an hour somewhere, or the watch was wrong. The clock in the Lincoln confirmed the time. He had left Pensacola at ten o'clock, no later, and should have been home before eleven. Where had he been? He suspected that the moon had led him all over the night-black county.

Streetlamps were sporadic in this part of Babylon, among the workers' houses. The ground was flat here, and the dwellings set far back from the road. Lights burned in only a few windows. A dog that was tied to a tree barked viciously.

Coming up on the left, beyond the field where the traveling circus set up every July, was the old Babylon cemetery. Nathan remembered now that Evelyn and Jerry had been buried early in the afternoon. He had been annoyed that their corpses had been located so quickly.

Lights along the side of the cemetery that Nathan had seen in his approach suddenly winked off, all three at once. This startled him, but no less than the fact that when he looked into the sky, he found that the moon had suddenly altered its position. It had seemed to follow him all the night, pinning him against the car seat, stabbing through a point just between his eyes. Now it shone not on him at all, but over the cemetery. On the drive home, the interior of the car had been bleached with the livid white light; but as Nathan glanced around, he found the interior of the car dark. The dash dials gleamed a pale lime green.

But all along this uninhabited road, the cemetery was whitely lighted. He could count the gravestones inside. The worn lettering was deeply shadowed, and he could make out names of families in town: HIGHTOWER, READ, TOBIN, LAMB, BLUE, and LARKIN.

Nathan tried to think whether these monuments looked the same now as when he had last driven by. HIGHTOWER was as he remembered it, and so was BLUE, because he could recall attending services at each graveside. He didn't know the READ, TOBIN, and LAMB families very well, though he assumed they had their plots on this near edge of the cemetery. But Nathan was almost certain that the Larkin plot was distant, on the far side, not here. As he drove past, he automatically slowed, and stared into the cemetery. With a clarity that ought not have been possible from such a distance, he made out the upturned earth of the new double grave, and marked out the less-recently spaded ground where Margaret Larkin lay buried. Nathan suffered an alteration of perception that sometimes accompanied heavy drinking: an expansion of time, in which hundreds of discrete sensory perceptions and trains of thought crowded every passing second. Nathan tried to remember how much bourbon he had consumed at the racetrack—no more than half a pint; how many beers with supper—no more than three. It was possible, though it hadn't occurred to him before, that he was drunk.

He was frightened and determined to get home as quickly as possible. Last time the streetlamps had winked out he had smashed into something that looked like Margaret Larkin. He stepped hard on the accelerator, but to his surprise, his foot sank to the floor without resistance. The car suddenly lost power. He threw his foot on the brake, but that too was ineffectual. The car rolled forward slowly. He pulled on the emergency brake but there was no alteration in speed. He threw the Lincoln into park, but the car only rolled to an easy stop, directly in front of the gates of the cemetery.

Turning the key in the ignition gave no response. He tried the turn signal, but this didn't work. Only the headlights remained, and the interior dash lighting. Nathan punched the lights out, but was so frightened by the intensity of the moon's pale glow that he pulled the knob out again immediately. The lights did not come back on.

He pushed buttons, turned the key again and again, twisted knobs, but all to no effect. Nathan pulled the keys from the ignition and stepped quickly out of the car.

He was momentarily blinded by the light of the moon. He stared up. It was twice as large as it had been only a few moments before, and so bright it wavered in his vision, wobbling like the sun. He cast his eyes to the ground, when it appeared that the moon was yet increasing in size. He didn't dare look at it.

There was a noise behind him, a wet slap against a solid surface. Something had knocked against the brick archway of the entrance to the cemetery. Without looking around, he pressed the catch of the car door, intending to retrieve the pistol that he kept in the glove compartment. The door would not open. He thrust the key into the lock; it turned and snapped softly off. He pulled on the front door, pulled on the back, and this proving fruitless, he beat on the window, wondering if he could break the glass with his fist.

Another wet slap made him turn around.

Margaret Larkin stood solemn and unmoving beside the brick archway. The moon, triangled in the corner of Nathan's eyes, was three times its normal size, and swelling by the moment. It shone directly on the figure beneath the cemetery entrance. Her eyes and mouth were closed, but slowly they opened on unreflecting blackness, the only black things beneath the black starless sky— all else around her was washed out in a cold white light. Blacks and browns, the red brick and the green foliage, were bleached to a slightly shadowed gleaming white. Nathan looked down at himself, at his hands and clothing, and found that he alone was in deep shadow. Behind him, the untenanted land across from the cemetery was unremittingly black, as if the moon shone there not at all. He couldn't make out the colors in his shirt or his trousers, could barely trace the nails of his hands. He held his arms out to the side but no light fell upon them.

He looked up again. Margaret Larkin had moved to the other brick post. Her gown—whatever garment it was that she wore

—had somehow altered its form. He glanced at it now, trying to make out how it was constructed, but his gaze was brought irresistibly up to those empty eyes and that gaping black mouth.

Suddenly full of anger, Nathan turned a little, and ripped the radio aerial from the car. He pressed it in so that it was three feet of sturdy sharp metal, and then hurried several steps toward the white motionless figure.

Without turning, Margaret retreated into the cemetery. Nathan pursued her into the violent white landscape. Behind him he could feel the moon growing still larger and brighter. The gravestones were diffused with reflected light; even the oldest gave back the chill illumination as though they were polished mirrors. They glowed beyond their physical boundaries. The graveled paths, the rank vegetation, the trees, the planted and the artificial flowers, were a dusty gray and began to lose their definition as Nathan grimly followed Margaret Larkin's retreat among the shimmering monuments. The apparition swept backward without stumbling, without flinching or moving aside for small obstacles, with only a slight fluttering motion of the arms and hands at her sides.

Nathan held the aerial menacingly before him, and tried not to notice that his arm and its metallic extension remained in deep shadow. He passed his free hand before his face, and for a moment the white landscape was blacked out.

All the tombstones glared suddenly brighter, so bright that for a moment he lost sight of the figure of the girl. He looked behind him. The moon, enormous, featureless, with a staggering incandescence, hovered directly over the cemetery. With anything so bright so close, he felt he should have been burned, but all he felt was a creeping chill across his shoulders, a prickly dampness peeling across his neck.

Nathan tried to adjust to the glare. It wasn't entirely like light, or great intensity of light; but rather the landscape appeared an overexposed photograph. Before him, the small monuments and the gravestones were of a dazzling and undifferentiated whiteness, while the dark trees, grass, shrubs, and earth, which ought to have been black in the night, were a shining gray with speckled shadow. Behind him was the moon, frigid and enormous, imparting a dense primeval phosphorescence to everything before him. Only his own body remained in shadow.

Nathan tried to call out but could not. He had heard nothing at all since the wet slaps against the brick. They echoed in his mind now, when all else was silence. He waved the automobile aerial in front of him, and its slender black length disappeared in the whiteness. He ought to have heard its metallic swish through the air, but did not.

The dazzling white figure of Margaret Larkin anchored suddenly at the head of the freshly turned graves of her grandmother and her brother, and though Nathan moved closer, she did not retreat. The mouth and eyes opened and closed mechanically, like those of a dying fish.

Nathan lunged.

The aerial pierced the figure, and it exploded, like a burst balloon. The phosphorescent whiteness disappeared in that same instant.

All Nathan's sense was transferred from his eyes to his ears. He could see nothing; the sudden darkness blinded him as effectively as the whiteness. His feet moved forward over the grave, and he kicked aside the flowers that the dead woman had left for her granddaughter.

Beside him, on other graves, he heard crickets and cicadas. Frogs croaked in a drainage ditch nearby. He could make out the barking of the tethered dog he had passed.

He turned to stare at the moon, but found it reduced to its normal size, partially masked by the thick foliage.

Nathan stopped, stared carefully down to the earth, where Margaret Larkin, or whatever it was that impersonated her, had stood. His eyes slowly grew accustomed to the night. A slightly gleaming liquid soaked the already damp earth, forming a small flat pool; and as he looked, the dark pool drained away into the turned earth.

Nathan did not move for several seconds. He felt the tip of the aerial, which had pierced the figure; it was damp. He wiped his soiled fingers on his trousers. Around him, the tombstones shone only faintly; he could read none but the boldest inscription on the newest monuments.

When he felt that his heart was beating less quickly, when he assured himself that he had suffered only a minor hallucination brought on from the anxiety of the last couple of weeks and the liquor he had consumed, Nathan stepped over the concrete curb of the Larkin family plot and onto the narrow gravel path. He realized then that he was in a different part of the cemetery, the farthest corner, out of sight of the road; he could not have seen this tomb when he was driving by. He wondered how quickly he could find his way back to the gates.

Once again, behind him, there was a slight noise. It was no wet slap this time, but still Nathan did not turn. A rumble, felt more than heard, broke against his ankles, swelled up through his legs, and registered sickeningly in his belly.

The agitation in the earth intensified, and the sound grew with it; a grotesquely rumbling tremor in the earth behind him.

Nathan turned slowly, and stared at the graves of Evelyn and Jerry Larkin. He cried aloud, but was not reassured by the sound, as before he had been frightened by its absence. On the right-hand side of the spaded ground, the clods of earth trembled and scattered. Splits appeared in the surface, and were quickly filled with loose shaking soil. The trembling strengthened, and the earth above the grave heaved from top to bottom, as if a hellish seesaw operated beneath. When the lower end was raised, earth flew against the pink marble monument that read LARKIN; and when the upper end came up, Nathan himself was pelted with the small clods. He backed against a small monumental stone to stand out of the way of the flying earth.

He wanted to run from that place, but was transfixed by the heaving earth of the fresh grave. In his fright he told himself that one of them, Evelyn or Jerry, had not been killed. It must be Evelyn: Jerry's head was cut off. The sword through the old woman's body had been insufficient; the overturning of the car into the Styx hadn't been enough. The coroner had been fooled and Evelyn Larkin buried alive. But after her funeral, when the mourners had gone away, she had closed up her wounds. She had cleared her lungs of the black water of the Styx, and pushed open the top of her coffin. She was clawing to the surface of her premature grave.

He waited for a hand to be thrust up through the earth, a grimy thin hand that had belonged to Evelyn Larkin, that was not yet dead. But it was no hand that appeared. The surface of the coffin, with the glint of a metallic handle on the lower end, broke the surface only a few feet from where Nathan stood. The coffin had been rocking itself to the surface of the grave.

He turned to run, but was arrested by a ripping, earth-muffled explosion behind him. He threw his hands over his face. The coffin itself had exploded; splinters and slats of wood, fragments of satin and gleaming hardware rained down all around him. He was knocked painfully in the forehead by a long splinter of painted board.

He staggered forward, teetered on the edge of the open hole. At the bottom of the space, torn out of the earth by the emerging coffin, he could see the side of the second casket, itself beginning to shake and worry itself upward.

The first coffin had exploded, had destroyed itself, and the body inside with it; and now the second was to follow suit. Nathan whirled about with the intention of running all the way across town, without pause, until he had reached his own home. Ben would be waiting up for him.

He had taken two shaky steps forward, when he was knocked solidly to the ground by a large dead weight falling across his shoulders. His first thought as he raised himself dazed was that the coffin—had there been a bomb inside?—had broken a branch of the live oak that stretched above. To lift himself from the ground he placed one hand firmly to the earth, but it pressed revoltingly down on another, thin and lifeless.

Nathan scrambled away. Turning, he saw the strangely reposed face of Evelyn Larkin only a few feet away. Her body lay twisted, in a soiled white shift, at the edge of the grave. The corpse, whole despite the explosion, had evidently caught for a few moments in the branches of the tree, and then dropped down upon him. Three dozen half-digested oysters boiled up out of Nathan's stomach.

He pulled himself farther away, found he had twisted his ankle painfully. He stuttered, saying nothing, not knowing what he had intended to speak, when there was only the dead woman to hear him.

Behind the old woman's corpse, the clods of earth above the other grave had begun to tremble.

"No!" cried Nathan, but he stared away from the grave, at the corpse of the old woman. A thin bile of black water bubbled out of her mouth onto the earth. He thought he could make out his name in the disgusting gurgle.

Nathan backed away, stumbling over a low concrete curbing surrounding a family plot. He wanted to stand and run, but remained as he was, in the sharp grass above an old sunken grave. The old woman's corpse was sprawled in a patch of bare earth littered with the fragments of her coffin.

The eyes of the corpse struggled to open. Nathan realized that they had been sutured shut by the undertaker. He watched the flesh of the lids as they were torn raggedly apart. The black pupils, reflecting the moon, gazed at Nathan.

The mouth clamped open and shut. More black water spilled out onto the black earth. Slowly, in a motion that was wholly uncharacteristic of Evelyn Larkin in life, the entire body trembled into motion, undulating with a ghastly sinewy grace. It had lain on its side, and now began to snake toward him, curving bonelessly through the dank weeds. The head arched back, and that terrible stare was directed away, but a second later, the head was thrown forward again hugging the earth, to look on him with calm malevolency. Black water flowed intermittently from the mouth, and the lean frail corpse whispered his name, ever more distinctly, as if learning to speak again.

Nathan scurried crablike away, his hands scraped by sharp stones and nettling vegetation. This close to the ground, he could feel the second coffin as it continued to work its way to the surface. Behind the sinuous advancing corpse of the old woman, Nathan saw the now violent seesaw motion of the ground above Jerry Larkin's casket.

Evelyn Larkin rose from the earth in a graceful spiral, a motion that was at once beautiful and hideous, because no one living had ever moved so.

Entranced, Nathan rose also. Evelyn Larkin, or rather her ambulatory remains, began to turn softly, in an easeful slow spin, her arms bent at the elbows and her hands folded lightly before her. Her head was tilted at a pleasing, almost coy angle; the linen grave-gown dropped in thick folds to the earth. Her bare feet turned without friction on the uneven ground. She would have seemed a fine picture of an old woman, dreaming in the light of the moon, had it not been for the damp earth that stained her grave clothes, for the torn flesh about her eyes, for the impure water that still poured from her mouth, blackening her chin and neck.

Nathan rushed forward, and pushed the corpse violently toward the open grave. His hands sank sickeningly into the soft flesh, and almost to his surprise, Evelyn Larkin's body was pitched backward. A second, less powerful shove knocked it over into the gaping hole. It lay still at the bottom. The open eyes stared up at Nathan, and black water spilled between the color-less lips that syllabled his name. But just to the side, and shaking clods of earth over the old woman's corpse, the second coffin broke through the surface of the earth. Nathan turned and ran.

He reached the cemetery gates, and heard behind him an-other explosion. The second coffin had freed itself, and in a few moments more, Jerry Larkin's corpse, animated, would be in sliding pursuit.

The door of the Lincoln stood open. The key he was sure he had broken in the door was in the ignition. He slammed the door shut and turned the key, staring all the while into the blackness of the graveyard. Not bothering to look ahead of him, Nathan slammed his foot on the accelerator, and barreled off in the direc-tion of John Glenn Avenue. Out of the corner of his eye, he had caught sight of an arm, thin and black-sleeved, reaching around the brick post of the cemetery gates.

PART VII

PRECARIOUS SAFETY

Chapter 38

Speeding toward his home from the horror in the cemetery, Nathan hadn't even the presence of mind to work out whether it had been real or imagined. His fright had been genuine, and he couldn't at first think beyond that. His mind whirled not on the animated menacing corpse of Evelyn Larkin, but flickered with images of other murders he might commit. He thought of strangling his father in his bed, drowning Ben in the pool, running down Ted Hale in front of the town hall, hanging Belinda from one of the ornamental pines on the patio. He had no motive for any of these crimes, but he laughed aloud thinking of the relief they would bring him. With all of them dead, he would be rich and untroubled.

Over and again, as the wheels spun down the pavement of Babylon's dark streets, the trembling rich images clicked across his mind, silent and bright and richly colored as a slide show in a darkened room: his father with bulging eyes and wagging black tongue, his brother listing beneath the surface of the water, the sheriff's broken body beneath the Lincoln, the gentle shadow Belinda's hanging corpse cast against the side of the house.

Nathan pulled the car into the lighted garage. He took the key from the ignition and held it close before his face. Outside the cemetery he remembered breaking the key in the lock; the key was whole now. Obviously it had never been broken; obviously then, all had been imagined.

He swung out of the car, ran to the edge of the garage, and swatted out the light. Above, in the black starry sky, the moon seemed absurdly gray and small; but it also appeared exactly the right size, and Nathan told himself that it had never been any larger than it was now, had never shone white and icy upon his back.

The episode was a mental fiction from beginning to end, or rather, only the beginning was real. He had taken a wrong turn somewhere in Pensacola; concentrating so on all that had transpired in the last two weeks, he had not noticed his mistake for some while. His discomposure on looking up and thinking himself lost had thrown him into a kind of trance, in which he had imagined—it was best not to think now of what he had imagined.

Nathan entered his house the back way, and was disturbed that Ben was in neither the den nor his own room. But drawn to his father's wing of the house by the sound of a television, Nathan was very much surprised to find his brother and his father watching Johnny Carson together.

The old man glanced at Nathan suspiciously, and greeted him with an almost imperceptible nod. Ben looked up sheepishly, and said: "Hey, Nathan, Daddy and I was just wondering when you would get back—"

"No we weren't," said James Redfield.

"—and I've been keeping Daddy company all the evening, we've been watching television and talking—"

"Nathan," said James Redfield: "Soon as it was dark, and 'fore Nina had even gone home, Ben came in here with a TV-tray and his supper on it, and sat down, and hasn't hardly got up since except to go to the bathroom, and I asked him what he meant by it, and he said—"

"Daddy!" protested Ben: "I didn't mean anything by it! Like I said, I was just coming in here to keep you company."

"Then why haven't you kept me company in the last ten years, that's what I'd like to know!" cried the old man. "Why are you suddenly starting up on it now?"

"Daddy," said Nathan, actually pleased with this argument, for it brought him further away from that silence in the cemetery, just as the vividly colored television screen provided a great and welcome contrast to the harsh expansive whiteness that had ruptured his mind: "Daddy, I don't think Ben had a ulterior motive in coming in here, just like I don't. We just thought you might want some company. But you don't really mind if we just sit down and watch a little TV with you, do you?"

"I s'pose not," said the old man crossly, and leaned back on his pillows. It was apparent that he still did not trust his sons to have come to his room without some deviousness in their minds, and that he was angry with himself for not being able to find it out.

Ben glanced at Nathan thankfully for backing him up, but Nathan nodded blandly in reply. Nathan realized that Ben had gone to his father's room because he was frightened of remaining alone. Since the deaths of Evelyn and Jerry Larkin, Ben had rarely left the house. He worried constantly that his part in the deaths of the grandmother and grandson would be discovered, and it required all his courage just to answer the phone during the day.

He hid whenever the doorbell rang, demanding that Nina say that nobody was at home. Every night he required of Nathan the reassurance that no one in town suspected them of the murders, and that there was no possible way to connect them with the overturned automobile at the bottom of the Styx. He had been out of his wits when he found that the Larkins' station wagon was lifted out of the river, but had been somewhat relieved by Warren Perry's arrest, for that proved that Ted Hale had no idea what had really happened. At the same time, Ben was sorry for Warren Perry, but reflected that since the schoolteacher didn't do it, he probably wouldn't be convicted of the crime. Ben had it in his head that the sword was only circumstantial evidence, and insufficient grounds for strapping Warren into the electric chair.

Ben Redfield was a man of small intelligence and he was fearful, nervous, and prone to whine. It was unlikely—and Nathan knew it—that Ben could hold up under the pressure of daily exposure to the world outside that air-conditioned house. Nathan was certain, for instance, that if he had allowed his brother to work for a few hours in the bank each day, Ben would begin to imagine that all and sundry knew of his guilt: the other tellers, the customers, the children who passed on the sidewalk and peered in through the plate glass window. It would be only days before Ben, breaking beneath this unsubstantial persecution, would confess all to Ted Hale. But kept inside, Ben moved hour to hour, protected and unbothered. He watched television, ate when and whatever Nina cooked, and swam in the pool. Nathan had even given him permission to go to the racetrack alone, so long as he promised not to lose more than twenty-five dollars, but Ben had refused to travel without his brother.

For his own peace of mind, Nathan had to assume that Ben would gradually overcome this nervousness, and in his unconquerable simplicity grow less apprehensive with the passing days. In hope of abetting this process, Nathan had, after the first night, not allowed his brother to sleep on the cot at the foot of his bed.

Tonight, however, when Johnny Carson was over and the two sons had taken leave of their bewildered father, Nathan said: "Ben, why don't you sleep in my room? The rollaway's still set up in there."

Ben knew better than to ask a reason for his brother's change of heart. He nodded with unvoiced thanks. But a few moments later, when they came to the door of Nathan's room, he ventured to say: "Nobody called. Nobody came by. Nobody called while you were gone, Nathan."

"That's good," said Nathan soothingly. "Listen, Ben, everything's gone be all right. Warren Perry's in jail, and all the 'tention in this town is focused on him now. There's no reason for anybody to look at us, no reason in the world. They'll probably let him go free, 'cause after all, he didn't do it, though I have to admit it'd be a lot better for us if they *did* convict him. But even if he does get off, they're not gone be coming around here after us. There's no reason for 'em to, Ben."

Ben could never hear enough of such reassurance.

"You'll be all right," said Nathan: "You'll come out of this. In another week, you won't ever remember what really did happen. You'll be thinking like everybody else in town, that it was Warren Perry who killed that old woman and Jerry Larkin."

"You think so?" said Ben hopefully.

Though having cause for fitful nightmarish slumber, the brothers slept peacefully that night, each comforted by the other's presence.

The following morning, they were both wakened by Nathan's alarm. Nathan sat up in bed, lighted a cigarette, and said to his brother, who turned groggily on his pillow, "Listen Ben, why don't we go down to Navarre for a couple of days, get away from here, it'll do us both good, and by the time we get back—everything'll be different. We'll *feel* different. You and I haven't gotten off together in a great long while."

Ben sat up suddenly. He could not recall when last his brother had spoken so affectionately to him, or made any invitation so ungrudgingly. "Nathan," he said quietly, repressing his excitement, "that sounds real good to me, but you know we cain't leave Daddy alone."

"I'll talk to Daddy this morning. He won't care if we go, so long as we get somebody to stay here while we're gone. We can see if Nina will stay, and if she cain't, maybe Ted'll let Belinda come over. Daddy'd just love to have a couple of days with Miss Pie all to himself. Hell, I'll drive up to Atmore and hire a nurse out of the hospital if that's what it takes. I got to get out of this town for a couple of days, and that's that."

"When you think we can leave?"

"I don't see why we couldn't go this afternoon. I got a little work that's got to be done at the bank this morning, and then I can probably get away. I'm gone go talk to Daddy."

James Redfield was willing to allow his sons to go off. His acceptance, however, was conditional upon either of the females agreeing to sleep over. He'd not be left alone in the house. In fact, he added at the end, he had just as soon they moved away forever, so long as they left Nina and Miss Pie behind, who were the only real comforts of his life.

Nina had arrived by the time that Nathan was finished with his father. Nathan offered her fifty dollars to stay the two nights. The black woman looked quizzically at him for a moment, wondering at the importance of the trip that would prompt such liberal persuasion. She agreed, saying: "You don't think I'd leave Mr. Red alone, do you—by himself, when you two go gallavanting off?" At Nathan's behest, she went directly to James Redfield's room, to tell him that she would stay with him until Nathan and Ben returned from the beach.

"When they coming back?" said James Redfield, with high-pitched curiosity.

"Thursday, Mr. Red." She paused: "You know what too, Mr. Red?"

"What?"

"Mr. Nathan told me he was gone give me fifty dollars to stay with you."

James Redfield considered this darkly. "Why you suppose . . ."

"I don't know," mused Nina. "They say they going down to Navarre. I s'pose they are. I don't know where else they might be going . . ."

Her well-understood inference was that Nathan and Ben Redfield were going anywhere on earth but Navarre.

"Nina," said James Redfield, in a lilting wheeze: "Those two boys were in here with me last night watching TV, and you know how long it's been since they did *that*. I kept expecting 'em to say something bad, to tell me that the bank was folding, or that you had gotten married and run off to Apalachicola, but they didn't say a word. I didn't like having 'em in here either—they made me nervous. I wanted you or Miss Pie in here with me—protecting me. I don't know where those two boys are going either, Nina. Just let 'em go, maybe then you and I can have a little peace around here."

Chapter 39

The business that Nathan Redfield had to get out of the way at the bank that Tuesday morning pertained to the acquisition of the Larkin blueberry property. On the Sunday previous, while Evelyn and Jerry Larkin lay naked on adjoining tables at the funeral home south of town, Nathan had been alone in the bank, working with the posting machine to alter the record of loan payments made by the Larkins over the past twelve months. The falsified card showed that Evelyn Larkin had failed to pay anything at all over the last seven months, and before that had made but partial payments on three occasions. Evelyn's copy of the card had been secured by Charles Darrish on Saturday night, immediately after he had heard of the deaths of the old woman and her grandson. His wife Ginny had accommodatingly informed him where Evelyn had kept all her records, and as her executor, nothing was more natural in the world than that he should ride out to the unprotected house and take all important papers into his custody, against the possible incursion of thieves and vandals. He understood then what Ted Hale had meant when he said that the house was troubled with damp rot.

Charles Darrish assured Nathan that the original loan card was destroyed, and Nathan had prepared another in its place, and turned it over to the lawyer. This was to be used only in extremity, for it wouldn't stand up under close inspection; anyone who examined it carefully would see that the entries had been printed up all at one time, though on two machines for contrast. But Nathan so little considered that subterfuge would be needed at all, that he prided himself on being even this circumspect.

The cards had been substituted, and to balance the books, Nathan had credited the payments he had subtracted from the Larkins to his own mortgage on the condominium at Navarre. It was necessary now however that he have certain papers drawn up, by the regular secretary at the bank, for the appropriation of the property. This must be accomplished anonymously if possible, and though Nathan stood over Mrs. Roland's shoulder, and watched carefully the typing, his name appeared on none of the documents.

He hurried the woman through, and carried the papers himself to Charles Darrish's office. He was back in the bank, thoroughly satisfied with himself, by eleven o'clock. Nathan had worried a little how Charles Darrish would take the deaths of the Larkins, but if the man suspected anything, he said nothing at all, and guarded himself so well, that he did not betray even the suppression of his suspicions.

Nathan had commented warily and briefly that the strange deaths fell right into line with their plans, making everything much easier; and that now their consciences need not even snag on the possibility that they were doing the old woman out of money rightfully hers.

"Yes," replied Darrish: "All this is easier now. It can all go quieter now that they're—not here any more."

Nathan said nothing at all to this, and Charles Darrish went on after a moment: "Nathan," he smiled and shut his eyes tight: "You go on down to Navarre just the way you planned. Take Ben like you said, and just sit still a couple of days. Don't call—"

"There's no phone," said Nathan.

Darrish nodded, and went on: "—and I'll take care of everything here. Everything can proceed. In a couple of weeks, all this will go through. I just want to put one more step between you and me and the company in Mobile, just to make sure that there's no way for somebody to stumble on the fact that it's you and me that owns it. I'm gone make a little trip to Atlanta. I'm gone fly up there tomorrow, and see what I can arrange. Probably I'll have good news for you by the time that you're back. Why don't you come back on Thursday sometime, planning to have dinner with Ginny and me? We'll have a little dinner, just the four of us, down at the White Horse. Now that you and I are going to be partners, in this and maybe other things too, who knows?—you and Ginny ought to make it up between you. I'm taking her with me tomorrow, let her go shopping, let her buy all the livelong day while I'm going about my business, and I'll take it up with her then."

Nathan nodded and smiled blandly: "I'd like that. You're right: Ginny and I ought to make it up, though I cain't really say that there was anything that much that was keeping us apart. But nobody's gone get hurt with what you and I are putting through right now, and Ginny's gone benefit from it too."

In all Nathan's dealings now, his aim was to discourage trouble. He had no particular wish to make it up with Charles's wife, for his enmity with Ginny had been long and satisfying, but it was possible she might someday be able to do him harm in these matters. Just so, he had asked Ben to accompany him to Navarre, not simply because Nathan was reluctant to be alone, but also that he might watch over his nervous younger brother.

What Nathan decided, on the walk from Darrish's office back to the CP&M, was that the lawyer knew something, suspected a great deal more, but had determined merely to concentrate on the business portion of the conspiracy—for conspiracy it certainly was—and to limit his guilt to only that part. What else had been done he consigned to Nathan's conscience and Nathan's culpability. Nathan knew that the man was only protecting himself by not trying to find anything else out, and this selfish motive re- assured the banker as no other would.

Nathan sat at his desk, signed a sheaf of drafts for the First National Bank in Pensacola, dictated three short letters required by the arrival of the morning mail, and then talked with Mrs. Roland concerning his absence over the next few days.

At the last, Nathan went through the files in his desk, to make sure that he had replaced everything that had to do with the Lar- kins, and that no scrap of paper remained that might be aligned with the altered records.

He slammed the drawer shut with a smile, turned the key in the lock, and stood out of the chair, lifting his hand in general farewell. But he stopped with a choked laugh of astonishment. Across the mahogany railing, at the end of the line of customers before the single open teller's window, a woman was standing in the middle of a puddle of water on the carpet.

"What is—" he cried in a small amazed voice, thinking that the roof had leaked there, without anyone having noticed. But he glanced at the ceiling above that spot, and the plaster was not discolored.

Someone had spilled something and not cleaned it up, but who had been dragging a bucket of water across the floor?

Nathan stared; the pool grew slightly larger, as if the water were pouring off the woman's body onto the floor. The thought even crossed Nathan's mind that she had failed to hold in her urine, and now was determined to ignore her misfortune with as much dignity as possible.

Nathan leaned forward over the desk, wondering how best to approach the woman, whether to call out, or tap her on the shoulder discreetly. Just as Nathan was turning to Mrs. Roland, from the corner of his eye he saw the woman in line turn her head toward him, smiling.

It was Evelyn Larkin. Her mouth was split in a meaningless grin, and black water spilled out of it, staining her featureless white shift, and splashing into the small pool about her bare feet.

Her mouth widened and contracted, and the water spilled faster.

Nathan staggered to the mahogany railing and leaned over it. Evelyn was no more than five feet away. She stood still with her back to him, but her head was twisted over her shoulder, and she stared and grinned.

"Get out of here!" Nathan whispered hoarsely.

Maintaining her mocking grin, Evelyn Larkin turned her head away, and faced forward to the man standing before her in the line. He had turned to stare at Nathan, and did not apparently notice that he stood beside a rotting corpse.

Nathan stepped awkwardly over the railing, grabbed the woman by the shoulders. Her flesh yielded beneath his grasp as it had the night before in the cemetery and he was sickened. Despite his disgust he swung her around to face him.

She grinned, and opened her mouth in a wide circle O. She laughed shortly, but the sound was cut. He stared into her mouth, and saw that black space fill suddenly with blood, welling up from the throat, a scarlet spring in that livid bloodless face. She spat it up all over him.

He drew back. She laughed again. Her mouth filled once more with the thick blood, and she spat in his face so that he was blinded by it.

Nathan wiped the noisome blood from his eyes, and screamed, "Goddamn! Goddamn you back to hell!"

He looked up into the frightened face of Annie-Leigh Hooker.

"Annie-Leigh—" he cried, "Annie-Leigh, I thought you—"

"Thought what!" she demanded. She advanced on him, now angry, embarrassed for his having yelled at her, cursed her, swung her around by the shoulders. "I don't know what you think you're doing! I come in here wanting to deposit a hundred and forty-seven dollars even, and you start yelling at me, and—"

"Annie-Leigh," Nathan pleaded, "listen, I'm sorry, I—" He was suddenly aware that he was being watched by everyone in the bank. There was no blood on him.

"Annie-Leigh," he began again, in a low voice that he tried hard to control, "I apologize. I think I've got a fever. It had nothing to do with you. I was having an hallucination of some kind, because—"

"Well," said Annie-Leigh severely: "You better go to the doctor about it right now, or you're not gone have any customers left. What do you do to people who want to take their money *out?!*"

Nathan rushed from the bank, and Annie-Leigh remained half an hour longer there, surrounded by the employees who apologized for Nathan, and gossiped about what might have brought on the attack. Eventually all agreed that it was but a momentary aberration, and that it had nothing to do with Annie-Leigh. Nathan ought to go to see a doctor, he ought to take a long rest, he ought to bribe everybody in town to keep his father from finding out that he had assaulted a customer in the main lobby of the CP&M.

Though she had been badly frightened at the time, by that afternoon Annie-Leigh was proud of the morning's mishap, because for once she was not only a relayer, but the subject of Babylon's hottest gossip. Annie-Leigh held court at the sporting goods store, and people in Babylon who couldn't tell a golf ball from a pup tent came in to hear how Nathan Redfield had threatened her with immediate death by strangulation while she was waiting in line, with a deposit slip already filled out, in the middle of the CP&M bank.

At four o'clock, Jay Neal dropped over from the sheriff's office with the perplexing news that during the night, someone had dug up and stolen the corpses of Evelyn Larkin and her grandson Jerry, buried only the previous day. The perpetrators, whether medical students or pranksters, had unaccountably destroyed the coffins afterward and left them strewn over half the cemetery.

Chapter 40

Two days served both to repair and refresh Nathan and Ben Redfield. The brothers spent a lazy quiet time of it in their condominium on the beach. Because it was the middle of the week, only one other apartment was occupied, and that by three Eastern Airlines stewardesses. The women came over the second night for drinks, and Nathan and Ben were so excited by their company, that although nothing more came of the evening, they were as pleased as if they had waked the next morning with all three in the bed between them.

At Navarre the sand is as white as sand may be. The vegetation is sparse, sharp sea grasses that make a desultory effort to hold down the shifting high dunes. This end of narrow snakelike Santa Rosa Island is little inhabited, and the mainland only a few hundred yards distant, is thick subtropical forest. Navarre has no permanent inhabitant, and even on July fourth weekend, no more than a hundred persons can be found in the few dozen houses that make up the unincorporated summer community.

The brothers' bedroom was on the second floor, and on one side they could see the soft blue water of Choctawhatchee Bay, nominally a freshwater basin, and on the other the fine green water of the Gulf of Mexico, sticky and clear and breaking all night long in noisy whitecaps. The moon was reflected off the Gulf.

The sky was wide and low and always bright, and they saw not a single cloud all the while they were there. It was a fine and important change from Babylon, where all water stagnates, and the sky is masked by crowding tall pines. The Larkins were dead, and would never bother them again.

Ben was reassured by his brother's constant proximity, and by their distance from Babylon; but he dreaded returning and often looked out the window, expecting Ted Hale's car to drive up with two pairs of cuffs dangling from the rearview mirror. Ben lay on the beach in the same position as he lay beside the pool at home; the sun beat the thoughts out of his head so that he hadn't the presence of mind to be fearful of the future.

Nathan's thoughts and evasions were more complex. He was troubled by what he termed "what he thought he had seen": the watery ghost of Margaret Larkin, and the animated corpse of her grandmother. He didn't dare call these visions up directly.

He told himself that he had been drinking too much over the past couple of years, and that this excess, combined with the strain of the past few weeks, had tripped an imaginative switch in his brain, to produce the phantoms. He thought he was being honest with himself in declaring that he hadn't a guilty conscience, that he did not feel upset that he had deliberately murdered three persons, and judged that he felt no worse now than he had about Jim and JoAnn Larkin fifteen years back.

In the cemetery he had been alone with the ghosts. He had been alone on the streets of Babylon when Margaret Larkin had exploded against the windshield of the Lincoln. These incidents were doubtless the residue of some long night of drinking six months back—nothing more. But some more recent night of drinking had triggered the stronger and more dangerous reaction, the transformation of Annie-Leigh Hooker into the corpse of Evelyn Larkin—more dangerous because it had happened in public.

Certainly he wasn't actually haunted; he couldn't admit for a moment that the ghosts were real. Rather than leaving the question there, on whether they were genuine or imaginary, he constrained himself to wonder only how long he would be inflicted with these terrible visions. He feared that he would betray himself, for though convinced that they were false and unsubstantial images, he might still be surprised by the sudden reappearance of Margaret or Evelyn Larkin in some populated place. His sole consolation was that he wasn't yet troubled by Jerry.

Nathan concluded by telling himself that he must simply stare down any apparition until it disappeared or shifted back into its proper form.

As part of this resolution to deal bravely with subsequent appearances of the murdered family, in whatever place they showed themselves, Nathan drank only beer in his time at Navarre. In explanation, he told Ben that he had lost his taste for hard liquor.

Late in the night, Nathan and Ben walked up and down the empty beach, toeing the tide line, and talked of all the things they'd do when their father was dead; and Nathan even told Ben some details of his intimacy with Belinda Hale. Ben, who had nothing of comparable significance to confide in return, merely expressed over and over his intention to say nothing about anything to anybody as long as he lived.

It was only when the nearly full moon seemed to expand a little when he brushed his eyes across it, that Nathan turned to go inside again. He asked Ben how many beers he had drunk, so that he might stop short of that number in future.

The following afternoon, Thursday, they carefully locked the condominium, and drove back to Babylon. The road all the way lay through thick forest, and neither brother said much. Both were occupied in repeating small personal rosaries of courage that they hoped would preserve them through to the end of all this unfortunate business.

Chapter 41

Nathan and Ben found all in Babylon as they had left it. Nina remained at the house after their return only long enough to gather all their clothing, stiff with sand and seawater and salt air, and throw it into the washing machine. Belinda Hale came out of their father's room, and suggested that they might both want to step in and speak to the old man.

Belinda preceded them, and went to her chair at Mr. Red's side. Nathan and Ben stood awkwardly in the doorway. "Hey, Daddy," they both said.

"Why you back so soon?" said Mr. Red, in a high-pitched whine.

"Daddy," said Nathan, attempting a little joke: "We just didn't think that you could do without us, and that's the truth."

"It's not the truth," said the old man: "You could at least have stayed away until Sunday. Miss Pie and Nina and me were having the time of our lives, weren't we, Miss Pie?"

"We sure were!" cried Belinda vehemently.

"Well, Daddy, we sure don't want to interfere with your pleasure, not at any time, so Ben and I'll just leave you alone to yourself with Belinda. Ben and I are having supper out tonight anyway, with—guess who?"

"Who?" shouted the old man, looking away.

"With Charles and Ginny!" blurted Ben, who hadn't spoken yet to his father, and felt that he ought to say something to him before they left the room.

Mr. Red looked up slowly, and glanced at his two sons. Then turning to Belinda, he said, as if they weren't there: "What I want to know, Miss Pie, is whose idea this supper is. I don't believe Ginny and Nathan have sat down at the same table since President Kennedy got 'ssasinated. You think you could find out?"

Belinda, not a bit disturbed by this impolite indirection, looked up at Nathan and said: "Nathan, your daddy—"

"I heard him," said Nathan. "Daddy," he said, with some little exasperation: "You can ask me a question direct and still have hope of getting it answered. You can ask me direct, and I will tell you that Charles Darrish is looking for a reconciliation between Ginny and me, and I for one am all for it. We don't have much kin in this town, we got so little it hurts, in fact, and it just doesn't make sense any more for Ginny and me to be dancing the warpath around each other like we have been."

James Redfield turned sourly away. "Well go on then. You having dinner over at Ginny's house?"

"No, Daddy," said Nathan: "We are meeting on neutral territory, down at the White Horse in just about thirty minutes, and I will give her your loving regards."

Half an hour later, Ben and Nathan were seated in the main dining room of the White Horse. They had been given the best table, across from the bar, in the bay window that looked out over the gravel parking lot. As they sipped at their beers, and talked of nothing, the sun went down on the other side of the building. The brief southern twilight passed before the waiter could refill their glasses.

The White Horse was the only restaurant in Babylon with any claim to quality. In laminated plastic, tacked beside the entrance, were two reviews it had received in the past eight years in Sunday editions of the Pensacola *News-Journal*. Both, in similar language by the same reporter, called the White Horse the best restaurant in the northern part of the county, well worth the drive up from Pensacola.

The White Horse was owned by Calvin McAndrew, and it would have made him rich if he had not spent every afternoon at the Cantonment dog track. His wife acted as hostess and waitress, and invariably dressed in a deep purple; their son John, in Belinda's class in high school, had been waiter for the past three years, and the twenty-one-year-old unmarried daughter was cashier. No one could remember having seen Jean McAndrew standing up, or in fact anywhere else but behind the register by the doorway. She knew everybody who came into the restaurant, and she knew no one else; and the joke in Babylon was that Jean McAndrew didn't have any legs.

Charles and Ginny were not more than ten minutes late, and Ginny apologized with wreathing pink smiles, and carefully explained that none of the clocks in the house worked on the nights around the full moon, and that she was certain that it all had something to do with the intensity of the moonshine on the gears and springs.

Ginny had particular smiles for Nathan that evening, and through their first two drinks did not even allude to the trouble that had been between them for more than fifteen years; but after they had all pondered the menu as if they did not know it by heart, and ordered what each of them always ordered at the White Horse, Ginny turned and laid her soft powdered hand atop Ben's. "You know, I am so ashamed of myself, I just lie awake in the bed at night, thinking how I've neglected you, Ben."

Ben laughed nervously, but it was clear to Nathan and Charles that Ginny was not talking at all about Ben, but about Nathan. It was easier and less embarrassing for them all if Ginny directed her remarks to the younger simpler man, the man with whom she had *not* been warring.

Ben, who had some idea that this was all a sham, at least on his brother's part, was afraid that Ginny's attentions to him would bring down Nathan's wrath, and he tried to draw back. But Nathan, directly across the table, signaled for Ben to allow Ginny's hand to remain, and so he suffered himself to be apologized to.

"Ben," said Ginny: "I just don't know what we're going to do with you. You're a grown man, and you don't do a thing in this world. Nathan and I are just going to have to put our heads together and find something that you're good at."

"All we need," laughed Nathan, "is somebody to pay him for lying around in the sun, 'cause he's awful good at that."

Charles and Ginny laughed too, and Ben blushed.

And so the evening continued, much talk being expended on

Ben and his general incompetence at anything productive, about the felicities of the condominium at Navarre (which Ginny admitted she coveted), about how big and busy Atlanta had become. At the broaching of the last subject, Charles nodded deftly to Nathan. Nathan interpreted this nod as a signal that all had gone well with their plans for the acquisition of the Larkin blueberry property. Two subjects were not brought up: Ginny and Nathan's past differences, and Warren Perry in jail for the deaths of the Larkins. Each had his reasons for avoiding the latter topic.

In relief that the evening was going well, and buoyed by Charles's indication that their project had prospered in Atlanta, Nathan had ignored his own injunction against hard liquor, and with Ginny and Charles switched to vodka martinis before dinner, and continued with the same to accompany his deep-fried seafood platter. The whole table was merry and voluble by the time their plates were taken away, and they had requested the memorized menus again, so that they might determine dessert.

The quartet, suddenly silent among the other diners in the place, stared at the menus before them but Nathan, for drunkenness, wasn't at first able to concentrate on the list of pies and shortcakes and ice creams. His back was to the rest of the room, and he faced Ben, seated deep in the bay window. John McAndrew stood behind Nathan, his pad raised and his pencil poised, silently urging the table on, for he had other customers. Ginny had spoken, and Nathan heard the young man scribbling across the pad. Ben spoke then, and Nathan was just at the point of deciding whether to go with the McAndrew's Special Strawberry Shortcake or McAndrew's Supreme Apple Pie à la Mode, when a drop of liquid splashed on his menu. It was thin watery blood, quickly blotted into the porous paper.

He looked quickly up, in the process overturning his water glass. At his side, and bending forward slowly from the waist, stood Jerry Larkin. Discolored blood dripped unrhythmically from a clumsily sutured gash across his neck. Jerry grinned. His mouth welled with black water that seeped out over his chin. His battered face was a colorless gray, and one cheek was smeared with graveyard soil. He was dressed in an ill-fitting brown suit with a white shirt beneath, stained and damp at the collar with blood. Jerry's bare feet, black with mire, were fixed in a spreading dark puddle of black water and blood on the red carpet.

While the others fussed with the overturned water, Nathan gripped the edges of his chair and told himself over and over that this was an apparition. Jerry Larkin's corpse, with the head sewed badly on by the undertaker, was only the accustomed waiter, John McAndrew, impatient for his order. John McAndrew's hands were not stained with blood and black water. The overwhelming damp stench that radiated from the upright corpse was only another trick of Nathan's senses. He tried to will Jerry away, and return John McAndrew to his place.

Jerry Larkin turned his grinning head slowly. Nathan stared at the straining sutures. Afraid they would break and the head plunge into his lap, he drove his chair back. "Excuse me . . ." he stammered.

Still sitting, he glanced at the three faces at the table, which stared back at him in immobile alarm. Nathan then remembered something strangely irrelevant: That, since Ginny and Charles had been out of town, they probably had not heard of the assault on Annie-Leigh Hooker.

In that same freezing moment, he wondered if Belinda knew of it, whether his father had found out; tried to imagine what the town was saying now about the attack, and how Ed Geiger had reported it. Nathan decided he wouldn't go back to work for a while, would take a leave of absence from the bank for a much-needed rest. Nathan turned his head and Jerry still grinned at him. The sutured lids, like Evelyn's, had been torn unevenly apart and loose flaps of flesh, the upper lids, hung attached to the fold of skin beneath the eyes. The corpse's stare was insolent and horrifying. The water with grainy black impurities continued to spill out of his mouth.

Nathan rose with an inarticulate stammer. The chair fell behind him. He stood unsteadily, staring at Jerry still, trying to think what actions or what words would dissolve the vision.

The pad and pencil Jerry's corpse held in its bloodless swollen hands dropped to the floor. With slow deliberateness, those hands that stank of earth and corruption rose and cupped the bruised chin beneath the grinning mouth. Dead Jerry Larkin pushed upward with slowly gathered force.

Nathan stared with dismal fascination at the gash that circled the neck. The sutures strained. The thin discolored blood spilled out faster.

One by one the sutures snapped. Others were pulled out as thread is ripped from the hem of a dress.

Jerry's two upraised hands rocked the severing head back and forth until it was torn free of the trunk. The eyes continued their insolent calm stare, the grainy water spilled out over the protruding black tongue. The corpse raised the head high, as if in triumph; but after a motionless pause, the body collapsed in a heap across Nathan's vacated chair. The head spilled forward, landed with a loathsome thud on the carpet and rolled beneath an unoccupied table.

Nathan stared wildly around. Eyes in the restaurant turned toward him. He realized tremulously then that no one else was seeing what he saw. He turned back quickly, hoping to find John McAndrew in his accustomed place by the table, but the headless corpse, draining blood and black water from the severed neck onto the carpet, still lay across his chair.

Nathan turned, resolved to get out of the White Horse as quickly as possible. The hostess moved toward him, Mrs. McAndrew in her close-fitting purple dress. He feinted to the right, in hope of reaching the door before she stopped him, and in the corner of his eye, he saw the arms of the purple dress raised in alarm.

The dress was no longer purple but a dingy gray. Nathan looked up: It was Evelyn Larkin advancing toward him, her mouth and eyes opened wide, grinning as Jerry had grinned. Black water poured from her mouth too, and she stained the carpet as she walked.

Nathan threw his hand over his mouth and whirled toward the door. Jean McAndrew had risen from her chair behind the cash register, and blocked his path.

No one in the restaurant saw that he was being pursued by the attenuated corpse of an old woman, who threaded her dripping way among the tables of diners.

It wasn't the cash register girl at all, but Margaret Larkin, with poised gravity, moving slowly and with infinite grace, between him and the door. Under the dim spotlight overhead, Nathan could see now that she was made of water, the same grainy black liquid that poured out of the corpses' mouths. The impurities whirled over her body and dress alike, and gathered more densely at the extremities, so that her hands and feet were almost black with them, while her head remained pale by comparison.

She opened her mouth wide as Nathan came nearer, as if to draw him inside it. The black minute filings swam more quickly over her body and she shimmered in the weak light.

He raised his hand to strike her, but in the same instant, Margaret's arm was lifted as well, and Nathan was clutched in a gelatinous vise, clammy and disgusting. He raised his other arm and was similarly stopped.

Margaret's head pulled back, and for the first time he smelled the noisome breath of the river in her. Her face urged upward to his.

With one great exertion, Nathan pushed sideways and forward, hoping to pin this noxious water-thing against the door-jamb. He succeeded, and through his clothing he felt the mass flabbily deform itself against the wood. He pressed harder; it burst, drenching him and the woodwork with the vile black liquid.

Not looking back, Nathan stiff-armed the door open and fled the restaurant. Standing in the bay window, Ben, Charles, and Ginny watched him rush toward the Lincoln, his figure faintly illumined by the rising golden moon, and listened to his crushing footsteps on the loose gravel.

PART VIII

FULL MOON

Chapter 42

Babbling incoherent apologies and explanations to Ginny and Charles Darrish, Ben Redfield hurried out of the White Horse after his brother. The Lincoln strained at the edge of the highway, its horn blowing and its engine revving high. Ben ran across the lot to the car and jumped in. On the reckless drive home, he sat fearful and silent, and did not even dare to tell Nathan that the headlights were not on. The more inexplicable or violent his brother's conduct, the less Ben was inclined to question it.

Ben followed his brother with amazement through the darkened house as Nathan turned on all the lights, and peered anxiously into the closets; but still Ben said nothing. He did not ask what Nathan expected to find, or why he had nearly frightened poor old Jean McAndrew out of her wits. On any other occasion Ben wouldn't have followed so close on Nathan's heels, expecting a sarcastic rebuke and a gruff dismissal, but on this evening when he had lagged behind in another room, Nathan called to him impatiently. At the last Nathan pushed open the door of his father's room, found the old man sleeping. Nathan walked silently across the carpet, pulled the glass doors shut, and locked them.

The feverish tour completed, Nathan brought Ben into his own room, and motioned him to sit at the foot of the bed. Then, to Ben's continued astonishment, Nathan went into the bathroom, propped the door carefully open, removed all his clothes, and laid himself in a tub of steaming water. The contrast between the temperature of the bath and the frigid air of the house was so great that Nathan began to sneeze.

"Nathan," Ben ventured to suggest, when his brother had allowed the water to drain out, and began to fill the tub with fresh, "you think you really ought to have it that hot? Steam cain't be that good for you—"

"I'm tense," said Nathan, in a small hot sharp voice: "I got to get rid of the tenseness in my joints."

Ben nodded as if he understood. He grew restless sitting on the edge of the bed, watching his brother lie back in a tub of water. After Nathan's eyes had closed for a couple of minutes in apparent peace, Ben rose quietly and went to the glass doors that looked out on the forest behind the house. The nearly full moon shone through the sparse branches of a dying pine.

"Ben!" his brother called out excitedly: "Ben! Where'd you go?!"

Ben ran to the bathroom door. "Nowhere!" he cried: "I was looking at the moon, I—"

"What's wrong with it?" Nathan demanded, and rose out of the bath. His skin was burned a harsh red, and steaming water coursed through the thick black hair of his chest. His features were contorted in fright, and he looked an anguished devil rising naked from hell.

"What?" Ben stammered.

"What's wrong with it? What's wrong with the moon, that you're looking at it like that? What's it doing?"

"Nathan," said Ben, trying to think of the correct reply to this nonsensical question: "It's just sitting there. It's not doing a blessed thing!"

Ben slept that night in Nathan's room, and to his mystification, not on the cot at the foot of the bed, but in the bed itself. Nathan's hand was clamped on his brother's forearm the night through. The door had been locked, and a chair set against the knob. The curtains had been drawn against the forest, and a lamp placed on the floor in the corner. It was kept on so that no shadows from outside showed through the material.

In the worried minutes before sleep, Ben tried to think of something to link Nathan's present fearfulness to the cash register girl at the White Horse. But Ben could imagine no reason why Nathan should be afraid of Jean McAndrew—unless she had somehow found out about Evelyn and Jerry Larkin, and was blackmailing him. But even supposing that to be the unlikely case, he still couldn't figure out against whom Nathan had barricaded the room.

But Ben followed his brother in everything, and Nathan's momentary moods had so strong an effect on him that he quickly gave over trying to reason it all out. Even though he had no idea what troubled Nathan, Ben set about to reassure his brother that all would turn out well.

Early on Friday, Ben telephoned the bank to say that Nathan would not be coming to work that day, but had decided to remain some time longer at Navarre. All that morning, Nathan sat quietly in the den and watched television. He even allowed Ben to leave him for a few minutes now and then, so long as the kitchen door was propped open and he could see Nina moving about inside.

After lunch, Nathan turned the television off, and moved out with Ben to the side of the pool. Here he lay on the chaise beneath the high hot sun, and thought out what had happened the night before. He had worked hard in Navarre to prepare himself for the apparitions and was furious with himself for having failed his first trial so miserably. The only comfort to be gleaned was that no one else had seen the specters. He alone was afflicted. He had wanted to avoid the ghosts, or ignore them when they did appear. He now tried to imagine that they would atrophy and fade. He looked forward to the end of the summer, by which time he would wonder if they had been anything more than vagrant dreams. Evelyn, Jerry, and Margaret Larkin lay dead and rotting in the Babylon graveyard.

His reaction in the White Horse had been inexcusably violent. He had throttled the fat cash register girl, who in his mind had assumed the form of Margaret Larkin. He was known to each of the two dozen witnesses; there was no way of keeping the story quiet.

He considered it best to lie low for a while, to give out that he was suffering a nervous breakdown caused by an overload of work at the bank, the assumption of all his father's responsibilities at too early an age. Better to have people think he was weak, than for them to imagine him a murderer. The bank would get along well enough without him, and his salary would continue to be paid. It occurred to Nathan that he had not been visited by the spirits of his victims in Navarre, but that all three had presented themselves not two hours after his return. He conjectured hopefully that he would be affected only if he remained in Babylon; out of the town, he might rest untroubled. Then he must simply go away for a while, a few weeks, a few months. James Redfield would probably not object even if he moved away altogether.

That would probably be best, he reckoned, simply to leave Babylon for good. Nothing kept him here except the bank and his father, the bank didn't need him and his father didn't want him. Ben would go along, because he might prove useful in case the visions did after all remain, and because it might be dangerous to leave him behind.

Nathan, reassured by this decision, called Ben out of the pool. Ben padded over.

Nathan shielded his eyes against the sun, and squinted up at his brother: "How'd you like to spend the rest of the summer down at Navarre? Just you and me. I think think it's about time we had a rest—everything that's happened and all."

"I think I'd like it," said Ben cautiously. "What's Daddy gone say?"

" 'Good riddance!' " cried Nathan, imitating his father's strained voice so that Ben laughed. Then he added: "We'll just get Nina to move in. I don't know why we haven't done that before, she lives all by herself anyway, it's not like she's giving anything up to come here."

At that moment, Belinda Hale stepped through the open glass doors onto the patio. "Hey ya'll. D'y'all just get back?"

Both men greeted her, but Belinda rode over their salutations: "Ben, why don't you go inside and talk to Nina for about five minutes, while I speak to your big brother?"

"Okay—" said Ben, looking to Nathan for approval.

Nathan nodded, but cautioned: "You let me talk to Nina about what we just said, Ben. Don't you say anything."

Ben nodded his head and disappeared.

"Nathan Redfield," said Belinda, as she came to stand by the chaise: "I hear that you have been laying hands on Annie-Leigh Hooker in front of two hundred and forty-seven seeing witnesses while my back was turned, in the middle of the CP&M!" She laughed at her little joke, but was disconcerted that Nathan's reaction was neither embarrassment, nor laughter, nor anger, but a kind of quiet fearfulness. Belinda had learned the afternoon before, from a source three times removed from anyone who had been at the bank that morning, of Nathan's attack on Annie-Leigh Hooker. However, this tale had been so garbled into a murderous attack that left Annie-Leigh on the floor of the bank bleeding, unconscious, and practically naked, that Belinda had credited very little of it.

"No—no," protested Nathan: "What you heard was wrong, whatever you heard, it didn't happen that way. I hadn't hardly touched Annie-Leigh. I—" He broke off and looked closely at the cheerleader. "Listen, Belinda, what else did you hear? You didn't hear anything about last night, did you, because—"

"Last night!" cried Belinda: "Nathan, d'you attack somebody else? What are you talking about? You're not starting to pick fights, are you? With high school girls?"

"No," said Nathan: "It's nothing. Listen Belinda, Ben and I are going down to Navarre for a while—"

"You just got back!"

"I know," he said: "But we're going down there again." He glanced away, and added nervously: "It's so nice down there this time of year."

"It's sand fly season on Santa Rosa, Nathan, and you hate sand flies you told me."

"They're not so bad this year, not bad at all. Anyway, Ben—"

"Nathan—"

"What?" he asked distractedly.

"Nothing," Belinda replied carefully. "When are you leaving?"

"Tomorrow. I'm going in to pack now, while it's still light out."

"You cain't pack in the dark?! Why?!"

"No—"

"Nathan, what is going on here?!"

"Nothing, Belinda. Nothing's going on, I just haven't been

feeling the way I should, and Ben and I are going down to Na-varre for a while, and just sit out in some sun—"

"You got some girl down there who's not as fat as I am, haven't you!"

"No—"

"Well," she said, in some small exasperation: "I don't know what's got into you now, but it sure is gone be dull around here without you. I'm in love with Mr. Red and everybody in Babylon knows it, and I'm not gone never leave him, but Nathan, I'm not gone like coming here so much when you're not home. I missed you the last two days. How long you and Ben gone be gone?"

"I don't know."

"Two weeks?"

He paused. "Maybe longer."

"Nathan," she said: "You go pack. I'm gone go talk to Ben. Maybe Ben'll tell me what I want to know. I have never seen you like this. If I can get away, I'll come down to Navarre and see you. I'll tell Daddy I'm gone go spend the weekend with my friend Clarisse. I went down there this morning to go shopping with her at Gayfer's, and she doesn't have a telephone, so Daddy won't have any way of knowing I'm not there with her, and I'll come down and see you, and maybe I can do something that will cheer you up. I'll lose five pounds, and you won't even recognize me!"

"That'll be real nice, Belinda," said Nathan and rose from the chaise. "Now, I got to go in and talk to Daddy for a bit, I'll be back—"

"You got to let me go with you. He's expecting me, and I got to let him know I'm here."

"You cain't stay though," said Nathan: " 'Cause we got to talk private—"

"All right, Nathan!" she cried: "But I have never heard of such secret goings-on."

When the door to his bedroom was opened, James Redfield looked up expectantly, but his face showed his disappointment that Miss Pie was accompanied by Nathan.

"I just came to speak," said Belinda: "Nathan's not gone let me stay, Mr. Red."

"Daddy, I want to talk to you for a minute."

James Redfield looked distrustfully at his son. "Why cain't Miss Pie stay in here? What you got to say to me that Miss Pie cain't hear? Miss Pie just got here and you are already sending her away?"

"Daddy," said Nathan earnestly: "I got to talk to you for a few minutes about family stuff that Belinda doesn't care anything about. I think you and me talking about family stuff is gone bore her worse than Ben would."

"I'm going!" cried Belinda, to avoid the argument that would quickly be raised between the two men if she remained. "I'm gone go in the guest bedroom and change in my new bathing suit that I bought in Pensacola this morning, which has got about half a foot of thirty-six-inch material in it, and I sure am glad your pool has got a wall around it, because my own daddy would arrest me if he saw me wearing it in public, and I'm gone find Ben Redfield a blindfold to put around his head, and the thing cost me eighteen dollars, which is about three dollars for every polka dot on it, and that's not counting the six percent sales tax—"

When she was gone, Nathan told his father that he had decided to remain the rest of the summer at Navarre. "Who's gone stay here with me?"

"Nina."

"Has she said she would?"

"I haven't asked her yet, but she will."

"Nathan," said his father: "You cain't do it. You're president of that bank, you begged me to make you president—"

"I didn't—"

"—and I did it against my better judgment. And now you are coming in here and telling me that you want to take off right in the middle of the yearly audit, and leave the place to wrack and ruin, well I'm just not going to let you—"

"Daddy, the bank's not going to wrack and ruin. It's just that I've been tired lately . . ."

"Tired? Nathan, you look like you spent half your life out on a logging track somewhere, felling pine trees by twisting 'em off in your bare ten fingers. You don't look tired."

"*Tired*, Daddy. You know what kind of tired I mean."

"Breaking down?" said the old man suspiciously.

Nathan nodded.

"You telling me you about to have a nervous breakdown, and that's why you want to go to Navarre?"

Nathan nodded again. "I've been on the edge. A couple of things have happened—"

"What?"

"Daddy, listen, I just got to get out of here for—"

"No!" cried the old man. "Nathan, you cain't up and leave the bank! You can take a couple of weeks off when the audit's over, but you got to be back at the beginning of August for the tax men. I don't know what you're thinking about. Besides, you're not going to leave me here with Ben, you—"

"Ben would go with me, Daddy."

James Redfield paused at this. "Nathan," he said slowly: "You are up to something. I know you're up to something, you and Ben, and I'm not gone be a party to it. You go away, you go away to Navarre if you want, or wherever it is that you're *really* going —but I'm gone appoint a new president of the bank—and you know I got the power and the right to do it. You go off now, and you don't ever step foot in the CP&M again. You go off now, and you will never see me again, and you will never see a penny of my money again. You understand?"

Nathan nodded, rose, and walked out of the room.

Behind him, the old man's voice called: "Send Miss Pie in here! Where's Miss Pie?!"

Chapter 43

After leaving his father, Nathan went directly to his room. There the curtains were still drawn, and though he suspected that the windows weren't locked, he hadn't the courage to pull aside the drapes to check. He was fearful of what might be standing just outside. He locked the door, looked carefully to make sure no one was hiding in the bathroom, and then moved quickly and repeatedly from the suitcase open on his bed to the chest of drawers and closet, untidily tossing in more clothes than he would ever need in Navarre.

At the last he wrapped a white handkerchief about his hand, took from the top bureau drawer James Redfield's pistol, and loaded it. Then from the folder which held his certificate of honorable discharge from the Air Force, Nathan took a sheet of CP&M stationery that bore his father's legitimate signature three quarters down. This page, which had been prepared during his father's first long illness for the convenience of his secretary, Nathan placed in the small manual typewriter on his desk, and typed out the following note:

> I have been sick for the past two years and there is no hope of my ever getting any better. I am constantly tortured with pain in my spine, and this pain has become unbearable. I have therefore decided to kill myself. I want to thank Nina and Belinda Hale for nursing me. If it hadn't been for them, I would have killed myself a long time ago. Nathan, when you read this, I want you to make provision for both of them out of the money I have left you. Fix it so that Nina doesn't ever have to work again, and see to it that when she graduates from high school, Miss Pie can go to any nursing school that she wants.

Nathan wondered why he had not made this essentially simple decision before, why he had allowed his father for so many years to constrict and sour his life. Tonight, when Belinda had left the house, he would go into his father's room, shoot him through the temple, and place the smoking gun in his lifeless hand. Ted Hale and Raymond Everage would find the note on the bedside table.

Everything would come to him: the bank, the oil leases, the freedom to leave Babylon. He could abandon the plan to get the Larkin blueberry farm, and let Charles Darrish have the whole thing if he wanted it. He and Ben would move to New Orleans or Houston or Atlanta, and never be bothered again. It occurred to him oddly now that the Larkins' murders had been a great waste; none would have been necessary if only he had got rid of his father first.

Nathan smiled in anticipation, read through the page again, and then slipped it beneath the blotter on the desk. Cautiously, he stepped out into the hallway, and moved quietly toward his father's room. He heard the old man's voice. The door was open, and a soft light burned inside. Nathan was thinking of some excuse to have Belinda leave the house, but he realized quickly that his father was speaking not to Belinda, but to someone on the other end of the telephone.

Nathan went close to the door and listened.

"No," he heard his father say: "I didn't. I thought he'd be home by now. Ginny, listen. Do me a favor and call Charles up at the office, and tell him to get over here as soon as he can. Yes, I think maybe something is wrong, but I don't know what . . ."

There was a long pause now; the old man's breathing became more labored. Nathan suspected that Ginny was telling his father what had happened at the White Horse the night before.

"Ginny," said James Redfield at last: "Call Charles. Get him over here right now. This minute, you hear me?" His voice was a hoarse whisper.

He hung up, and Nathan returned to his room, with altered plans. He did not trust Charles Darrish to remain on his side, especially if the lawyer discovered that James Redfield had decided to change his will in favor of Ginny.

He pulled out his father's suicide note, and slipped it into the typewriter again. Between the first paragraph and the signature he added these lines:

I have recently discovered that Charles Darrish, who has been acting as my lawyer for the past twenty-two years, has been embezzling funds from my estate, and has actually tried to kill me with an overdose of my medicine. He planned to suppress my most recent will, in favor of one which left the bulk of my money to his wife Ginny. I have decided that it is necessary to kill him before I die, so that I may insure the financial well-being of my two sons, Nathan and Benjamin Redfield.

A slight scratching at the glass doors made Nathan jump. But boldly he moved toward the drapes, and pulled aside one corner of the material. He was relieved to find that it was only the tip of a dead pine branch that had brushed against the glass.

Just around the corner of the house from Nathan's bedroom, Belinda and Ben splashed about in the pool. Dusk gathered about them, but their eyes became accustomed gradually to the failing light. Though she knew that James Redfield waited for her impatiently, Belinda remained with Ben in order to quiz him on Nathan's reasons for wanting to leave town. Ben proved as evasive as his brother, but the girl was determined to get at the truth before she left that night.

James Redfield was frightened. He suspected his sons of some devilment that he was helpless to discover on his own. He feared that Nathan had sent Miss Pie home, and was nervous to think that he might be alone in the house with them.

Still Belinda did not come, though he lay breathless and sweating, constantly listening for her footsteps down the carpeted corridor. He marked the passing of time by the diminution of light. In this part of the house, the air conditioning was turned off. The glass doors were opened, and the cool air of twilight blew lazily through the screens.

The wind through the pines gradually sent him off into a light troubled sleep. He was awakened by some slight disturbance in the room. James Redfield turned his head on the pillow. By the intensity of darkness, he realized he had slept for half an hour or more.

The wind no longer blew lazily, but with some force through the screen. It was chill and unpleasantly moist. He lifted his head groggily from the pillow, expecting to hear the first drops of rain. The room was dark, the patio outside scarcely less so. The sky beyond the waving black foliage of the pines was a deep blue; but no storm clouds had gathered, which would explain the dampness in the air.

He held the confused notion that someone had come through the screen door. He wondered if perhaps Belinda weren't standing in a dark corner of the patio, having entered the room, and gone out again, not to disturb him. He started to rock himself up into a sitting position, so that he might call. His tilting head, turned toward the patio, caught the slightly gleaming outline of a human figure traced in water on the screen, as if someone— of small and slight stature—had leaned up against it while very wet, leaving water in thousands of the tiny squares of mesh. He moved his head to see the outline more clearly, but it disappeared, and though he turned this way and that, he could not find it again. In the failing light, he noticed a trail of water, small puddles that glistened faintly on the carpet, leading from the patio screens to the door into the hallway.

James Redfield cried out feebly: "Miss Pie! Miss Pie!"

The full moon rose over Babylon.

Chapter 44

Friday morning, Charles Darrish thought hard about what he had witnessed at the White Horse Inn. Nathan Redfield had lost control, assaulted the McAndrews: mother, daughter, and son, and probably would have laid hands on the father if he had been around. This tallied uncomfortably with the report that Darrish had just received of Nathan's attack on Annie-Leigh Hooker in the bank. It was particularly disturbing that this assault had taken place only a few minutes after Nathan had left Darrish's office.

Over a sandwich and coffee in the drugstore, Darrish became convinced that Nathan Redfield was out of his wits and had killed Evelyn and Jerry Larkin. A few minutes more, and he had credited Nathan with the murder of Margaret Larkin as well, not to mention the desecration of the cemetery.

A man who opened graves couldn't be trusted with a box of wet matches. Charles Darrish decided to drop Nathan Redfield.

When Darrish returned to his office, he knelt before his safe, squinted at the dial, and twirled the sequence of twelve numbers that opened it. He took out the papers relating to the proposed acquisition of the Larkin blueberry farm, and carefully cut them up with a large pair of rusty scissors. Then he made several phone calls to halt the plans that he had set in motion for the establishment of Panhandle Enterprises, Inc., as they had dubbed the dummy holding company. Because he had performed his part carefully, he was able to do this without arousing suspicion in those who had helped him, and in a manner that could not easily be traced later. He had never told Nathan with whom he was dealing, and though Nathan thought that all Charles's representatives were in Mobile, they were in fact in New Orleans and Birmingham. He and Ginny had traveled to Atlanta on other business entirely.

At the very last Charles took out the forged loan payment card that Nathan had brought him. He compared this with the original that had been preserved in a hidden well in the rear of his desk. He burned the forgery in an ashtray, poured the cinders into an envelope, folded the envelope, and with a splintered broom handle pushed it to the bottom of his wire wastepaper basket.

A final telephone call at six o'clock, to a man who had spent the afternoon on a golf course, served to cut Darrish off completely from his complicity with Nathan Redfield. He could now safely deny that he had had any commerce at all with his wife's cousin.

Just as Darrish was preparing to go home, his wife telephoned, and related James Redfield's importunate plea that Darrish go right over to him.

"Charles," Ginny said: "James sounded scared. Especially after I told him about what happened at the bank the other morning, and then last night at the White Horse—"

"Listen, Ginny," said her husband: "I think James has got every right in the world to be scared, because I think Nathan killed all three of the Larkins."

There was a long pause.

"Why didn't you tell me this before?" demanded Ginny at last.

"Because I didn't want to see you upset. Nathan's your cousin, Nathan's family, even if he's not close. I had to make sure before I said anything."

"I wish you had said something sooner," said Ginny hotly: "Maybe Evelyn and Jerry wouldn't be dead now."

"No," he said: "They would be though. I didn't know enough

at first to know what Nathan was about. I don't think at the time we even knew Margaret was dead, did we?"

"Yes," said Ginny dryly: "We did."

"Well," went on Charles unperturbed, "there wasn't enough to go on. Now I think there is. Nathan attacked those people in the restaurant, knocked Jean McAndrew right up against the door, and looked about to throttle her, or something worse, right there in front of forty paying customers, and it was right then that I was pretty much sure that something was wrong."

"Why didn't you say something then?"

"I wasn't *really* sure, so I came in here today, and I thought it all out, made a few phone calls, that's all. I called the bank this morning. Nathan's at home. He didn't come in. They had already heard about what happened at the White Horse. I think they're hoping he'll stay away. They asked me if I'd go over and talk to James about all this."

"You are gone go over and tell James Redfield that his oldest son went and laid three people at the bottom of the Styx? And one of 'em was a fourteen-year-old pregnant girl? And—" She paused significantly: "And I bet it was Nathan that got Margaret pregnant in the first place . . ."

"I imagine it was," said her husband: "And I thought you might want to go over and talk to James about it all."

"No," said Ginny flatly. "There's probably nothing about those two boys that James doesn't already suspect, except that I don't want to be the one to tell him."

"I don't much care whether you *tell* him or not," said Charles slowly: "But I do think you ought to get him out of there."

"What?"

"Get him out of there. Nathan told me that he was after the Larkin farm for the money it would bring. He'd get a lot more money if James was to die sudden. Last night Nathan pushed a girl near about through a glass-paned door, and the other day he nearly ripped Annie-Leigh Hooker's shoulders off her back, and I think it would be a good idea if you got James Redfield out of that house. It wouldn't do any good to talk to Ben, those two are so close. I don't think Ben would leave if Nathan was pointing a double-barrel at his appendix scar."

"You really think something might happen to James?"

"I do, I sure do."

Ginny said nothing for a moment, but at last remarked: "I guess this really is serious, isn't it? Now, I think you're right and we're gone have to get James out of that house, but I don't know if I'm gone be able to do it by myself. If I can get to Nina though, maybe the two of us together can convince him to come away with us. But Charles, even if we do get him out of there, you think there's any proof? I mean, can Ted Hale arrest Nathan and hold him? I sure would like to see Warren out of jail, poor thing is wasting away like a little black puppy-dog with ringworm, but I don't want to go dragging James Redfield out of his own house in a fireman's carry, and then have to let him go back when Ted Hale laughs in your face about Nathan."

"Ted's bound to have heard about Annie-Leigh Hooker and I imagine he knows what happened last night at the White Horse too. And when I start painting a picture of Belinda sitting on a couch with the man who might have killed Margaret Larkin, Ted's not gone start talking to me about evidence."

"All right then, Charles. I'll go by Nina's place and pick her up. If Nathan's at the house I may have trouble getting in. He was friendly enough last night, but after what happened, he may not throw open his arms when he catches sight of me on his front step. I may have to hide in the car, and send Nina in on foot."

"But you're gone try?"

"I'm gone try. I hate to do it on a Friday. I hate to start any project on a Friday 'cause it always comes out wrong, and starting a project on a Friday, you might as well be walking around inside the house with an open umbrella over your head, it's that kind of luck. But if what you say is true, and it was Nathan that killed Evelyn and Jerry and Margaret, then I'll do everything I can to see him strung up."

Chapter 45

At the other end of the darkened patio from James Redfield's room, the iron gate was pushed slowly and quietly open, and a dark figure moved stealthily across the flagstones. The old man's weak eyes could just discern the awkward outline of a large woman. It paused at the screen.

"Who's that!" cried the old man.

The screen slid open, and the figure moved into the room. James Redfield reached for the light.

"No!" hissed the intruder.

"Oh," sighed James Redfield: "Nina—thank goodness—what you doing here? Why you coming in like that, fit to scare me into a silk-lined casket? Somebody else—"

"Shhhh! Mr. Red," whispered Nina earnestly: "I come to take you away . . ."

"What? Where you gone take me? What you talking about, Nina?"

"Mr. Red," said Nina: "I got to get you away from this house. Just for the time being now, I—"

"Why?!"

"Mr. Red," the old woman cried: "You think I'd ask you to come away with me in the dark if I didn't just *have* to do it?"

James Redfield paused, and without another word of argument, began to raise himself in the bed. Nina hurried forward with the wheelchair.

"How are we gone get out of here?" demanded the old man, as he was shifted into the chair. "Do you plan to wheel me all the way to the center of Babylon?"

"Miss Ginny has got her car outside. We're gone go to her house for a while."

Nina pushed open the screen, and maneuvered the wheelchair over the metal tracks. James Redfield peered ahead into the darkness. Another dark figure hovered at the iron gate of the patio.

"Ginny," he whispered hoarsely: "Is that you?"

"James," she cried excitedly back: "We got to get you away from here! You don't have to worry—we're gone bring you back just as soon as we can."

She pulled open the iron gate.

"Ginny, what did Nathan do?"

"Shhhh! We want to get you out of here without anybody seeing that you're gone, or who it was that took you."

"Then let's go. Don't hang around. Somebody was just in the room checking on me, and they'll be back. I don't know who it was, but they'll be back."

The full moon shone bright above the pines that grew dense in the yard, and its white-gold rays shattered into nervous spots of light on the needle-carpeted ground. Nina pushed the wheelchair urgently across the uneven ground. Frequently the wheels caught and turned in small ruts and holes so that Ginny had to bend to lift the front of the chair. They proceeded silently. From the other side of the house, they heard the muted voices of Belinda and Ben and the occasional splash of water in the pool. "Miss Pie," the old man whispered twice, and said nothing more. Two of the lights had been turned on around the pool, and their harsh glow broke fitfully across the gravel roof.

Nina ran over a large pinecone, and the chair tilted, threatening to toss James Redfield out. The two women struggled to right it, holding their breath in suspense against the accident. In that brief moment, they heard, not far from them, a strange unsettling noise. Something was being dragged across the carpet of brown needles. They stared around them, and found that the noise had its equal echo on the other side of them as well. Without a word Nina pushed the chair quickly forward, and Ginny ran to the car and pulled open the back door. She opened the trunk too, and cried "Hurry, hurry!" in a frantic whisper.

Nina hastened the chair forward.

Though Nina and James Redfield were not thirty feet from Ginny, they appeared but dark shadowed figures among the black trees. The moonlight dappled their movement, now illuminating one of the old man's flurrying hands, now brightening on the black woman's contorted mouth.

But further back, through the trees and nearer the house, Ginny Darrish could see something else—the prone body of a white-robed woman snaking, in motion that was elegant and unhurried, across the ground. As she stared, Ginny caught sight of another figure, a man, in dark clothes but with a pale featureless head, moving at the same pace, in a glide that was just as sinuous and inhumanly graceful. They slipped quickly and without apparent effort among the thin trunks of the pines.

Nina had laid James Redfield across the back seat and folded the chair in the open trunk. "Miss Ginny!" she hissed twice: "Let's go! Let's go!" She slammed the trunk closed.

Ginny shook herself, and ran around the car, got in, and started the engine. She backed recklessly in the cul-de-sac, scraping the finish of Belinda Hale's blue Volkswagen.

When she pulled on the headlights, Ginny and Nina beside her shrieked. Caught in the white light, against the white brick of James Redfield's patio, were a man and a woman. They rose from the earth in a soft spiral, and stood erect. They turned their dead expressionless faces a moment into the harsh light, then slipped through the open iron gate.

Chapter 46

Ted Hale had spent all morning, and the greater part of the afternoon in the county sheriff's office in the Escambia County Courthouse in Pensacola. Over a long lunch at a seafood restaurant on the municipal pier, he had discussed with the county sheriff, the county coroner, and the county district attorney, the case of the murdered family in Babylon. The deaths of the grandmother and her two grandchildren had attracted attention all over Florida and in neighboring states, and it had been decided that the trial of Warren Perry ought to go forward as soon as possible, in order to assuage the public's longing for a culprit.

Hale felt duty-bound to say he thought the schoolteacher not guilty of the crimes. He found it difficult to push this opinion, however, since he had no one to blame in Warren's stead, and because he was known to have "harbored" the suspect for many months previous to the murders.

The points in favor of Warren's innocence were two: His fingerprints had not been found on the sword, and his mother, however reluctantly, backed up Warren's claim that he was in Atmore by eight o'clock, at which time Warren's uncle, Mr. Henry Harp, was certain that Evelyn and Jerry were alive in his garden on Palafox Street. Overwhelmingly against Perry was the fact that no other suspect had presented himself, coupled with the necessity of bringing someone to trial soon.

Just as Hale was taking leave of his friends in the sheriff's office, a call came through to him from Babylon. Briefly, Charles Darrish told him what he suspected of Nathan Redfield. He had murdered Jerry and Evelyn Larkin, and, just as Evelyn had said and as none of them had believed, he had tied Margaret Larkin to her bicycle and drowned her in the Styx.

Hale accused Darrish of scandalmongering and demanded his proof. Darrish said he didn't have any, but told, without implicating himself, of Nathan's scheme to get the Larkin blueberry farm for the possible oil beds that lay beneath it. And, as clincher, he related with some embellishment Nathan's attack on the cash register girl at the White Horse.

"Now," said Darrish: "You know what happened the other day in the bank, when Nathan laid his hands on Annie-Leigh Hooker, when she wasn't doing a thing but waiting in line to make a deposit."

"Yes," said Hale grudgingly: "I heard. I heard from several people, but I didn't give it much credit. I know Nathan, and I know he doesn't attack customers. I also know Annie-Leigh Hooker, and I know what she and Ed Geiger can do to a story. I thought it was something about like Nathan tripping on somebody's foot and falling against the girl, that's all I thought it was."

"Other people saw it," said Darrish: "And you ought to have listened careful. Nathan jumped the rail, and just about pushed his thumbs through her windpipe. And Margaret Larkin was Annie-Leigh Hooker's best friend. He might have been out to get 'em both. Ted, I wouldn't be saying all this if I didn't feel that I had to, because Nathan is Ginny's cousin, and it's not gone be doing this practice one bit of good in the world to have my wife's cousin languishing on death row through the next five sessions of the Supreme Court."

Hale replied grimly: "Yes."

"Now," said Darrish, no longer in the voice of persuasion: "Ginny right this very minute is on her way over to the Redfield place with Nina to get James Redfield out of the house and safe. Now Nathan may be just fine, and this may be something pressing on his brain and he cain't help it, but until it's cleared up, we just thought it was best to get James out of there. I don't think we could do anything with Ben, Ben's not gone leave Nathan no matter what."

"Charles, listen. Belinda's probably over there too." Hale sounded frightened, and his fear proved that he had in some measure accepted Charles's accusations. "Does Ginny know enough to get her out of there?"

"Yes, if Belinda's there with James, she'll get her away too. But Ginny's gone try to do it without Nathan finding out. I'm proud of her. I'd be scared out of my britches to go over there right now, thinking what I think about Nathan Redfield, and trying to spirit his daddy out of the house in a wheelchair."

"Listen," said Hale: "I'm on my way up there right now. You stop Ginny, and I'm gone to make sure everything's all right. Nathan won't do anything in the next forty-five minutes, that's all it's gone take me to get there. He won't be scared to see me, but if it's Ginny, he'll know something is up. I don't want him to do anything. If it's like you say, and it's something that's pressing on his brain, Ginny might start it all over again. You ought to keep her away."

"I cain't," said Charles simply. "She's on her way there now. She's probably already strapping James Redfield in his chair. You just better get up here quick as you can."

Chapter 47

Nathan's plan now was simple. He would put on his bathing suit and join Belinda and Ben in the pool. When Charles Darrish arrived, Nathan would feign surprise but offer to take him in to James Redfield. Then he would go to his own bedroom for the pistol and the suicide note, and return. He would shoot Charles Darrish through the heart, then quickly place the pistol against his father's temple and pull the trigger.

The shots would no doubt bring Ben and Belinda running. Nathan would pretend to have arrived there only seconds before, and would allow one of them to find the suicide note on the bedside table.

Three times he went over these actions in his mind, and then satisfied, changed into his bathing suit. He carefully unlocked the door of his room and peered out into the hall. This short carpeted corridor opened only onto his and Ben's bedrooms and the bath that they shared. At the other end was the wider hallway that led from the den to James Redfield's separate wing. Nathan could just make out the angled glow of the outside lights, ricocheting off the den walls and through the archway. Nathan wondered whether Belinda had gone down to his father's room again, but that thought snapped off when he stepped into a small puddle of water in the middle of the carpet. It was thick and impure, and stained his foot black. He glanced, terrified, down to the end of the hallway. Just as he did so, the door opposite his father's slowly closed and clicked shut; this was the door to the guest bedroom. It was Belinda who had just entered that room, where she changed her clothes, and it was Belinda who had tracked muddy water into the house—he dared believe nothing else.

Nathan stepped into the den, and approached the glass windows that opened onto the pool. When he saw that Ben swam alone, he turned back with confidence, and stepped quietly to the end of the hallway. He paused at the door of his father's darkened room, and carefully eased the door shut. Then he squeezed open the door of the guest room, with the intention of persuading Belinda to return to the pool.

The room was unlighted, but the curtains across the glass wall had been drawn open. Nathan glanced uneasily at the moon rising above the trees outside. As before in the cemetery, it seemed a featureless sharp disk, but now it was full. Belinda stood silhouetted against the black glass.

"Well, Miss Pie," said Nathan with soft derision: "Do you think—"

It wasn't Miss Pie, but Evelyn Larkin that turned slowly to face Nathan. Black water spilled iridescently out of her mouth into a shining puddle at her feet.

She came forward in a slow turning glide; her feet moved not at all, and she skimmed across the thick carpet, her arms raised in graceful menace.

Unthinking, Nathan stepped forward to meet her; he grabbed Evelyn by both upraised wrists and slung her onto the bed. Her putrescent flesh coated the palms of his hands, and he wiped it frantically away on his pants, while twisting his head about in the darkness, trying to remember if there was anything near with which he might pound the old woman's corpse into immobility. Evelyn's body had flopped onto the bed like a hooked fish in the bottom of a boat, and now in a sidewise rocking motion was trying to right itself.

Nathan picked up a small pottery vase that stood on the dresser, and turned toward the bed.

"Nathan!" cried Belinda: "What the hell are you doing?"

He looked down. Belinda lay on the bed, encircling her bruised wrist with her other hand, and whimpering. "You hurt me, goddamn it, Nathan, what did you think—"

"Belinda," he cried: "I thought—"

"Nathan, get out of here. You cain't push me around like that. You hurt me—"

He moved forward, but she twisted farther up on the covers.

He rushed to the door, and flicked up the light switch. He turned to her, and began apologetically: "It was the dark, Belinda, I thought you were—"

"A burglar! How many burglars you know are fat as I am? How many burglars you know wear a two-piece bikini?" The top of her new suit had been dislodged in the brief scuffle, and now she pulled it up again to cover her breasts. "I was just standing at the window trying to think of a going-away gift for you, or trying to think of some way to keep you from going. Nathan, I was just telling myself how much I was going to miss you, and that I wasn't gone have the heart to do a handstand when you were gone."

He stood by the door, with his hand still on the switch. "Come on back to the pool, and we'll sit with Ben a while, and then I'll be all right. I just—well, you see why I need a little vacation." He laughed shortly, but Belinda only looked askance.

"No rough stuff," she warned him.

"No," he replied meekly. "I won't touch you—"

"Unless I tell you to," she added archly.

He smiled, and stepped back for her to pass before him into the hallway. He turned out the light, and pulled the door shut without looking back into the darkened room.

"You think I ought to see if Mr. Red is all right?" whispered Belinda, nodding toward James Redfield's closed door. Evidently she had forgiven Nathan, for her tone was confidential.

Nathan shook his head. "He's probably asleep, and you'd wake him. And if he sees you, he'll talk you into staying, and I want a little of you to myself." Putting his arm on her shoulder, Nathan led Belinda down the long corridor, through the den, and out onto the patio. Ben sat on the far side of the pool, with his legs beating idly in the water.

"Ben," Nathan called: "Why don't you run inside and pour Belinda and me out a drink? Strong, okay?" He smiled.

Ben jumped to his feet and ran past them into the house.

Belinda and Nathan walked to the diving board, but just as Nathan was gallantly helping her to step up on it, Belinda turned and pushed him into the pool.

"Nathan," she said sweetly when he came spluttering up: "I just couldn't have faced myself tomorrow morning, if I hadn't done that. I just *had* to get you back. But I promise that I'll be good to you for the rest of the evening."

Nathan paused in the water, open-mouthed, as if trying to decide whether to be angry or not. But then he laughed, and motioned Belinda in. She dived; they met at the bottom of the pool and kissed. The sharp mercury light was dim so far down, and they turned slowly in the water with their eyes closed.

Just when Nathan was sure that he would have to rise to the surface for breath, Belinda's sharp nails gouged deeply in his neck. He opened his eyes to protest, and found himself staring into the filmed pupils and bloodless face of Evelyn Larkin. Her mouth was open, from having pressed against his, and black water poured out of it like a cloud of ink. Her arms reached around and dug into his shoulders. She pulled him closer, and for a brief moment he stared at the floating torn flesh about her unfocused eyes, and even began to count the torn sutures he saw there.

He breathed in water, and gagging, broke free. He beat up to the surface at an angle, fearful that Evelyn would grab his legs and pull him down again.

He spun out of the water, and swam frantically for the side of the pool. He scrambled out, and impulsively turned to see what had become of the dead woman.

Belinda broke the surface of the water, wiped the wet hair from her face, and grinned: "What's the matter, Nathan? Cain't hold your breath? You're smoking too much!"

He shook his head, bewildered; he tried to see through the disturbed water whether Evelyn Larkin was still somewhere beneath the surface.

Belinda swam toward him, and he automatically extended his arm. She smiled and gripped his forearm, and he pulled her out of the pool.

Belinda opened her mouth to speak, but a vile mixture of black water and blood spewed out over him. He jerked out of her grasp, and stumbled backward, falling into one of the flower beds that edged the house. Evelyn Larkin advanced on him.

He had cut his hand open on one of the large sharp white stones that formed the border of the bed. Nathan picked this up, and raised himself, staring all the while at the old woman's corpse. Evelyn moved slowly toward him, reaching out.

He lifted the stone high—

It's Belinda, he thought.

—and brought it down hard on her temple. There was a sickening soft crunch, and that whole portion of Evelyn's head gave way, falling inside itself, and oozing an oily gray putrescence and black water where blood should have flowed.

The corpse staggered aside and collapsed in a twisted heap at the edge of a row of azaleas. It stared with its remaining eye at Nathan. A little stream of thin gray matter bubbled out of its temple.

Nathan stared up, for he realized that the quality of light had altered. The mercury lights were black, as if shorted; but the full moon was directly above, and shone with the harsh livid light that had prevailed in the cemetery. It began to grow larger.

Nathan looked down. All the patio, the pool, the shrubbery was a washed-out white-gray, a colorless poisonous phosphorescence, like that produced by decaying fish. All but his own body, and whatever lay outside the patio, was now so lighted. He looked down at himself, and he appeared as if in deep shadow; and beyond the white brick walls the forest was black and unseen. The enlarged moon, bright as the sun, had wiped the stars from the sky.

"Nathan!" cried Ben behind him, his voice full of terror.

Nathan whirled around. Ben stood in the black shadow of the den, just inside the open doorway, the two drinks in his hands thrust outside into the harsh light of the moon.

"Ben," said Nathan: "I don't—"

The two glasses dropped out of Ben's hands and smashed on the flagstones.

Jerry Larkin lurched out into the supernatural moonlight. His ill-fitting suit was stained with earth, and as he moved forward, a few needles of pine straw dropped out of his coat. The gash circling his throat was more ragged than before, and the head had been so much knocked about that the features were scarcely identifiable. The crushed skull showed through along one side, where the ear had been ripped off. The jaw hung slack and uneven. The flesh had been scraped from one side of the face; there the eye dangled on the end of the distended optic nerve.

The corpse reached out for Nathan.

Nathan dodged to the side, heading for the flower bed beside the glass doors. There were other stones he could use. He knelt to pull one out of the earth, and turned to find that Jerry was closer than he anticipated. Still kneeling, he hurled the stone, but it fell short, and landed on the corpse's foot. The sharp rock cut through the melting flesh, snapping the bones, and as Jerry continued to advance, part of the foot was left behind.

Nathan crawled aside, toward the open door of the house. But in the bright, bleaching light he did not see the broken glass on the ground, and cut his wrist badly. He lifted his hand automatically to his eyes. Blood poured out, but it was scarcely visible in the deep shadow that prevailed over his body.

Nathan had instinctively taken the broken glass in his hand, and now he raised himself, grasping it so tightly that it cut into his fingers.

He made a menacing gesture toward the advancing corpse, which paused momentarily, but then continued forward.

Nathan made another feint, lifted the shard of glass, and brought it down to sever the optic nerve. The dangling eyeball fell to the stones.

The corpse limped toward Nathan on its mangled foot.

Nathan bounded forward and upset Jerry onto the hard surface of the patio. Before the corpse could right itself, Nathan had jumped solidly onto its chest. He felt a sickening crush of bone beneath him, and his feet sank into the flesh. Nathan dropped to his knees, and—

Thinking, *This is Ben.*

—drew the sharp edge of the glass, again and again, across the gash in the corpse's neck. The head was soon detached, and spun off a little to the side, an unrecognizable gray lump of liquefying bone and gore.

Nathan stood and staggered backward toward the house. He stared up at the moon, which remained engorged. He turned at the door.

Margaret Larkin stood just within the doorway, water pouring off her body into a pool of phosphorescence at her feet.

Nathan moved frantically sideways, pushing hard against the wall of glass, his face turned toward the pool. Belinda's body lay at the edge of the azalea bed. His brother's corpse was sprawled on the flagstones. There was a wide pool of almost colorless blood between the trunk and the head, which stared up at the moon in opened-mouth astonishment.

Nathan had been tricked, and tricked again.

Margaret Larkin stood before him, her small gray form erect in solemn triumph.

Chapter 48

It was dark when Ted Hale reached Babylon. On the feverish drive from Pensacola, he had become convinced that Nathan Redfield had indeed committed all three murders, and that it was possible he would do more. Hale realized that all along, out of friendship, he had tricked himself into thinking that Nathan was guiltless. He had refused to examine Evelyn Larkin's hysterical accusations, had not even allowed himself to make the simple connection that it was Nathan's sword that had killed the old woman, and sliced her grandson's head off. But once he admitted the possibility that Nathan was guilty, certainty followed quickly on.

He was not sure what to do now. It was not possible to arrest Nathan, for there was no evidence against him; but following the two attacks on young women, Annie-Leigh Hooker and the cash register girl at the White Horse, it was not really judicious to let him roam Babylon's streets. But this was a question he set far behind his principal priority now: that of making sure that Belinda was safe, and well away from the Redfield house.

Once he had passed the Babylon town limits, his temptation was to put on his blue revolving light and the siren, but he refrained. He first stopped at his own house, ran inside shouting for Belinda. He waited five miserable seconds in the darkened kitchen, but there was no reply to his summons. He ran from room to room, calling her name, ever more loudly and with ever more despair.

He drove next to the Darrishes. From the front walk, through the thin pink curtains of the living room window, he could see James Redfield installed in the corner of the plush rose sofa, while Nina stood at attention behind him. Hale knocked loudly, and was immediately let in by Charles Darrish.

Hale glanced round the room, and was distressed not to see Belinda.

"Hale," said James Redfield, and the sheriff looked at the old man. He appeared at once angry, distressed, and very ill. His wheezing was so protracted he could hardly be understood: "You know what Nathan did?"

Hale nodded dismally. "Where's Belinda? Didn't you bring Belinda out with you?"

"They wouldn't let me!" cried the old man.

Ginny appeared out of the darkness of the hallway. "She was over there in the pool, Ted, but we couldn't go after her, because we had to get James out of that house without them seeing, or I don't know what would have happened. I just know she's all right, I'd have gone back there myself for her, but I knew you were on your way. Go on over there." There was something hesitant and defeated in her manner; her words afforded no reassurance.

"Call first," suggested Darrish, and picked up the receiver of the phone just beside him. "What's the number?"

Nina told him, and Darrish dialed. He held the receiver out to Hale. Everyone in the room could hear the ringing, and held his breath. Hale wouldn't take the receiver: six, seven, eight rings and his eyes began to glaze.

"Maybe they're in the pool," said Nina: "They cain't hear the phone when they're in the pool."

Ten rings, and Ginny said: "She's on her way home now. Maybe she's on her way to find you, thinking that James got kidnapped. Maybe Nina's right and they're all just in the pool." Hale looked at her, as if he didn't understand what she said. "That's it, Ted," she said, without inflection: "She's in the pool, or she's out looking for James."

Ginny and Nina exchanged troubled glances; this Hale caught. "What is it!" he demanded: "What is it you're not saying?!"

"Nothing," said Ginny: "Nothing. I know she's all right. You go on over there. Call home. Maybe she's at home!" Charles had hung up the telephone.

"Mr. Hale," said Nina slowly: "I'd go on over to the house if I were you. Belinda was there just a little while ago, and Mr. Nathan and Ben are there, but there's somebody else there now too."

"Who'd you see over there? Who else would be over there?" cried Hale. "What'd you see over there?"

"Nothing," said Ginny: "We don't know what we saw. But we saw something. I don't know, but I think you'd better get on over there."

"Go on, Ted!" cried the old man, in a quaver: "I don't know what would become of me if anything happened to Miss Pie! We got to take care of Miss Pie!"

"Charles," said Hale: "You come with me. It might be better if I didn't go over there alone, and you said that Nathan trusted you."

"I don't know," said Charles with some hesitation: "I think—"

"Go with him," urged Ginny: "It might take both of you to handle Nathan—"

Though Charles Darrish still hesitated, Ted Hale pulled him out the front door, and then pushed him toward the cruiser. In little more than two minutes they were on the road that ended in the Redfield cul-de-sac.

Hale stopped the car just at the point where the house was visible through the trees, but he parked on the left side of the road, beneath a wide overshadowing live oak.

"Why don't you go on to the house?" demanded Charles.

"I want to get to the house quiet, on foot," said Hale. "I don't want him warned that we're coming."

Charles Darrish wiped his sweating hands nervously over his pants legs.

"Charles," said Hale: "I want you to go to the front door, but go slow, and I'll run around the back way. I'll go in through the garage. Now get the pistol out of the glove compartment and stick it in your pocket."

Charles made no move, so Hale took out the gun and handed it to the lawyer.

The police radio began to crackle loudly, and harsh voices came over, but Hale paid no attention. "Let's go," he said loudly.

Charles Darrish opened the cruiser door, and still staring nervously at the sheriff, stepped out into the street. When the lawyer had retreated out of the range of the police radio, the noise of an approaching car was suddenly audible. He turned toward the Redfield house, and saw the International Scout hard upon him. Its lights were not on, and Darrish saw Nathan Redfield's moonstruck face through the windshield, wild and star-ing.

Darrish jumped, but he was caught in midair. His head smashed open on one of the headlights. He was pressed against the grille for a second, while the Scout moved thirty feet for-ward, but then he rolled down to the pavement. The left rear wheel rolled solidly across his back, and snapped his spine.

As Hale climbed out of the cruiser, his vision had been blocked by the low-hanging branches of the live oak, but he had heard the sickening thump. He ran out into the darkened road, and staring after the vehicle, saw Darrish's broken body lying directly beneath a streetlamp. Hale rushed to it, and saw at once that the man was dead.

Hale ran his hands for a moment across Darrish's twisted back, and then stood bewildered. He glanced toward the Red-field house, and then broke into a run. He headed around the front of the house toward the garage, staring up at the harsh lights that shone above the swimming pool. But brighter than these was the moon, shrinking and whitening as it rose. There was no sound but the buzz of a faulty mercury lamp.

He ran into the garage, slipped along between the wall and the side of the Lincoln, and rushed through the open door onto the lighted patio.

Blood still drained out of Ben Redfield's body, and spilled over in a little sullen stream into the swimming pool. Belinda lay motionless beneath the azaleas, her face and neck covered with blood. He leapt over Ben's body, and crouched at his daughter's side. She breathed faintly.

He lifted her tenderly in his arms, resting her bloody head against his shoulder, and whimpering, retraced his steps. But, because the way was better lighted, he went to the back of the house now.

The bedrooms of the Redfield house were dark, but the moonlight shone deep into them, spectrally illuminating the furnishings.

To his right, in the forest, dry wood snapped. Automatically, Hale paused and listened intently. An animal dragged itself across the deep-laid pine straw; but it moved too quickly to be wounded, and only a wounded animal, Hale thought, would move in such a fashion. The sound was picked up, echoed with only slight variation, a moment later. As the two animals—whatever—moved farther on, going toward the north, he gradually lost the sound. Another twig broke faintly, as if to click off the diminishing volume.

Hale took a cautious step forward, but no more, for he was arrested again by another sound, a wet slap against a tree trunk, that was no easier to identify. More slaps, a quick half dozen, as if a sopping towel were being slung against the pines; but the slapping moved northward and was soon lost to Hale. He tried to imagine what bizarre procession would produce so strange an accompaniment, but could not. What had Ginny Darrish and Nina seen?

He realized then how long he had been distracted by these uninterpretable movements in the forest. Belinda's breathing had grown shallower. Hale hurried toward the cul-de-sac. In a minute more he was at his cruiser, trying to open the back door without disturbing the burden in his arms. Glancing up the street, he saw his two deputies standing over Charles Darrish's corpse. They raised their heads slowly and stared at him.

Chapter 49

Nathan had fled the patio into the garage. Inexplicably, the door to the Scout was opened, and the key was in the ignition. He jumped in, slammed the door shut, started the vehicle, and backed screeching into the driveway. He headed up the darkened road toward the center of Babylon, and stared at the moon, dreading to see it expand once more. He ran over some animal, a very large dog or perhaps a doe that had wandered across the road, and the thing falling beneath the back wheel had almost caused the Scout to tip over. Only then did he realize that his lights were not on. He spun through town without meeting another car.

Soon enough, Nathan thought grimly, Ted would find the bodies of Ben and Belinda, and soon enough, the highway patrol would be after him. Now he was headed south, toward the coast and Navarre, where he had been untroubled by the visions. Freedom from the ghosts that existed only in his mind was all that was important now to Nathan. The police would find him easily enough in Navarre, he had no doubt of that, but his only requirement now was to be as far as possible from Babylon. The moon shone above the Scout, but Nathan could not see it.

Nathan was nearly overwhelmed with relief when he passed beyond the municipal limits of Babylon and slowed the Scout a little, almost beginning to enjoy the ride. Despite the earliness of the hour no other car was on the road, but Nathan was pleased with this unexpected solitude. When he reached that point in the four-lane highway where trees on the median masked the opposing two lanes, he thought uneasily of the night earlier in the week when he had been mistaken in the road, and found himself coming upon the Babylon cemetery. The moon shone brightly over the dense unbroken pine forest on either side, and Nathan studied the trees and roadway carefully to make sure that he was still on the highway that led south. He had just decided that he was, smiled and relaxed, when just ahead there appeared, without a warning sign, a sharp bend that ought not to have been there.

He slowed to a careful twenty miles an hour, and maneuvered the curve apprehensively. His headlights, turning across the vertical plane of dense pine, suddenly glinted on metal. His entire frame shook with a fear that was beyond wonder or surprise. With his hands on the wheel, unable to turn, and his foot on the accelerator, unable to slow, he was headed north, no more than a mile out of Babylon. The Styx River bridge lay just ahead.

Nathan braked. There was no mistaking his location or direction. The full moon now shone through the windshield, and on the far side of the river, he could just make out the Larkin farmhouse, glowing white among the dark pines. Sweating and suffocated, he rolled down the window. The dead moist air that hung above the Styx invaded and filled the vehicle.

A wet slap broke against a tree only a dozen feet from his open window. He pivoted his head that way, saw nothing. He lifted his foot from the brake, and made a quick turn in the road.

The lights of the Scout, panning across the trees, picked out two low white spots, like phosphorescent balloons, in rapid movement toward the highway.

He slammed his foot on the accelerator, and once more turned the curve. He would return to Babylon, give himself up, and be protected by Ted Hale. If these were phantoms of guilt, then he'd be rid of them once he had surrendered.

He took the bend more quickly this time, spun around it, and barreled south toward Babylon, leaving whatever it was in the forest well behind him. The road curved slightly all the way back, three quarters of a mile, no more. He ought to be passing Nina's house in less than a minute. His mind strayed in fearfulness, back to the bridge and what had waited for him there, and when his consciousness snapped back to the road, he looked anxiously ahead, for he knew he ought already to have passed the town limits. But the forest was unbroken on either side, and Babylon wasn't beyond the next curve in the road—nor the one after that. The trees were towered and black and crowded the roadway; the moon shone high overhead.

Nathan checked the mileage gauge. It was just ticking off seven tenths. He drove faster, as attentive to the gauge as to the road. A full mile of the winding highway, the dense unbroken forest, and Babylon was not in sight. From the Styx River bridge to Babylon, there was no turnoff, no way of getting lost. Where was he? His mind had wandered, he had passed through Babylon without noticing, and was probably half way to the coast by now. Because of the position of the moon, he knew he was headed south. His mind played one trick on top of another.

After five or six miles more of unchanging undifferentiated forest, through which he traveled with increasing speed and distraction, Nathan was vastly relieved to come upon a dirt track that led off to the right. He slowed. Visionary landscapes didn't have driveways, and he was somewhere, on some real road. Nathan was feverish, and all his fears for his uncertain future concentrated in the single sharp desperation to know where he was. He had told himself that if only he drove long enough, he'd come to a place or a sign that would point his location.

He stared at the house at the end of the dirt track. It was

familiar, and if he could figure out where it stood, he'd know where he was, how far from Babylon, how near to Navarre.

The house was unlighted, a two-story farmhouse surrounded by tall pines. The Scout had already shuddered past it when Nathan realized that this was the Larkins' blueberry farm. He twisted with shock back to the road. The Styx was twenty yards ahead. Evelyn and Jerry Larkin's corpses blocked the near end of the bridge, horrible in the Scout's wavering headlights. Jerry's head was unrecognizable, not one feature remained intact. He stood lopsided on one whole foot, and the torn stub of the other. His dark suit made the battered corpse that inhabited it the more terrible by contrast. Evelyn, though deteriorating, was still recognizable as the woman who had quailed before Nathan in the lobby of the bank. But her dress was ripped, and beneath it the deeply gouged flesh showed like that of a rotting animal carcass, prepared by a clumsy country butcher.

Nathan tried to brake. But a hand was laid on his arm, tiny, but bloated and wet. He turned. Margaret Larkin, her watery visage swimming with black impurities, her eyes and mouth opened wide on black nothingness, leaned forward across the seat, pressing her face against his. She still looked like a young girl, but she stank of the river.

The Scout smashed into the two corpses, then broke through the thin plank railing and plunged into the Styx.

The vehicle fell on the passenger side, and Nathan was knocked unconscious for a few seconds. The Scout slowly righted itself as it sank.

Nathan came to. The black water swirled above his waist. Somewhere in his panicked mind, he told himself that nothing he had seen had been real. Margaret Larkin was not on the seat beside him; he had imagined her hand on his arm, her rubbery face. It was only necessary that he free himself from his foundering vehicle.

The Scout was sinking slowly, he'd have time to open the door and swim away, but perhaps not more than fifteen seconds.

He pulled out his left hand from where it had caught behind him, and felt for the door handle. His legs churned slowly in the deepening water beneath the dash. He had caught the handle and was pulling up, when an arm, a human arm, was driven through the window and against his face with such force that he was knocked away from the door. He fell beneath the water, and when he came up struggling, he saw that it was Jerry Larkin's corpse that flailed outside the window, both black-clad arms reaching in and blindly grasping. The pulpy featureless head was detached from the straining corpse, and bobbed against the windshield.

Water slapped through the open window around Jerry's arms. Nathan scrambled away from the sightless reach of his victim's corpse, and frantically jerked the handle of the passenger door behind him. It wouldn't give. He started to lower the window, but another hand, mealy and stinking of death, was jammed into his face. Evelyn Larkin was pushing wildly through the slightly opened window. Her ragged broken fingers clutched at Nathan's face. The full moon was reflected dully in the filmed pupil of her single eye, as she urged her rotting face forward. Her jaw sagged open, and a gleaming black snake twisted up out of her throat, and slithered through the window, falling into Nathan's lap.

At the same time, her hand caught at the side of Nathan's head, but he pulled away, and sustained searing pain for the effort. He dropped below the reach of the two corpses' flailing arms, onto the floor of the vehicle, and held himself there until he was drowned.

Ted Hale rode in the ambulance that took his daughter to the hospital in Atmore. She had sustained a bad concussion, which left her unconscious for almost two days. When the wounds in her face healed sufficiently, they might begin to think of plastic surgery to deal with the scars.

Within an hour of Charles Darrish's death, and even before Ginny had been told of it, Deputy Jay Neal discovered what had become of Nathan Redfield. The damaged bridge, and the Scout, only half submerged in the Styx, gave evidence of that. Why he had been heading south, *toward* Babylon, and why he had drowned when escape would have been so easy, were mysteries much speculated upon.

The corpse was charged with five murders: Margaret Larkin,

Evelyn Larkin, Jerry Larkin, Benjamin Redfield, and Charles Darrish; and Warren Perry was immediately released from jail. The motives for the crimes were obscure and ambiguous, but with what turned up only a day later, everything was laid to insanity.

The badly decomposed corpses of Evelyn Larkin and her grandson Jerry were washed up on a sandbar near the junction of the Styx with the Perdido. What was taken to be Jerry's head was deposited only a dozen feet away.

Of all Nathan Redfield's crimes, this was the most disturbing and incomprehensible. Evidently he had dug the corpses of his victims out of the graveyard, maliciously destroyed the coffins, and thrown the bodies into the Styx. When Ted Hale came to identify Evelyn and Jerry Larkin, he had asked the county coroner if he knew what the strange black grainy residue was that coated them. Dr. Dickinson said it was no more than river silt.

However, no one could tell how it came to be that when the county coroner pried apart the tight rotting fingers of Evelyn Larkin, he found Nathan Redfield's severed ear resting on the blackened palm.